I0525775

Apache Tears

a

NOVEL

BY

GORDON MUSTAIN

&

STONEY LIVINGSTON

i

Copyright 1996 by Gordon Mustain and Stoney Livingston

First printing: Bookworld (April, 1996)
Second printing: iUniverse (August 1, 2000)
Third printing: Chokonen

Dedications

To **Cheryll**. Just because.

To those peoples native to America, and especially the **Apache**, who gave me the inspiration and insight to contribute to this work. Those early days of my youth in Arizona gave me a feeling for the land, the animals and the people that will remain with me forever.

Thanks, **Ma**. I couldn't have done it without the trust and freedom you bestowed upon me in my youth to roam and explore the desert. My limited experience of ranch life and the ``old ways" of doing things, and a way of life almost extinct, are sad but treasured memories.

To **Wendy, Kristy** and **Cassie**.

I am grateful for the meeting with **Gordon Mustain** and the bond that has grown between us. You're a good writer, Gordon. Maybe we can do this again sometime.

Special thanks
Sam & Bobbie Stinson
Jay Savera
Bill & Sheila Pattison
Peg Files
Andy Cozine

Stoney Livingston

Dedications

To Val , for all the reasons, spoken and unspoken, you made it possible.
And to **Stoney**, who refused to take no for an answer.

Special Thanks to
Sam, who was there with encouragement when it counted most, way back when
Jay, for all the help
Peg, for relighting the fires
And to **the Tinde** for the lessons they have taught me about courage, honor, suffering, dignity, humility, and the power of the Mother's love.

Gordon Mustain

Authors' Note

Whenever one endeavors to write a character, a culture, and/or a spiritual milieu other than one's own, there is always the risk of unintentional offense to some in the culture portrayed. We sincerely hope this is not the case, but given the potential, we feel it important to clarify our intent and our conventions in writing **Apache Tears**.

Although considerable research on the Apache, and on the Chiricahua Apache in particular, went into writing **Apache Tears**, it is in no way intended to be a "true", or anthropologically correct portrayal of the Chiricahua Apache or their spiritual beliefs and practices.

It is, rather, a work of fiction, a set of characters and events which might have occurred in some nearby quantum parallel reality. There is no Chiricahua Reservation in the Chiricahua Mountains in southeastern Arizona. Once, when Cochise was still their chief, they had been granted such a reservation. But like too many treaties, this one lasted only until ranchers and miners discovered that the land the government had ``given away" was valuable. The government's forced eviction of the Chiricahua from this last central and most sacred remnant of their traditional homelands initiated the final ten years of the 500 year war they had been fighting to retain them.

It follows as self-evident, that had the Chiricahuas retained that reservation and evolved as a culture still rooted in the heart of their traditional homelands, they would have been a different culture than they are today. The culture depicted in **Apache Tears** is a fictional speculation on what that culture might have been, and the characters fictional characters who might have grown out of such a culture.

Where we deal with the history of the Chiricahua people we have made every effort to be accurate. Regarding the spiritual aspects of **Apache Tears**, a couple of notes are in order. There are more than 550 different Native American tribes. Each has its own unique spiritual cosmology, ritual practices, ceremonies, and beliefs. But woven throughout the diversity of traditional Native American spirituality are a set of common core beliefs which unite them, much as the diverse sects of Christianity are linked by common core beliefs:

The earth is sacred. All things are conscious and worthy of respect. All things and beings are related. The spiritual world and the real world are not separate ``worlds'' but are component realms of this world we live in. Life is the result of interplay between the forces of these realms. Just as one has a responsibility for one's physical presence in the physical realm, one has a corresponding responsibility for one's spiritual presence in the spirit realm. The spirit realm is ultimately the more powerful realm because it is the source of the physical realm. Spiritual power is neutral in nature. How it is used determines whether it is good or evil. Spiritual entities of many kinds, rock spirits, mountain spirits, water spirits, wind spirits, animal spirits, plant spirits, ancestral spirits, are all willing to help us in our daily lives if we develop the respect and humility necessary to ask for their help.

These are not only core beliefs shared by nearly all Native American tribes, but are core beliefs shared by nearly all shamanic peoples around the world. There are certain shamanic ceremonies and rituals, and shamanic healing practices which have a similar cross-cultural commonality. It is to these and other such commonalities that we have tried to be true in the writing of **Apache Tears.**

Like many Native American tribes, the Chiricahua have been understandably reticent in revealing many details of their spiritual beliefs and practices. There is little in the literature detailing specific rituals, healing techniques, or ceremonies. The Gahan, or mountain spirits, have been openly confirmed as important deities, as has Ussen been identified as the Giver-of-All-Life. Beyond these, and a brief mention of the White Painted Woman coming of age ceremony for young women, all ceremonies, rituals, prayers, chants, healings, and spiritual teachings in **Apache Tears** are fictional creations, written to be true to the spirit of the Chiricahua people, and to the spiritual commonalities described above.

In short, we have tried to write the spiritual parts of **Apache Tears** authentically without attempting to be factual. It is a book intended to honor all Native Americans, and the Chiricahua Apache people especially, for their suffering and their enduring dignity, for what they have taught us in the past, and for what they still have to teach us.

Finally, we owe a personal thanks to the Chiricahua people. One cannot study their history and culture, visit the land on which that history occurred and out of which that culture grew, and not be changed, not begin to get hints of that earth-born power which sustained them through 400 years of war. Experiencing such a deep love for a land, and the return of that love from that land, however faint, is an enriching experience for which we are grateful.

Gordon Mustain & Stoney Livingston

PROLOGUE: THE WOUNDS

Dawn, July 15, 1967 --- Republic of South Vietnam

Sergeant Clayton Minor Price sat on the edge of the sandbag bunker and folded his map, then gazed out over the emerald green landscape below the hilltop.

The bright Vietnamese sun inched over the horizon. It was already hot. Soon, he knew, it would be a hundred degrees, with humidity to match. Corporal Billy Horse sat next to him cleaning his rifle, softly whistling the Marine Corps Hymn as he always did while preparing for a patrol.

Clay watched as Billy carefully worked on the inside of the M-14 receiver with an old toothbrush. Billy was full-blooded Apache from the reservation in southeastern Arizona, near the ranch on which Clay had grown up. The two had met as children and had become fast friends. At age twelve Billy had performed a ceremony in which he and Clay – along with two other Apache friends, Elmer Pipestem and Oscar Gosheyun – had become Blood Brothers. Five years later, Clay and Billy had joined the Marine Corps on the ``buddy system.'' Their time in Vietnam had brought them even closer.

As he finished reassembling his rifle, Billy suddenly stopped

1

whistling and looked up at the cloudless sky, head cocked as if listening.

``Something buggin' you?'' asked Clay.

Billy pulled out a pack of cigarettes and offered Clay one. ``Just a feeling.''

``What kind of feeling?''

Billy thought for a moment. ``You remember the Secret Place, on the reservation?''

``Yeah.''

Billy took a drag on his cigarette. ``Those last few months of school, before we left for Boot Camp, I spent a lot of time out there. Alone with Wolf. Sometimes the spirits would speak to me. Not always in words. Sometimes it would just be a feeling that would start me thinking.''

``Something *is* bothering you.''

Billy didn't answer for a long time. Finally, he sighed. ``Something about this patrol, Clay. I don't think you should go.''

Clay smiled. ``You've been here too long, Billy. It's just another daylight patrol. Probably be like ninety percent of 'em – a blank.''

Billy's face took on a look of concern. ``Don't go, man. Let Standifer take the squad.''

Clay field-stripped his cigarette butt and stood. ``Too late now. We're mountin' up. C'mon, let's go. We'll talk about all this when we get back.''

7:58 A.M., July 15, 1967

``Where the hell are they? I can't see anything!''

The staccato sound of AK-47 automatic rifles rattled from the jungle to their right front. Someone tossed a grenade. It exploded harmlessly in the dense vegetation. The branches over Clay's head fell to the ground as the enemy fired a burst blindly at them from somewhere in the jungle.

``Corpsman! Corpsman up!'' It sounded like McCreery in the

third fireteam.

Clay looked to his left, at Menenghello, his second team leader. ``Hold your team here. I'll take the first and third teams and we'll try to flank 'em to their left. Keep the corpsman with you. Get on the radio and advise the skipper that we may need some help. Take care of Mac's injured."

Menenghello nodded and turned to his radio operator.

Clay moved in McCreery's direction at the double in a half crouch, his M-14 at the ready. ``Mac, where the hell are you?"

``Over here, Clay. Brown's hit in the leg bad. Where the hell's the corpsman?"

Clay knelt next to McCreery, who worked feverishly at applying a web belt tourniquet to Brown's left thigh. ``He'll be here in a second." He threw himself to the ground as the small arms fire intensified in their direction.

With his cheek on the ground, and his face turned in McCreery's direction, Clay said, ``I'm gonna take Brown's M-60 and the rest of your team. We'll join up with Billy's team and try to flank the gooks on their left. You stay with Brown."

McCreery looked to his right. ``Shooter, you and Worm go with Clay."

Clay got his feet under him and moved further to the right in a crouching run, Brown's machine-gun held at low port-arms, an eighty-round belt loaded, the loose end of it draped over his left arm to keep it from dragging the ground. Worm and Shooter appeared from the thick brush to follow at his heels.

Billy had his ear to his small PRC-6 radio as Clay approached. ``The rest of first platoon will be here in about twenty minutes," said Billy, moving the radio from his ear.

``Let's try to flank 'em on their left," said Clay. ``I'll take the lead with the machine-gun, Worm and Shooter behind me, then your team. Got it?"

Billy nodded. ``Lead out. Let's get it done."

Clay moved to his right, Worm and Shooter not far behind.

They had gone about seventy-five yards when they ran into the ambush. The VC had allowed Clay and Worm to pass the ambush point. In his haste, Clay had been careless.

When the VC opened up, Clay felt the bullet strike him in the side before he heard the report of the rifle. The impact of the slug drove the breath from his body. He fell to the damp soil, gasping for air. He clutched the M-60 as he rolled for the relative safety of a large tree trunk. The ground around him churned from the impact of VC bullets, creating miniature tremors in the earth that Clay felt in his chest.

He held his side and drew air into his lungs as he tried to determine the seriousness of his wound. He was bleeding, and he felt pain, but he didn't think the wound was life-threatening. He was more concerned about the squad and the number of VC.

He saw Worm on the ground and bleeding as the VC continued to shoot at his prone figure, most of the bullets missing their mark.

He raked the jungle across the clearing with a long burst from the M-60.

``Hang on, Worm!'' he yelled.

He fired another burst and was getting to his feet when Billy burst into view.

``Clay! Clay! You all right?'' Billy shouted.

Clay watched, horrified, as bullets from an AK-47 on full automatic ripped into Billy's stomach. Billy squeezed off one round from his M-14 as he fell.

``No!'' Clay charged into the small clearing where Billy had fallen. ``No!'' He fired his M-60 in the general direction of the VC. He felt bullets strike his arm and side. They felt like hard punches. Then there was excruciating pain. He held onto the machine-gun and remained standing.

I'm dead. So this is how it feels to die. I'm not going out alone. Jesus, just let me get some more.

He squeezed the trigger and staggered towards the hidden VC. Another bullet struck him in the side, knocking him to the ground. He lost the machine-gun. He pulled a grenade from his pocket flap and

4

removed the pin. He threw it feebly at the sound of approaching voices. In his weakened condition, the grenade traveled only fifteen yards. He heard shouts of fear – then the explosion. The deadly fragments whizzed over his body as he buried his face in the damp soil.

He crawled to his machine-gun, clutched it tightly and struggled to his feet, determined to kill more VC before he died. He staggered and fell to one knee. His vision blurred. He shook his head and focused on a tree in front of him. Unsteadily, he regained his feet. A movement in the brush drew a twenty round burst from his gun. A body fell to earth.

Clay felt the strength leaving his body. All firing had ceased. *Where the hell is everybody?*

He turned and staggered back to Billy, who lay bleeding on the jungle trail, most of his small intestine outside of his body.

``Oh shit. Oh God. No!" Clay knelt next to him and stared for a moment at the portion of Billy's small intestine lying on the ground like some evil and purple serpent. He placed his M-60 next to the dying man and gingerly picked up the intestine and put it on Billy's stomach. Tears filled his vision. He covered the exposed intestine with his helmet.

``God, it hurts, Clay"

``Billy. . .Goddamnit, don't you die on me, you sorry sonofabitch."

Billy coughed and winced with pain. ``You don't look so hot yourself."

``I feel like shit."

Billy's body jerked with pain. ``I'm dyin', brother."

The tears on Clay's cheeks cut swaths of tan on an otherwise bloody face. ``What the hell were you doin', steppin' up here like that? Goddamnit, Billy – why?"

``I saw you go down the first time..."

Clay searched the sky. ``Please, God. Don't let him die. I swear, I'll do anything; I'll even believe in you. . . just let him live." He turned his gaze back to Billy's face. ``I love you, brother. Don't leave me.

5

Please hang on. I'll go for help."

He stood to search for help and fell unconscious over Billy's body.

One Year Later: Pre-dawn, July 15, 1968 --- Republic of South Vietnam

``What yo' medicine-man instincts be tellin' you about this here party we be attendin' today, Doc?"

Frank Redhawk ignored the question as he completed his fourth check of the contents of his medical corpsman kit spread on a poncho on the ground in front of him. Only when he was finished did he look up at Snake, who sat with his back against the bunker, loading his rifle.

``I don't like it," said Frank. He turned back to his preparations, re-packing the contents of his medical kit methodically. He knew lives might depend on his ability to find what he needed instantly.

``Me neither. Don' like fightin' with no Marvin the ARVN on my flank. We get in shit, an' ol' Marvin gon' mess up bad an' we gon' hafta go save his ass, or he gon' bug out an' we gon' be in the middle of the griddle, Jack – with no slack – and that's a fact." Snake picked up his rifle, inserted the loaded magazine, and let the bolt slam home, chambering a round. He snapped the safety on.

Frank looked up at him. ``We're still in the compound, man."

``Shit, Doc, I carry locked an' loaded on the streets in Detroit. An' tha's home. Compound or no compound, we in a war zone. I damn sure carry locked an' loaded here."

Frank shrugged and went back to his work. Snake was the closest thing to a friend he had in the platoon. Despite their outwardly different demeanors – Frank withdrawn, efficient, uncommunicative; Snake brash, talking a steady stream of high-energy jive, constantly breaking the rules and getting away with it because he was the best night point man in the platoon – despite these surface dissimilarities, Frank sensed in Snake a secret suffering, isolation and anger not unlike those he carried within himself. Frank was comfortable with Snake in a way he couldn't be with the other men.

6

``Saddle up!" It was Gunny Parker, the platoon sergeant.

Frank closed the last flap on his kit and looked up at Snake.

The black man shrugged. ``I guess if the man say dance, we best be dancin'."

11:08 A.M., July 15, 1968

``Corpsman up! Corpsman up!"

In a crouch, Frank fought his way through the thick tangle of underbrush towards the voice, his medical kit held to his chest to keep it from snagging. He'd long since dumped his pack. Mortar shells exploded all around him, throwing geysers of dirt and shredded vegetation high into the air. With each explosion he had to fight the impulse to dive to the earth.

``Corpsman! God, Corpsman!" Another voice, filled with pain and fear, screamed off to his left. It was further away. Frank continued in the direction of the first voice. His breath came in short, sharp gasps.

``Over here, Doc!" It was Gunny Parker. Snake lay on the ground next to him, a bloody mass of torn flesh where the right side of his face had been.

Frank fought through the last of the underbrush and dropped to his knees beside his friend. Everything else disappeared from his awareness. Snake's right eye hung from its shattered socket on strings of muscle, and lay on the mass of crushed bone and shredded flesh which had been his cheek. It moved with involuntary contractions of the muscle strings as his friend looked up at him with his good eye.

``Ah, Doc," he whispered.

``Hang in there, Snake." Frank felt for Snake's pulse with one hand, opening his kit with the other. The pulse was weak and irregular. ``You hit anywhere else?" Frank pulled a battle dressing and morphine from his kit.

``Back of my head hurts." Snake took a sudden deep breath and let it out slowly. ``Motha's put a hurtin' on me, Doc." His voice was weak. ``But I was right about ol' Marvin. Done bugged out again."

A mortar round went off nearby. Shrapnel ripped through the

brush and whined overhead. Both Frank and Snake were lifted off the ground and slammed back down by the concussion. Snake screamed as his eyeball rolled to the hollow next to his nose. ``What's wrong with my eyes, Doc?'' Snake's voice was faint and filled with terror. ``I can see but everything's crazy.''

``Just take it easy while I check out your head. Don't move.''

He slipped the fingers of his right hand under Snake's neck and worked them gently up under the back of his friend's head. Something warm and soft gave way around his fingers and Snake's body went rigid for an instant before it collapsed again. Snake exhaled one long, final time, and died.

Frank felt it like a kick in the solar plexus. He choked back the instant grief which surged up in his throat, choked it back and shoved it down to be consumed by the fires of his rage. He withdrew his hand slowly and wiped Snake's brains from his fingers onto the earth. With his scissors, he cut one of Snake's dog tags from the laces of his boot and put it into his dead friend's mouth, closing his jaw onto it. He looked at Snake's face for a long moment, seeing all the details, using the vision to seal off the churning maelstrom of rage, grief, and guilt inside. He should have gotten there sooner. He should have moved faster. He should have known more.

``Doc!''

He should have been able to do something. He should never have let himself care as much as he did. He should have cared more.

``Doc, goddamnit!''

Frank looked up slowly. It was Gunny Parker.

``We're pulling back to the mouth of the canyon. The CO wants you to stay with me until we get there. All the wounded are being brought to the same place.''

The words came to Frank from far away. He nodded to show he understood. He was afraid to try to speak. He didn't know what would come out if he opened his mouth. He looked back into the face of his dead friend. Dry, withered tears burned behind his eyes. He put the strap of his medical kit over his shoulder and across his chest, the kit resting on his hip. He leaned down and picked up the body of his friend, getting him across his shoulder, then followed the Gunny as they began to retrace their steps.

They had managed twenty-five yards when the mortar round went off about fifteen feet to Frank's right and behind him. He screamed in anger and pain as he felt the shrapnel rip through his right thigh, breaking both bones, before the concussion slammed him forward onto his face.

``You okay, Doc?'' Gunny Parker crawled back towards him.

``Broken leg,'' Frank managed through the pain. ``May have nicked an artery. There's a lot of blood.'' He rolled on his back, his kit already open. He cut the leg of his uniform away from the wound. Jagged ends of bone protruded through the lacerated flesh, obscenely white against the pulsing blood. A jagged tip of bright silver metal flashed in the sun. A wave of dizziness came over Frank and he shook his head to clear it. The movement sent a jolt of pain through the wound and his whole body broke into an intense sweat.

``Let me give you a hand.'' Gunny Parker took the tourniquet from him and put it on his thigh, above the wound.

``Thanks,'' Frank said. ``I'll be okay. You go on.''

``Sorry, Doc, but I got my orders. You're supposed to stay with me. I'll carry you.''

``You can't carry both of us.''

``Snake's dead, Doc. We'll send somebody back for him.''

``No, damnit! He hasn't got anybody else. I'll stay with him.''

``I don't have time to screw around, Doc. . .''

``Then get out of here, goddamnit!''

``Not without you, you sorry shit.'' Gunny Parker grabbed Frank by the arm and started to pull him up.

Frank couldn't suppress a grunt of pain. ``Wait a minute,'' he said, his breath coming in quick, short pants. ``I'm gonna have to splint it.'' He suddenly knew what he would do. ``Bring Snake over here.'' Frank pulled his belt off. ``I'll splint my leg to his and if you're so goddamn set on following orders, you can drag us both.''

Gunny Parker looked at Frank for a long moment, and then shook his head and grinned. ``You're a crazy son-of-a-bitch, Doc. You want to give yourself some morphine before we start?''

Frank shook his head. ``I've only got three amps left. Somebody's going to need them worse than me before this thing's over.''

It took nearly twenty minutes to drag Frank and Snake back to a dense stand of trees near the mouth of the canyon where temporary headquarters had been established. The Gunny left him with the other wounded and dead.

Frank let his eyes close and listened to the sounds of the battle. Pain pulsed through him. Nearby, a wounded man moaned, and then cried out. Frank opened his eyes. He fumbled with the belts tying him to Snake. He wanted to crawl to the moaning man and help. He couldn't make his fingers work on the buckles. He tried to sit up. An instant roar of pain engulfed him. His vision went dim. He fell back.

``Frank.''

He opened his eyes. It was a corpsman from one of the other platoons.

``You got anything left in your kit?''

Frank struggled to think. ``Some,'' he managed. ``Take it.''

``You're losing a lot of blood, man. You want me to start some plasma?''

Frank shook his head. ``See about the others.'' His voice was cracked, his throat and mouth dry. His vision dimmed again. He closed his eyes and felt his medical kit being removed. He drifted, caught himself, and forced his eyes open again. The other corpsman squatted beside him, going through his kit.

The mortars started again. Six quick explosions walked through the grove towards them. Frank watched the corpsman's head come off his shoulders, a look of surprise still on its face as it hit the ground and rolled. Bright gouts of blood erupted from the neck as the body collapsed in slow motion. Frank clamped down hard on the scream of horror which reverberated through him. But he could not hold back the

10

bile that roared up from his gut. He turned his head and vomited, the spasms slamming shock wave after shock wave of pain through his body. He lost consciousness.

After a timeless period he became aware of someone pulling on his arm.

``What the hell we got here, Siamese twins?"

The voice came from far away. Frank tried to open his eyes. They would not respond. He felt himself being lifted, heard grunts and heavy breathing. ``I'll take 'em both. Get somebody else. Let's move! Those choppers can't sit there all day."

Frank felt himself being carried. Each impact of the lurching, heavily laden walk sent a new wave of pain tearing through him. He clamped his jaws tight against it. He would not cry out. He lost consciousness again.

CHAPTER ONE: THE PATHS

Early Morning, June 18, 1979 --- Bar-X Ranch, west of the Apache Reservation, Southeastern Arizona

Clay cinched up the saddle on the pinto in the early morning sun. It was not yet hot, but he knew it would be another scorcher by ten. He fed the excess cinch strap back through the ring and patted the horse gently on the withers.

``Aren't you going to take more than just a canteen and some salt and pepper?"

Clay turned to his mother who stood near the coral fence. ``Just that and my guns, Ma. I want to do it like Billy and I used to."

``That was twenty years ago. You don't have to do that now."

Clay smiled. ``We didn't have to then. It just seemed more like the olden days."

``It still doesn't make any sense to me, son."

``It doesn't to me either, Ma, but something is calling me up there in the mountains." He nodded to the east.

``Well, you sure picked a good horse for it," said Mr. Foster.

Clay smiled at the old man. ``He looks so much like Elmer's old horse, I couldn't pass him up. You sure you can spare him? I don't have any idea how long I'll be gone. Maybe a day. Maybe a month."

``Not a whole lot going on around here this time of year. You take him. He's a tough little bastard. You're as good a judge of horseflesh as your father was."

Clay's father had been made foreman on the Bar-X the year Clay was born. Clay had been in Vietnam when he had heard about his father's tragic fall from a horse during a summer thunderstorm in 1966. His father had died of massive head injuries. Mr. Foster had given Clay's
mother the foreman's cabin as her permanent residence for the rest of her life.

Clay stuffed his Winchester rifle into the saddle scabbard, and strapped his single-action Colt to his left hip. His skinning knife hung on the right side of the gunbelt. He looked at his mother. ``Take care of my GTO, will you? It may be old but it's one of the best-running cars in the state."

His mother nodded.

``You sure as hell didn't visit long with your mother." Mr. Foster's voice was gruff. ``I mean, hell, you only graduated from that damn university a week or two ago."

Clay smiled. ``I'll be back."

``What are you looking for up there, son?" asked his mother.

Clay squinted into the brightening sun. ``I don't know for sure. Maybe I just want to be there again. Maybe I'll go into Om'nitche and look up Oscar and Elmer, if they're still there. I'm not sure. I just know I've gotta go."

Cora Price stepped forward with a sad look on her face. She hugged her son. ``I know you loved Billy, Clay. I hope you find peace out there."

Clay said nothing as he hugged his mother. The saddle creaked noisily as he mounted the pinto. He rode east from the ranch, turned, and waved once silently.

Mid-Morning, June 18 --- Apache Reservation

Apache Tears

The heat shimmered in waves from the blued barrel of the Winchester as Clay aimed the rifle. He blinked a drop of perspiration from his eyelid and squinted to hold back the moisture long enough to draw a bead. His sweaty left index finger took up the slack in the trigger. The .44 caliber slug boomed into the canyon.

He saw the buck fall as the slow-moving, heavy bullet struck it just behind the shoulder. Like a starving cougar, Clay charged the two hundred yards to the fallen animal, never taking his eyes from the spot where the deer had fallen. It was the way he hunted. He didn't wait like other hunters for the animal to bleed and become too weak to move, or to move slowly away and leave a blood trail. If the wound was not fatal, he didn't want to have to track the animal down. He would finish the deer before it could get out of sight, and before there was much suffering.

The brushy terrain restricted long-range vision, and he had been lucky to spot the white tail at two hundred yards. Clay breathed heavily as he neared the spot where it had fallen.

A quivering manzanita bush caught his attention. He switched the rifle to his right hand and removed the single-action Colt from his holster with his left. It was quicker for close-in work. He stepped around the bush. The deer's legs jerked spasmodically and it died quietly. There was no need for a second shot.

Clay holstered the pistol and leaned his rifle into the bush. He pulled his staghorn-handled knife from its sheath and slit the dead animal's throat. The canyon was still. A turkey vulture hovered silently in lazy circles high above in the hot morning air.

He turned his attention back to the dead buck. He slit the animal open and removed the entrails. He worked as one who had done it before, but long ago, and had forgotten the subtle tricks that made the task easier. As he continued to work in the hot sun, he remembered. He pulled the skin tight, so that when his blade touched the meat just beneath the hide, it fairly fell away.

Thoughts of the deer swirled in his mind, visions of a gentle, frightened animal. He put down his knife and looked away from the

14

carcass. Remorse filled him. He hadn't needed to kill this deer to survive. He could have ridden back to the ranch. He could have packed food in. He could have stayed away. There was no longer any need to live off the land.

He looked back at the exposed flesh of the deer, the skinned hide still attached at the spine but laying on the ground above the animal's back. He searched the desert west of him and turned his eyes to the east where the mountains lay; where the Secret Place was. Slowly the sadness left him. He was a boy again, Apache, not white.

He remembered Billy explaining a deer would give itself willingly to someone who was worthy. He looked down at the carcass. ``I'm not sure if I'm worthy, but I thank you anyway, old friend." He trimmed away the last of the hide.

He cut two thick steaks from the loin. The rest of the carcass he cut into thin strips to dry in the sun. The thinner the slice, the quicker it would dry. From a saddlebag he removed a large tin of pepper which he liberally spread over the exposed strips of meat. It would help keep the flies away as the venison dried in the sun. As he hung the strips on the branches of a nearby palo verde tree, he added some salt for flavor and to speed the drying process. The palo verde allowed the sun's rays to penetrate to the meat better than the cedar or mesquite.

He carried the deer's head to a large mesquite tree and wedged it into a fork in the branches, careful not to damage the large rack, then stepped back and looked at it. *Why in the hell am I doing this?* He had no answer. A distant howl penetrated his awareness. It started out low and crept slowly up the scale of sound, then suddenly stopped. Clay looked to the east, the direction of the sound. *That didn't sound like a coyote, but it must be. There aren't any wolves up here.*

He returned to the deerskin. He cut a portion from a corner of the deer hide and worked the buckskin carefully, scraping it and fitting it to the sole of his foot, then marked the edges he wanted trimmed with his knife. He wasn't certain he could make Apache moccasins, but there was no better way to find out than to try. He made a crude needle from one of the bones, and cut strips of rawhide to use as thread. He knew he should tan the hide, but he had neither the time nor resources. He hoped wearing the moccasins as they cured would keep them soft. He felt closer to Billy as he stitched the knee-high footwear.

It was sunset when he tried them on. The right one was a little tight, but it would stretch with time. They were comfortable, but he was not sure how long the comfort would last. His old friends seemed nearer. He could almost talk to them. He knew it was only in his mind, but it felt good.

He built a small fire and cooked his steak. Meat didn't last long in the desert unless it was dried. His jerky would be ready to move by late afternoon the next day. The Arizona sun and dry air made better jerky, faster than anyplace on earth.

After eating, he lit a cigarette and moved to his horse, hobbled Indian style only ten yards from his fire. The short length of rope tying the horse's front legs together left the horse free to move around, but prevented it from running, or wandering too far. He patted the pinto on the neck and offered him a handful of oats from the saddlebag. The horse snorted and accepted the offer.

``Looks like you and me for a while, horse. The way I have it figured, your bag of oats will last about as long as my carton of cigarettes if we both tone down a bit. We'll go into Om'nitche when we run out, okay?''

The horse looked at him, soothed by his voice. Clay fieldstripped his cigarette. ``Goodnight, horse.''

Late Morning, June 20 --- Apache Reservation

Clay rode east, toward the Secret Place where he, Billy, Elmer, and Oscar had sealed their brotherhood in blood, his Wellington boots dangling from the saddlehorn, his roughly made moccasins comfortably unfamiliar in the stirrups.

He wondered if anyone else he had known on the reservation had died in Vietnam. Clay had felt Billy's spirit nearby for a long time after his blood brother's death, but as the years passed, a distance grew, until he rarely felt it anymore. He still thought of Billy often, but

16

thinking thoughts was not the same as feeling spirits. Since the fall of Saigon in 1975, Clay had felt no spirits at all, only mocking ghosts – until now. The Secret Place drew him, and he once more felt Billy's spirit, somewhere nearby.

A lone eagle circled overhead. Clay stared into the sky. *Is that you, Billy?* There was no sign from the silent flier.

In the late afternoon, he stopped to water his horse at a small stream. A piece of white quartz caught his eye and he reached down and picked it up. A large scorpion, uncomfortable in the bright afternoon sun, arched his back and crooked his tail, warning Clay to replace his cover. Clay didn't like scorpions. His normal reaction would have been to smash it, but something stopped him. *No need for killing on this day,* he thought. He carefully replaced the rock and moved back to his horse. Again he heard the long, deep howl from the east, and looked up. *That's really strange. Sure sounds like a wolf, but I swear I read somewhere that there weren't any wolves left up here.*

It was almost dark when Clay rode into the Secret Place, a large, lush, bowl-shaped meadow with a stream running through it. From a large beaver pond at the northern end of the meadow, the stream flowed south, bordered on both sides by oak, sycamore and pine. At the southern end of the basin, the stream veered west and disappeared beneath a deep, crystal-clear pool. It was a place of serene beauty, equaled by no place else on earth in Clay's mind. It was timeless. It seemed nothing had changed.

A red-tailed hawk peered at Clay from a rocky ledge overlooking the stream on the west side of the basin. Clay took it as a good sign. It was his favorite bird. He gazed back at the majestic creature, wondering what it was thinking. The hawk cocked his head sideways as Clay dismounted the pinto two hundred feet below his position.

``I'm no danger to you, my friend," said Clay softly, as his moccasins touched the sandy soil next to the stream's edge. The bird took wing at the sound of the soft voice below.

Clay found no need for a fire that first night. It was warm

enough to be comfortable with his blankets wrapped around his body. Sleeping on the ground in the mountains of his youth, surrounded by the secret night sounds from his past, he was at peace with himself and the world for the first time since Billy's death.

In the morning, Clay woke to bird songs, splashed cold water from the stream on his face, and thought how lucky he was to be alive. Sitting in the early sun, he ate some of his venison jerky. He looked for the hawk but the bird was nowhere to be seen. *He'll be back.*

The days turned into weeks and still Clay stayed in the Secret Place, living on venison jerky and water, with occasional supplements of wild chokecherries and acorns. He felt good.

Using a pool in the river as a mirror, he shaved almost daily with his knife. He didn't like facial hair. There had been a time once, for about six months, when he'd worn a mustache. He'd only done it out of defiance to his battalion commander's wishes. He had never intended to make it a permanent fixture.

Each day, Clay sat for hours and watched the animals, especially the hawk. There were times when he felt that if the large bird would only move a little closer, he would be able to read its mind. On occasion, he talked softly to it. The bird would cock its head to one side and remain motionless. Daily, Clay tore off a small strip of venison jerky and placed it atop a boulder near the stream, not far below the hawk's rocky perch. Daily, the bird ignored the offering.

Mid-Morning, July 14 --- The Secret Place

Clay looked at the last three strips of his jerky, then looked up at the hawk, perched in his usual place. ``Okay, bud, I'm gonna try this one more time." He walked over and placed a strip of jerky on the top of the boulder near the stream and retreated a few steps. ``Okay, hawk, I'm waitin'."

From somewhere within the hills nearby, the strange, wolf-like howl began again, softly. It grew in volume until the basin vibrated with the sound. As the sound faded, the hawk swooped down upon the

18

rock. It grasped the meat firmly with its talons and tore at it with its beak. After devouring the meat, the hawk looked at him and screeched loudly.

Clay smiled. *Well, I'll be damned.*

Mid-afternoon, July 14 --- Outside of Om'nitche, the largest township on the western side of the reservation

Frank Redhawk sat hunched over his battered oak desk, finishing up his Paramedic Monthly Summary Report for the Tribal Council. He shook his head and sighed as he signed it. He put it in an envelope and tossed it onto the sofa across the small, crowded mobile home living room-office. He leaned back in the chair, rubbing his face with his hands.

It was always the same. Eighty percent of his calls in the past month had been to patch up the ugly results of domestic violence, or fights between young men on the reservation. And as always, nearly all the reports on those calls contained the depressing notation: *Alcohol Related.*

He looked around the office at the equipment and supplies the Tribal Council had provided since he had come to them with his proposal five years earlier. So many parts of his dream had become reality. *Yeah, all but the important parts*, he thought. *The parts about actually being able to make a difference. Like the Nam. Just like the Nam.*

Frank stood and stretched. He stepped around his desk and to the door. At six one and a hundred eighty-five pounds, Frank moved with the lean, conditioned grace of a mountain cat, even with the slight limp left after the shrapnel wound.

He opened the door and stepped out onto the wooden deck that was his porch. He inhaled deeply and looked east, his eyes following the scrub oak-covered foothills as they folded quickly up into the Chiricahua range. Nine-thousand-foot peaks towered towards the flat, dark bases of white cloud-islands, drifting through the summer afternoon sky.

A slight movement to his right caught his attention. A young, healthy coyote trotted out of the brush and across Frank's field of vision, heading towards the mouth of a draw just east of the trailer. The coyote stopped and looked directly at Frank.

Neither Frank nor the coyote moved for a long moment. The coyote lifted his muzzle in a series of short, sharp yips, looked back at Frank, turned and trotted into the draw and out of sight.

Somewhere to the southeast, over the mountains, thunder rumbled. A restless breeze rustled the dry rabbit brush and rattled the brittle leaves of nearby oaks. Frank watched, listened, and waited, but the moment was past.

The shrill shriek of his emergency line jerked Frank around. In half a dozen strides he was through the door and at his desk, answering the call. He was already running down a checklist of what he would need to take as he jotted down the details. He was out the door and in his truck within ninety seconds of taking the call.

``Damnit," he muttered, fighting the wheel, pushing the truck as fast as he dared over the rough dirt road. He knew exactly where he was going. He had been there before. He hated domestic violence calls. Frank hoped the Tribal Police got there before he did. He had no great desire to have to do his job and theirs, too.

On a badly washboarded downhill curve with a hundred-foot drop-off, the truck got sideways and another jolt of adrenaline hit him as he got it straightened out without slowing down.

``Some damn dream," he muttered as he hit the main gravel road through the reservation. He flipped on his lights and siren, and increased his speed.

The dream had its earliest origin three days after the end of his sophomore year at the University of Arizona in Tucson. His great uncle, Henry Laughing Bird, had come to his house while his mother was at work to tell him that his cousin, Billy Horse, had been killed fighting as a Marine in Vietnam. The next afternoon, Frank had enlisted in the Marine Corps with the express provision that he be sent to

20

Vietnam.

After fourteen weeks of Boot Camp in San Diego, and another six weeks of Advanced Infantry Training at Camp Pendleton, he had come back to Tucson on a 10-day leave before shipping out to Vietnam.

The meeting with his mother still left a bitter taste when he thought about it. Everything had been fine until he told her he wanted to drive down to the reservation to spend a couple days with his father before heading back to Camp Pendleton.

``There's nothing for you there,'' she had said. ``You call him your father, but what kind of father would ignore his son all these years?''

``I don't know,'' he'd answered. ``Maybe that's what I've got to find out.''

The argument had been short but intense. For the first time, Frank had been unable to completely control his anger. He had left that morning for the reservation.

He found his father in a small, weathered clapboard BIA house on the outskirts of Om'nitche, the main reservation settlement. It was not what he had expected. The house reeked of the sickly-sweet smell of cheap wine and the sour odor of old vomit. His father, looking eighty years old, had been unconscious on the living room floor surrounded by empty bottles, overturned chairs, plates of half-eaten food and filthy, worn-out clothes.

Unable to wake his father from his alcoholic stupor, Frank had driven up into the hills to his great uncle's place, and there, from Henry Laughing Bird, he had learned the truth.

After Frank's mother had left her husband and taken Frank to Tucson when he was seven years old, she had apparently forbidden his father to have any contact with him. The drinking had started not long after, and in spite of every effort by Henry and other friends, it had continued.

``He just gave up after that,'' Henry had told him. ``He'd hoped to be able to pass on to you everything he knew about the old ways.

21

When he realized he wasn't going to be able to do that, I guess he just felt there wasn't much left."

``Couldn't you have helped him? You're a healer."

``I'm sorry, Frank. I tried. But he has given up. And now he considers me a foolish old man living in the past, talking with spirits, and trying to hide from the power of the white eyes' world."

Frank's anger had exploded at that point, in a diatribe against the white world in general, and the federal government in particular. When he had finished, Henry smiled gently at him.

``And yet you are going off to fight their war. Going off to kill other men on their behalf."

Frank was stunned. He had never looked at it from that viewpoint before. He had simply found his life in the white world increasingly intolerable, and the news about Billy had fueled his anger to the point he was no longer sure he could control it. He knew the anger had to be vented somehow, and revenge for Billy's death had beckoned seductively.

``Billy chose the warrior's path," Henry had said quietly. ``He prepared himself well here, in the old ways, before he left. He knew the price he might have to pay. He understood that a desire for revenge only weakens a warrior's spirit. He would not want that for you. We spoke of you often before he left. He considered contacting you to see if you wanted to enlist with him. But in the end, he agreed with me. Yours is not the warrior's path."

``Then what the hell is my path?" Frank had asked. ``What the hell am I supposed to be doing?"

``Do you remember the coyote pup with the broken leg you brought to me when you were six?"

``Yeah. I wanted you to heal it and you said you couldn't, but that I could."

``And you did. The coyote came to you. Pain always carries with it the wisdom to know where to go for healing. Only men refuse to acknowledge that wisdom."

``But I didn't do anything. I just fed it and petted it and talked to

22

it. I think I hated you then for not telling me what to do."

``You knew what to do. You did all that was necessary. You loved it. It healed and returned to the wild."

``What are you trying to tell me?"

``If you have to go to Vietnam, don't go to fight someone else's war. You are a healer. Don't try to walk anyone's path but your own."

Frank checked the speedometer and his watch. He was still five minutes away but he knew if he drove any faster there was a good chance he wouldn't get there at all.

He had spent the last two days of his leave with his great uncle. For the first time he felt he had found someone he could talk to about his life and his uncertainties. Henry offered neither explanations nor excuses for his parents' behavior. Nor did he offer Frank ready-made solutions. Rather, in his turn, he told Frank stories about the old days, helped him recover some of his fluency in the language, and taught him a couple of simple ceremonies he could use to help cope with his anger and continue looking for his own answers. For his part, when Frank returned to base he put in for a transfer to Navy combat corpsman training and was accepted.

Frank downshifted and got on the brakes hard as he turned off the main road. He bounced across a dry wash and started up the rutted track that led the last half-mile to the cluster of ramshackle houses in the distance.

Pulling up in front of the house, Frank cut the motor, grabbed his bag and the oxygen tank, and got out. A small knot of silent people stood in front of the open door of the house. From out back he could hear sounds of breaking glass and metal pounding on metal. The tribal police had not yet arrived.

Great. He started for the door. *Nothing like working without backup to keep you on your toes.* The small crowd parted silently as he approached and entered.

The woman, in her early thirties, was sprawled awkwardly on the floor of the living room, one leg bent back under her. Frank knew from the faint bluish color of her skin that it was bad. He crossed to her and knelt down, setting his bag and the tank within reach. Everything but the woman disappeared from his awareness.

He quickly, but gently, straightened her leg, then checked for a pulse. It was very faint and irregular. Ugly purple bruises were already apparent on her throat. A quick examination confirmed his fears. Her trachea had been crushed. She was unconscious and no longer even attempting to breath. He opened her jaws, and using a pen light from his breast pocket, quickly examined her throat for signs of internal bleeding. There were none.

``Hold on," he said softly, opening his bag to get a sterile flexible breathing tube. He tore off its wrapping, and with infinite care worked it into her mouth and down into her throat. The tube forced the crushed walls of her trachea open again. He took a deep breath and put his mouth over the open end of the tube and blew into it, hard. Her chest rose.

He started CPR. Soon a thin, whistling sound indicated she was starting to breath again on her own.

``That's my girl. Just keep it up now. You're going to be just fine." He stopped the CPR and rechecked her pulse. It was stronger and more even now. He grabbed a fitting from his bag and rigged it over the end of the tube and connected it to the oxygen tank. He was setting the pressure on the regulator gauge when he heard the back door of the house slam open.

``Get away from my wife, you son-of-a-bitch!"

Frank glanced up in time to see the husband charging at him, rage on his face, an axe raised over his head. Frank rolled away as the ax came down, slamming into the floor where he had been kneeling. Before he could get to his feet the man swung again, and though Frank avoided the blade, the handle caught him heavily on the crown of his head. He stumbled and fell backwards against the wall, stunned.

A quick glance at the terror on the faces of the people outside the front door told Frank there would be no help coming from that quarter.

As the man passed his wife's body, advancing on Frank again, he kicked the oxygen tank clattering across the room, ripping the breathing tube from her throat.

``No!'' Frank yelled, then rolled away again as the man buried the axe head in the wall. The man cursed, struggling to free it. Frank got to his feet and retrieved the oxygen tank. He quickly knelt again next to the woman. Before he could re-insert the tube, the wrenching sound of the axe coming free from the wall made him look up.

Again the man advanced on him, the axe raised, wordless sounds of rage and pain snarling from his throat.

``No!'' Frank screamed again, standing to meet the charge. ``No, goddamnit!'' He swung the oxygen tank as hard as he could, and heard the sickening crunch of a skull fracturing as it impacted against the man's head. Blood poured from the man's ears and nose as he collapsed slowly and finally onto the floor.

Blood from his own wound ran in Frank's eyes. He wiped at it as he knelt next to the woman again. He felt for a pulse and found none. The color of her skin told him all he needed to know, but he ignored it.

``You're going to make it,'' he whispered. He re-inserted the breathing tube. ``You're going to be okay. You're going to make it.'' He was still doing CPR when the tribal police finally arrived five minutes later. It took three of them to get him away from her body and out of the house.

He refused their offer to take him to the reservation hospital and asked one of them to get his bag. He didn't want to go back in the house.

``We'll have to keep the oxygen tank, for evidence,'' one of them said.

``Just get my bag.''

When he had the medical bag, Frank got in his truck and drove slowly back towards the main road. A great, echoing, painful emptiness wrapped itself tightly around him. He instinctively reached for his rage, but found only an unbearable grief. He didn't know where he was going. He just knew he had to go somewhere. He had to find a way out of the emptiness and pain.

Late Afternoon, July 14 --- Apache Reservation, Henry's cabin

Henry Laughing Bird's sod-roofed, pine-log cabin was backed up against a redrock outcrop, nearly hidden in a dense stand of pine at the sixty-five-hundred-foot level in the Chiricahuas, half-a-mile from the closest road. Frank had walked most of the distance from the road, and stood in shadow now, on the trail near the cabin. He watched the old man sitting on a log in the sun darning a pair of socks, fifty feet away.

What am I doing here? He doesn't need my troubles. Frank turned and started silently back towards his truck.

He had taken only three steps when a coyote, out of sight in a draw off to his left, broke the late afternoon silence with a series of short yips. Frank turned towards the sound. He waited. But there was only the intermittent whisper of the wind moving through the pine boughs overhead. After a moment Frank sighed. He glanced back at the cabin one final time. Henry had put down his sewing and was standing now, looking straight at him.

Frank held the eye contact for a long moment. He felt a strong, warm pull towards the old man battling the emptiness and despair around him. Without making a conscious decision, he found himself walking towards the cabin. Henry watched him silently until Frank was within ten feet or so. The old man smiled an infinitely sad and gentle smile.

``You look like you might have had better days, nephew."

Frank stopped, a little ashamed of the tears his great uncle's words had started, but as they ran down his cheeks they felt somehow long overdue and very important.

Henry watched for a moment, then nodded and motioned for Frank to follow him as he turned and walked towards the door of his cabin.

Apache Tears

Once inside, the old man steered Frank into one of the chairs next to a battered but still sturdy wooden table in the middle of the one-room space.

From a nail pounded into the unfinished log wall, Henry took down a blue porcelain-covered basin and dipped water into it from a large wooden bucket. He set the basin on the table, then moved across the room to an old trunk sitting against the wall next to the open door. From the trunk he took a washcloth-sized piece of soft, tanned buckskin, a porcupine quill, some long black hairs from a horse tail, two buckskin strips about an inch wide and two feet long, and a fan of mocking bird and raven feathers. He put these on the table next to the basin.

He began a soft, rhythmic hum that seemed to come from deep in his chest as he moved deliberately across to the south wall which was nearly covered with hanging bunches of dried plants. Frank recognized the first bundle the old man took down. It was dried sage. But while the four leaves Henry took from another bundle looked vaguely familiar, Frank couldn't identify the plant for certain.

``What are the leaves?" Frank asked as Henry placed them on the table along with the sage. The old man merely shook his head and continued to hum as he stepped over to a screen-covered cupboard made from an ancient wooden apple box nailed to the log wall. He brought back a cracked but still serviceable ceramic mortar and pestle and a large box of wooden kitchen matches. These too, he placed on the table.

Frank noticed his tears had stopped. The vast emptiness around him was filling with the comforting rhythmic pulse of his great uncle's humming. He found himself uncomfortably aware of a previously unnoticed throbbing pain on the top of his head.

The old man lit a match and picked up the bundle of sage. He held it over the flame until it began to smolder. He shook out the match and put it on the table, then blew gently on the sage, without interrupting his humming, until it was glowing brightly and generating clouds of sweetly pungent smoke.

27

Apache Tears

He motioned for Frank to turn around and sit facing the table and the east wall, his back to the door. When Frank had done so, Henry circled in front of him. With the fan, the old man wafted clouds of sage smoke up and down Frank's legs, arms, and torso, and across his face and the top of his head.

Henry circled to the south, repeated the process on Frank's right side, moved to the west where he did Frank's back, and finally to the north where he did Frank's left side. By the time the process was completed, Frank had relaxed into the clean scent of the smoke, and with that relaxation came a lessening of the pain.

Henry used the fan to waft smoke across the items on the table, across the basin, and finally around himself. When he was done, he held both the fan and sage out and up to each of the four directions. He then dipped the smoldering end of the sage bundle into the water in the basin, extinguishing it. He returned the sage to the wall. The fan went back into the trunk.

At the table, Henry put the buckskin piece in the water and worked it until it was soaked. He used it to clean the blood from Frank's face and from around the wound. His touch was the gentlest Frank had ever felt.

When he was satisfied, Henry rinsed out the buckskin. He took the basin to the door and emptied it, then refilled it and returned it to the table. He put the buckskin back in the basin, then put the four leaves in the mortar and crushed them into a powder. He held the mortar up to each of the four directions, then returned it to the table. With one hand he steadied Frank's head. With the other he took a pinch of the powder and sprinkled it in the open wound.

Frank flinched and gasped at the sudden, intense burning sensation in the wound. He was amazed when the burning disappeared in a matter of seconds, and with it, all the pain. It wasn't numb, the way a local anesthetic would work. It simply didn't hurt any more.

Henry let go of Frank's head and picked up the porcupine quill and one of the long horse-tail hairs. He threaded the hair through a slit in the fat end of the quill and pulled it about a third of the way through.

Sutures, Frank thought. He braced himself against the expected pain. But as Henry put the first suture in place and tied it, Frank found there was no pain to resist. He felt the quill pierce his flesh on both sides of the wound, and felt the horsehair being pulled through and tied. But it didn't hurt. *Whatever the hell that plant is,* he thought, *it has some damned interesting properties.*

Henry quickly put the rest of the stitches in place. When he was finished, he took the wet buckskin out of the basin and folded it into quarters. He emptied the rest of the contents of the mortar onto the square and rubbed it with his fingers, working it into a paste and into the texture of the buckskin.

Again, he steadied Frank's head with one hand, and with the other, placed the buckskin, with the herb down, over the wound. Again, Frank experienced an intense but brief burning sensation, which was gone in a matter of seconds. Henry used the buckskin strips to tie the bandage in place.

Finished with the bandage, Henry returned the rest of the items to their places, emptied the basin, and got a blue porcelain-covered cup out of the cupboard. He filled it with water. From a worn buckskin pouch at his waist, almost identical to the one Frank wore, he took a three-inch-long quartz crystal. He held the crystal up in front of him, focused his attention on it, then simultaneously blew sharply on it and gave it a squeeze. He used it to stir the water in the cup, and left it in the cup as he offered the cup to each of the four directions. He took the crystal out of the cup, returned it to his medicine pouch, and gave the cup to Frank, motioning for him to drink.

Frank did so and returned the cup to the table. The old man looked deeply into Frank's eyes for a long moment, then nodded once. He motioned Frank to get up and led him over to the single rough bunk.

``I'm not really. . ." Frank started, but the old man shook his head again.

``There will be time for words. They will get in the way right now." He motioned Frank into the bunk.

A great weariness came over Frank, a weariness like he used to

29

feel after battle, a weariness so deep that every thought, every motion, required a conscious effort of will. He sat down, rolled onto his side, and pulled his feet up onto the bunk.

Henry picked up a folded blanket from under the bunk and covered Frank. ``Sleep,'' he said.

Frank let the weariness pull his eyelids closed, and ceased struggling against it. He was safe for the moment. For the moment that was enough.

Dawn, July 15 --- The Secret Place

Clay awakened before the sun was above the eastern rim of the Secret Place. There was a slight chill in the early morning air. He sat up, wrapping his blanket around his shoulders and listened to the whisper of the wind in the trees and the murmur of the stream. The pinto snorted for his morning ration of oats.

``Sorry, horse. No more oats.'' Clay shrugged. ``No more jerky either. We finished off the last of 'em both yesterday.'' Clay tossed his blanket aside and put on his moccasins. They were holding up better than he had expected. He strapped on his gunbelt and walked down to the stream. Kneeling next to it, he scooped some water up in his cupped hands and drank. The water tasted sweet, but wasn't exactly filling. He closed his eyes and splashed the cold liquid over his face. He wiped the water from his eyes and opened them and stared into the face of a Mexican gray wolf, no more than fifteen feet away.

It was not gaunt and hungry-looking like the few he had seen in Mexico; it looked as well-fed and cared for as a pedigreed dog. Adrenaline pounded through Clay. The large male wolf stood motionless, the expression on his face neither menacing nor curious. He showed no sign of fear.

Unconsciously, Clay's hand drifted slowly to the pistol on his hip. Something he could not identify in the wolf's eyes caused him to stop the movement.

He felt an impulse to reach out and touch the animal, but something held the urge in check. The eyes seemed to talk. Clay knew he was fantasizing, yet knew he was not. For several minutes the two faced each other, neither moving.

Suddenly the wolf broke his stare, turned, and retreated into the brush, disappearing with a crash of small branches. Clay sat on the ground next to the stream, his body quivering from the built-up adrenaline. He didn't move for a long time. When his heartbeat slowed, and the other effects of the adrenaline faded, he shook his head. Maybe he had imagined it.

He looked at the tracks in the soil. *There had been a wolf. But maybe I saw the tracks subconsciously and imagined the meeting.* He shook his head again and splashed more water on his face. He looked again. The tracks were still there. He could still feel the wolf's eyes on him.

Clay stood and moved the thirty yards back to his camp. He approached the pinto, speaking softly. ``Must be time to get the hell outa here, horse. I'm startin' to hallucinate. Out of food anyway. Time to go huntin', and I don't hunt here."

Hunting was forbidden in the Secret Place. There was no law, except that the Blood Brothers had agreed to such an arrangement. The animals here had their right to be left in peace.

Early Morning, July 15 --- Henry's cabin

Frank woke to the smells of pine smoke and coffee, and to the exquisite sounds of two mockingbirds carrying on a remarkably varied musical dialogue in the pale light of early morning outside the cabin.

He sat up slowly, swinging his legs over the edge of the bunk, and looked around the cabin. He was alone. He closed his eyes, sensing the events of the prior day about to intrude on his consciousness. He struggled to hold onto the purity and tranquillity of the moment.

He managed it for a time, but inevitably, the images of the call, and what had followed, returned. They carried with them a deep, aching grief. He reached up gingerly to feel the buckskin bandage on his head, and was both surprised and relieved to find, after probing with increasing pressure, that there was no real pain at all. Only a slight

31

tenderness.

The echoing emptiness which had engulfed him, and from which he had feared he might never escape, was also gone. In its place he sensed some new quality in his awareness which he could not yet identify, some subtle change which carried with it a hint of new strength.

He pulled his fingers through his shoulder length black hair, undoing the sleep tangles as best he could. When he was finished, he got to his feet and stretched until his vertebrae popped, then walked to the open cabin door.

The sky was a cloudless blue, the air cool, fresh and still, carrying as yet no hint of the hot summer hours to come. A green-on-green carpet of wild grasses sloped out and slightly down from the cabin to the pine trees which bordered a half-circle clearing a hundred feet across. On the right side of the clearing a small creek, no more than three feet wide, flowed from a spring high up in the redrock formation behind the cabin, out across the meadow, and on into the pines.

Halfway between the cabin and the creek, his great uncle sat on the splitting stump, his back to the cabin. A battered sheepherder's coffeepot hung over the small fire in the fire-ring just to his right. The old man was looking up into a tree in front of him. Following the positioning of his head, Frank spotted one of the two mockingbirds filling the morning with their song. It took him a moment to realize that Henry was the other.

A quiet smile spread across Frank's face. For a time he lost himself in the magic and musical communication between the old man and the bird.

Frank had no idea how old Henry was. He had not seemed to change much in the five years Frank had lived on the reservation; the same long, gray hair worn straight with a red-cloth head band, the same raven-black eyes that so often danced in quiet amusement, the same slight, five-foot-nine build, even the same clothes – faded long-sleeved denim shirts and blue jeans, beaded belt, Apache moccasins, and turquoise nugget and bear-claw necklace on a buckskin thong.

Apache Tears

From Frank's earliest reservation memories, Henry had simply always been there. He seemed somehow eternal. Frank felt a momentary sense of guilt for having taken his great uncle so much for granted.

That, at least, I can change, Frank thought. *Starting right now.* He reached down and opened the buckskin medicine pouch Henry had given him so long ago. He took out a roughly triangular-shaped piece of shiny, jagged metal, an inch to an inch-and-a-half on a side.

He held it in the palm of his hand, moved it slightly, and watched the rays of the sun run like liquid fire along its convoluted edges. With the exception of the medicine-pouch, which Henry had given him, Frank knew of nothing it would be harder to part with than that bit of twisted steel. He closed his hand around it in a fist and smiled. He stepped out of the doorway and walked towards his great uncle.

Henry looked back over his shoulder at Frank and smiled. ``Have some coffee,'' he said, indicating a cup on the ground next to the fire pit.

``Morning,'' Frank replied. ``Smells great.'' He continued to the fire and squatted down, using a twig to tip the pot and fill his cup.

He looked up to find Henry watching him intently. He could feel the touch of the old man's gaze as it traveled over his entire body and back to his face.

Henry nodded in approval. ``You're better this morning.''

``Thanks to you, uncle.'' Frank looked down at the grass for a moment, then away at the pine trees. ``I learned something last night, and just now, standing in the doorway watching you.''

The old man waited silently while Frank sipped his coffee. ``I'm not really proud to say it, but I think I've always sort of taken you for granted, somehow. I mean, I've appreciated everything you've done for me. What you've taught me. But for the most part I think I've tended to sort of file it away as interesting. Under cultural heritage or something. Most of it I never really tried to use much. It never seemed quite real. . . until last night.''

Frank looked back at the old man. ``I have a lot to learn from you, uncle, if you will accept my apologies. And if you will teach me."

He held out the bit of shiny metal. ``It's the shrapnel that broke my leg in Nam. Except for my boots, it's all I've got left from there." He paused, momentarily uncertain whether that bit of metal could ever mean anything to anyone but himself. He shrugged. ``I couldn't throw it away," he said.

Henry accepted the shrapnel almost reverently. He held it in his open palm for a moment before closing his hand around it.

``I am honored by your gift, Frank Redhawk. There is great power in it." Henry held it for a moment, his head cocked to one side as though listening intently. ``Great power," he repeated, and put the metal carefully in his own medicine pouch.

``As to apologies," the old man continued, ``a bear does not apologize for doing things the way a bear does. You are a young man. You have been walking your path the way a young man does."

Frank nodded, and looked away at the pines again. He sipped his coffee. ``Will you teach me?"

``What I can," Henry answered quietly. ``But in the end, you will have to walk your path alone."

Frank was silent for a long time before he spoke again.

``You said once that my path was the healer's path, and I've tried to walk it. But it seems lately like the more I do, the harder I try, the worse things get." He paused for a moment.
``Yesterday. . ." he started, then stopped again, then continued. ``I just don't know if I can go on trying to be a healer if it means killing my own people."

He told his great uncle about the call, and what had happened.

``I will do a ceremony to honor the spirit of the man who died," Henry said quietly when Frank had finished. ``In his death he taught you the beginning of a great truth."

``I don't understand."

``There is more to healing than fixing up broken bodies." Henry moved from the stump to squat in front of Frank. ``Let me look." He

34

untied the thongs holding the bandage in place and gently removed it. He stood and peered down at the wound. ``Good,'' he said.

Frank reached up and gingerly explored the wound by touch. He couldn't believe what he was feeling. The wound had completely closed overnight.

``What were those leaves?'' he asked. ``I've never seen anything heal so fast.''

``Do you remember the sacred place of the water spirit? The place I showed you and Billy and Elmer, a long time ago?''

Frank nodded.

``The plant grows there, along the creek.''

``Nowhere else?'' Frank asked.

``Nowhere else.''

Frank sensed an excitement coming to life. ``Maybe I could get someone from the U of A to identify it,'' he said.

``Why?'' the old man asked.

``Do you have any idea what it could be worth to the people if we could put it on the market? It would mean jobs, income, a new hospital. . .''

Henry broke into peals of laughter, and Frank stopped, puzzled. ``What?'' he asked.

Henry shook his head. ``It is a gift from the water spirits. It can not be sold. It is difficult to even give it away. My grandfather gave it to the white-eye soldiers a hundred years ago. But it does not work for them.''

``Why not?'' Frank asked.

``They would not speak to it,'' Henry said.

``I don't understand.''

``The white eyes would not speak to the plant's spirit. My grandfather told them they had to ask it to work for them, but they said they did not speak to plants. So it never worked for them.''

Frank again touched the healed wound. ``It will do this to me,'' he said, ``but it won't work on a white man?''

Henry nodded. ``I asked it to help you last night. You will

35

understand, in time."

``Let's go over it once more,'' Frank said, but Henry declined with a shake of his head.

``Too many words.'' The old man patted Frank on the shoulder. ``Come.'' He motioned to the creek. ``You have time to bathe before you leave.''

``Where am I going?'' Frank asked.

``Do you think you can still find the water spirit place?''

Frank thought for a moment, then nodded. ``Yeah.''

``Good. I need more of those leaves. I would like you to get them for me.''

``Sure,'' Frank said as they approached the creek bank. He sat down and began removing his worn jungle boots, blue jeans, and western shirt. ``Any particular reason it has to be today?''

``It is where your path leads. Tomorrow it might lead somewhere else. Then I would have to make the trip.''

Early Afternoon, July 15 --- The mountains southwest of the Secret Place

``Horse, we been out here more'n seven hours and haven't spotted sign fresher than three days old. You think somebody's tryin' to tell us something?'' Clay felt uncomfortable. It was more than just his hunger. He was not yet ready to be away from his sanctuary. He felt as though he'd left a large part of himself inside the Secret Place. The more the modern world entered his consciousness the more uneasy he became. It was too soon. It was not yet time to return to the outside world.

He turned his horse back toward the Secret Place. In deference to his stomach, he took a different route, riding slowly and looking for fresh signs of game.

His luck was no better on the way back. He reached his old camp and unsaddled the horse, more comfortable in his mind, but quite uncomfortable in his stomach. He looked from the pinto to the stream, then back to the horse. He sighed.

``As much as I dislike the idea, horse, I'm gonna have to fish, leave this place, or starve. I hate fish, but I'm gettin' mighty tired of plants. I'm no vegetarian."

The horse stared at him.

``Yeah, I know. They're dirty little critters. Just because they live in water, people think they're clean – well, they're not."

Clay walked to his saddle where his Winchester lay carelessly across the horn, barrel pointing skyward. He took off his moccasins, picked up the rifle and levered a round into the chamber. ``Damn! I hate fishin'."

Mid-Afternoon, July 15 --- *The mountains north of the Secret Place*

The sun was hot. Frank was glad he was nearly at the crest of the last ridgeline he had to cross to reach the place of the water spirits. It had taken longer than he'd expected to cover the seven miles from Henry's cabin, and the canteen the old man had loaned him had been empty for the last half-hour.

He was pushing his way through the final tangle of manzanita and scrub-oak between him and the ridge crest when he heard the sharp crack and boom of a big-bore rifle. Frank froze for a moment, replaying the sound, trying to determine its direction. It seemed to come from the valley, which fell away from the ridgeline in front of him, from the place of the water spirits.

The old familiar anger rose in him again as he moved quickly but silently in a half-crouch from shadow to shadow up onto and across the ridgeline. A tall rock formation a hundred yards to his right gave him a landmark he recognized. He knew that from atop it he would be able to see virtually the entire valley.

He made his way towards the rocks, careful not to present a silhouette to whoever was shooting. Another shot boomed and echoed off the surrounding hills. Frank cursed under his breath. He had no idea who was down there, but from Frank's viewpoint, whoever was doing the shooting was defiling a sacred place. And the fact that prior to the first shot, this had been the first day in longer than he could remember

37

when he'd been entirely free of the anger that plagued him, made his anger worse.

He climbed quickly and gracefully up into the rocks until he reached the vantagepoint he'd been seeking. He stretched out prone in the shadow of an overhang and edged forward until he could see down into the valley. A third shot cracked and echoed. What Frank saw turned his anger to rage. A white eyes, barefoot with his blue jeans rolled up around his knees, was leaning a rifle carefully against a tree. Frank watched as the man waded several yards into the stream, reached down, and retrieved a dead trout floating on the surface.

There had been times in Vietnam when Frank had desperately wanted a weapon with which to unleash the fury, which had burned in him after the worst battles. But never had he wanted one as badly as he did at this moment.

As the white man made his way back to the creek bank, Frank took in the other details of the scene: the pinto horse tethered to a tree with a lariat; the deerskin bag hanging in another tree; the saddle, bedroll, and cooking gear on the ground near a cold fire-pit: the pistol, holster and belt next to a pair of moccasins on the stream bank. Looking first to his left, then to his right, Frank mentally mapped out a route down to the makeshift camp which would both keep him concealed and allow him to periodically see what the white man was doing.

The white man unceremoniously tossed the fish on the bank and climbed out of the stream.

Frank slid backwards away from the edge of the rock. When he was certain he would not be seen, he got to his feet and climbed down out of the rocks.

Not this time, he thought fiercely. Path or no path, healer or no healer, he'd had enough.

CHAPTER TWO: THE REUNION

Mid-Afternoon, July 15

Frank eased through a dense thicket until he could see the white man squatted at the fire-ring preparing a fire, no more than thirty feet away, his back to Frank. He had put his moccasins on and was wearing the pistol now, the holster tied down on his left leg. Frank judged him to be no more than five feet-ten and about a hundred and seventy pounds. His dark, auburn hair covered his ears and rubbed on the collar of his denim shirt.

Frank backed silently out of the thicket, and circled left, keeping to shadows whenever possible. Any sounds he made were indistinguishable from the background sounds of the stream and the afternoon up-canyon wind, which rustled through the pines.

He reached the tree where the rifle leaned, stepped around it, picked up the Winchester and levered a round into the chamber. He held the rifle aimed squarely at the white man's back.

Nearly simultaneous with the sound, the man pivoted quickly around without rising and looked at Frank long and hard.

``That rifle ain't for sale, buddy.''

Frank motioned to the man's moccasins with the Winchester. ``You a member of the Wannabe Tribe?''

39

``If you don't put down my granddaddy's Winchester, you're gonna wannabe somewhere else." His left hand drifted casually to his holstered Colt.

Frank pulled the trigger on the rifle. The man jumped backward as the bullet kicked up the dirt in front of his left foot. Frank re-cocked the Winchester and said, ``Real easy, put the pistol on the ground and move away from it."

``Okay, I'm convinced. But you owe me twenty cents for the bullet." He gingerly removed the pistol from the holster and placed it gently on the ground, taking care that no dirt made its way into the moving parts.

``Now the knife."

``Prick." He removed the knife from its sheath and placed it next to his Colt.

``Now, back away from it."

Frank saw the man study him, watching his eyes for any sign he might be bluffing.

``And what if I like it where I am?"

``Where you are is in my house, and this time I've got the gun, white eyes. Now, back away."

Slowly, the white man stood and backed up three small steps.

``Further."

He took three more steps.

``Further."

The man glanced over his shoulder. ``That puts me in the water."

``Further."

The white man mumbled, almost inaudibly, ``Crazy goddamned Indian. Got no respect of any kind for footgear," and backed into the stream until his knees were covered by the cool rushing water.

``You're one of the more intelligent white eyes I've met." Frank moved slowly to the knife and the pistol lying on the ground, keeping the Winchester pointed at the white man's chest. He picked up the weapons, stepped back to the tree, and placed them at the base of the trunk. ``Now, what are you doing on the reservation illegally?"

``The only thing that makes it illegal is the fact that you've got the Winchester. If I had it, it'd damn sure be legal enough."

``I take back what I said about your intelligence. That sounds a lot like what the white eyes used to tell my grandfather – about anything they wanted to do."

The man smiled. ``I guess you got a point there. Wasn't exactly thinking in those terms. My apologies. Now, can I get the hell outa this water?"

``What are you doing on the reservation?"

``Until you came along, I was fixin' supper."

``If you want to eat it, I suggest you answer my question."

``If you'll let me get out of this water, it would be a bit more comfortable to talk. You got all the weapons." The white man's eyes lingered on Frank's jungle boots. ``Christ, didn't you ever hear of the Geneva Accord?"

``Okay, move up onto the bank and sit. Cross-legged."

He waded out of the water and sat in the prescribed position with obvious difficulty.

``Now, talk."

``I'm really not into this cross-legged bullshit. How about if I at least stretch one leg?"

``Cross-legged."

The man sighed and looked up into Frank's gray eyes. ``Where the hell does an Indian get gray eyes?"

``I damn sure didn't get them 'cause my grandmother was a rapist."

The intruder's eyes narrowed. ``I'm tired of this game. What the hell do you want?"

``I want to know what you're doing here. And I don't mean fixing supper."

He shrugged. ``It's kinda personal. Why don't we just let it go that I'm up here to poach fish 'cause I love the smelly little bastards."

``Those smelly little bastards are my brothers."

41

Again the man shrugged.

``If that's the way you want it. I was hoping there might be some reason not to shoot you. I hate digging graves.'' Frank brought the rifle to his shoulder and sighted in on the bridge of the white man's nose.

``Hey, you drink whiskey?''

``Is that what you want on your tombstone?''

``All right, goddamnit – I've been coming up here since I was a kid. Whenever I wanted to get away from it all, I've always had this place. I've never even seen an Indian up here before, except for me and my friends.''

``Native American.''

``How about we forget the ethnic bullshit? You got a name? Mine's Clay Price.''

``How did you find this place?''

``My dad was foreman on the Bar-X, just southwest of here. I used to ride out here all the time. Had a lot of friends on this reservation.''

``Apparently, you never learned much from your `reservation friends', or you wouldn't be using a short-barreled buffalo gun to fish.''

``I don't fish for sport. I'm hungry. And I don't own anything smaller than my granddaddy's old Winchester.''

``Give me some names.''

``Elmer Pipestem, Oscar Gosheyun, Billy Horse – what the hell is this, some kind of inquisition?''

``One of those guys doesn't live on the reservation anymore. Which one?''

``Billy's on a different reservation now. He was killed in Vietnam.''

``And where were you when he was over there dying to protect your right to trespass on my reservation?''

``I was right there with him, you asshole. Billy was a friend of mine. We went in on the buddy system. You're startin' to get too damned personal, and you're beginning to piss me off.''

42

Frank swung the rifle smoothly to the left and pulled the trigger, knocking a small branch from a tree across the stream. He jacked the lever repeatedly until the magazine was empty. Without speaking, he tossed the rifle to Clay. ``Second Battalion, Third Marines. 1968. Corpsman with Echo Company. Billy was my cousin.''

Clay stood without invitation and approached Frank, his anger overcome by his memory of Billy. ``If Billy was your cousin, how come I never met you? Hell, I've got more time on this reservation than most Apaches.''

``My mother moved us to Tucson when I was a kid. I was at the University when I heard about Billy. What I was learning seemed pretty insignificant in comparison to what was going on over there.''

``I was tryin' to stuff his intestines back into his body when he died.''

Frank offered his hand. ``Frank Redhawk.''

Clay took the offered hand. ``Clayton Minor Price, and don't you ever call me anything but Clay.'' He smiled.

``Wouldn't dream of it,'' Frank said. He nodded towards the fish next to the fire-ring. ``Didn't mean to interrupt your dinner, but this is a sort of special place, one that makes shooting of any kind seem kinda sacrilegious.''

Clay walked slowly towards his pistol. ``I don't normally shoot up here either, but I was hungry. How 'bout you? You hungry?''

``I'm not much of a fish eater, but,'' Frank motioned towards the buckskin bag hanging in the tree, ``If you haven't eaten that whole deer, I could stand some venison.''

``Sorry. It's all gone.'' In one swift movement, the Colt was in Clay's hand. It recoiled as the big .44 slug left the barrel. He turned to Frank. ``I hate the damn things, too, but there's a fresh one in the stream for you if you want it.''

Frank glanced at the stream and saw the trout floating on its side on the current. He turned and looked at Clay long and hard, then, without a word, waded into the stream and retrieved the fish.

He brought it back to the bank and laid it gently on the grass.

Still without speaking, he opened his medicine pouch and took out some pollen, throwing a pinch of it to each of the four directions over the fish. He chanted a prayer in Apache, repeating it four times, then turned to the stream and threw the last of the pollen into the water. He picked up the fish then, and – wading back out into the current – set it gently into the water and let it go.

Frank waded back to shore and climbed up the bank. He walked up to Clay and without pausing, punched him in the jaw – hard.

Clay staggered backwards a few steps. He caught his balance and rubbed his jaw with his right hand.

``You crazy son-of-a-bitch. What makes you so sure I won't blow your goddamn brains out?''

``I'm not, but I wasn't bullshitting when I said those fish are my brothers.''

``Hell, man, I was just trying to get you something to eat.'' He looked at his three fish laying on the ground. ``They're not real big, but I guess we can split 'em. And don't give me that Apache shit about not eatin' fish. I heard that from Billy, and he's the one taught me how to shoot 'em like that.''

``Billy learned better, when he grew up. You call it what you want. I don't eat them.'' He paused, studying Clay carefully. ``But thanks for the thought.''

``Look, man, I don't even know why I'm really up here. Billy's been on my mind a lot lately and I just felt like I had to come. I tried to leave this morning to do some huntin', but I couldn't stay away. I hate fish, but I'm hungry. I'm going to eat what I killed, but I won't kill any more here. You've got my word.''

``Fair enough,'' Frank said.

``I never should have been shootin' up here in the first place, and I don't need you or anyone else to tell me that.''

``Like I said, one of the more intelligent white eyes I've met.'' Frank smiled for the first time.

``You sure you don't want some of this fish?''

``Go ahead. There's a chokecherry thicket back up the stream, and some bear lilies. No offense intended. But I really do consider those fish my brothers."

``Goddamnit!'' Clay moved to his three fish. He picked them up gingerly and moved to his knife at the base of the tree trunk. He ignored Frank as he dug a shallow hole and buried the fish. Only when his task was completed did he turn to the other man. ``Where the hell did you say them chokecherries were?''

Late afternoon, July 15 --- The Secret Place

The sun had moved well into the west by the time the men had finished their impromptu meal. The fire, in which Frank had roasted the bear lily roots, had burnt down to a few coals. Frank got up and walked to the stream and filled his canteen. He brought it back to the fire and sat down again, handing it to Clay.

``When did you go over there?'' Frank asked.

``Billy and I first got there in October of '65. We got back to the States in November of '66, and were back over there by February of '67''

``How long were you there, all together?''

``Let's see, I extended my second tour by six months.'' Clay drank from the canteen and handed it back to Frank. ``When I got back to the States, some captain thought I was officer material. I went through MARCAD and then flew jets – between my carrier time and DaNang – about two more years. So it adds up to a little over four and a half years.''

``You must have been there when I was, in '68.'' Frank took another drink and set the canteen on the ground between them.

``I was there the first nine months of '68.''

``I didn't make it quite that long. Got there in January and was Med-Evaced out in July during Operation Party Crash. July 15th, I think.'' He looked at the date on his watch. ``Damn, that's eleven years ago today.''

Clay thought for a moment. ``Operation Party Crash?''

``Yeah, the name was about as dumb as the operation. We got

cut to pieces on that one – all for some asshole colonel's precious body count.''

``Most of the bodies I counted were Marines.'' said Clay. ``I was in the unit that came in to bust you guys out. Christ, I even picked up two at a time. There were these two guys strapped together at the leg like Siamese twins.''

Frank looked at Clay long and hard. He closed his eyes. His leg ached where the shrapnel had broken it. He heard a voice echoing in the caverns of his memory. *What the hell we got here, Siamese twins?* He looked at Clay again.

``You okay, man?'' Clay asked.

``Say it again.'' Frank's voice was subdued but intense.

``Say what?''

``The two guys with their legs strapped together. Give me the details.''

Clay screwed up his features. ``Let me think. One of 'em was already dead. Half his face was blown away. The other guy had been hit in the thigh. His leg was broken and bleeding all over the place. It looked like somebody had splinted it to the dead guy's leg. I had a hell of a time getting them both to the chopper.''

Frank took a deep breath and let it out slowly. ``I wouldn't be here now if you hadn't.''

``What the hell are you talking about?''

``The dead man was black, tall and lanky. His eyeball was hanging out of its socket.''

A wave of recognition flooded into Clay's consciousness. ``Jesus Christ. I can't believe this. You had to be the other guy. I remember thinking he was an Indian at the time.''

The two men stared at one another for a long time, neither moving. Frank finally spoke. ``It seems a bit anticlimactic, but I guess I owe you some thanks.''

``Start with the forty cents for my two bullets.'' Clay grinned.

Frank dug in his pocket and pulled out a handful of change. He counted out forty cents and handed it to Clay. ``That's a start. You've

46

got at least a month of dinners coming whenever you say the word." Frank offered his hand.

Clay accepted both the money and the offered hand. ``I still can't believe this."

``Me either. But the old ones say Power works in its own way and time. Maybe we were supposed to meet."

``Could be," Clay answered. ``But I don't put much stock in divine providence."

An uncomfortable silence settled between them. Clay broke it.

``What have you been doin' since you got out?"

``After I got wounded, they flew me to the Navy hospital in Yokosuka, and then back to Oak Knolls. I was there until October of '69. My right leg healed up almost half an inch shorter than it had been, so they discharged me. They figured it was cheaper than tailoring all my uniforms."

``You been here ever since?"

``No. At first, I just traveled a lot, all over the west. I couldn't seem to find anything I really wanted to do. Then I heard about two kids here on the reservation who got thrown from a horse. Died before the Tribal Police could get them to the hospital because there wasn't anybody on the force with more than basic first-aid training.

``I talked it over with the Tribal Council, went back to the U of A and finished my last two years with a degree in physiology, then came out here and set up shop as a paramedic, and started training some help. That was five years ago. How about you?"

``You went to the U of A, too? Next thing I know you're gonna be tellin' me your birthday is January 17."

``What year?" Frank asked, a serious look on his face.

``Screw you. I've had enough coincidence for a while."

Frank laughed. ``It's the wrong month anyway. So you went to the U of A?"

``For the last four years. I worked as a cropduster part time to help pay expenses. Just graduated last month in engineering. Haven't really decided what the hell I'm gonna do yet."

``Married?"

``Nah, never really found the right one, I guess. You?"

``Huh uh. Every time I'd think something was getting serious, either I'd start feeling trapped, or the girl would decide she didn't want to play house with a reservation Indian."

``Native American, remember?"

``Touché. That's part of the problem. The damn historical conditioning goes so deep that even we can't keep it straight sometimes."

Clay pulled a pack of cigarettes from his shirt pocket. ``I don't see that labels are all that important. Smoke?"

Frank took a cigarette from the offered pack. ``Thanks." He rolled the end of the cigarette between his thumb and index finger until some tobacco came out into his hand. He tossed it out in front of him towards the stream, then lit the cigarette and held out his lighter for Clay.

``Maybe you're right about labels," he said. ``But when you live with other people putting them on you long enough, you get a little sensitive."

Clay accepted the light.

Frank put the lighter back in his shirt pocket, then stood and stretched. He looked at his watch. ``It's getting late. I've got to gather some plants for my uncle, and get 'em back to him before too much longer. How long you planning on staying up here?"

``I don't really know. I could start back any second now. You want some help gatherin' those plants? I'm a plant gatherin' fool."

``No, I think I can handle it. I saw what I needed up near that chokecherry thicket. But, if you've had enough of this place for a while, we could head back together. My truck's parked near my uncle's place. You could leave your horse there and we could run into Wilcox for the first installment on that month of dinners."

``Sounds like a plan to me, Doc."

The use of the nickname caught Frank by surprise. ``I haven't been called that since I left the Nam."

Clay smiled. ``You're still doctorin' folks, ain't you?''

``Yeah, I guess I am.'' Frank hesitated for a moment. ``And sometimes it seems to be just about as useless, too.'' He shrugged. ``But you gotta do what you gotta do, and patchin' people up seems to be what I'm stuck with. Why don't you get saddled up while I get those plants? My uncle's place is only about seven miles from here but it'll be a lot easier if we do it before dark.''

``Consider it done,'' Clay answered.

Sunset, July 15 --- Pinery Canyon, the Reservation

The sun had just dropped below the horizon when Frank and Clay paused on a rocky ridgeline covered with scrub oak, juniper, and buckbrush. Frank took his canteen from the saddle horn as Clay wrapped the reins of the pinto loosely around a branch, and reached up for his own saddle canteen.

They drank deeply, then stood together silently, looking out over the wide, flat expanse of Sulfur Springs Valley, stretching westward from the reservation boundary for twenty miles to the foot of the Mule Mountains. Across the valley to the northwest, the Dragoons reared their rugged way towards the gold and pinks painted on the undersides of broken clouds by the setting sun. A light breeze meandered through the brush around them, cooling their bodies through their sweat-stained shirts.

A half-mile or so below the ridge on which they stood, a dirt road wound its way between foothills from the south northward, roughly following the course of a dry, rocky stream bed lined in places with large old cottonwood trees.

Frank pointed to a draw, just north of them, which led down off the ridge. ``We can get down to the road there. It's only a mile or so to the cut-off to my uncle's place, then about another mile by road back up to the tree line.''

``You mean to tell me we just came all this way down just to turn around and go back up?'' Clay asked. ``Damn, I thought you said you'd been a corpsman, not a second lieutenant.''

Frank laughed. ``Sometimes the quickest way isn't the shortest. We could have cut across but it would have been rough going with the horse, and we'd have been cutting trail after dark. This way it's just a walk in the park."

``Yeah, an uphill walk. But I see your point. What the hell, it'll just make that steak dinner taste that much better."

Frank took another small sip, then recapped the canteen and put the strap back over the saddlehorn. ``Shall we do it?"

``Lead on," Clay answered.

They made their way north on the ridgeline and then down the draw to the road. By the time they reached it, the colors had disappeared from the sky and the light had begun to fail. A three-quarter moon, already visible above the crest of the Chiricahuas to the east, promised plenty of light for the rest of the walk.

They moved along the road with the practiced gait of men who had learned to cover long distances on foot without exhausting themselves. They spoke little, both content to savor the magic of that special time between day and night when the onrush of darkness seems to stall, and for a time all good things seem possible. In the cottonwoods across the streambed to the west, birds chattered their final songs of the day as they settled into their roosts.

They'd covered another half-mile, and were coming around a bend between two closely set hills, when Frank stopped.

``Damnit," he said. ``Would you look at that."

Seventy-five yards to the left of the road, half-hidden by brush and junipers, a bonfire burned, the flames dancing in the darkness, throwing glowing sparks and embers high into the air. A late-model pickup with a cabover camper was partially visible in the light of the flames.

``That's no Apache campfire," Clay said.

``Not a sober one, anyway," Frank answered, disgust evident in his voice. ``Why don't you go on. I've gotta check this out and see if I can't talk some sense to whoever it is. Until the rains get here, things are so dry the whole damn reservation is a tinderbox."

``You got that right," Clay answered. ``You sure you don't want me to go along? Or wait?"

``No, it's probably just a bunch of kids. No offense, but with a white man there they'd probably feel duty-bound to give me a hard time. The road makes a big loop up ahead. I can cut across and catch you."

``Whatever you say, Doc. But I'd appreciate it if you didn't waste too much time. Those berries and roots weren't bad but they're wearin' a little thin already."

``You got it. See you shortly."

Frank moved off the road towards the fire, picking his way carefully through the buckbrush. He wanted to be able to survey the scene before he made his presence known.

He could hear Clay moving on up the road with the horse, and smiled in the darkness. As unexpected as it had been, and badly as it had started off, he was glad he had met the white man. He sensed a kinship between them that might go deeper than their shared Vietnam experiences and their separate relationships with Billy.

He quickly covered the ground between the road and the clearing where the camper was parked, and squatted in the brush to look things over. What he saw triggered a warning flare-up of his anger.

The camper was parked parallel to the streambed, nose pointed north. The big fire crackled and burned in a poorly built fire-ring behind the truck. Two rifles leaned up against the side of the camper and a young white man squatted with his back to the fire, facing the door of the camper, whittling on a cottonwood branch with a large hunting knife, a half-empty fifth of whiskey on the ground at his side.

``Come on, you asshole, hurry up," the young man yelled towards the camper. ``Maybe it was your idea, but that don't mean you can take all night."

Frank clamped down on the anger. *No sense making a big deal out of it,* he told himself. *Probably a couple of kids from Wilcox with a camping permit.*

51

Because of the fire danger on the reservation, Frank had argued before the Tribal Council against the issuance of any such permits until the summer rains started, but he'd been voted down. The money from those permits was an important part of the reservation budget. Campfire restrictions were printed clearly on the back of all such permits, he knew, but he also knew that few people took the time to read them. Still, pointing them out was all he needed to do to get most people to cooperate.

He stood, and stepped out into the clearing. ``Evening."

The man spun around at the sound of his voice.

Something in the look on his face triggered a second warning in Frank's consciousness.

``Your fire is a bit big for as dry as things are," Frank said.

The man looked at the fire and back to Frank, confusion evident. Frank walked slowly towards him.

``Hey Charlie! We got Indian company out here," the man called towards the camper. He got to his feet, his eyes darting from Frank towards the rifles against the camper and back again.

Frank's warning signals were sounding full blast now, and he changed directions slightly, trying to put himself in position to cut the man off from the rifles.

A second man's voice roared from inside the camper. ``Ouch, goddamnit! You bitch!" It was followed by muffled sounds of a struggle that set the camper swaying on its springs.

The man by the fire made a break for the rifles and Frank reacted instantly, catching him as he reached for the closest weapon. Frank didn't hesitate. He spun him around and hit him, hard, feeling the man's nose break under his fist.

Another cry of pain from the man in the camper was followed by a woman's voice, screaming. ``Pinda lickoyi bastard! Help! Help me!"

Frank hit the man again, sending him sprawling in the dirt. Quickly, he threw one of the rifles as far into the darkness as he could, grabbed the other, jacked a round into the chamber, and headed for the

52

door of the camper. He heard a shot from inside and was reaching for the door when it slammed open into him, knocking him off balance, the rifle falling from his grasp.

The other man jumped out of the camper, a .357 magnum revolver in his hand. He fired a quick shot in Frank's direction which went wide of its mark, and Frank charged, crouched low. His shoulder slammed into the man's midsection, knocking him backwards against the rear of the truck. Frank grabbed the man's right wrist, holding the pistol out and away, as he crouched and slammed his shoulder up and forward again into the man's diaphragm. He heard the air forced out of the man's lungs with a sudden explosive burst at the moment of contact and knew he had won.

The pistol fell from the man's hand and he doubled over, trying desperately to breathe. Frank reached down for the pistol and saw the pointed toe of the first man's cowboy boot just before it impacted his face above his right eye. Frank's head snapped back and he sagged to his knees, stunned. Something hit him hard on the back of the head and he collapsed, trying desperately to hold onto consciousness as the world seemed to spin and go dark. He tried to roll onto his back but his body would not respond. He could hear the harsh breathing of the first man standing over him.

``Charlie! Charlie, you OK?''

Frank could hear the second man groan as he managed to pull air back into his lungs.

``Charlie, goddamnit, what do I do?''

``How the hell do I know?'' The man's voice was groggy. ``Tie the son of a bitch up. I can't think yet.''

Frank managed to stay conscious but quit trying to move. He knew he was in trouble now, and his only hope might be surprise. He heard one of the men enter the camper.

``Jesus Christ, man, you shot her! She's bleeding all over everything!''

``She bit me, asshole. Just get the rope out here.''

Frank heard him come out of the camper and waited until he felt the man grab one of his wrists before he made his move. He rolled towards the man, trying to catch his legs, but his body still responded too slowly, and the man managed to step away. Frank felt himself being kicked again, in the ribs this time, and the pain shot through him. He rolled over and struggled to get to his hands and knees, but collapsed again. He felt the bite of the hemp as the man yanked his arms behind his back and tied his wrists tightly.

``What are we gonna do, Charlie?'' There was fear in the man's voice.

``Will you stop with your whining?'' the one called Charlie growled. ``Just let me think for a minute.''

``My old man's gonna have my ass, man! There's blood all over in there.''

``For Christ sake, shut up. The blood will wash. Give me a drink. Just relax. We got all night.''

``I told you we shouldn't pick her up. I told you she was trouble.''

Charlie fired the pistol into the air. ``You give me anymore of that `it's all my fault' shit and I'll put a bullet in you too. You were damn sure anxious to get your turn on top of her.''

``Yeah, but I never figured …''

``That's your problem, Brucie boy, you never figure anything right.''

Frank lay still, listening, letting his strength return, very carefully testing the bonds on his wrist. They were too tight to offer any encouragement. He figured Clay probably had heard the shots and would come back to investigate, but Frank had no idea how long it would take him. He knew it was risky, but he moved slightly, trying to get a look at the one called Charlie. Things had happened too fast for him to be sure he could recognize him again.

``He's moving,'' Bruce said, fear in his voice.

Frank heard someone walking towards him and tensed his whole body against the anticipated impact of another kick. Instead he felt someone grab his hair and yank his head back.

``You awake, asshole?'' The one called Charlie looked down at him. Even with the blood running in his right eye, Frank got the look he wanted. He would never forget that face.

Frank remained silent. Charlie slammed his face back into the earth. ``Sit up pus-face, unless you want me to shoot you in the back.''

Frank struggled into a sitting position, wincing at the pain in his ribs, which told him at least one of them was cracked if not broken. Charlie squatted in front of him and put the muzzle of the .357 hard against his nose.

``You made a big time mistake walkin' in here,'' he said. ``Who are you?''

Keep him talking, Frank thought. *Play for time.* Clay was his only hope now. It was hard to keep the rage and hate out of his voice as spoke. ``Frank Redhawk,'' he answered, looking into the pale blue eyes of the young man with the dirty blonde hair, squatted in front of him.

``What are you doin' here?'' Charlie demanded.

Frank gestured towards the fire. ``Your fire was too big. Things are so dry around here it's dangerous. I was going to ask you to make it smaller.''

``Looks like things were a little more dangerous than you thought, don't it, Chief?'' Charlie said. He pulled back the hammer on the pistol, cocking it.

``Jesus Christ, Charlie, wait a minute,'' Bruce cried. ``There's gotta be something else we can do.''

Charlie stood and kicked Frank in the stomach. He took a swig from the bottle in his left hand, then turned towards his friend.

Clay had continued up the road towards Frank's truck, but something about the size of the campfire behind the camper caused him to stop after only a couple hundred yards. It was a large fire, a white man's fire. Maybe the vehicle was broken down. With his mechanical experience, it would be foolish to go on without at least checking to see if he could help. He turned his pinto around and started back towards the truck.

55

Apache Tears

As he nudged the little horse into the cedars flanking the dirt road, he heard shouts. The sounds were partially muffled by the thick stand of trees, and he was unable to clearly distinguish the words, but the fear and urgency were quite clear, even at his distance. It sounded like a woman's voice.

Immediately, he tried to conjure up a scenario to explain what he was hearing. Before he had time to complete his thought, he heard a muffled shot. Instantly, his moccasined feet were on the ground and the Winchester in his hand. He looped the pinto's reins over a cedar branch and headed for the edge of the treeline. He heard another shot, this one not muffled. He levered a round into the chamber of his rifle as he ran.

It seemed to take forever to get to a position where he could clearly see the campsite. After a time, he heard another shot. He crouched behind a large cedar and took in the scene before him. The fire burned fifteen yards to the rear of the pickup. Between the fire and the pickup, Frank lay prone, face down, unmoving, his hands tied behind his back. A young man stood over him, a pistol in his hands. The man turned his head to the right and said something to someone out of Clay's range of vision. *There's at least two.*

Clay moved to his right until he could safely cross the open space between the cedars and the dry streambed bordered by the large cottonwoods. He worked his way back down the stream bed until he was even with the front of the pickup, then left his cover and moved up next to the driver's side of the vehicle. He inched his way down the side of the camper until he could see the second man standing about five yards to the rear of the bumper, a rifle in his hands. *Two confirmed – could be more in the camper. I thought I heard something in there.* He moved to the corner of the camper, trying to pinpoint the exact set of circumstances under which he labored.

From where he stood, he could see Frank. He was sitting now. Dark, half-coagulated blood oozed from a wound on his forehead, forming a large dark socket in his right eye as it collected and dried there. The first man squatted in front of Frank, pushing the large revolver against his friend's nose.

56

Frustrated with the situation, which confronted him, Clay waited for a chance to make a move without endangering Frank. He remembered Billy's death as clearly as if it had happened this morning. His adrenaline pounded in his temples. He wanted to kill the man with the pistol and get it over with. *This is the goddamned United States of America. We don't do that kinda crap anymore. There must be another way.*

The man squatting in front of Frank cocked the pistol.

Oh shit. Clay drew a bead on the back of the man's head. Before he could pull the trigger, he heard the second man plead, ``Jesus Christ, Charlie, wait a minute. There must be something else we can do.''

Charlie stood and kicked Frank in the stomach. He took a swig from the whiskey bottle and turned to his friend. ``What's the matter, Brucie? No ... ''

Clay read the fear on Charlie's face as the younger man saw him and pulled his pistol upward. Clay pulled the trigger on his Winchester. The heavy slug smashed into Charlie's left kneecap, and he shrieked in agony as he went down, dropping the pistol. Clay stepped to the second man and struck him in the face with the barrel of the Winchester, sending the hunting rifle and the man both downward in separate directions. He levered another round into the chamber of his forty-four and waved his weapon in a broad arc as he rushed to Frank's side.

Bruce started to get up.

``Go ahead if you feel lucky,'' said Clay softly.

Charlie was out of action and writhing about in the dirt, his kneecap smashed. Bruce lay still as Clay unsheathed his knife and cut Frank's bonds.

``I got these two, Doc. You okay?''

``Yeah,'' Frank said, rubbing his wrists and hands quickly to get the circulation going again as he got to his feet. ``But there's a woman in the camper that's been shot.''

He started for the truck at a run, motioning towards Charlie. ``Get a tourniquet on that guy's leg.'' He jerked open the door and stepped up into the camper.

It took a moment for his eyes to adjust to the semi-darkness before he saw the figure on the bunk. She was Apache, no more than fifteen or sixteen years old. She had been shot in the stomach.

He didn't hesitate. Grabbing the top sheet, which had been kicked onto the floor, he started tearing off strips. The girl moaned and Frank heard the fear in the sound. He looked at her while he worked. ``You're gonna be okay,'' he said softly. ``I am Tinde. I'm a paramedic. We'll get you to the hospital.''

The girl was naked, and when Frank had the makeshift bandages in place, front and back, he covered her with a blanket. He checked her pulse quickly. ``What's your name?''

She did not respond. She simply turned her head away, face distorted by the pain.

Frank knew they had to move quickly. ``I'll be right back,'' he told her. ``Try not to move.'' He jumped back out of the truck, running over in his mind what had to be done.

Clay stood over Charlie, who lay on his side, moaning in pain, hands tied behind his back. Clay had used the man's belt to put a tourniquet on the injured leg, above the knee. Bruce sat cross-legged about five feet away, hands tied behind his back, whimpering, tears streaming down his cheeks.

``She's gut-shot. We've got to get her to my truck. I've got plasma there.'' He glanced at the fire. ``Let's get that fire out and get out of here.''

Clay snatched Bruce to his feet. ``Start kicking dirt on that fire, punk.'' As Bruce moved to comply, Clay grabbed a five-gallon can of water on the ground near the camper.

``You got the weapons?'' Frank asked.

Clay answered as he poured water on the fire, sending clouds of steam up into the dark night. ``I got a rifle and a pistol, and these guys don't have anything else on 'em. I checked.''

``There's another rifle I tossed into the brush, but we'll get it tomorrow,'' Frank said, running to the cab of the truck. He looked through the window. He moved quickly back to Charlie and squatted next to him. ``Where are the keys?'' he demanded, checking the tightness of the tourniquet.

Charlie winced. ``Eat shit, Geronimo,'' he snarled between gritted teeth.

Frank jerked on the tourniquet, jarring the shattered knee and Charlie screamed.

``Where are the keys?'' Frank asked again, his voice ominously quiet.

``In my right pocket.'' Frank barely heard the words. He rolled Charlie onto his back and pulled the keys out quickly. He turned towards the fire, which was out now. Clay came towards him, and Frank tossed him the keys.

``Can you drive and keep an eye on these two?''

Clay caught the keys. ``My pleasure.'' He turned to Bruce. ``You heard the man. Get in the cab.'' He grabbed Charlie under the armpits and unceremoniously dragged him to the cab, paying no heed to the injured man's screams.

Frank grabbed the rifle and pistol off the ground. ``About a mile up the road there's a turn off to the right. Take that. About another mile and you'll see my truck.''

``You got it. Here, take my Winchester with you.'' He tossed the rifle to Frank as he moved to the driver's side of the cab.

Frank re-entered the camper and crouched next to the girl. ``It won't be long now,'' he said softly, taking her hand. ``Hang on.''

At his truck, Frank used the radio to notify the reservation hospital to get the doctor and prepare the operating room. He gave Clay an ampoule of morphine. ``Stick that in Charlie if you get tired of his yelling.''

``It's music to my ears. You keep it. He ain't getting it from me.''

Frank got back into the camper, and with disciplined quickness, he got an IV started, injected the girl with a dose of morphine to ease her pain, and signaled Clay he was ready.

59

It was only five miles into Om'nitche, but with the rough road, Clay had to drive slowly to keep the truck from bouncing around too badly.

Sitting in the center of the bench seat, Bruce looked over at Clay. ``What are you gonna do with us, man?"

Clay glanced at him briefly. ``If I can talk Frank into it, I'm gonna hang your ass."

``Hang us? What the hell for, man?"

Clay looked over at him again, holding the look longer this time as the truck moved slowly down the road. ``You stupid shits. If I gotta tell ya, I may not even wait for Frank's permission." He returned his eyes to the road.

``But I didn't do anything," he whined. ``It was Charlie's idea."

``Shut up, asshole," Charlie snarled through his pain.

Bruce turned to his friend. ``It was your idea. I told you we shouldn't do it."

``Shut up, damnit. I've got connections, remember?"

``How the hell's your dad gonna get us out of this? He doesn't even know where we are, and this sonofabitch is crazy," he nodded in Clay's direction.

``He's bluffing."

``You keep thinking that." Clay reached over and with a closed fist hit Charlie's injured knee.

Charlie screamed.

``Hey you crazy shit, his old man's a U.S. Senator."

Clay smiled. ``Is that a fact?" He reached over and hit Charlie's knee again.

CHAPTER THREE: THE VISION

Pre-dawn, July 16 --- Om'nitche

Frank sat on the steps outside the main entrance to the reservation hospital as the first faint hint of light appeared above the mountains to the east. His ribs had been taped so that breathing was no longer quite so painful, and the gash above his eye had been cleaned up, but he was gripped by a bone-deep weariness.

The girl had been in surgery three-and-a-half hours. The doctor had said that he thought she would be okay. Two tribal police guards had accompanied Charlie and Bruce on the emergency helicopter evacuation to a Tucson hospital where the white men were to be turned over to a U.S. Marshall.

Clay and Frank had spent the better part of another three hours talking with, and writing reports for, Eddie Vasquez, Chief of the Tribal Police and a close friend of Frank's. Clay hadn't liked it when Eddie had impounded his Winchester as evidence, but he'd gone along finally.

When Eddie was finished with them, Clay had left to try to find Oscar and Elmer. Frank had stayed at the hospital to fill out his paramedic report. He waited now for Eddie to finish his business with the doctor, hoping to catch a ride with him back to his truck.

Frank sighed deeply. He knew he should be pleased the girl was going to be all right, and proud that Dr. Hardesty had said his actions had saved her life. But he couldn't. Instead, he struggled against a numbing apathy, which deadened all his emotions, even the anger, which had been his companion for so long; apathy and a vague sense of foreboding he couldn't seem to shake.

He looked east towards the crest of the mountains standing in barely visible black silhouette against the first faint hint of dawn. *I used to love the dawn,* he thought, *for the peace and unspoken promise it held.* Now dawn seemed just another deceit, promising little but further despair.

He was startled to hear his name spoken softly from the shadows on his left. He turned towards the sound. Henry stepped into the light, motioned for Frank to follow him, and without waiting for a response, turned and disappeared back into the darkness.

Puzzled, Frank got to his feet and followed. He caught the older man in a few strides. ``What's going on?''

Henry continued walking as he answered. ``We have much to do, and little time. We must hurry.''

``I don't understand.''

``The Gahan spoke to me last night.''

The Gahan, Frank thought. *The Mountain Spirits. The most powerful Apache deities from the old way.* He had heard the stories but had never considered them as anything other than cultural myth.

``How did you know where to find me?'' he asked.

``I told you. The Gahan spoke to me.''

Frank's confusion grew as Henry led him around behind the hospital and down into a wash where two horses were tethered to some creosote bushes.

``I don't want to be impolite, uncle,'' Frank said, ``but I can't just take off right now. I've got a lot of things. . .''

Henry cut him off with a short, sharp hand motion, palm parallel to the ground. When he spoke, his words carried a hard-edged authority Frank had never heard from him before.

``We have no time for foolishness. The Gahan do not speak except on matters of greatest importance. Come." He handed the reins of one horse to Frank, and immediately swung into the saddle of the other with an ease that belied his advanced years.

Frank started to protest once more, but again the sharp hand motion cut him off. Without having made the decision to do so, Frank found himself mounted. He followed Henry up the wash at a fast trot.

Questions raced in circles through Frank's mind for a time, but as the darkness gradually faded into a half-light and Henry urged his horse into a smooth, distance-eating lope, the questions disappeared. It took all of Frank's attention to keep pace.

They followed the wash east, then turned southeast up and over two ridgelines, climbing ever higher through the foothills. Henry led them into the mouth of a canyon Frank had never seen before. The walls grew progressively steeper and the canyon narrower as they rode. The old man nudged his horse into a still narrower side canyon and they slowed to a walk. In places the walls came so close together, Frank's knees brushed against them as his horse climbed carefully up the steep water-worn bedrock.

They emerged finally onto a broad, pine-dotted ridgeline and Henry once more picked up the pace. He led Frank east and south across the flat terrain, and then down a gentle slope, into what Frank recognized as the northern end of the small valley in which he had met Clay, the day before.

Though the sun had not yet appeared, the light was nearly full when they reached a roughly circular grassy meadow surrounding the spring-fed beaver pond, which was the stream's source.

Without words, Henry dismounted and quickly unsaddled the sweat-darkened buckskin mare he rode. He slipped the bridle off over her ears and turned her loose. Frank followed suit. When he was done, he joined Henry on the west bank of the stream just below the beaver dam.

Henry sat down with his back to the stream, indicating Frank should sit facing him. Once in place, Frank started to ask another question. Once more Henry cut him off.

``There is great power circling all around you, Frank Redhawk, but you can neither see it nor use it yet. You do not understand what is happening. I could see the power but did not understand myself, until last night. The Gahan have not spoken to any of the Tinde for many years. Few of us even remember the old ways. Fewer still follow them. I have tried to do so, and last night I was honored. The Gahan spoke of the circle of our people, the Tinde, nearing completion. It is a time of many changes. You are at the center of them, Frank Redhawk. You will complete the circle.''

Frank shook his head in confusion. ``I am sorry, uncle, I don't understand. I have no power as you speak of it.''

``You do not know what power you have because you have no spirit name. The spirits cannot speak to you until you have a spirit name. That is why we have come here. The Gahan have called for you.''

``But I do have a name. Frank Redhawk.''

``Enough! These are not matters about which one argues. I have told you, there is great power circling about you. You will either learn to see it and use it, or it may destroy you, and perhaps all the Tinde with you.''

The feelings of foreboding, which had been growing throughout the ride, intensified. Frank shivered. Up on the ridgeline to the west, a pack of coyotes started a yapping chorus.

``You must have a spirit name in order to claim your power,'' the old man said. ``No one, not even the Gahan themselves, can force you to accept what is offered. And claiming such power is never without danger. But refusing it is far more dangerous. If you are to find your spirit name, we must complete the preparations before the sun touches the water behind me. The choice is yours.''

The old man fell silent then, but his eyes never left Frank's. It seemed to Frank, his great uncle's gaze was somehow penetrating deep inside him; plumbing depths he never knew were there. Frank hesitated, becoming aware of the fact that he was profoundly frightened. The realization made him angry. He was too old, and had seen far too much, to be frightened by old stories and superstitions. But the fear was there. And there was something, some indefinable presence that tugged at the outer edges of his consciousness. The coyotes' singsong chorus continued.

``We do not have much time,'' the old man said softly.

Frank remembered the despair, apathy, and rage he had been battling for so long. Somehow the fear he was experiencing now seemed less threatening. He knew he could not go on the way he had been. Something had to change. And he *had* asked Henry to teach him the old ways.

``What do I do?'' he asked, finally.

Henry smiled at him. ``You must be cleansed in preparation. Take off your clothes.''

As Frank began removing his boots, Henry walked to his saddle and untied a buckskin bag and a tightly woven willow basket, which had been coated with pine tar to waterproof it. He dipped some water from the stream into the basket and set it on the ground in front of Frank.

Continuing to disrobe, Frank watched as the old man opened the buckskin bag and removed some yucca blossoms. Beginning a song Frank had never heard before, Henry crushed and threw a few of the blossoms to each of the four directions.

He reached once more into the bag and took out a handful of crushed yucca root and stirred it into the water, creating a sudsy foam. Henry handed the basket to Frank, who stood naked now in the early morning light. ``Offer the basket to the four directions. Ask the spirits to bless it, then scrub yourself well with the suds.''

As Frank complied, Henry sang another song, which Frank had never heard. Frank tried to follow the words but found he could not do so and complete his own prayers at the same time. He focused on his own task. When he had finished the prayers, he scrubbed his body thoroughly. There was something both soothing and invigorating about the feel of the yucca suds. Henry's voice became a rich, deep, background murmur, barely distinguishable from the sounds of the creek.

When Frank was finished, Henry took the basket from him and emptied it onto the ground between them, asking the earth to accept the gift.

He led Frank into the sacred waters of the stream and had him stand facing east. Using the basket, the old man poured water over him. Frank flinched at the first touch of the cold water but the chill quickly passed. Henry sang another song, asking the sacred water to accept the pain and sorrow and evil and ignorance being washed away, and to transmute it into harmonious, life-giving energy. He repeated the pouring and the song three more times, turning Frank to each of the four directions. Just as the first rays of the rising sun filtered through the pines onto the pond, stream, and meadow, Henry led Frank out of the water and onto the grassy bank.

When Frank was seated in a patch of sunshine facing the rising sun, Henry sat down in front of him. He placed the empty basket between them.

``You are cleansed now, and empty like the basket. Your father the sun fills you with a new light of understanding which will lead you towards your spirit name. But there are some final words of the old way that must be spoken first."

Henry paused and closed his eyes. He tilted his head to one side as though listening to something very far away. When he finally spoke, it seemed to Frank the old man's voice was touched with some powerful hint of eternity itself.

``I have told you the stories of Ussen, Giver-of-all-Life, and of White-Painted Woman. I have spoken to you of the Gahan and how they always stand ready to help the Tinde who live honorable lives.

``Now it is time to speak of beginnings and endings, the circle of life. Ussen grants you life and you arrive from the body of your mother. In the early days you ride the cradleboard, protected and cared for by your mother and her power. These are the days of the rising sun, days of laughter and joy.

66

``Then you leave the cradleboard and enter a time of much learning and begin to care for yourself. But you are without a spirit name and without power. These are the days of the morning sun, long and filled with many wonders.

``When the days of the morning sun have passed, you enter the time of action, of hunting, and marriage, and war. These are days of much power, the days of the afternoon sun.

``When you have grown old and your hair white, like the mountains in the time of the snows, you enter the days of the evening sun. These days are filled with memories, and with much wisdom and sound counsel.

``These are the four times of a man's life. You have passed through the days of the rising sun, and the days of the morning sun. You have entered the days of the afternoon sun. But you have no spirit name, and therefore you have not had power. Your life has been hard. Without power a man can not find his center.

``Now you are prepared to seek your spirit name. You must leave behind your fear and self-doubt. In the days of the afternoon sun, if your wife or children are killed and it gives you cause for great grief, and you say, `I am wronged, and I cannot go on,' then you will be weakened and dishonored. Your enemies will attack. You will fall, just as the deer who is weakened in battle with the wolves, and lags behind the herd, falls to the wolves while the rest escape.

``But if you say, `I am wronged, and I am angered by this, and my anger gives me strength for action,' then you will be honored for this by the people. They will follow you in action. By your anger and strength they will know the depth of your grief. And your enemies will run away as the wolves run away when the wounded buck turns on them and attacks, killing many with hooves and antlers.

``These things you must know in the time of the afternoon sun. That is why I speak to you in this way.

``Without power, none of this will be possible. Your fear and self-doubt will consume you. That is why you must complete the rest of this naming ceremony correctly.

Apache Tears

``In the time of the afternoon sun, every choice you make will be your choice: to hunt deer or to hunt antelope; to live in peace or to war; to follow your leader to a new location or to remain behind alone. No one else will make such choices for you. You may seek counsel, but the choice must be yours.

``When confusion besets you, you must rely on your power for wisdom. The power you are granted with your spirit name will always be yours. You may call upon it at any time.

``You may sometimes ask for power from other sources, from the Gahan, or the wind spirits, or the water spirits. Sometimes you will receive it, sometimes not. But your naming ceremony power will be with you always. You need only call on it in the manner in which you are instructed.''

Henry paused. He threw pollen from his medicine pouch to the four directions as he sang another ancient song. He took the basket to the stream and dipped water into it then returned to sit in front of Frank.

``Now it is time to speak of the closing of the circle. It is time to speak of death. You have learned well to heal bodies. But you have also learned that healing bodies does not always forestall death.''

Henry took his knife from the sheath he wore on his belt. ``Ussen fills your body with the spirit of life as the stream fills this basket with water. When the basket is old, and cracked, or when it is injured badly in battle or hunting, as I injure the basket with my knife, thus, then the spirit drains away to rejoin Ussen as this water drains away to rejoin the stream.

``A healer of the Tinde knows that healing the body is only part of his task. He must also convince the spirit to return. He knows he cannot force it, he can only coax. If he has power and is persuasive, the healing is done. If he is not, the person will die, though the body may be healed.

``Only when a death is dishonorable, according to the ways of the Tinde, only then does the spirit become trapped in this world. It must then live in great discomfort and sorrow and anger for many gatherings of the mescal. Such spirits spread disharmony and sickness

68

among the Tinde, until the proper ceremony has been done to return them to Ussen.

``For one who would have power, honor in life must always be more important than death."

Henry returned his knife to its sheath and sat silently for a long time, looking at Frank. Finally he nodded.

``Now I have spoken all you must hear of these things. It is time to speak of your search for your spirit name. You must take great care. Follow these instructions exactly.

``When I leave, you will dress yourself and climb there," he pointed to a rock formation up the side of the ridge behind Frank and to his right. ``You will sit with your back to the rock, facing the place where the sun rises. You will stay there four days. You will not eat. You will come down to the stream and drink once with each rising of the sun, and once with each setting of the sun. Four swallows only.

``Four times each day you will sing your prayers to the spirits of the four directions; once when the sun rises, before you drink; once when the sun is at its highest point; once when the sun sets, before you drink; and once when the moon disappears. You must not sleep."

Frank found the rhythms of the old man's words almost hypnotic. He worried briefly that he would not be able to remember everything, but the concern passed as his great uncle continued.

``Spirits may come to you in many forms. Some may try to frighten you away. When fear stalks you, you must hold tightly to this."

He handed Frank the piece of shrapnel to which had been tied a mockingbird feather, a bit of coyote fur, and a bear claw. A hole had been drilled in the metal and a leather thong threaded through it. Henry gestured, and Frank tied it around his neck, the shrapnel hanging in the center of his chest.

``You must hold to that and neither move nor look away. If you do either, you will be in great danger. If you do as I say, you will be safe.

``Some spirits may speak to you. You must not answer. One will ask you why you do not answer. Only then may you speak. You must speak these words as I speak them: `I am of the Tinde, but I have no spirit name. I do not know when spirit words are meant for me.'

``Then you must wait and listen carefully. The spirit will give you a name, and a song with which to call your power. When he calls you by your spirit name, you may speak and ask what questions you wish. But be very careful to remember your song. Without it your name will be of little use.

``When the spirit is gone, you will continue as before. But instead of the songs I have taught you, you must sing your power song. On the morning of the fifth day I will come for you."

Henry stood and faced the new day's sun. He sang a song from somewhere deep in his chest, a sonorous, rhythmic wordless chant. He shifted his gaze from the sun to the surface of the stream and knelt beside it. He dipped his hands into the sacred water, stood, and turned to Frank. He crouched in front of Frank and touched one wet hand to Frank's forehead, the other to his stomach just below his navel.

The old man stood again then. Frank looked up at him, silhouetted against the morning sun. Golden fire leaped from the edges of the old man's form. It seemed to Frank that his great uncle grew steadily larger until he was nearly three times his normal size. When Henry spoke, his voice boomed around the meadow, echoing off the hillsides.

``The Gahan have summoned you, Frank Redhawk. Go now and seek your spirit name."

Henry turned and walked away from Frank, towards his saddle. As he moved, he seemed to shrink again to normal size. He made a low whickering noise in his throat as he walked. Before the old man reached his saddle, both horses reappeared out of the pines.

By the end of the second day, Frank was beginning to wonder what he was doing. He had followed his uncle's instructions faithfully. The hardest part had been sitting in one place for so long, though he had struggled more than once with a near-overpowering hunger. Plenty of animals had come and gone from the stream and pond during the

70

time, and Frank had felt a deeper kinship with them than ever before. But there had not been a single incidence of anything he could classify as unusual, much less supernatural.

The doubts plagued him for a time, but in the end he decided to stay. On the second night the spirits began to arrive.

The moon had just risen when an eagle, taller than a man, swooped out of the darkness and landed on the ground in front of Frank with a great rustling of feathers. The eagle screamed angrily, turning its great head from side to side, looking at Frank first out of one piercing yellow eye, then the other. Only when it finally flew off into the night, did Frank realize he had ceased breathing. He pulled great gulps of the cool night air into his lungs. Adrenaline pounded in his ears. When nothing more happened for a long time, he began to wonder if he had fallen asleep and dreamed the visit.

No sooner had the question occurred to him than twin mountain lions emerged soundlessly out of the shadows. Frank felt a new jolt of fear as they prowled around him, sniffing at his feet and hands, coughing and growling. Somehow Frank knew they were talking together about whether to kill this strange-man creature, dump his spirit back into the stream, and carry his body off to their lair. One of them snarled, lethal fangs flashing in the moonlight. Frank slowly moved his left hand to the piece of shrapnel and clutched it tightly. He kept his gaze focused on a spot between the two lions and was able thereby to watch both without looking at either.

One of the big tawny cats sat in front of him and reached out with a paw towards his foot. It hooked a claw into his boot and tugged. Frank heard the nylon insert rip. The sound startled the cat, which jumped backwards. After a moment longer, they, too, turned away from him and faded back into the shadows.

Frank did not move for a long time. His mouth was dry and his muscles ached from the tension. After several minutes he reached down slowly and felt his boot. There was a tear in the nylon that had not been there. He knew he was not dreaming.

His rational mind ceased struggling against his senses. What

71

was happening couldn't be happening, yet it was. He knew it was futile to deny it. He could only wait. He kept going over his great uncle's instructions, certain now they were far more than ``cultural heritage,'' and that in some indefinable way his entire future hung on following them carefully.

Just before dawn, a beaver appeared. It was no larger than most beavers, but it showed no fear of him. It sniffed at his legs, and spoke.

``Why do you sit there under this tree I wish to cut down?''

Frank fought an impulse to answer. He waited, trying to control the trembling which gripped him.

``You are a very rude man not to answer me. Do you not know who I am? I am Beaver. I have much power to give. Many healers call upon me. Am I not worthy of an answer?''

Still Frank remained silent, waiting, hoping it would ask him why he did not answer. In the old ways, he knew, the beaver had great healing power. But the question did not come. Instead the beaver sniffed at his leg again.

``Perhaps you are not of the Tinde,'' the beaver said. ``I shall have to save my power for one with better manners.'' It turned and ambled away into the darkness.

Frank felt a keen sense of disappointment. His great uncle had told him his path was the path of a healer. He had been certain the beaver would ask him the key question, but it had not. *Maybe I'm really not Tinde,* he thought. *Maybe I spent too much time in the world of the Pinda Lickoyi. Maybe I am not worthy of power.*

As the dawn emerged from behind the eastern mountains and pale light made its way down into the valley, Frank stood and stretched. He searched the ground carefully around the rock where he had been sitting. He could find no tracks other than his own. For a moment he doubted the reality of the night's experiences. Until he remembered his boot. He looked down. The nylon was torn. Frank took a deep breath and let it out slowly. He didn't understand what was happening, but most of his doubts as to its reality disappeared.

He made his way down to the stream. He sang his songs. He

cupped his hand, dipped it into the stream, and brought it to his lips. He drank his four swallows slowly. He understood why the People considered water sacred.

The third day was more difficult by far. Many times he fought off the clutches of sleep. Waves of hunger rolled over him, causing the world to spin. The heat of the midday sun tormented him. His throat constricted with thirst, making breathing difficult. He drifted back and forth through the events of the past two days, and then further back.

Once he was certain his mother and her Mormon missionary friend were standing at the bottom of the rock formation upon which he sat. She screamed up at him, cursing him, while the missionary prayed for his soul's salvation and laughed.

Late in the afternoon he heard artillery fire in the distance. He watched dead friends fight futilely against endless hordes of black-pajama-clad Orientals rushing down out of the pines across the valley. He heard voices to his right. ``Corpsman! Corpsman, God, I can't see!"

``Corpsman up! Corpsman up! They're all dead!"

Tears streamed down his face as the words echoed over and over. ``Corpsman up! God, they're all dead! Corpsman up!"

A coyote climbed onto a rock about ten feet from him. It sat on its haunches and looked at him. ``You couldn't save them, could you?" it asked, and grinned.

Frank wanted to scream, but dared not. *I tried, damnit. I tried.* The tears came again.

The coyote approached him. Frank didn't move. It sniffed at his ear and whispered. ``You loved them. That's all you could do." It turned and walked away.

At sunset, Frank tried to sing his songs, but his voice was cracked and hoarse. All that came out were a few tortured sounds. He fell twice on his way down to the stream. He bathed his face and neck. It took all his willpower to limit himself to four swallows of the water.

Back on his rocky ledge, as darkness came, he began to shiver. It got progressively worse until, by the time the moon appeared, his body ached from the spasms. The moonlight seemed to somehow warm him and he began to relax.

Then came long battles against the sleep that tried to overcome him. At one point he drew his knife and braced it on his knee with its point against the soft part of his throat beneath his chin. Twice his head nodded and the tip of the knife drew blood.

When the moon had disappeared again, and he had once more sung his songs, he heard noises all around him. He knew the spirits were coming again.

A creature with the body of a man, the wings of an eagle, and the head of a deer appeared before him and shouted at him in a language he did not understand. When it had gone, another came. This one, too, had the body of a man, but the head of a wolf. He carried a great bow and a single shining golden arrow, which he fired at Frank. Only with great effort did Frank keep from crying out as the shaft passed through his body and the rock behind him and returned to the quiver of the wolf-man. Then he, too, disappeared.

The darkness closed in around Frank. He took comfort from it. He wrapped himself in it, wanting the invisibility it offered. He was frightened, and more alone than he had ever been. A heavy, almost suffocating depression settled on him. He wasn't sure he could go on.

He was certain these spirits had represented great powers, yet none had asked him the critical question. He knew somehow now that none would. He was not worthy. He had waited too long to try to claim his Apache heritage. He had come too far from the world of the white eyes. He had lost both. He had fallen into a crack between worlds from which he would never escape.

Suddenly his father was standing before him, lit from within by a pale golden light. At the sight of him a great anger erupted in Frank's gut and roared upwards through his chest. He clenched his teeth to keep from shouting the curses that shrieked through his consciousness. With his fists, Frank pounded the rock upon which he sat.

His father smiled a sad smile. ``It was all I could give you,'' he said softly. ``Use it wisely.'' He turned and disappeared into the darkness.

What, Frank wanted to yell. *What did you give me?* And then he heard his great uncle's words again:

``But if you say, `I am wronged, and I am angered by this, and my anger gives me strength for action,' then you will be honored for this by the People and they will follow you in action. By your anger and strength they will know the depth of your grief. And your enemies will run away.''

The anger eased but Frank held onto a part of it and stored it away in his heart next to a love for his father he had not known was there.

The stars moved down from the heavens and sat with him as the remaining hours of darkness passed in a quiet peace Frank had never before known.

With the dawn of the fourth day, Frank tried three times to stand, and three times his legs buckled under him. On his fourth try he used his anger as a crutch and managed to make it down off the rocks before his legs gave out again. It didn't matter. He crawled the rest of the way to the stream. With the rising of the sun, he lay on his back and weakly sang his songs. When he had finished, he rolled over and dipped his cupped hand in the water. As he sipped, he felt a change taking place inside him. Something old and worn and sad had left him in the night. The sacred water seemed to spread out through his body, filling empty spaces, cleansing wounds he had forgotten, making whole parts of himself he thought had been broken forever. It filled him with a new and different strength. When he got to his feet, the trembling weakness in his legs was gone.

He took tobacco from his medicine pouch and made a wordless offering to the four directions and to the sacred stream. He turned and climbed back towards the rocks. A sense of anticipation grew as he made his way slowly up the slope. *It is the fourth day. It will be today, or tonight.*

The morning was filled with a symphony of bird songs and an endless parade of animals coming to drink the sacred waters. Deer and elk grazed side by side. A mountain lion lolled in the sun grooming herself in the fastidious way of all felines, watching her cubs cavort in the grassy meadow. Beaver worked industriously on their dam and fish jumped in the pond, covering its surface with endlessly interlocking circular ripples.

The coyote from the night before appeared on the rocks below where Frank sat, a freshly killed rabbit in its mouth. It ignored Frank while it ate, then turned to look up at him and grin before trotting off. Frank laughed, even as he struggled against the hunger the coyote had re-triggered.

With Frank's noon songs, great billows of cumulus clouds built over the peaks east of him, rising ever higher into the clear blue of the sky. Their bases spread out as they moved towards him. Distant thunder rumbled off the mountainsides. The bases of the clouds turned a dark, steel gray. Lightning flickered through their writhing masses. A restless wind tossed the trees and bushes in the valley. The birds fell silent. The beaver disappeared into their conical dens. The fish sank to the bottom of the pond. The animals left the open meadow, seeking shelter.

The clouds moved over the valley, blotting out the sun. A great stillness descended on the earth. Frank moved back closer to the rocks behind him. He noticed his breathing had become shallow and quiet. Huge, cold drops of rain began to fall, singly at first, then faster, painting a mosaic of splatters on the rocks.

There was a blinding flash of light followed instantly by an explosive crack as a bolt of lightning hit the rock formation above and behind Frank. Every hair on his body stood out straight. A tingling wave of energy surged through him. Adrenaline poured into his system and he clutched the shrapnel on his chest and fought the impulse to run.

Another flash and another crack and the rock he was sitting on split open. He felt himself falling into a great darkness as the mountain swallowed him.

The falling sensation gradually waned, but Frank could neither move nor see. Only his sense of touch convinced him he had not died. With every inch of his body he could feel the cool, grainy texture of rock. It was not crushing him, but seemed to move with his breathing.

It was as though he were encased somehow inside the mountain itself.

At first it seemed the silence, too, was absolute. But after a time Frank became aware of a deep, slow, ponderous, rhythmic pulse; so slow and deep that he did not actually hear it with his ears, but rather perceived it with his entire body.

He knew he should be terrified, but he was not. The rocks encasing him emanated an indescribably profound love, wordless, unconditional, and eternal.

His heartbeat, his breathing, his thoughts, every bodily process, slowed inexorably towards a harmonic resonance with the bass rumble, which pulsed through him. A mild wave of anxiety arose. *I am dying,* he thought, but he experienced no fear.

With a hesitant patience he waited, for what could have been an instant, or an eternity. Then, as he felt himself move in some mysterious way into a state of perfect balance with the mountain around him, a wave of pure bliss floated him gently upwards and away from his body.

He found himself in a dimensionless space, and images of the Tinde swirled around him: a raiding party, dressed in the old way and armed only with bows and short lances, in victorious battle against dark-bearded men in suits of armor and firing ancient muskets; a cluster of summer wickiups all ablaze and Mexican soldiers moving among the bodies of the people – men, women and children – taking scalps; a hunting party moving out of a village filled with the laughter of children and the quiet words of women going about their work; the great leader Mangas Colorado sitting in council with blue-clad soldiers, promising peace in return for peace, and the great leader later, dead in a pool of blood on the ground next to the army camp fire, a horse soldier corporal reloading his pistol; a joyous celebration of the White-Painted Woman ceremony in the sacred place, a Great Gathering of the people, blessing the passage of their young girls into womanhood; the great Tinde leader Cochise looking at the bloated bodies of his son, his wife, and his nephew, hung by the white-eye army officer who had lured them into the army camp under the white flag of truce; images of his people dead of starvation and food poisoning on the reservation near Fort Bowie because the white-eye agent traded their healthy cattle to nearby white-eye ranchers, and substituted diseased cattle in their place; old Nana, perhaps the greatest of all the warriors, leading a pitiful, sick and hunger-weakened band of eighty of the Tinde off the reservation on foot to escape a small-pox epidemic, fighting a twelve-hundred-mile running battle against white-eye horse soldiers, leading his band into the Chiricahuas only to find their springs and streams poisoned, and then on into the Sierra Madres of Mexico, where they wanted only to be left alone to hunt and heal themselves, and hounded out and back north and eventually back to the reservation at Fort Bowie, having lost only two men in battle to the horse soldiers' seventy, but having lost thirty-two of the Tinde to starvation; scenes of Geronimo, healer-turned-war-chief, leading a band off the reservation after all their farming implements had been confiscated because they violated white-eye prohibitions against certain religious ceremonies, raiding a white-eye ranch for horses with which to reach the mountains in the south so they could hunt and bring food back to the people; scenes of the reservation in the Chiricahuas in the 1920's and 30's, BIA agents backed up by Marshals with rifles, forcibly taking children from their parents to be placed in off-reservation missionary-run boarding schools; scenes of the children being whipped for speaking the language of the Tinde, and forbidden to speak of their religious ways – all these images whirled around him and he knew they were part of who he was.

The grief, the torment, the betrayals, the anguish, the pain, the hopelessness, all vied for possession of his soul, but his anger protected him. He let it grow into an implacable resolve in which he wrapped himself as the images faded.

From somewhere his father's voice came, echoed, and faded: ``Use it wisely-isely-isely.''

He became aware again of the mountain's rumbling pulse. The profound sense of love that accompanied it mixed with his anger, softening it, strengthening it. The pulse began to change, to fluctuate slowly, to coalesce into near-recognizable sounds, which became words in his mind.

``This is wisdom, man of the People. Anger must never be without love. This is wisdom."

He waited. More words came. ``The circle of the Tinde is near completion. A great sickness of the spirit is upon them. For a hundred passings of the white wind from the North, for a hundred seasons of rebirths from the East, for a hundred cycles of summer rains coming from the South, for a hundred gatherings of the Mescal in the West in the shortening days of the dying sun, the spirit of the people has been draining away. It must be restored soon. If not, then though ten-thousand bodies may live, the Tinde will die and be no more. This you must do. For this we have summoned you."

Frank waited, but no more words came. There was only the quiet, implacable, eternal power of the mountains gently lowering him again into his body, cradling him in the cool, grainy touch of their embrace. Frank drifted, aware of nothing else, until he opened his eyes.

He was lying on his side, his cheek against the rock. A soft breeze caressed him with the fresh scent of rain-wet pine. The sun had disappeared behind the ridgeline to the west. Above the eastern peaks, cloud formations flamed orange and red. He sat up and looked down into the valley. Deer grazed on the edges of the meadow near the pines. On the far side of the pond a coyote drank, sat back on its haunches, and raised its muzzle in a long, wavering, haunting wail. It howled again and was answered from the south, from the ridgeline behind Frank to the west, and finally from the north.

Frank joined their chorus with his evening songs. When he had finished, the coyote drank again before moving off into the trees and up the eastern slope.

The colors on the clouds faded to pinks and mauves. Darkness crept down from the west, past Frank, and into the valley. The breeze died, was reborn, rustled softly through the trees around him as though seeking somewhere to rest, and then was still again. Gradually the birds settled into their roosts and ceased their final protests against the coming of the night. A deep silence took possession of the sacred place.

Frank did not try to think. His clothes, still damp from the afternoon rain, chilled him and he began to shiver. He did not mind and so did not resist. He merely waited. The words of the Gahan echoed in his consciousness. He marveled at the love he felt for the rocks upon which he sat, for the mountains that surrounded him. He smiled as he sensed the return of that love, magnified a thousand-fold. He knew as long as these mountains remained, he would never again be alone.

The moon was well above the eastern horizon and bathing the rocks around him in blue light when he first heard the snufflings and gruntings in the trees to his left. He knew it was a bear, and from its sounds, a large one. His heartbeat quickened and his hand went to the shrapnel at his breast. He was not frightened of bears, but wasn't entirely comfortable with them, either.

The sounds came closer and circled around below him and up to his right. He caught glimpses of the great mass of the creature, the silver-tipped fur luminescent in the moonlight. It was a large grizzly, the greatest of all bears, with courage and strength beyond reckoning, sacred above all animals to the people. At some level, Frank knew the last grizzly in Arizona had been killed forty years before. At another he knew that this data was irrelevant. He had no doubts about the reality of what he was seeing.

The Bear circled him cautiously, never coming clearly into view, and finally stopped in the shadows to his right.

``Why are you shivering, man of the people? Have none of my brothers given you fur to keep the night chill away?''

Frank dared not speak but he felt himself relaxing very slightly. He experienced the beginnings of an affection for this spirit who, alone of all the spirits, had shown some awareness of his discomfort.

``Why do you not answer me, man of the Tinde?''

Frank's heart raced. He took a deep breath and let it out slowly. ``I am of the Tinde,'' he said, his voice a hoarse whisper, ``but I have no spirit name. I do not know when spirit words are meant for me.''

There was a long moment of silence, and then the massive Bear climbed up the rock formation into the moonlight, stopping no more than ten feet in front of Frank. It was a magnificent beast, an ancient male, covered with scars. He stood on his hind legs and swayed from side to side, towering twelve feet above Frank.

``Then, man of the Tinde, I shall name you Walks-With-Bear, for I see your courage. I see your honor. I see your scars, and I see that your spirit does not drain away. I see your love for the people and your respect for the ways of the spirit. I see the power of the Gahan in your heart. I see your love for your mother, the land. I am honored to share my power with you.''

The great creature dropped back onto all fours and walked towards Frank, stopping about four feet away. Frank could feel the warmth of the Bear's breath, could smell the clean, pungent odor of its musk.

``I am hungry, Walks-With-Bear. I have come to this place to dig bear lilies. I would be honored by your company.''

The Bear's massive presence filled Frank with a warm, scintillating energy. He felt an immense joy and love for this creature. ``It is I who would be honored, grandfather,'' he said, getting easily to his feet, the physical ordeals forgotten, their effects vanished.

When the great grizzly had finished feasting on bear lily roots, it rambled along in the stream, overturning huge rocks with an astonishing ease and topping its meal off with the crayfish delicacies it discovered.

Frank kept pace on the bank. Despite a question he ached to ask, he held his silence, waiting respectfully until the Bear had finished eating. Finally the big beast seemed satisfied.

``This is a good place to come,'' the Bear said. ``I have been away a long time.'' He moved into the center of the stream and lowered himself into the water, rolling from side to side. He stood again, and shook his massive frame, water droplets flashing like a crystal aura in the silvery blue light. He shook again, and then broke into an ambling run towards the bank.

He leaped out of the water with an agility that astonished Frank, shook himself again, and rolled in the meadow grass, lolling finally at Frank's feet.

``Join me, Walks-With-Bear,'' he said. ``It would be good to talk.''

Frank seated himself next to the ancient grizzly. ``I have many questions, grandfather,'' he began, ``because my ignorance is great. But I have a confusion through which I might not hear your answers.

``My great uncle, Henry Laughing Bird, has told me my path is the path of the healer. The Gahan have given me a healer's task. You have given me my spirit name and have offered to share your power. I am honored, but I am also confused. I know little of the old ways yet, but I have always believed your power to be the power of the warrior...''

The great beast cut Frank off with a snarling roar. With a sudden swipe of one massive paw, it ripped Frank's chest open, knocking him onto his back. Blood spouted into the moonlight. The bear was on its feet in an instant, towering over Frank.

Pain and terror saturated Frank's consciousness for several long seconds, before the ancient beast lowered its massive head and began licking at the wounds. In moments they were healed, the pain gone, and the terror replaced by an absolute trust.

The Bear laid down next to Frank again. ``The power of the warrior, Walks-With-Bear, and the power of the healer are the same Power. Your ancestor, Geronimo, knew this truth. It served him well.''

Frank sat in silence for a long time. ``I am honored by your teaching,'' he said finally.

The Bear got to his feet. ``Come, Walks-With-Bear, let us return to your place on the rocks. The moon is nearly gone and it is time for you to learn your power song. The Gahan have given you a great task.''

Frank's Bear song was not a song at all, in any traditional sense. It was, rather, a deep, guttural growling that started in his chest and was modulated by irregular constrictions of his throat. Learning it had been complicated at first, but after a couple tries he had managed to duplicate the sound the Bear was making by way of instruction. After a few repetitions he had mastered it, and it seemed now as natural as speaking.

``You sing well, Walks-With-Bear. When you call, I will hear.''

Frank looked at the ancient beast seated on the rocks to his right. The moon hung low over the ridgeline behind him. Its light had taken on a liquid quality, reflecting off the silver tips of the grizzly's fur in a shimmering blue-white aura.

``I will try always to call upon your power wisely, grandfather.''

The Bear nodded in silent acknowledgment. Lifting a scarred muzzle towards the stars, the Bear snuffled at the night's delicate air currents. ``The moon will be gone soon, and then I, too, shall go.''

``Have I time for one final question, grandfather?''

``I have been waiting for you to ask it.''

``The Gahan have told me I must recover the spirit of the Tinde. I have accepted the task, but I don't understand it. How am I to know what to do?''

``Listen to your heart. In your heart the Gahan will guide you. Follow your path. Dance with the opportunities chance provides. In these matters, intentions are more important than plans, the moment more important than concerns about tomorrow.''

The great Bear stood and raised its big head to once more read the night air. The moon was half-hidden behind the ridge and a line of dark shadow edged down the slope towards them.

``It is time, Walks-With-Bear.''

Before Frank could respond, the old grizzly turned and moved off into the trees. Frank listened until the last sound of its ambling gait faded into the cricket-accented silence of the night.

Frank sat without moving. He listened to the crickets, felt the texture of the rock upon which he sat, and watched the shadows move past him, down into the valley and up the eastern slope. When the last of the moonlight was gone, he sang his Bear song to the four directions. Somewhere on the other side of the mountains, thunder rumbled faintly. He looked up at the stars. They seemed to have crept down close to the sacred valley, doming it with their brilliance. Frank floated on the bliss of near perfect solitude.

Dawn, July 20 --- The Secret Place

At first light, Henry Laughing Bird rode into the valley, leading Frank's horse. Frank made his way down out of the rocks to meet the old man at the stream below the beaver dam.

Henry grasped Frank by the shoulders and studied him silently and intently. Frank felt the familiar pull of that compelling gaze. At length the old man nodded his head once, and smiled. ``You have done well, nephew. Let us gather some berries and break your fast. When we have eaten we will talk of your experiences."

The sun was well up by the time Frank had finished telling his story of the four days and nights. Henry had listened intently, asking an occasional question to elicit more details about some particular event.

When Frank had finished, they sat across from each other in silence. The cool water rushings of the stream, interwoven with the songs of many birds, filled the morning.

``You have truly been honored," Henry said finally. ``You have been given a great responsibility, but you have also been granted much power."

``I would be more comfortable, uncle, if I knew for sure how to use it," Frank answered. ``I don't even know where to begin."

``You have already begun. You began when you agreed to seek your spirit name. Now you have your name and great power as well. You will know how to use it when the time comes." The old man paused. ``And that time may come sooner than you expect." He got to his feet.

``Come. There are many things happening which you must know about. We will go to my cabin. We can talk as we ride, then you must sleep."

``There were times I was certain I could not stay awake," Frank said. ``Now I am not certain I can sleep. I feel a tremendous sense of urgency."

Apache Tears

The old man laughed, the buoyant sounds bouncing off the walls of the valley. ``You will have no problems with sleep, Walks-With-Bear. Just sing your power song. Bear knows all the secrets of sleep and dreams."

CHAPTER FOUR: FRIENDS

Shortly after dawn, July 16 --- Om'nitche

After leaving Frank at the hospital the night of the rape, Clay had walked into Om'nitche for breakfast at the town's only cafe.

Now, an hour later, Clay squinted against the rising sun as he walked from the cafe to Oscar's house on the edge of town. Though the coffee and food had helped, he was tired. It had been a long night at the hospital, and he was irritated about having to leave his Winchester with the Tribal Police.

He wondered if he should forget about seeing Oscar until later, but he thought of the pinto tied to a tree. The horse would need water soon. Of course, he could go back to the hospital and ask the reservation police to give him a lift to the horse, but he did want to see Oscar.

He hesitated as he approached the front of the house. The early rays of light bounced from the spotless windows to the neat rows of snapdragons planted before them. The house was white, trimmed in cocoa, the wood-frame construction a far cry from the wickiup Clay remembered Oscar living in when he was a kid.

He walked up the swept dirt path to the door. He hesitated. He hadn't seen Oscar for so many years – and he had written to him only

86

one time since Billy's death, to tell him how it had happened – perhaps another time would be better. He shouldn't just come barging in. He needed a shave and a bath. The smell of his own body was apparent to him as he stood before the door. He turned to leave.

A tanned six-year-old face peered around the edge of the curtain behind the window. Clay smiled and waved. The face showed a white smile. The door opened.

``Are you looking for someone, mister?''

This was an older face, a woman's face. She had no smile, but neither did she frown. She had a look of reserved curiosity about her. Her straight black hair framed a strong face with high cheekbones and piercing dark eyes. She acted as though it were a commonplace occurrence for a stranger to show up at the door at dawn.

Clay faltered. ``Well, ma'am. . . I was going to call on Oscar. . . but I just realized that it's a little early for making social calls. I can come back later.'' He felt stupid.

``Who should I say is calling?'' She opened the door a bit wider, and he could see she was wearing a housecoat.

``My name's Clay, but you folks aren't up yet. I'll come back later if it's all right with you.'' His gunbelt added to his self-consciousness.

The woman's expression changed. A hint of recognition entered her eyes. ``You're Clay Price, aren't you?''

Clay hid his surprise. ``Yes, ma'am, but you have me at a disadvantage. Are you Mrs. Gosheyun?''

She opened the door fully. ``Yes.'' A warm smile covered her face. ``Please come in. Oscar has talked of you often. He calls you his only white brother. Please.'' She stepped to the side and motioned him in.

He entered, still voicing apologies for the early intrusion. She ignored his rhetoric. ``Please sit down. I'll wake Oscar. He'll be so happy to see you.'' She left him standing there as she moved down the short hallway to their bedroom.

The little face stared up at him, a toothy grin covering a large portion of the brown. Clay smiled. ``What's your name?''

``Billy-Clay, what's your name?''

Clay's heart went to his throat. ``Did you say 'Billy-Clay?'''

The boy's grin expanded. ``Billy-Clay Gosheyun. My father says I am named for two great warriors. Are you going hunting?'' The little man looked at Clay's holstered pistol.

Clay knelt next to Billy-Clay. ``I was thinking about it. How old are you?''

``I'll be seven next month. You wanna see my rifle?''

``You've got a rifle of your own?''

``Yes, but I can't touch it unless I'm with my father. When he gets up, I'll show it to you.''

Clay rubbed Billy-Clay's hair. ``I can hardly wait.'' He heard fast footsteps in the hallway and turned to see Oscar rushing to him, clad only in his undershorts.

He barely had time to stand before Oscar was hugging him and patting his back, tears streaming down his face. Clay was overcome, and he felt tears in his own eyes. They danced around the room, oblivious to the presence of the others. They stopped only when Mrs. Gosheyun cleared her throat in a manner intended to advise her husband that he should get dressed and make a more proper entrance.

They broke their embrace and Oscar stepped back to look at his Blood Brother. ``We all thought you were dead, Clay. I can't believe it's you, man. You look great! I was so proud for you when we heard about the Congressional Medal of Honor.''

Suddenly Clay was embarrassed by Oscar's lack of dress and his mention of the Medal. ``You look pretty good too, my friend, except those are about the scrawniest pair of legs I've ever seen.'' He smiled.

Oscar looked down at his scantily clad figure. ``Oh. I forgot. Don't you go anywhere. I'll be right back. Oh, this is my wife, Carla. Give me one minute.'' He disappeared down the hallway.

Clay wiped away the moisture in the corner of his eyes. He offered his hand to Carla. ``Pleased to meet you, Carla.''

88

Apache Tears

Oscar and Clay sat in the livingroom, talking about old times as the smell of cooking bacon wafted from the kitchen. Oscar's two older girls, ten-year-old Consuela and eight-year-old Tina, had yet to appear. They were in the bathroom, combing and primping for their important guest. Billy-Clay had put up a short fight, but after displaying his rifle for Clay's approval, he was at his mother's side in the kitchen. The two men were left alone.

``So how long have you been a fireman?'' asked Clay.

``Close to ten years, now.''

``Long time. Don't you get bored?''

``No. There's something new all the time. I'm a smokejumper and crew leader during the summer, and a fire captain the rest of the year.''

``Sounds like you've worked hard. To tell you the truth, I would have thought you, of all of us, would have been the one to goof off. You were always playing practical jokes and aggravating folks. Here you are, probably the most settled down one of the bunch.'' Clay paused. ``How's Elmer doing?''

Oscar studied the throw rug on the hardwood floor. ``Not so good, Clay. He's been on the bottle for about four years.''

``For what? I mean, what caused it?''

``Lots of things I guess. He got married about five years ago. A year later, his wife had a stillborn child – she damn near died in the process. The doctor said she couldn't have any more kids, and that was the beginning of the end for Elmer – the end of his marriage – his smile – his caring for about much of anything.

``He doesn't work – hell, he doesn't even have a hobby, unless you call drinkin' a hobby. He waits for that government check, and as soon as he gets it, he's back in the bar. When funds get low, he buys package liquor and takes it home with him.''

``Can't you do something to help him?''

``I've tried. We've all tried. I thought maybe if my kids were around him more, he'd take to them and think of them as his second family. It had the opposite effect.'' Oscar shook his head. ``There isn't much can be done for him now, Clay. If there's any doing to be done, Elmer has to do it himself."

``What about his wife?"

``She tried to help. She hung in there for a long time, but when she saw how hopeless it was, she divorced him."

``How long ago?"

``The divorce was final in late June."

``Last month?"

Oscar nodded.

``I guess I can't fault her for not tryin', can I? Where'd she go?"

``She had no place to go, so we. . . Carla and I. . . sort of . . . "

``Took me in."

Clay looked up at the sound of the woman's voice.

The woman who stood there was three inches shorter than Clay's five-feet-ten. Her hair was raven-black and worn straight. It fell loosely below the small of her back. Her high cheekbones accented a pair of dark eyes made more prominent by their largeness. Her nose had none of the angular look that distinguished most of her sisters, but was smaller and rounded. Her thirty-year-old figure was lithe and muscled, tanned by her maker at birth.

She offered her hand. ``I'm Maria Pipestem. I've heard a lot about you from – from Oscar and from Elmer."

``Pleased to meet you, Mrs. Pipestem." He stood and shook the offered hand.

``Maria. Please."

Clay nodded. He felt uncomfortable. Something in her eyes when she looked at him disturbed him.

``Breakfast is ready," Carla called from the kitchen.

Breakfast had been pleasant enough, though Clay had been apprehensive when Maria had been seated next to him for the meal. Once, when she stood to get more coffee, her leg had brushed his lightly. He was certain it had been accidental, but he was acutely aware of her presence. Everything she did seemed to magnify itself in his

90

mind. He was grateful when Oscar suggested a walk after they had finished their coffee.

They strolled in the dusty streets of Om'nitche, recalling days of joy, long-since past. The morning sun warmed their backs.

``I don't understand something, Oscar."

``What's that?"

``Now, don't misunderstand me, damnit, but that Maria is one of the finest-looking women I've ever seen in my life. There's got to be more to this booze business than her losing a kid and not being able to have anymore. Was she messing around on him?"

``I've got to admit, Clay, I'm a little disappointed in you. Maria was one of the most faithful wives you'll ever want to meet. Just because she's good-looking doesn't mean she's going to bed with every big shot that looks her way.

``She didn't want to marry Elmer in the first place, but her parents were poor, and her father wanted her out. Elmer didn't really want to get married either, but he felt sorry for her. He knew how she was treated at home.

``I know that sounds like a shaky way to start out a marriage, but after they settled into Elmer's place, and she got pregnant, I could see the change in both of them. They could hardly wait for the baby to get here.

``Elmer built a special room onto his wickiup; got it all set up and ready to go. Used wood-frame construction – looks odd as hell. I never saw a man more excited about the birthing of a baby.

``That night, in the hospital, when the baby was born dead, Elmer lost it. He went out in the hills with a couple bottles and didn't show up again for two days. When he got back, he heard about Maria not being able to have any more kids, and this time he disappeared for a week. He's never been the same.

``Maria's a damn good woman, Clay. It's not her fault she's good-lookin'."

Clay picked up a rock at the edge of the road. He tossed it into the trees on his left. ``You know, Oscar, you're right. I probably never would have thought of her sleeping with anybody else if she wasn't so damn good-lookin'. I guess that doesn't say much for me, does it?"

``The white man doesn't have a monopoly on those kinds of thoughts. There's talk around town since she moved in with us. Carla gets little snide remarks from some of the women."

``Carla's a mighty fine looking woman herself. I don't know how you or Elmer either one did so damn good. How does Carla put up with it? Does she get jealous?"

Oscar laughed, his dark hair bobbing. ``Not Carla. Maria is her best friend. Besides, Carla believes in the old ways. If she ever caught Maria in my bed, she would personally cut her nose off."

Clay smiled and winced playfully. ``Damn. That nose is too pretty to cut off."

``Are you interested?" It was asked lightheartedly.

``Not me, my friend. She's Elmer's woman. We're Blood Brothers, remember?" answered Clay.

``Ex-woman."

``Not as far as I'm concerned. She's still his woman, and maybe we can get them back together if we work on it."

``Give it up. You wouldn't recognize him now."

``Maybe not, but I'm going to visit him later. Right now, I need a lift to my horse."

``Horse? What horse?"

Clay related the story of the night before. When he finished, Oscar looked at him silently for a moment.

``Is Angela going to be all right?"

``The doctor says it's too early to tell, but he thinks so."

``That's a blessing, anyway. Angela is a good kid. Ever since her parents died, she's been stuck with that useless drunken uncle of hers. I'll stop in and see her later."

``You know, Oscar, this whole thing about me being here is strange. I don't know what made me come after all these years, but out of the blue, I just felt like I had to come. I can't explain it."

``You don't have to, man. It's good to see you."

``It's good to see you, brother. Things have changed so much, and yet they remain so much the same."

``Yeah, I know what you mean."

``Last night, I had the weirdest feeling as I came up on that camper and saw that guy pointing a pistol in Frank's face. It was like. . . well, it was like I was drawn to that spot by something – just like coming out here in the first place."

``Well, let's hope it doesn't take Divine Guidance to get you out here for your next visit." Oscar started back to his house. ``C'mon, let's get the truck and get going. I've got a horse trailer. I'll drive you down to Mr. Foster's place. I haven't seen the old man for years."

They drove the gravel road for some distance in silence before Clay spoke. ``You know, Oscar, I'd give a million bucks to turn back the clock fifteen or twenty years."

``I've thought about it too, brother. We could get Billy back. Elmer too. He's gone too for all practical purposes. Yeah, it would be nice to start over from about age fourteen, wouldn't it?"

``Maybe we can with Elmer."

``What the hell are you talking about?"

``Wait until you see my horse. He looks just like that little Roman-nosed pinto Elmer used to have. Same personality, too." Clay saw the small stand of cedar where the horse was tied. ``That's it, right up there. He should be off the road about twenty or thirty yards."

Oscar pulled the four-wheel-drive Bronco off to the side of the road and shut the engine off. He sat unmoving behind the wheel as he studied the little black-and-white pinto. ``I'll be damned. It takes me back in time just to look at that horse."

The pinto whinnied softly as he recognized Clay's scent.

Clay lifted the five-gallon water can from the back of the Bronco and watered his horse. He removed the saddle and rubbed the pony while Oscar fed him the small portion of hay they had brought along.

``I can't believe the resemblance," said Oscar softly. ``It's uncanny."

Clay smiled. ``What do you think? How about instead of taking me back to the Bar-X, you just give me a lift back to town? If I could use your place to shower and shave, I'd like to ride this little critter over to Elmer's and visit with him for a while. I'd sure like to see him."

``You know you're welcome to use my place anytime you want. You don't have to ask." Oscar couldn't take his eyes from the horse.

Mid-morning, July 16 --- Oscar's residence

Clay whistled off tune as he stepped into the saddle, rubbing his clean-shaven face with the back of his hand as he nudged the pinto forward. Oscar and his family stood beside him. Maria had left before the two men had returned with the horse.

``Good luck, Clay."

``I'll let you know how things come out."

Clay sat easily in the saddle as the pinto cantered to the east. The little horse was eager for exercise. Clay let him change gaits at his own will. The pinto moved into a trot, then back to a canter, then quickly to a lope. Soon, he was at a half-gallop. Clay reined him back. ``Whoa, little fella. Save some of that energy. You ain't still mad about me leaving you tied up all night, are you?"

The pinto slowed to a walk. Clay patted him on the neck.

A mile east of town, Elmer's wickiup came into view, complete with its odd-shaped wood-frame addition, tall television antenna and three chickencoops. Four old and battered pickup trucks dotted the landscape around the house. Only one of the trucks had tires, and all but one of those were flat. Clay shook his head. He reined up and sat the horse quietly as he took in the corral behind the house. He could make out two horses, a bay and a roan. They looked well cared for.

``Hello, the house," Clay raised his voice.

For a moment, nothing stirred but a gentle breeze passing through the scrub oak near where Clay sat atop the horse. He saw a dirty curtain move near the door. The door opened a few inches.

``Who the hell are you? And where did you get that horse?"

Elmer's gruff voice filled the air. He opened the door and stepped into the frame, a lever-action rifle held at his hip.

``Helluva way to greet a brother."

Elmer bent forward, straining his eyes to focus on the man and horse thirty yards from his door. ``Who the hell are you, white man?"

Clay felt a sadness. Perhaps he shouldn't have come. ``If I'm a white man, so then are you, brother. We shared blood in the Secret Place a long time ago."

Elmer moved towards him, stepping from the shade afforded by the ocotillo extension over his front door. He still showed no sign of recognition.

``You gonna keep me in this saddle all day, Elmer? It's getting hot just sittin' up here."

``I'll tell you when you can get down." Elmer moved closer.

Clay saw the gruff expression on Elmer's face collapse when recognition took hold. The man fell apart. He dropped his rifle and ran to where the pinto stood. The sudden move frightened the horse and Clay reined him in sharply. He dismounted quickly and let go of the reins.

``Clay! Is it really you?" They collided in a strong embrace. Clay could smell the heavy-sweet odor of cheap wine on Elmer's breath. It oozed from his body in the form of perspiration. It was all about him. Clay ached with sorrow for lost friends and lost lives.

Noon, July 16 --- Elmer's residence

They sat across the battered old kitchen table from one another, the white man, and the Apache. They stared into each other's bloodshot eyes as they talked. A bottle of bourbon sat on the table between them. Elmer had dug into his special reserve for the occasion. The bottle was almost empty.

On shaky legs, Elmer stood, knocking his chair to the floor. ``I got more whiskey. Don't worry about that." He moved to a cupboard.

``Hell, Elmer, don't you think we've had enough? It's barely noon, fer Chrissakes."

``What's the matter? Can't you hold yer likker anymore?''

``My friend, I can hold my likker and yer likker.''

``Tha's more like it. What say we drink until one of us passes out?''

``What the hell for?'' Clay was way beyond what he wanted to drink.

``So we can see who can drink the most.''

``Who gives a damn?''

``I do.''

Clay shook his head. ``Damn, Elmer, this ain't goin' according to plan at all. Let's quit drinkin' and sober up.''

``Why?'' Elmer sat the unopened bottle on the table and, after three attempts, righted his overturned chair and plopped into it, almost falling to the floor. He caught himself with one hand and pushed his way semi-upright.

``That's why. Hell, you can't barely sit up, much less stand,'' answered Clay when Elmer stopped tottering.

``Tha's okay. It don't make no difference. How much you want for that horse?''

``What horse?''

``The one you rode in here on. What the hell horse you think I'm talkin' 'bout?''

``Oh. That horse.'' Clay shook his head again. A feeble plan worked its way into his gray consciousness. ``I'll tell you what, Elmer, ol' buddy. I'll make you a bet. If you win, you can have the damn horse.''

``Iss a deal. Wait a minute. What do you get if you win?''

``You don't touch a drink of any kind of goddamn booze fer a month – nothin' – no whiskey, no beer, no wine – nothin'.''

Elmer screwed up his angular features as he considered Clay's challenge. ``What's the bet?''

``I say I can drink you under the table.''

Elmer grinned. He shrugged his large shoulders. ``You can't win. I've got too much practice.''

``I'll take a chance. What the hell you got to lose? You wanna step outside – see the horse again? Help you make up yer mind?''

Elmer looked suddenly very sober and very sad. ``I know what you're trying to do, brother. It won't work.''

``If the spirits are with me, it'll work.''

Elmer studied Clay. Suddenly he grinned and twisted the cap from the bottle. ``Give me yer glass.'' He laughed. ``You know, it's a long walk back to town.''

Clay glanced at the amber liquid in the bottle. He looked up to the ceiling. *Mr. Foster, I hope you ain't too fond of that horse, but I don't know any other way.*

Early afternoon, July 16 --- Elmer's residence

Clay crawled on his hands and knees from the house. He found the pinto standing next to the water trough. ``Move over, horse.'' He raised himself to the edge of the trough and slid into the green water, moccasins, gunbelt and all.

The tepid water did little to sober him. He slithered over the edge and fell to the ground. The pinto stood only a few feet away. ``Damn, horse, I'm drunk. Oh shit.'' He vomited on the ground, the foul liquid mixing with the horse dung at the edge of the trough. He wiped his mouth with the back of his hand and reached for the corral fence to aid him to his feet. He staggered and fell into the fencepost, striking his head. He fell on his back and stared into the bright sky.

Oh shit. I'm gonna die out here in this damn corral. Who's gonna take the horse back to Mr. Foster? What the hell am I doing? Damn!

He rolled onto his stomach and pushed his torso upward. He struggled to get a foot under him and was able to manage the standing position after only two attempts. He hugged the fencepost for support and shook his head. He staggered to the pinto and picked up the reins.

``Come on, horse. I think I'll walk for a while.''

He glanced at Elmer's open door as he moved past the front of the house. *At least I got him in bed. He'll be all right.*

Clay stumbled and fell. Again he vomited. He struggled back to his feet and started for town again. He could hardly wait to tell Oscar the news. Only a hundred yards from the house, he sat under a scrub-oak and waited for the dizziness and the nausea to pass. He leaned back against the tree and passed out.

Early evening, July 16 --- Oscar's residence

Clay opened his eyes and took in his surroundings. The room was small, but it was clean. He became aware of Billy-Clay's voice in another room. Where was he? No, he knew where he was. How did he get here? He couldn't remember. He moved to sit up. His head exploded with pain. He dropped back into the pillow. The pillow had a feminine smell to it, not perfume, but somehow it smelled of woman.

He discovered he was naked and blushed at the thought of someone else undressing him.

Maria walked into the room. ``How do you feel?'' Her expression was stern.

``Naked. Who undressed me?''

``Carla and I. You were in no condition to undress yourself.''

``Where's Oscar?''

``He had to go to work just after you left.''

Clay rolled his eyes to the ceiling. ``How did I get here?''

``I found you up near Elmer's place. I got you on your horse and brought you home.''

``What were you doing up by Elmer's place?''

``Taking care of the horses. You don't think Elmer does it, do you? If it was up to him, they would starve.''

``Elmer wouldn't kill a fly unless it was eating his food.''

Maria looked down at him and tossed her head. ``Good ol' Elmer, the harmless town drunk, is that it?''

``Maybe it used to be, but he won't be drinking for a while.''

``He will drink until he dies, Mr. Price. He has no hope. For anything. He has only the bottle. The bottle and his government check. And you helped nothing by going out to his place and getting drunk

98

with him."

Clay sat up. He quickly pulled the sheet up as it fell to his waist. ``Now wait just a minute here. This isn't what you think. I didn't just go out there and get drunk with Elmer."

``Is this what you look like when you're sober?"

``Where's my clothes?"

``They're outside, drying. I had to wash them. They were full of horse dung and vomit."

Clay was humiliated. He lay back in the bed. ``I'm sorry I bothered you. I wish we could have started out a little differently. I guess it looks like I'm just another one of Elmer's old drinking buddies, but we go a lot deeper than that. A lot deeper. As soon as my clothes are dry, I'd appreciate it if I could have 'em."

She turned and walked to the door of the room.

``By the way, lady, you've got mighty pretty hair," said Clay.

She looked back over her shoulder at him. Her lips twitched in an almost imperceptible smile. ``You've got nice legs."

Clay turned beet-red as she left the room.

Evening, July 16 --- West of the reservation
``What the hell were you thinking when you started drinking with him?" asked Oscar as he drove south on the two-lane highway. The Bar-X lay before them.

Clay had said nothing of the bet. He wanted to be away from the women. ``Oscar, you think Elmer would keep his word to a Blood Brother?"

``To a Blood Brother, probably, but I doubt to anybody else."

Clay told him the story, finishing it as they pulled into the ranch yard.

Oscar smiled. ``You crazy fool. Why didn't you tell Carla and Maria? They both think my old brother is no better than Elmer. Less, even."

``You can tell them. I felt a little funny even staying there after I found out they undressed me. It ain't like they've never seen a man, or I haven't been naked with a woman, but there's something about being undressed when you're unconscious. I mean, hell, they were probably giggling and making jokes and who knows what all."

Oscar laughed. ``You haven't changed much. That's good to know." He looked around. ``Is that still your mother's place over there?"

``Yeah, that's it."

Clay and Oscar visited with Clay's mother, and later, with Mr. Foster. The old man remembered the young Apache who had warmed up the roundup meal with his jalepeno peppers. The two laughed and talked like father and son. Clay was happy to once more experience the closeness of ranch life, and at the same time sad that it was a way of life rapidly disappearing from the west. He wondered how Elmer was doing. He thought of Angela Stillwater and the two white men. A vision of Maria flashed through his mind. He shook his head.

``You okay, Hon?"

He looked up at his mother who sat at the hearth of the cold fireplace. ``Yeah, Ma. I was just clearing some crazy thoughts out of my head."

``As hard as you were shaking it, I'll bet you cleared 'em out real good."

They all laughed. Clay stood. ``I've gotta go back to the reservation and check on Elmer."

``Bring him back to the ranch with you, Clay. He's always welcome here." said Mr. Foster. ``You was all a fine bunch of boys. It would be good to see Elmer again."

``I'll ask, but I don't think he'll come."

Clay had told them of Elmer's problems and about their bet.

``You know, Clay," said Mr. Foster. ``You never did let me pay you for those last two roundups you worked for me before you left home."

Clay looked at the old man. If he hadn't loved his father so much, he could be closer to Mr. Foster. He thought the old man understood that a little bit. ``You've more than paid me over the years, Mr. Foster. I appreciate all you've done for my mother, and for me when I was growing up.''

``Your dad helped me through some rough times. He stuck with me when I didn't have a dime. I didn't do any more than any man would have done.''

``Just the same, I say we're square. Matter of fact, I probably owe you more than I'll ever be able to pay.''

Mr. Foster stood from the kitchen table and moved to the large mahogany desk at the north end of the livingroom. He opened a drawer and removed a small ledger book. Clay watched silently as he thumbed through the pages. ``Ah-hah, here it is. Seems like I've owed you a little over seven hundred dollars for more'n seventeen years now. Tried to give it to your mother, but she wouldn't have anything to do with it. Said it was yours, not hers.''

``You don't owe me the money, Mr. Foster, but I know you, so I'll take you up on it. How much do you want for that pinto I took onto the reservation?''

Mr. Foster raised an eyebrow. ``Let me see. . . with interest, I figure you got enough to buy that little horse and about a month's worth of feed.''

Clay stepped forward. He offered his hand. ``Thank you, Mr. Foster. I appreciate it. Can I take him with me now?''

``He's your horse, son. You don't expect me to board him here for nothing, do you?'' The old man took his hand and grasped it warmly.

Clay looked over to Oscar. Oscar shook his head. ``I know. I know. We load him back in the horse trailer, right?''

Clay smiled. ``Let's go.'' He turned back to his mother. ``I'm taking my car, Ma. I'll see you in a few days.''

His mother stood and hugged him. ``Stay out of trouble. And stay away from all those pretty Apache girls. They can be meaner than hell, you know.''

Apache Tears
Late night, July 16 --- Oscar's residence
The throaty rumble of his GTO vibrated in his chest as the old car purred into Om'nitche behind Oscar's Bronco. It was almost midnight when they parked next to the white-and-cocoa house. Clay was excited. He stepped from his car to the horse trailer. Oscar followed him.

``You going out to Elmer's tonight?" asked Oscar.

``Hell yes. You coming along?"

``I can't. I've got the watch in about fifteen minutes. I'll be off in forty-eight hours. If you can keep him straight that long, I'll move in as reinforcements."

``I'll ride bareback. Is it okay to leave my tack in the trailer?"

``As long as you want. I've got to go. I'll see you in a couple of days."

``Later."

Shortly after midnight, July 17 --- Elmer's residence
The interior of the odd-shaped wickiup was lit with an eerie gray light as Clay approached Elmer's residence. As Clay got closer, he realized the light was coming from a blank television screen. Black-and-white dots of snow flittered across the tube, unnoticed by Elmer who sat at his kitchen table, smoking a cigarette and sipping from a glass. Clay's heart fell as he saw Elmer put the glass to his lips.

Through the opened door, Clay said, ``A man never breaks his word to a Blood Brother."

Elmer looked up, startled by the sound of Clay's voice. ``That's right, he don't. And a Blood Brother doesn't assume that he has just because he's drinking from a glass. Get in here, you old war-horse"

Clay strode through the front door. Elmer remained sitting. He motioned Clay to the chair across the table. ``Sit. You want a drink?"

``Elmer. You lost a bet."

Elmer looked at Clay with a smile in his eyes. ``I'm drinkin' water, brother. That don't mean you got to. Hell, I've got plenty of wine, beer and whiskey layin' around. No sense lettin' it go to waste for

102

the next four weeks."

``You serious?"

``I'm serious, Clay. The spirits were with you." He held up a hand so Clay could see the trembling. ``It won't be easy for a few days, but this is one test I'm not going to fail. Sit. Drink. It won't bother me. It will only make me stronger."

``I really don't want another drink for awhile, Elmer."

``Don't bullshit me, Clay. I know you like your whiskey. Even as a kid you loved the stuff."

Clay sat at the table. ``Yeah, maybe so, but I had a belly full of it lately. Thanks just the same."

Elmer sat and pushed a full bottle of bourbon to Clay's side of the table.

Clay cleared his throat. ``Elmer, really. I'm not into a bunch of whiskey tonight. I've got something outside I'd like to show you."

``It'll wait. Drink. Make me strong. I'll drink water with you and show you how strong I am."

``Elmer, I'll take your word for it."

``Drink! If you are my brother, and you were sent here by the spirits – drink."

Clay opened the bottle.

Early morning, July 18 --- Outside of Om'nitche
The mesquite branch tickled Clay's nose as he lay on his back in the early morning sun. He brushed the branch from his face and drifted into a state of semi-consciousness, trying to remember where he was. He could see Elmer, holding a glass of water to his lips, smiling as he urged Clay to drink more whiskey. More beer. More wine.

He remembered Elmer stepping outside in the light of day and finding the pinto. More beer. Elmer rode the horse round and round the house, shouting and shooting his rifle. More wine. Elmer fed and groomed the horse and drank water from his own glass. For Clay there was more whiskey.

There was no passage of time, only variations of consciousness.

103

How could one man have so much booze in his house? If the damn place ever caught fire, it'd blow the southeastern part of the state right off the map.

Again the branch tickled his nose. He grabbed for it with his eyes closed and jerked it to him, touching the hand, which held it loosely. He came immediately awake and sat upright. ``What the. . .''

He looked into the smiling face of Maria Pipestem. ``What are you doing here?''

``Tickling your nose with a mesquite branch. What are you doing here? I see you haven't changed your ways. You smell almost as bad as you did last time.''

Clay rubbed his face with his fingers. Several days' growth of beard rose above the surface to greet his fingertips. ``Oh Jesus! Where's Elmer? What day is this? Where am I?'' He looked around to get his bearings.

``Elmer's fine. He's sleeping with your horse.''

``My horse?'' Clay moved his tongue around the inside of his mouth. It was dry.

``The pinto.''

``That's Elmer's horse. I remember trading him for that roan he had out back. What do you mean – he's sleeping with the horse? In the corral?''

``Not Elmer. He doesn't like sleeping in corrals. The horse is in the house. Tied to his bed.'' Her smile grew.

Clay stood shakily. ``What are you smiling about?''

``You, Mr. Clay Price. You.''

Clay became self-conscious. ``I've seen better days. One day I'll see you sober and you'll be sorry. I can explain all of this. I really can. I know it looks kinda bad, but there is a pretty good explanation. I think.''

She looked radiant to him as she stood there, smiling. The short-sleeved cotton top of white with red trim and her cotton skirt of red with black trim emphasized her shiny raven hair as it flowed down to the small of her back.

``How do you know the horse is tied to the bed?''

``I helped him tie it there. I rode in early this morning to feed the horses and give them some exercise. Elmer was so tired he was rum-dum. The house was a mess. Empty bottles and cans everywhere. And not even a hint of booze on his breath. I couldn't believe it."

``You mean he still hasn't touched a drop?"

``You drank it all." She laughed. ``He doesn't even want a drink. He says you and he are going to change the world. You have driven the evil from his life."

``We are? I did?"

``You have. He's like the Elmer I once knew. We had a long talk. He loves you and Oscar. He wants to make amends for the way he has lived for the last four or five years. We are at peace now."

Clay felt a strange constriction in his chest. ``I'm happy for you. I'm happy for Elmer. Now, where am I? And where is the house?"

She pointed to the roan, tied to a nearby mesquite. ``Why don't you just ask him? Give him his head and he'll take you home."

``How did he get here?"

``Elmer says you rode him out early this morning. You said you were going to town to get some more whiskey. I guess you must have changed your mind."

``Yeah, I guess I must have." He walked to the horse, his empty stomach growling and his head in pain. His knees seemed to rattle and wobble. If only he could make it to the horse, he'd be all right. The landscape began to spin. He went down on one knee.

He felt her hand on his shoulder. ``Be still. Don't move around until your body has a chance to catch up with your mind."

``Please. Go away, Maria. I'm fine. Thank you. I'm fine. I'll be okay. Go to Elmer. He needs you." The ground rushed to meet his face.

Late afternoon, July 18 --- Elmer's residence

The smell of horse filled the room. Clay liked the smell. He opened his eyes to see Elmer standing over him, grinning from ear to ear. ``So, the white man lives," said Elmer. ``They must be making them tougher nowadays."

Clay reached for him. ``You no good sonofabitch! I oughta kill ya!" He fell from the bed as Elmer jumped out of reach. On the earthen floor, only inches from his eyes were two moccasined feet – woman's feet. He became aware of his nakedness and her presence in the room at the same time. He bounced back onto the bumpy mattress and pulled the blanket up to his neck.

``What are you doing here?"

``I brought you back. You were sick." Maria smiled.

``I suppose you helped Elmer undress me too?"

``Elmer was asleep." Her smile broadened.

Clay pulled the covers to his hairline to cover his change of color. ``That's two for your side and zero for mine." He mumbled into the blanket.

``You still have pretty legs. A little white, though."

``Elmer, make her go away until I can get dressed."

``What for, brother? She's seen more of you than your mother."

``For cryin' out loud, Elmer. Don't you have any sense of decency? The woman is your wife. Tell her to leave the room while I dress."

``She's not my wife anymore, Clay. I can't tell her what to do. You white men caused that problem – liberated women."

``It's your house. Tell her to leave."

``She's my friend now. I can't tell my friend to leave."

Clay lowered the blanket to his chin. ``Aren't you two going to get back together?"

``Not us. We never should have gotten married in the first place. I like her better as a friend." Elmer winked. ``You better not let this one go, Clay. She's too much woman to stay single forever."

``Are you crazy, Elmer? What are you talking about?"

Elmer turned to Maria, then back to Clay. ``I see it in her eyes, brother. Are you blind? The woman has a thing for you."

Clay looked past Elmer to Maria. She stood silently behind him. ``Maria, would you please leave the room while I get dressed?"

She looked at him, then at Elmer. ``Elmer, you talk too much."

Apache Tears

She left the room.

CHAPTER FIVE: THE INVESTIGATION

Early evening, July 18 --- Elmer's residence

Clay watched Maria's every move as she prepared the evening meal. He was torn between his desire to know her and his loyalty to Elmer. There seemed to be something wrong about wanting to be with his Blood Brother's ex-wife. It was more than sexual. It was more like a closeness – a spiritual closeness.

Oscar's Bronco slid to a stop outside of the front door in a cloud of dust. He ran into the small house.

``Just in time for supper, Oscar,'' said Elmer.

``I ate early.'' He turned to Clay. ``They let those white boys go. The people are madder'n hell, and so is at least half the Council. This may not be a good place for a white man for a while, Clay.''

``Let 'em go?'' Clay stood. ``How could they let 'em go? They shot that girl. She was raped at least once. What do you mean 'they let 'em go'?''

Oscar shook his head. ``I don't know the details, but I heard some nasty talk. You better go, Clay. There may be a few hotheads out there that don't really care who your friends are.''

``Where's Frank?'' asked Clay.

``I'm not sure, but he may be at the Council meeting.''

``I want to see him before I tuck my tail between my legs and sneak off the reservation."

``I wouldn't chance it, Clay. People are talking revenge."

``Are they crazy? I helped bring them in."

``That doesn't matter now. I've never seen the kind of anger this thing's stirred up."

``I'm gonna see Frank before I go anywhere."

``I'll go with him."

Clay turned to Maria, surprised by her offer. ``I don't think so."

Elmer rubbed his chin. ``I'd think that one over, Clay. Her great-uncle is a mighty powerful man on the reservation. He's a healer. Got lots of big medicine. There are people out here who fear Maria more than they would your pistol, and that's a fact. Less chance of trouble if she goes."

``Let's go before it gets any later," said Oscar nervously.

Maria turned off the stove and stepped through the door in front of the men.

She rode in the back seat with Clay. Elmer sat next to Oscar in the front. ``Don't hurry, Oscar," she said. ``Frank won't be there."

``What? How do you know that?" asked Oscar.

``He's in the hills."

``Your uncle again?" asked Elmer.

Maria nodded. ``Yes."

``Then why didn't we eat supper and wait for Frank to come in out of the hills?" asked Clay.

She faced him. ``Oscar is right, Clay. You won't be safe here until this matter is resolved. Oscar or Elmer can call you when feelings die down."

``This isn't right. Maybe if I could just talk to that police chief, what was his name? Vasquez, yeah. He seemed like a nice enough guy."

``Please, Clay. No."

He looked into her eyes and saw that she knew more than she would tell him. He tapped Oscar on the shoulder. ``Just get me to my

109

car, Oscar. I'll call you from Tucson. I'll find out what's going on through the U.S. Attorney's office and see if we can't get this thing reversed or whatever they call it."

Maria touched his forearm. ``Forget it, Clay. It's not your fight."

He faced her. ``Why? Because she's Apache? Would you say the same to me if a white man shot Elmer or Oscar, or his wife, or you? It's everybody's fight. We're all Americans, for crying out loud. All of us. There must be some mistake. I'll get it straightened out in Tucson and they'll be back in custody in a day or two."

Maria shook her head.

Dawn, July 19 --- *Clay's apartment, Tucson, Arizona*

Clay sat at the dinette table, sipping a cup of black coffee as he studied the old black-and-white photograph. The early morning sun peaked through the opened curtain, casting golden rays of light onto the glossy picture, causing him to turn it to the shadow momentarily. They were all there, The Blood Brothers, with their horses and their rifles. Clay smiled. It looked like a frame from a western movie.

He studied the background and picked out the Bar-X ranch house in the distance. He remembered the day the picture was taken. It had been the day before spring roundup when they were only fourteen years old. He wished he could find the one they had taken at the end of the roundup – they weren't quite as bright-eyed and bushy-tailed in that picture. They had been a tired bunch of little cowboys.

He sipped his coffee. It was cool. He dumped it in the sink and poured a fresh cup. He sat and looked into the picture. He was there. He smelled the horses and the fresh rope. He felt the spurs on his Wellington boots. Even then he wore Wellingtons.

He shook his head. *That was a long time ago, in a world that no longer exists.* He thought of Oscar and Elmer and Frank Redhawk. *Well, maybe it does exist – a little bit.* He wanted to talk to someone, anyone who could bring back the old days, the days when life was uncomplicated, when he had his friends, and when there had been no war.

Apache Tears

Something told him Frank Redhawk was such a man, a man with whom he could share these kinds of thoughts, a man who would understand.

His mind drifted to Susan, and he wondered what she was doing. *Probably getting ready for work,* he thought. He hadn't seen her since graduation. She was younger than he by almost eight years, but at age twenty-six, she was older than most of the college girls, and he had taken an interest in her. And even though the interest was mostly physical, it was an interest. Clay shook his head. That relationship was going nowhere, and he had known it from the start.

He lit a cigarette and questioned his purpose. What was he doing with his life? He was long past the point where he thought he could make any major changes in the world. He wasn't even sure if he could make a minor contribution; wasn't sure he even wanted to. He felt somehow less than other men his age. He had no wife, no children, no prospects.

He looked around his apartment. The furniture belonged to the apartment complex. It was conservatively modern and of cheap construction. The coffee table in front of the sofa sat unevenly due to a broken leg improperly repaired by a previous tenant. The refrigerator was old and scratched. It kept food cold – too cold, often freezing anything on the top shelf. It was noisy and expensive to run. The breakfast bar between the small kitchen and the front room was chipped on its top edge. The carpet had once been gold ochre, but was now a faded brown, the shag frayed and shaded with indelible dirt.

The bedroom was much the same. Nothing was his. Whatever he owned of value was stored at his mother's place on the Bar-X, with the exception of a few photos, his clothes, two pistols and a few miscellaneous items. What had his life been worth? *What is the worth of a man? How is it measured?*

He shook his head as he often did when he wanted to change his line of thinking. *Boy, are you feeling sorry for yourself, or what? Think of the guys sitting in VA hospitals, knowing they'll never leave. You're pretty damn lucky if you stop and think about it, Price.*

111

Apache Tears

Thoughts of the night Angela Stillwater was raped flooded into his consciousness. He flashed to Elmer and wondered at the change in him; all because of a pinto horse and a belief that Clay had been sent by the spirits. The horse, the spirits, and Clay had given him the strength to become a man again – just like that. It was all crazy. Nothing made any sense.

Then there was Maria. Clay shook his head. He didn't want the thought to go any further. It persisted. He saw her rounded, un-Apache nose, and her large ebony eyes as she sat next to him in Oscar's Bronco and told him it was not his fight. He felt an uncanny attraction for her. He couldn't pinpoint exactly what the attraction was, but it was strong, and he feared it was beginning to affect his thinking about other matters.

He thought of the two young men he and Frank had taken into custody. Bruce was a whiner and a follower. He was not much of a man, but maybe someday, if he lived long enough, he would grow into one. Charlie on the other hand, was a totally different matter. He would never change. He was one of those rare types that was truly mean – mean and vicious to his core. Charlie was dangerous, and the only thing that would ever change him was death. Clay shivered at his thoughts.

He picked up the telephone and dialed information. ``Tucson, please. The newsroom at KDWI.''

He hung up the phone and redialed. ``Hello. I'd like to speak to Teresa Chatla.''

A woman's voice said, ``This is Teresa, may I help you?''

``Teresa, you may not remember me, but we had a communications class together at the U of A a couple of years ago. The name's Clay Price.''

The voice warmed. ``I remember you, Clay. You were in engineering of some kind. I couldn't figure out what you were doing in that class.''

``I took it as an elective.''

``So what can I do for you?''

``This is going to sound a little strange, but I don't want to say

112

anything over the phone. I'd rather meet somewhere when you can spare about thirty minutes."

``Hold on, let me check my schedule." There was a pause, then she said, ``How important is it?"

``Pretty important, or I wouldn't be calling you. I imagine you're pretty busy, but you're the only news reporter I know, and I think what I have to say will interest you."

``Can you make it to The Chuck Wagon at one o'clock this afternoon? We can grab something to eat while we talk."

``Which one?"

``Broadway and Treat."

Clay glanced at his watch. ``I'll be there. You remember what I look like?"

``Enough to pick you out."

``See you at one."

``It's nice talking to you. I'll see you then."

1:00 P.M., July 19 --- The Chuck Wagon restaurant, Tucson

Clay sat in the booth with Teresa. She was Navajo, with a small strain of Mexican blood from somewhere deep in her past. She had been a serious student from what he could remember of her, except for that one time, during the last week of school, when the class had decided to go to the Purple Dragon instead of conducting their studies in the classroom. Even the professor had gone to the local college bar with them. Clay had learned something of her background that afternoon as they sipped twenty-five cent beers and talked of plans for the future. She had laughed and smiled a lot that day.

Teresa had stuck to her plan, and was already pretty well known in the city as a reporter for one of the local network TV stations. Clay trusted her as much as he trusted any reporter, which wasn't very much, but he needed help from somewhere.

Teresa wasn't his idea of what a news reporter should look like, but she held her own when she appeared on the TV set. She was tall, five feet ten or so, and her fine, high cheekbones and angular features shouted her heritage. She still wore her hair straight, and though it wasn't as long as Maria's, it was long. *She will have to change that,* he thought. *If she is ever going to make it to the big-time, she will have to wear it differently. It makes her look too much like the Indian she is. Too many white viewers out there with leftover prejudices.*

Teresa sipped her coffee. ``So tell me, Clay, what is this all about?"

He told her about the rape and shooting, and about the apprehension of the two men. He told her about Charlie's father being a U.S. Senator. and about the charges being dropped.

She stared at him as he finished his story. ``Senator William's son?"

Clay nodded.

``I saw a little blurb on him a few days ago. It was just a short piece about how he had been injured in a hunting accident."

``A hunting accident?" asked Clay.

``I'm sure that's what it said. I'll look it up when I get back to the newsroom. What is it you want me to do?"

``I don't think I'm going to be able to get much in the way of information from the U.S. Attorney's Office. After all, I'm the guy who shot one of them. If you could just find out what they used to justify dropping the charges, I'll know where to go from there. I can't just sit back and let this slide."

``I'll do what I can. How can I reach you?"

He gave her his home phone number, as well as his work numbers.

``You stay pretty busy, don't you?"

``Not really. Not now that school is out. I guess I'll have to look for a permanent job now that I'm part of the establishment."

``I wish you luck. It's tough out there."

1:00 P.M., July 20 --- The Chuck Wagon restaurant, Tucson

The following afternoon, Clay sat in the same restaurant and waited for Teresa impatiently. He had arrived early. When she had called with news from the U.S. Attorney's Office, she had sounded troubled. He looked up from his coffee cup just as she approached his table with a hurried walk.

Quickly she sat across from him and opened her briefcase. She pulled several papers out of the case and placed them on the table in front of him. ``I'm not supposed to have these, but I've got a friend in the U.S. Attorney's office." She said nothing as Clay studied the documents. She ordered coffee and waited.

Clay finished reading and looked up at her. ``There's not a word in here about rape."

``The doctor who treated her didn't examine her for rape, nor did he take any smears or any other form of physical evidence. There is no witness to the alleged act except the girl, and she hasn't come forward yet."

Clay gritted his teeth. ``She will."

``Don't be too sure."

``What do you mean by that?"

``The senator's son says Jack Stillwater, her uncle, sold her as a prostitute."

``Her uncle sold her as a prostitute? What kind of garbage is that?"

Teresa shrugged. ``I don't know, but without physical evidence, or a complainant, as far as the U.S. Attorney is concerned, there's no rape. Unless you count statutory, and the two men both say they thought she was over eighteen. Jack Stillwater told them so. As Angela's guardian, he's agreed not to prosecute for obvious reasons."

``What about his crime? Has anyone talked to Stillwater?"

``That part of this whole thing is an Indian matter, and the Apache will never see this report. It's from the U.S. Attorney's Office."

``Did the U.S. Attorney talk to this Jack Stillwater guy themselves?"

``I couldn't find where they had. I think they're going to wait and see how things turn out with Angela. They don't like to get too involved in Apache matters if they can help it, especially if the criminal and the victim are both Apache."

``Do you think the girl went along with this willingly?"

Teresa shook her head. ``I don't think so. She was an honor student at a boarding school. The Bureau of Indian Affairs insisted that she return to the custody of her uncle in the summers. She fought it, but as usual, the BIA won, and she was sent back to the reservation."

Clay shook his head. ``Poor kid. What about the shooting? How did they pass that one off?" asked Clay.

``Accidental." She handed him another report.

``They won't get away with that. The girl will say otherwise."

Teresa shook her head. ``I don't think so. If this goes to trial, it'll all come out into the open, and the girl will be disgraced. I think we've heard the end of it from the legal system's point of view."

``How can the U.S. Attorney ignore her uncle using her as a prostitute?"

``It's easy. It's not in his jurisdiction until he receives a complaint initiated by the Tribal Police. The U.S. Attorney isn't going to initiate an investigation if he doesn't have to. Right now, all he's got are statements from Bruce and Charlie. The thing between Jack Stillwater and Angela is strictly an Indian matter. He may contact the girl when she gets better, but with Charlie Williams and Bruce Stinton involved, he's probably going to suggest to the Tribal Police that Jack Stillwater and Angela have more to lose than the two white men."

``Stinton? Stinton of the Stinton ranch?"

``One and the same."

``Great. His old man has almost as much political power as the senator."

``Maybe more."

Clay stared up at her. ``So that's it, huh? Just like that? It's all over and done? Let's forget about it?"

``No, not just like that. I'll keep looking, but I can't compromise my source in the U.S. Attorney's office."

``That doesn't sound real promising."

``What else can you do?"

``I don't know, but there should be some way to get justice out of all of this." He shrugged. ``Thanks for all of the work you put in. If I can ever help you out, just let me know."

``Thanks, Clay. Who knows? This may turn out to be something before the dust settles."

``Never can tell. I hope something comes of it for you. If you get anything more, don't hesitate to call. You've got the numbers."

Mid-afternoon, July 20 --- Tucson Medical Center, Tucson

Clay approached the hospital room warily. His heart beat at almost twice its normal rate. He wasn't sure what good it would do to confront Charlie Williams, but he felt helpless and insignificant sitting in his apartment. Maybe he could get the man to confess. *That's stupid, Clay. The only way this guy's ever going to confess is through torture.* His mind conjured up visions of torturing Charlie Williams. He was smiling as he stepped into room 721.

He was in the room before he saw Charlie's visitor. He quickly turned to leave, but it was too late. The man had seen him. He motioned to Clay. ``Please. Do come in. Charlie will be glad to see you."

Clay stepped nervously closer to the bed, hidden from Charlie's view by the partially drawn curtain. ``I'm not so sure of that, sir." He recognized Senator Williams. *Damn!*

Charlie looked up at him as he stepped around the edge of the curtain. The young man's eyes widened with fear momentarily until he realized Clay was unarmed. He looked at his father. ``That's the guy, Dad. He's the one who shot me."

The senator shifted his gaze from his son to Clay, uncertainty written all over his face.

Clay raised a hand. ``I'm not here to cause any trouble, Senator." He noticed the elevated stub of Charlie's leg.

The eyes of the older Williams narrowed. ``Precisely why are you here?"

Clay stood next to the senator. ``To tell you the truth, sir, I'm not really sure. I just heard that charges against your son have been

117

dropped. Since I was there, and saw what really happened, I found it hard to believe. I guess I just had to talk to Charlie here and get it straight from the horse's ass, so to speak."

``Now you see here, young man ...''

``Wait a minute, Senator Williams. Hold on just a minute. I don't know what kind of garbage your son has been telling you, but unless he told you he raped and shot a young Apache girl, he lied. I've always respected you as a senator and a politician. Even though I may have disagreed with you at times, I always thought you were honest.''

Clay looked the senator square in the eyes. ``I was there. He raped and shot the girl.''

The senator looked away from Clay's stare. ``I don't think you should be in here, young man.''

``Very well, sir. I'll leave. But I'm telling you right now, old Charlie here isn't out of the woods. You may be able to pull strings and make the U.S. Attorney dance with your political power, but he committed more than one crime that night. He assaulted a paramedic. I saw it. If the paramedic won't press charges, I will.''

``You can't press charges without the victim's testimony. I've heard nothing of an assault on a paramedic,'' said the senator.

``I was thinking more about him trying to shoot me with his pistol.'' Clay looked down at Charlie, who remained silent. ``I'll see you in court, Charlie.'' He turned and left the room, feeling stupid for having come in the first place, and even more foolish for the way he had spoken to the senator. He walked slowly down the long hallway towards the parking lot.

``Young man.'' Clay turned to see Senator Williams walking briskly towards him.

``May I have a word with you?'' asked the senator as he stopped at Clay's side.

Clay shrugged.

The senator pointed to the cafeteria across the hall from where they stood. ``Please. I'll buy you a cup of coffee.''

Clay followed him into the cafeteria. They sipped their coffee silently for a few moments, each waiting for the other to speak. Finally, Clay said, ``I don't mean to be rude, sir, but you called this meeting. What do you want to talk about?''

``My son, Mr. . . I'm sorry. What is your name?''

``Price. Clay Price. I wouldn't forget that name, sir. You're going to hear it a lot in the future.''

The senator ignored Clay's remark. ``Mr. Price, my son has suffered a severe trauma with the leg wound you inflicted upon him.''

``Excuse me, sir, but I should have shot him between the eyes, then we wouldn't be having this conversation.'' Clay sipped his coffee, feeling more in control.

``I don't think that's called for, Mr. Price.''

``You didn't see the girl, sir. I did.''

``I'm sure it was tragic, but the court has seen fit to dismiss the charges under our laws. Our country, in order to remain civilized, must operate within the framework of the law.''

``That's what I intend to do, sir, operate within the framework of the law.''

``You have no case, Mr. Price. My son and his friend have told me what really happened. I have done my best to keep this incident low-key, but if you insist on playing out your charade, I'll have you arrested.''

``You'll have me arrested?'' Clay smiled. ``For what?''

``Shooting my son.''

``What was I supposed to do? Step closer and make it easier for him to shoot me?''

The senator leaned across the table and spoke softly. ``Do I have to draw a picture for you, Mr. Price?''

Clay's confidence level began to subside. ``Maybe you'd better. I'm kind of stupid when it comes to lying.''

``There can be no charge of rape for reasons I choose not to divulge to you. It might be harmful to the girl and her family, and is none of your concern.''

Clay looked into the senator's sky-blue eyes. ``If there's any

119

reason in the world he can't be charged with rape, you'd better convince me senator, or you're going to find his name all over the headlines in tomorrow's paper." Clay thought of Teresa Chatla. He doubted she would help him, but she might.

Senator Williams cast a quick glance around the busy cafeteria. He pulled a two-page document from his inside suit pocket. Carefully, he spread the paper on the table so that Clay could read it. ``This is just a copy. I have the original in a safety deposit box."

Clay read the document slowly, going over every line twice. He looked up at the politician who sat silently across the table from him. ``How do I know this is Jack Stillwater's signature?"

``Really, Mr. Price. I wouldn't stoop to forgery, even to keep my son out of jail. I'm a man of integrity."

``So Jack Stillwater sold his daughter to your son and his friend for twenty dollars?"

The senator nodded. ``What you have left is a shooting – at this point, an accidental shooting. The bullet was never recovered from the scene. It passed through the girl's body. The way it glanced off her rib, it flattened and created quite a large wound. The doctor's report indicates that the bullet came from a large caliber weapon, probably, fired at close range. The exact size of the bullet cannot be determined. No ballistics tests can be run."

``So?" Clay became concerned at the direction of the conversation.

``So, Mr. Price, the Tribal Police report indicates that you had a large caliber rifle and pistol in your possession when you brought the girl to the dispensary."

``They know the rifle was a forty-four. It didn't make that hole in that girl."

``They didn't keep the pistol. They don't know if it was a twenty-two or a forty-five, or a .357 magnum."

``So I'll show it to them."

``It's too late, Mr. Price. You've had an opportunity to change pistols."

120

``So what?"

``So when my son and his friend, Bruce, tried to stop you from having your way with the girl, a struggle ensued and your pistol went off, the bullet striking the girl."

``Who would believe that?"

``Everybody, Mr. Price. My son and his friend have admitted to the police that they paid for the girl's services, but let's be honest, they're young – in their early twenties. I think most judges would go lightly on two young men whose greatest crime was receiving the services of a prostitute. What do you think?"

Clay shook his head. ``Sounds pretty good to me, Senator. You've got me convinced that I wanted to be third in line with an Apache prostitute."

``My son has lost his leg, Mr. Price. He will be disabled the rest of his life. I think he's paid any debt he may owe society for a misdemeanor, don't you?"

Clay nodded. ``Yeah, I do – for a misdemeanor. Now when's he going to pay the rest of his debt?"

``We have a criminal justice system in this country, Mr. Price. It's not perfect, but it works well. Let it work."

``Angela Stillwater will talk."

``I think not. She would be disgraced. Perhaps you should learn more about the Apache, Mr. Price."

Clay had no respect left for the handsome, silver-haired man who sat opposite him at the small table. ``I've seen the justice system in this country work. I saw all kinds of U.S. Government justice in Vietnam. But, you know, I think you've just convinced me that man can sink to lows I never even dreamed possible."

Clay stood, dumping what remained of his coffee onto the table, some of it running over the edge and onto the senator's Italian silk suit. ``Have a great day, senator. Oh, I'm so sorry about the coffee. I've gotta be going now. Send me the cleaning bill."

Senator Williams jumped back from the table and dabbed at his trousers with a napkin as Clay left the cafeteria.

121

Late afternoon, July 20 --- In the air, northwest of Tucson

Clay pulled the stick back on the Stearman cropduster, kicked the rudder hard right and applied full throttle as he narrowly missed a power pole. *Damn! That was close. I've gotta get my mind on business or I'm gonna end up planted in one of these fields, myself. Anything but this old Stearman probably would've come apart on that maneuver.*

He tried to concentrate on the end of the field below, but found his eyes fixing on the neat rows of green. He blinked his eyes several times. *Jesus, Clay, what the hell are you trying to do? Even a beginner knows you never focus on the rows – quickest damn way in the world to wind up in a coffin.*

He pulled back on the stick as he realized he was brushing the plants with his landing gear. *What the hell is wrong with me?* Again his mind drifted.

A bright red Cadillac loomed before him as he approached the road at the end of the field. *Shit!* He pulled back on the stick and felt the rugged little plane jerk its nose abruptly to the sky. He leveled the ship and looked down to see a clenched fist at the end of an arm, protruding from the driver's window, daring him to land the plane and fight it out like a man.

He pushed the throttle to full power and climbed skyward. He had made his last pass for the day but he wasn't ready to land yet. He felt the need to prove to himself that he still had the ability to do it right before he landed at the field in Marana. At three thousand feet above the ground he leveled out to allow the Stearman to pick up speed. He did a few barrel rolls and a few picture-perfect Immelmans, then put the ship into a short but steep dive. He pulled back on the stick and let the blood flow to his feet as the little craft made a perfect loop in the sky.

When he landed, Tubs, the owner of the company, met him at the end of the taxi ramp. ``What the hell's the matter with you, Clay? I saw you doin' aerobatics again. I told you, that costs money. That damned old airplane don't fly on water, you know. And it's way too old for that kind of crap. One of these days, you'll collapse a spar, and I'll be picking you out of a cotton field. I don't want to do that, Clay. I seen too many 'dusters go that way."

Clay removed his flight goggles as he walked to the hangar. ``I'm sorry, Tubs. I'll pay for the fuel."

``It ain't just the fuel, son. I'm gettin' worried about you. You been with me a long time, and this past couple days, since you got back from yore mom's place, you been actin' kinda spacey. You okay?"

Clay stopped just outside the hangar and studied Tubs. His real name was Vernon Tubbitts, but everyone called him Tubs. He was short and stubby, and in his late fifties. He worked as hard as any man Clay had ever known to maintain a business that he long ago should have abandoned. But Tubs loved airplanes, and he loved cropdusters. He still flew on some days, whenever his arthritis would allow. Clay had come to care for Tubs over the four years that he had known him. He was good people.

``I do have something on my mind that I can't quite get straightened out. Do you think you could get Shorty to help out around here for a while – just until I can get my mind back into the cockpit?"

``You got money problems? You need some money?"

Clay smiled and put his arm around the older man's shoulders. ``No, Tubs. Thanks. I don't need any money."

Tubs looked up at him, a serious expression on his face. ``Oh, my God. Yer in love. That's it, ain't it? I should have known. Only a woman can turn a pilot as good as you into a brainless bowl of mush. Hot damn! I can hardly wait to meet her. What's the lucky girl's name?"

Clay smiled to himself. It would be so much easier to let Tubs think he was in love. It would save a lot of explaining. ``You gotta be one of the most perceptive guys I know, Tubs. Her name is Maria. Maria Pipestem." *Why did I pick that name? I could have made one up.*

``Pipestem. What kind of name is that? Indian?"

Clay nodded. He was into the lie now. ``Yeah. Apache."

``No kiddin'? Don't that beat all. Well, by golly, it'll take someone as wild as an Apache to tame you down, son."

``She's wild in her own sort of way I guess." He reflected for a

123

moment on her image in his mind. ``And she's intelligent, and she's the most beautiful woman I've ever known.''

``Hot damn! You *are* in love. When do I get to meet her?''

``I don't know, Tubs.'' He became thoughtful. ``I don't know.''

Early evening, July 20 --- Northwest of Tucson

Clay pulled onto the freeway to Tucson, and watched in the rear-view mirror as a red Cadillac cut off another vehicle in order to make the turn onto the Tucson on-ramp.

He remembered the Cadillac at the end of the field, the one he had almost hit with the Stearman. There appeared to be two men in the car. He slowed his speed and watched in his mirror as the Cadillac slowed and maintained a constant distance. He pushed the accelerator pedal to the floor and the old GTO roared to life. He watched in the mirror as the Cadillac diminished in his vision to a dot, then disappeared.

Early morning, July 21 --- Clay's apartment

Clay stared blankly at the name in an article from a two-month-old issue of Leatherneck Magazine as he sipped coffee in his apartment. ``Colonel William Purvis, U.S.M.C., promoted to brigadier general and transferred to the Office of Naval Intelligence in Washington, D.C.'' The article went on to give a brief background of Clay's old wing commander.

Clay picked up his phone. After several attempts, he made contact. ``Hello, Bill?''

``Yes. Is that really you, Clay? How are you doing?''

``I'm doing fine, sir. Congratulations on your star.''

``Thanks. But cut the formal crap with me. You're the one with the Medal, remember?''

``That was a long time ago.''

``It doesn't make a damn bit of difference how long ago it was. We never forget that medal.''

``Well, thanks, I appreciate it.'' He felt self-conscious whenever anyone mentioned the Medal. ``Bill, a strange thing has happened out here on an Indian reservation. It involved Senator Edward Williams' son. Now, I think the good senator is whitewashing the whole thing. And someone is following me around. It's like cops and robbers. I was hoping you could help me find out a few things.''

``I'll do what I can, you know that. Why don't you start at the beginning and bring me up to snuff?''

``Well, you see, I ran into this ex-corpsman on the reservation out here. He's an Apache. Well, anyway, we met and talked about things, and on the way into town we came across. . .''

CHAPTER SIX: DOWN FROM THE MOUNTAIN

Dawn, July 20 --- The Secret Place

As Frank and Henry rode back from Frank's vision quest site to Henry's cabin, Henry told Frank about the charges against Charlie and Bruce being dropped, and about the unrest growing on the reservation.

``Danny Blue and some of his friends are talking revenge," the old man said as they neared the cabin. ``The words are empty of anything but anger at the moment, but they are dangerous words, nonetheless."

Frank knew Danny fairly well. He was twenty-four, single, and had one of the few college degrees on the reservation. He was also the leader of the reservation chapter of the American Indian Movement. Frank liked Danny, but knew him to have a short fuse and a violent temper, especially when it came to whites. From the depth of his own anger at the news about Charlie and Bruce, Frank knew Danny would be enraged. He agreed with his great uncle. That kind of rage would make Danny's talk dangerous indeed.

``I'll get Eddie and Oscar, and we'll talk with him," Frank said. ``Maybe between us we can cool him off until we figure out what kind of options we have."

126

They rode up to Henry's corral, set back in the trees, just south of his cabin. They dismounted, unsaddled the horses, watered them, and rubbed them down.

Henry closed the corral gate and he and Frank walked towards the cabin.

``It is not just Danny who is talking this way,'' Henry said. ``There are others. And it is going to get worse.''

``What do you mean?''

``Angela Stillwater is dying.''

``What?'' Frank reached out and stopped his great uncle. ``I thought you said she was recovering.''

``I told you the doctor said her wounds were healing well. But yesterday morning, she learned about what has happened with the two Pinda Lickoyi. She quit speaking and closed her eyes. The doctor asked me to see her, so I went.'' The old man's years seemed to settle on his face as he took a deep breath and let it out slowly. ``She has decided to die. Her spirit was already wandering far from her body. I walked with her for a time. Her pain is great and there is little in this world to hold her. When I was certain she would not come back, I told her I would honor her decision by doing the proper ceremonies when the time came, so she would not remain trapped here.''

Frank turned around and headed for the corral.

``Frank Redhawk.''

His great uncle's voice stopped him, but Frank did not look back. ``I've got to go to her. Maybe with my Bear song I can. . . I don't know. I have to try.''

Henry walked to him and put his hand on Frank's shoulder, gently turning him back towards the cabin. ``The Bear has given you great power, it is true. But you need not be with Angela to use it. You have been through much. Your body must have rest or it will fail you. Come in and lay on the bunk. Sing your Bear song and hold her in your mind. If it is not too late, you will find her.''

Once on the bunk, Frank became aware of how physically drained he was. He closed his eyes, created an image of Angela in his

127

mind, sang his Bear song, and quickly fell into a deep, but uneasy, sleep.

He dreamed he walked across vast, open stretches of desert under a full moon. He called for Angela. The sound of his voice was swallowed by the immense stillness of the night. He wandered and called with an urgency that clutched at his throat, and a despair that finally choked him into silence. He climbed a small hill and sat down on the rocky ground. A coyote with amber eyes emerged from the creosote and sat in front of him.

``She is gone, Walks-With-Bear.''

``I know. But I had to try.''

``Even Bear cannot do the impossible. It is a give-away of power to try.''

``What would you have me do, then? Nothing? She was young. She never got to live her life.''

``Who are you to make such a judgment? The coyote lives eight, perhaps ten cycles of the summer sun. The tortoise, a hundred or more. Do you judge the coyote's life less full for its shorter length? She lived her life. She completed her circle. Do not waste your time and power attempting to change what cannot be changed.''

``I felt I had to try,'' Frank said stubbornly.

``You felt you had failed,'' the Coyote answered, and grinned. ``It is your weakness. You can not stand to fail.''

``It is a strength, not a weakness,'' Frank responded, anger rising.

``It is your weakness,'' the Coyote repeated. ``I chase eight rabbits for every one I catch. I fail seven times for every success. But I do not judge myself. I do not waste my power wishing I'd been faster, or stealthier. I do not waste my power continuing to chase a rabbit, which has outwitted me, or sought sanctuary in the prickly pear patch. Instead, I honor the rabbit for its power, and continue on my way. I save my own power for the next opportunity. Think on this, Walks-With- Bear.''

The Coyote stood, lifted its head in song to the moon, and

128

trotted off into the night.

Frank stood to follow and found himself on the edge of a large, circular open area surrounded by cottonwood trees. Many of the Tinde were present, gathered in groups, around small fires. Tension filled the still night air. Flickers of lightning lit the undersides of massive cloud formations piled above the eastern mountains.

Frank approached the clearing. Those in the group closest to him turned towards him. He recognized Oscar, and Eddie, and Danny Blue. Maria was with them. An anxiety arose in him at the sight of their familiar faces. He wanted to turn and run. Maria beckoned to him.

``Come," she said.

``Speak to us," Oscar said.

``The People are waiting," Danny said, challenge in his voice.

The others in the clearing turned towards him. Terror gripped Frank. Their faces were contorted with pain. Their flesh grew old and sagged off their bones as he watched. They began a great anguish-filled wailing. Maria walked towards him.

``Come," she said again. Her features aged rapidly as she approached. Her skin wrinkled. Her hair turned white. Her shoulders stooped and her step became slow and labored.

Frank awoke to a hand gently shaking his shoulder.

``Come," Maria said, leaning over him. ``It is getting late. Henry has a meal prepared outside. We must talk."

Late afternoon, July 20 --- Henry's cabin

Deep late-afternoon shadows were creeping out of the pines and across the clearing by the time the three had finished a meal of coffee, venison, cornbread, watercress, and baby carrots from Henry's small garden. They had eaten in silence, in the old way, and when they had finished, Frank told them about his dreams.

Maria and Henry looked at one another, and the old man nodded.

She turned to Frank. ``The people are gathering. They are waiting for you."

129

``To do what?" He looked first at Maria and then at his great uncle.

``To speak to them," Maria said.

Frank kept his eyes on Henry and the old man nodded again.

``What am I supposed to say?"

``Speak what is in your heart," Henry answered.

``Uncle, my heart speaks to me in feelings. I have no words for them."

Maria reached out and placed her hand on Frank's forearm. ``What do you say to someone who is injured when you arrive to help?"

``That's different. . ." Frank started.

``Is it?" Henry cut him off. ``Do you not say the words that will get them to hold on, to reassure them, to let them know you care? Do you not say the words needed to get them to fight for their life?"

They sat in silence for some time before Frank spoke. ``Bear said your counsel was good, uncle. He is right. You speak the truth."

``Your brother the coyote also speaks the truth," the old man said softly. ``In this matter of the Tinde, many kinds of fear will circle you. You will need many kinds of courage."

Again a silence settled on them. Frank thought about the Bear's lesson concerning the nature of power, and remembered how quickly his emotions had been transformed from terror to trust, from uncertainty to confidence.

He thought about Maria's words: ``The people are gathering. They are waiting for you." The anxiety of his dream returned. The desperate need of the people pulled at him. He tried to imagine himself talking to the gathering he had seen in his dream. No words came, and the anxiety increased.

He heard the Bear telling him, *You must listen to your heart. In your heart, the Gahan will guide you.* He put the palms of his hands flat against the earth. A strength and confidence flowed up through his hands, his arms, his shoulders, and into his chest, filling the hollow the anxiety had created. No words came with the strength but he knew they would be there when he needed them.

``How is it, uncle, that the people are already gathering? How is it they are already waiting for me?''

``In the old ways, when the Gahan spoke, messengers were sent out. The people gathered to hear what had been spoken. Maria has been seeing to this throughout the day. Other messengers are continuing the work.''

``I'm confused,'' Frank said. ``You told me yourself that there are few followers of the old ways left. But in my dream I saw many people gathered.''

Henry laughed. ``Brother Coyote taught us long ago that men can be stubborn, and must sometimes be tricked into doing what is necessary.''

``I don't understand.''

Again, Maria reached out and touched Frank's arm. ``A few of those who gather do so to hear the words of the Gahan. Most gather to hear you speak on the matter of Angela and the two Pinda Lickoyi.''

Frank looked from Maria to his uncle. ``I am still confused.''

``They are the same matter, nephew. The matter of the Gahan, and the matter of the Pinda Lickoyi. You can not speak about one without speaking about the other. As the water of this stream is the same water, which falls from the sky, these two matters are the same. As the air we breathe is the same air which gave life to our fathers' fathers, these two matters are the same.

``The Gahan speak of great power at work, for it is the way of the Gahan to deal with such power. Men see the manifestation of this power in specific events, for it is the way of men to concentrate on the events of their lives rather than on the forces behind them.

``Once the people walked comfortably in both worlds. Now they have forgotten how to walk with the spirits. If you would talk to them about matters of the spirit, you must do so in terms of events in their lives. In this way they may come to remember lost songs. In this way they may begin to recover their power.''

Frank sat with his palms still resting on the earth. He closed his eyes and considered his great uncle's words. *They are the same, the*

131

matter of the Gahan and the matter of the Pinda Lickoyi. They are the same, the Bear had said, the power of the warrior and the power of the healer. This is wisdom the Gahan had said, anger tempered with love. They are the same, the air I breathe and the air Cochise breathed. They are the same, the anger, betrayal and grief the Tinde felt when Mangas Coloradas was murdered, and the feelings now about the charges being dropped against the two Pinda Lickoyi. They are the same.

Frank knew now what he must say to the people. The knowledge brought with it a great sadness, for he knew it might mean many deaths. But it also brought hope.

He opened his eyes. Great cloud masses writhed overhead, tinted a fiery red by the setting sun. Breezes moved in fits and starts through the pines around the cabin. He raised his left hand to the shrapnel at his chest and grasped it. He looked first at Maria, then at his great uncle. ``It is time," he said, and got to his feet.

Maria suggested the horses, but Frank wanted to walk. He was drawing a strength from his direct link to the earth.

They covered the distance in silence. The shadows of dusk became the darkness of night as they walked. Lightning flashed occasionally, illuminating the land with an almost eerie incandescence. Thunder rumbled like an afterthought.

They topped a small rise, and stopped, looking down on the fire-lit scene in the cottonwood grove below. The trees grew in a rough circle at the mouth of a large draw where it opened out to the west onto the flat land. The trees in the center of the grove had long ago been cut down, leaving a large clearing. Beyond the grove, the lights of Om'nitche were visible a couple miles to the northwest.

The flickering red-orange light of several fires in the clearing lit the trees from below, throwing dancing shadows upward into the night. Large groups of people gathered around each of the fires. Other smaller groups were scattered throughout the trees and among the collection of cars, pickups and four-wheel-drive vehicles parked on the western edge of the grove. Thirty or so horses were tethered to a picket line set up on the northern edge of trees.

Apache Tears

The subdued sounds of tense conversation mixed with the rumbles of the thunder and the rhythms of a single drum accompanied by a few old voices in an ancient chant. From the small groups around the vehicles, an occasional sharp, angry word, or bark of nervous laughter, broke through the background. Frank saw moonlight flashing off bottles being passed around in the dark.

``I want to enter from the east," Frank said to his great uncle. ``We can circle north and come down the draw."

The old man smiled, and stepped aside so Frank could lead.

Frank stopped in a mass of shadow at the mouth of the draw. The sounds were louder, the eastern edge of the grove only thirty yards away. He squatted and put his hands palm down on the sandy soil. *Before you speak, honor those who honor the spirit. They have power to weave with yours.*

Frank stood and faced Maria and his great uncle. ``I do not yet know all the words I will speak. But death will be one. Without your teaching, uncle, and without your help, Maria, I would not know how to speak this word without fear. I honor you, and ask your blessing."

The old man took pollen from his medicine pouch and threw it to the four directions. He grasped Frank by the shoulders. ``I am Two-World-Walker, Walks-With-Bear. You have my blessing."

``I am honored," Frank responded.

Maria began a soft but intense keening sound, uttered from high in her throat. A rush of feather rustlings sounded overhead and Frank saw a large, dark bird swoop over them and up onto a branch near the top of one of the cottonwoods.

She turned to him and placed her hands on his shoulders. ``I am Eagle Dreamer, Walks-With-Bear. You have my blessings."

``I am honored."

Frank turned back towards the clearing, hesitated, and stepped out of the shadows.

The nearest groups in the trees became aware of him before he reached the edge of the grove, and Frank felt their eyes on him as he

133

walked. He recognized several faces, some he had treated, others from Tribal Council meetings. He didn't speak. He was following the sound of the drum and it drew him towards the fire near the center of the clearing. He could hear the groups falling in behind him as he made his way through the trees. Adrenaline pumped into his system. Sweat broke out on the palms of his hands, and under his arms.

Other groups turned towards him. A murmur spread through the grove and out to those smaller groups near the vehicles. Frank reached the edge of the clearing and stepped into the firelight. Shadows danced around him. The sounds of voices died away except for a small group of old people gathered around the drummer near the central fire. They continued their chant. Frank joined in as he walked to their fire, the words coming back to him from some forgotten night of early youth.

``We are blessed in the Mountain Way,
The Gahan sing songs in our hearts.
We are strong in the Mountain Way,
The Gahan sing songs in our hearts."

The repetitions of the ancient prayer calmed him as he approached the circle of old ones around the seated drummer. The circle opened, making a place for him. Henry and Maria joined the circle to either side of him. They continued the chant four more repetitions. When they finished the fourth, the drummer stopped and the voices fell silent. The crackling of the fires and the shuffling of the last groups to enter the clearing were the only sounds.

Frank stepped into the center of the circle and offered his hand to the old man who sat there with an ancient drum. The man accepted the offered hand and got to his feet. Frank gripped the man by the shoulders, and nodded. The man returned the nod and stepped out of the center and back into the circle.

Frank turned slowly, meeting the eyes of each of the men and women who formed the circle. He nodded to each. He recognized most of them, but it was also as if he were seeing them all for the first time. He saw them not as quarrelsome members of the Tribal Council, or pitiful farmers trying to scratch a living from alkaline soil with too little water. He saw them not as relics, not as hopeless remnants of a beaten people. He saw them instead as proud and fierce warriors holding onto their ancient ways in spite of a hundred years of subjugation, a century of white eye attempts to destroy the spirit that made the Tinde the Tinde.

``I honor you, who honor the spirit,'' Frank said, and was startled at the power and strength in his voice. ``I honor your wisdom and your courage. I honor your rage and your grief. I honor your strength. I am honored to be part of your circle.''

The old ones nodded in acknowledgment, then stepped back to join the crowd that filled the clearing around Frank.

Frank walked slowly around the fire, keeping it to his back, looking at the people who pressed in around him. He saw Oscar and Carla and their kids. He saw Eddie Vasquez and his wife and two girls. He was surprised to see Elmer, and more surprised that he did not look drunk. He saw Danny Blue and a group of his young friends, a common anger turning their faces sullen. He saw people filling the clearing, and packed in among the trees. He tried to estimate the size of the crowd. Five hundred? Six hundred? He couldn't be sure, but it was more people than he'd ever seen gathered in one place on the reservation.

Frank continued circling slowly clockwise. Thunder rumbled to the east. ``Most of you know me as Frank Redhawk.'' The words seemed to dance like fire-cast shadows in the silence as he walked, waiting for the next words. ``Last night I was given another name, a spirit name. My great uncle, Henry Laughing Bird, has taught me that in the old way a spirit name is not often shared publicly. But the Gahan have sent me to speak to you of spiritual matters. I would honor your willingness to listen by telling you my spirit name. I am Walks-With-Bear.''

A snort of laughter erupted from somewhere back in the trees. A jolt of fear went through Frank.

``Hey, Frank. You sure it ain't Sleeps-With-Bear?''

There were a few nervous laughs but a murmur of disapproval from the crowd quieted them. Frank's left hand went to the shrapnel at

135

his chest. He continued walking. ``The Gahan gave me a vision of the Tinde last night, and spoke to me of a sickness of the spirit that was upon them.''

``Come on, Frank. People look up to you, man.'' It was Danny Blue. ``What are you doing, walking around talking all this spirit world stuff? Angela's dead, man. And those two Pinda Lickoyi bastards are walking around free!''

There were a few angry shouts of agreement. Frank walked up to Danny and stopped about five feet in front of him.

``What words would you have me speak, Danny Blue? Revenge? Retribution?''

``How about justice?'' Danny snapped. The chorus of support swelled. A quick series of lightning bolts stepped down the Chiricahuas towards them, the thunder arriving before the light could fade.

``What words do you want me to say?'' Frank asked again, gesturing to the crowd this time. ``Do you want me to say we should go and find those white eyes, and kill them? Would that be justice?''

There was a chorus of ascent, louder than before.

``One of the white eyes is the son of a U.S. Senator. They will come after us. They will arrest some of us, five or six. They will send us to the Pinda Lickoyi prison, and perhaps execute us. Would that be justice?''

There was a confused murmur in the crowd.

``The Tinde will lose five or six of their finest young men, and one of their finest young women. The Pinda Lickoyi will lose two rabid skunks. Will that be justice?''

``We can't just stand by and do nothing this time,'' Danny shouted angrily.

``You speak the truth, Danny Blue. But, is it not also true that there is nothing you can do to see justice done? Has that not been so for a hundred years and more? Is it not true that no Pinda Lickoyi has ever been jailed for raping a woman of the Tinde? Does this war, between a demand for action and an inability to act, not sit at the very center of every Tinde heart? How can this not be a matter of a sickness of the spirit?"

``You're twisting things around, Frank, trying to make it look like there's nothing we can do," Danny protested.

``We don't have to go after those two white eyes," someone yelled from the trees. ``There's plenty that come on the reservation every day."

Another angry chorus of support erupted. Frank tried to speak but could not be heard. His left hand went to the shrapnel. He looked around. Henry was standing with his eyes closed, lips moving in a silent chant. Maria moved up close to Henry. Across the fire Frank could see Oscar and Eddie and their wives trying to quiet the crowd around them.

Frank knelt down and put the palms of his hands to the earth. To the east, near the mouth of the draw, a pack of coyotes began a frenzied chorus. They were joined quickly by a pack to the south, another to the west, beyond the cars, and another to the north. As the volume of coyote cries increased, the volume of the crowd cries faded. When the crowd was silent, the coyote chorus died away, and the night was once more filled with the crackle of the fire and chirp of crickets.

Frank stood. ``There is something that can be done." He paced again around the fire. ``One thing. But it cannot be done with hearts full of revenge. It cannot be done without speaking of the past, and of the spirit world."

``The old ones have been practicing the spirit way for hundreds of years. Where did it get us?" Danny yelled.

The crowd moved back as Frank walked quickly to Danny. Frank grabbed him by the upper arm and pushed him into the clearing near the fire.

``The question is not where did it get us, nephew, but where did it get them. Your grandfather's father, at your age, could run on a summer afternoon from here to the Stronghold in the Dragoons with a mouth full of water and never swallow it. You can't walk from your wickiup to your pickup without swallowing from that bottle of wine you guzzle on like a starving child at his mother's dry teat. What is the difference between you, nephew? Your grandfather's father and his brothers could cover a hundred miles on foot in a night, and fight a running battle with white-eye soldiers all the next day. You talk of revenge but you have the courage of a rabbit. You can't fight your way out of the alcoholic fog long enough to realize you are dying." He took the wine bottle from Danny. ``You speak contemptuously of the spirit way and seek your power in this." Frank threw the bottle into the fire. ``The only power you will find in a bottle is the power to welcome death. That is not the power of a warrior. It is the only power left to a slave." Frank pushed Danny from the clearing, back into the crowd.

``All of you. I ask you. What is the difference between us and our grandfather's fathers? Why are we no longer capable of their feats of strength? Of endurance? Of courage? Is it diet? They lived and fought on roots and the flesh of horses, which had collapsed in exhaustion under them. Half starved and sick, on foot, they could out-run a company of Pinda Lickoyi soldiers on fresh mounts. What is the difference? What have we lost?" Frank paced around the fire.

``We lost our power. Our spirit power. We gave it away in exchange for our lives."

``We would not be here tonight if our grandfathers had not done so." It was the old drummer speaking.

``You speak the truth, uncle. But many gatherings of the mescal have passed since that decision was necessary. The world of the Pinda Lickoyi, and the world beyond, have changed. We have changed. We have grown strong in numbers. There are three times more of us now than there has ever been. But we have grown weak in spirit. The Gahan spoke to me of a time of great change for the Tinde. A time that demands we reclaim our power. That time is now."

``We'll never reclaim any power with a bunch of empty spirit talk," a voice called.

``If I want to hear spirit talk I'll go to the mission," called another.

``He didn't fight in Vietnam. He'll never fight for Angela."

``Take your spirit world back to the mountain. Angela wasn't killed by ghosts."

Anger roared in Frank. He struggled with it. He sang his Bear song, tentatively at first. Henry motioned and Frank followed him to the east edge of the clearing. The crowd parted before them and they passed on through the trees towards the mouth of the draw. Voices continued to pulse around Frank in angry counterpoint, but he was only marginally aware of them. He sang his song, more powerfully now. Those around him backed away. Henry disappeared into the crowd. Frank stopped at the very edge of the grove, facing east. He continued his song and the shouting died away. Lightning flashed and cracked on the ridgeline just east of them, the thunder drowning the sounds of his song.

A massive form ambled out of the shadowy mouth of the draw and towards the grove. There were gasps and mutters as people began to realize it was a bear. Frank stepped out of the grove and walked to meet the huge beast. Several lightning flashes came close together, illuminating every detail of the ancient grizzly as it stood on its hind legs.

From somewhere off to the south edge of the grove a rifle cracked and flashed. Then again. And again. The Bear did not react. Lightning once more lit the scene as Frank approached and the Bear dropped back to all fours and nuzzled Frank's chest. Frank turned towards the crowd. He stood beside the Bear, his left hand on the great creature's massive neck.

``I am Walks-With-Bear." His voice boomed in the darkness. ``I have been honored with the spirit power of the Sacred Bear. I did not come here to argue with you about revenge, or to hear your insults. I came to speak with you about a time of great change, a time of healing for the Tinde. But I cannot force you to hear my words. The choice is yours."

A buzz of whispers surged through the crowd. ``Stay," called a voice. ``Speak to us," called another. ``We would hear the words of Walks-With-Bear."

Frank walked back towards the grove, the Bear at his side. The only sounds as he moved through the trees were the shufflings of the crowd surging away in front of him and closing in again behind. Frank reached the clearing. The great Bear paced beside him as he circled the fire once before stopping on the east side. The horses on the picket line shied and stamped their feet.

``There is no need for me to speak to you of the great power we once knew as a people. The fierce pride with which we walked a land that spoke to us with every footstep. The long years of war and suffering. The courage. The starvation. The death. The betrayal. The grief. No need to speak to you of the hundred years of hopelessness, the despair we suffered as the white eyes took our children and did everything they could to destroy our ways, our language, our spirits. These things you all know in your hearts.

``I come, rather, to speak to you of a way to end this hopelessness. A way to turn Angela's death into a new beginning. A way to turn the white eyes' release into justice. It will not be an easy way. It will demand the strength and endurance of our ancestors. It will demand a courage strong enough to face death and not turn away. It will not be possible unless we reclaim our spirit power, our spiritual center. It may not be possible even then. But this I know. If we do not act, if we do not try, the spirit of the Tinde will die and we will be no more. The Gahan have spoken of a circle of the Tinde which must be completed. A sickness of the spirit which must be healed, or the spirit of the Tinde will vanish forever."

``What is this way of which you speak, Walks-With-Bear?" Frank recognized the old drummer's voice.

``The time has come to retake our land. To tell the white eyes they have broken the spirit and letters of our treaties one time too many. To tell them we no longer recognize their self-assumed power over us. It is time to take this land they have given us, defined by the borders they drew, and to declare it ours, as a sovereign people. To declare our right to defend our borders with arms if necessary. It is time to tell the white eyes that we are prepared to die, every man, woman, and child of us, rather than go on living as subjugated wards of a condescending, paternalistic, culturally intolerant white-eye government. It is time to redeclare our independence. In this way we can begin to reclaim our power. The Gahan have spoken. They make their power available to us. They demand only that we choose honor, even in the face of death."

The great Bear growled and stood to his full fifteen feet. He swayed from side to side, looking out over the crowd, then dropped again to all fours. The horses snorted and stamped.

``Someone came among us long ago, speaking as you do, Walks-With-Bear." The old drummer spoke with respect. ``He spoke of a spirit vision, and a new spirit way. The Ghost Dance Way. He promised that the power of the Ghost Dance would stop white eye bullets and bring back the deer to the mountains, and the buffalo to the prairies. It did not do so. It excited the young men. It angered the white eyes. Many of the people suffered, many died."

``Once more you speak the truth, uncle, and I honor you for your wisdom. But the Gahan do not speak of a new spirit way. They speak of the old way. And they do not make these promises. They say only that they make their power available to us. It is we who must be worthy of it and make use of it. They promise only that if we try to live with honor, the spirit of the Tinde will survive, and that if we do not find some way to do this, then the spirit of the Tinde will be no more forever."

``The white eyes will send the army onto the reservation." Another of the old ones spoke. ``Many of us will die, and the rest will be sent away from these mountains as Geronimo and his people were sent away."

``You may be right, uncle. But I think they will not respond this way immediately. Not if we have prepared well, and have made it plain we are ready to die rather than submit. The white-eye world has changed. There are many among them who would not stand by and let such a thing happen. Many of their ally countries would bring pressure on them. But you may be right. In the end, the army might come. That is why we must not walk this way with revenge in our hearts. We must

141

not give them any justification to send their soldiers. And that is why anyone who chooses to walk this way, must do so by their own choice. If, in the end, they do send their soldiers, we must die rather than submit. Only in this way will the spirit of the people live on."

``What about those who do not wish to walk this way?"

``The reservation is large. It can be split between us. Those who wish may continue living as they live now."

``How would we live, without the government money?" It was a woman with four small children clustered around her, hanging onto her skirt.

``For four hundred years before the white eyes came, we walked this land, and honored it. The land fed us and clothed us. It sheltered us. It healed us when we were sick. It made us strong when enemies were all around us. Now we try to use the land in the way of the white eyes. We no longer honor it. It no longer whispers to us its secrets. If we walk once more with honor, the land will once more honor us. Not in the old ways of hunting and gathering. We have grown to be too many to support in those ways anymore. We cannot go backwards. But in new ways, in ways we can not yet even dream, the land will honor us with balance and abundance."

Lightning crashed onto the ridgeline nearby and cold, heavy drops of rain began to fall.

``Think on these things, brothers and sisters. Think on them well. Speak about these matters among yourselves. Consider them for three days. At sundown, three nights from tonight, we will gather here to speak of them again."

Frank walked towards the east, the Bear at his side. The crowd parted silently before him as he moved through the trees and disappeared into the shadows at the mouth of the draw. The rain began to come down harder. Lightning played along the ridges above him. He turned to climb up out of the draw, retracing his steps towards his great uncle's cabin. He walked, unaware that the Bear had left him, aware only of the rain, which mixed with the tears on his face, and of the earth beneath his feet. His left hand went to the shrapnel on his chest. He held it tightly as he walked, stumbling occasionally in the darkness.

Late night, July 20 --- Henry's cabin

Frank reached the cabin and built a small fire in the fireplace. He sat near it on the floor, staring into the flames. The rain and walk had emptied him of grief. He was tired now, and drained. He had no idea what effect his words might have. He didn't worry about it. He had done what he could, had spoken the words that were in his heart. For the moment it was enough to gaze into the flames and feel their warmth penetrating his wet clothes to ease the chill which gripped him.

Henry and Maria arrived after a time. Neither spoke. The old man got a pot of coffee going over the fire Frank had built. Maria paced the small cabin with a nervous energy while she dried her hair with a towel Henry had provided. Frank noticed the rain had stopped.

When the coffee had boiled, Henry poured three cups and Frank joined the others at the small table. They sat in silence for a time before Frank spoke.

``I tried, uncle,'' he said quietly. ``I was frightened, angry, confused. But I spoke only words which came from within. I spoke only those words which seemed to me the truth.''

``You spoke with great wisdom and courage, Walks-With-Bear. You spoke well. Your counsel was good.''

``But did anyone hear? Did it do any good?''

The old man shrugged. ``In every healing there is a time of uncertainty. You do what you can, then you wait. If you see something else you can do, you do it, then wait some more. Healing cannot be forced. You have shown the people the path. Now they must decide whether or not to walk it.''

Frank nodded. ``It is such a narrow path. With death on both sides.''

``It is the path of the Tinde, nephew. The path we have been walking for five hundred years.''

Frank thought about his great uncle's words. He felt a kinship stretching back in time, with the warriors who sat in the councils of

Mangas Coloradas, of Cochise, of Nana, and Geronimo, warriors who discussed the same issues, who faced the same terrible decisions. That sense of kinship strengthened him and the exhaustion, which sat heavily on him, lifted a bit.

Maria finished the rest of her coffee and set the cup on the table. ``I have seen the effect of your words, Frank. The Eagle's gift sometimes allows me to penetrate through the uncertainty of things. What you have proposed will come to pass. The decisions are being made. I could feel them as I walked here. It is only the outcome which remains uncertain.'' She toyed with her empty cup. ``You will need help.''

Frank nodded. ``I know. There is so much to be done.'' He shrugged. ``But until I know how people decide, I don't know who I can count on, except you two.''

``Contact the white man, Clay Price. He is a strong man with a great love for the people.''

Frank studied her carefully as he considered her suggestion, then shook his head. ``No. I believe, as you do, that he is a good man. But he is white. This is a matter for the people.''

``I think you should reconsider,'' Maria said softly.

Again, Frank shook his head. ``It would ask too much of him. It would put him in conflict with his own people. He fought well for them, and suffered. I cannot ask him to oppose them.''

``As you wish,'' Maria answered. She got to her feet. ``I must go. The messengers to the other parts of the reservation should have returned by now.''

``Take the buckskin mare,'' Henry said. ``She is good in the dark.''

When Maria had gone, Frank and Henry sat sharing a comfortable silence for a long time. Finally the old man got up and crossed to the fireplace. He banked the coals against the remaining night hours. From his trunk by the door he took out a buffalo robe and two blankets, spreading them on the floor near the fireplace.

``We must sleep,'' he said. ``Dealing with great power takes its toll on the body. Over the next days you will have to speak many times. Some will challenge you. Some will oppose you. You will need your strength. Between now and the Great Gathering you have called, you must sleep every night, even if you feel no need. Sleep is a strong ally for a healer, particularly one who sings the Bear song."

CHAPTER SEVEN: THE RETURN

Shortly before midnight, July 21 --- Clay's apartment complex

It was late when Clay returned home. He had stopped at a bar and tried to take his mind off recent events by watching a baseball game on the big screen TV at The Sports Pub. He was irritated by his lack of accomplishment since he had left the reservation. There seemed no place left for him to go with his investigation. Short of carrying out his own sentence on Charlie and Bruce, there was nothing he could do. Perhaps with his findings in hand, Frank could convince the girl to press charges. That appeared to be the way to go at this point.

He parked his car in the parking lot of the large apartment complex and stepped into the warm desert night. As he looked towards the stairs leading to his apartment, he noticed a shadowy figure standing under the stairwell. The image of a red Cadillac in his rear-view mirror flashed through his mind. He slipped quickly out of sight of the stairs and circled around the building.

His heart pumped loudly in his ears as he moved stealthily up to the darkened stairwell from the blind side. He stood at the corner of the building, the stairwell an arm's reach to his left. He waited for a movement. He heard nothing. Maybe whoever it was had left before he

146

was able to get around the building. He held his breath. He sensed the presence of the person, around the corner, only a foot or two away.

He leapt around the corner with the quickness and grace of a cat. He pushed on the dark form and grabbed for an arm once contact was established. He twisted the arm and moved in close to the body from behind. He felt long hair brush against his hand as he twisted the arm.

``What the … ``

``Clay!"

He released his grip and stepped out of the stairwell. ``Maria?"

She stepped out of the darkness into the light cast by the lamp at the far corner of the building.

``Are you all right?" he asked.

``I'm fine. You're very good."

``What are you doing here?"

``I've got to speak to you," said Maria. ``I know it's late, but this is important."

``We can get in my car and find a restaurant, or, if you think I'm honorable enough, we can go up to my apartment."

``Your apartment is fine. I don't feel comfortable in this dress. I wore it to be inconspicuous but I'm afraid it's having the opposite effect. At least I feel like it is."

Clay stepped closer. ``Did you bring anything else? How did you get here? How long have you been waiting?" He touched her arm. ``C'mon, let's get up to my place."

``I have a suitcase under the stairs. I've been here since this morning. I rode the bus. Does that answer your questions?"

``Have you eaten?"

``I didn't want to take the chance of missing you."

He picked up her battered suitcase, which looked as if it had been handed down for several generations – violent generations – and moved to the stairs.

She followed closely. At the door, he fumbled for his keys, acutely aware of her nearness. He glanced at her twice during his search, then displayed a key with a sheepish grin. ``See? I do live here."

Inside the apartment, he emptied his refrigerator. She refused most of what he placed before her, but finally agreed to eat some cheese and bread.

He watched her as she ate, trying his level best to be as inconspicuous as possible. He ate small bites of cheese with her to put her at ease. He knew she was hungry and he wanted her to eat.

``Why do you stare at me, Clay?"

``I'm sorry. I didn't realize I was so obvious."

``You've been drinking again, haven't you."

Clay sighed, ``I had a few drinks with dinner, but nothing like what I had on the reservation. It seems like I'm never going to make a very good impression on you, am I?"

``I didn't know you wanted to. Is that why you stare at me?"

He took a bite of cheese. ``No, Maria, that's not why I stare at you. I stare at you because I have no upbringing and no class, and if I could stare a little bit longer, I think I could confirm that you're the most beautiful woman I've ever seen."

``Is physical beauty so important to you?" she asked.

``Not as important as it used to be when I was a kid. But the first thing we notice about anybody we meet is their physical appearance."

She looked into his eyes. ``Perhaps that is also the last thing you notice. Perhaps even the only thing."

``You don't believe that, or you wouldn't be sitting here with me at midnight."

She smiled. ``Perhaps there is hope. I came on matters not connected with your ideas of women. They are of far greater importance than your opinion of my physical appearance."

Clay stood from the table. ``Somehow this conversation got turned around. You're trying to make me out to be some kind of pervert or something. That isn't what I meant at all. I haven't even thought of you in those terms."

``In what terms do you think of me?" she asked disinterestedly, as she tore a piece of bread from the loaf.

Clay smiled at the way she tore the bread. ``As a work of art.''

She looked up at him, stopping in mid-chew. She continued to chew until she was able to swallow. ``A work of art? I should listen to you very carefully. That is one thing I didn't hear today, as I stood around in this foolish dress, waiting for you to come home. It seems every man here found me attractive, or defenseless, or sexy, or cute, or something even more explicit.''

Clay avoided her gaze. Unfortunately, she was right about most men. ``I'm sorry I wasn't here.''

``It was a good education. I'd forgotten how different white eyes are. Now I am reminded.''

Clay busied himself making coffee. ``If you're going to put me in the same category with all the rest of the white men in the world, how about if we just talk business?'' He turned the coffee maker on, his back to her as he spoke.

``If I put you in the same category with all other white eyes, I would not be here tonight. I have a strong belief in you. You are going to be good for my people.''

``For your people? What are you talking about?''

She pushed the bread and cheese to the side of the table. ``Have you had time to find out anything about the two rapists?''

Clay sat at the table. ``Quite a bit. And none of it is good. What's going on down on the reservation?''

For two hours they exchanged knowledge and information, each struck by the magnitude of what the other was saying, each knowing that an event of great consequence was taking place, even as they spoke.

At three o'clock, exhausted, they fell asleep. Not in Clay's bed, or on the sofa, but on the floor in the small livingroom, side by side, both of them fully clothed.

Early morning, July 22 --- Clay's apartment

Clay awakened to the woman smell of Maria. He opened his

eyes slowly, as if he feared even the movement of his eyelids might waken her. She was already awake and looking at him, her face only a foot from his.

``What are you staring at?'' he asked.

``You. You too are beautiful, in your own way.''

``I think you learned too much from the white men yesterday.'' He smiled.

``I'm being serious. You sleep the sleep of a cat, but it is a restful sleep. You are a good man, Clay. The way you sleep tells me so.''

``Well, you're just as pretty in the morning as you are in the evening. There are very few women who can say that.''

``You don't understand what I mean about beauty.''

``Neither do you. You want some coffee?'' He wanted to reach out and pull her to him.

``Yes, please.''

He stood and moved to the kitchen.

They drank their coffee quickly then breakfasted at a nearby restaurant. Clay studied her as she sat across from him in the booth. She had changed into a white cotton short-sleeved top and a loose-fitting turquoise cotton skirt. She drew more looks than she would have with the yellow summer dress, but Clay knew she was more comfortable with her Apache attire.

``You ever been up in a small plane?'' he asked.

``No, why do you ask?''

``I'd like to take you up in one. Today. Right now.''

``I have many things to do. I must return to the reservation.''

``I'll take you. I can fly you there in about thirty-five minutes.'' He waited patiently for her answer. He wanted to share his experiences with this woman. He wanted to know her. He felt closer to her than any woman he had ever met, and yet he could find no explanation for that feeling.

When she answered, it was as though she read his mind. ``You want very much for me to go, don't you?''

He looked at his empty plate. ``Only if you want to. I would think you'd like it. There's nothing like the freedom of flying.''

She placed a hand over his. ``I'd like very much to know this thing which brings you so much pleasure. When can we go?''

Clay tried to hide his smile and appear nonchalant. ``Let me put in a call to Tubs and I'll be right back.''

Shortly after noon, July 22 --- Tubs' hangar, Marana Airstrip

``You guys were gone so long, I was gettin' worried,'' said Tubs as they stepped into the old hangar.

``We decided to do some sightseeing southeast of here.''

``It's pretty down there this time of year. Kinda romantic,'' said Tubs.

Clay gave him a warning glance.

Tubs stood silently while Clay filled out his flight log. Clay signed the book and stood. ``Thanks, Tubs. I may need the plane again soon. Is that okay?''

Tubs gave Maria a knowing wink and said, ``You just give me thirty minutes' notice and she's yours.''

``Thanks, Tubs. We'll see you later.''

Maria followed him to the convertible. ``Does this mean you are not taking me back to the reservation?''

``You bet I am, but I'd like to talk to Frank Redhawk first. You feel like a late lunch?''

She smiled up at him as he opened her door. ``Sure.''

Early afternoon, July 22 --- A restaurant in Tucson

``Excuse me a minute.'' Clay stood from the table and dug into his pocket for change. ``I'm going to call Frank. I'll be right back.''

``Wait, Clay.'' Her voice was firm, not pleading.

He sat back down at the booth. ``What do you mean, `Wait'?''

``I didn't tell you everything you should hear before you call.''

Clay listened as Maria told him about Angela's decision to die, and of Frank's spirit name. When she finished, he sat there, staring at

151

her.

``Do you believe everything you just told me?'' he asked, after a lengthy moment.

``It is all true, Clay. Every word.''

``But the thing with the bear… Come on, there hasn't been a grizzly in those mountains since before I was born. You should have made him an Arizona Brown or Black. Even if I accepted all the other stuff, I know there isn't a grizz within three hundred miles of the reservation. Is the part about the girl dying true?''

He thought he detected the beginnings of a tear in one of her eyes, but he wasn't certain. She nodded. He stood to make his call, a look of determination in his eyes as he thought of Angela.

After several unsuccessful attempts to reach Frank, he opted for a call to Oscar. He heard his brother's familiar voice in the phone.

``Hello.''

``Oscar, this is Clay. I'm at a pay phone, so let's make it quick. I've just talked to Maria, and she's told me some pretty tall tales, about Frank and a grizzly bear and some pretty heavy-duty decisions being made. What in the hell is going on out there?''

``I'm not sure myself, Clay. I was at The Gathering. It happened. I saw it, but I don't understand it.''

``Hell, there hasn't been a grizz in that part of the state since before we were born.''

``It was a grizzly, Clay. I saw it. It may not make much sense. Hell, none of it makes much sense, but I was there. I don't know what's going on. I think Frank may be losing it. He's talking some real strong talk. It could mean a lot of trouble. Maybe you could come out and talk some sense to him – bring him back down to reality.''

``You mean they really are talking about independence?''

``Real seriously. And this thing with Angela is what set it off.''

``Oscar, I saw a confession signed by Jack Stillwater where he admitted selling Angela to those two guys for twenty bucks.''

``A confession? Old Jack can't even speak English, much less read it.''

``Are you sure?"

``Positive."

Clay paused. ``I'll tell you what. I'll come down and talk to him. I've got to see this grizz with my own eyes anyway. I better get going. I don't have much change on me. I'll talk to you later. Give Carla and the kids my greetings. Elmer too."

``I'll see you, brother."

When he returned to the table fifteen minutes after leaving, Maria was waiting patiently, an empty coffee cup before her on the table. ``What's the matter? Our waitress quit?" asked Clay.

``What did Frank say, Clay?"

He scooted to the rear of the booth. ``I couldn't reach him. I talked to Oscar."

``What did he say?"

``There's something weird going on, Maria. I don't know what it is, but I've known Oscar a mighty long time. Maybe somebody put something in your drinking water or something. He told me about a big grizzly bear that walked with Frank. He asked me to come back to the reservation and talk to Frank." He looked hard into her eyes.

``I told you of this."

``Yeah, you did. I'm sorry. I guess it's not your fault. Whatever has affected you has got to Oscar, too. Are you guys smoking too much peyote?"

``Please take me to the bus station, Clay."

His heart sank. *Damn. Why did I say that?* ``Maria, try to look at it from my point of view. I mean, I believe more in the spirits than I do in the Christian God, but this thing with the grizz is takin' it a bit far, don't you think?"

``I'll go by myself. I'll need my suitcase from the trunk of your car." She stood.

He dropped some money onto the table and followed her through the door and into the parking lot. ``Okay, okay, you win. Let's talk."

She said nothing, but opened the door and sat silently in the

153

bucket seat.

Clay sat behind the wheel. He looked over to her and saw that she was staring through the windshield at the bland brown side of the restaurant wall. ``Maria, I'm taking you back to the reservation. I'm not letting you take a bus."

She looked at him. ``Clay, I tried to tell you there were things going on that you would not understand. When I told you, you did not understand."

``I understand murder."

``What do you mean?"

``Angela Stillwater. She's dead, and the guys that did it are home free as far as the U. S. government is concerned."

``There is nothing we can do about that right now. I just want to go home, Clay."

``Do you mind if we stop by my apartment so I can pick up a couple of packs of smokes? It's not far from here, and I hate buying them from a machine when I have a carton at home."

``I don't mind."

They drove the half mile to the apartment in silence. Clay parked the car and hurried up the stairs to his place. When he unlocked the door and stepped inside, he knew someone had been there since this morning. The photograph of the Blood Brothers had been moved.

He rushed to the bedroom and checked his weapons. They were there, but they too had been moved. He quickly checked the rest of his apartment. There was no doubt in his mind. Someone had searched it in his absence. *All right, goddamnit. I've had enough of this crap.*

He picked up a suitcase from the closet and filled it with his best clothing. He pulled a large duffel bag from the corner of his bedroom and stuffed it with the rest of his things. He added his two pistols, a double-action .357 magnum Smith and Wesson and a .44 Colt, then went into the livingroom and took the picture of the Blood Brothers from the shelf. He looked at it briefly before packing it into the duffel bag.

Almost as an afterthought, he returned to the bedroom, opened a drawer and removed a small elongated box, hinged on one end. He opened the box and stared at the Medal and the ribbon with its white stars on a field of light blue. He hadn't looked at the Medal for years. To look at it was to re-live too much pain. He saw Billy laying on the damp trail, his intestines covered by his helmet. He saw the spattered blood on his own arms and hands, smelled the cordite in the air, and heard Billy's last words.

Clay wiped his eyes as he removed the Medal from the box and stuffed it into his shirt pocket. He rushed downstairs to the old GTO and Maria.

``Why did you bring your suitcase and that bag?" asked Maria.

``Somebody paid me a visit while we were gone. An unauthorized visit. It's time for me to move."

``Are you going to the reservation?"

He looked at her and grinned. ``You bet I'm going to the reservation. When my own elected officials start spying on me, it's time to go to another country."

Maria returned his smile. ``Frank will not be glad to see you at first, but he'll come around. Be patient."

``I think he'll be glad to see me. I'm going to bring him a present. Two of them."

The smile left Maria's face. ``No, Clay. You can't do it. It isn't your place to do it."

``If I don't, nobody will. When this independence business gets heated up in a few days, those guys will have personal protection provided courtesy of the taxpayers. If they're ever going to face the music, this is the only chance we're gonna have to see that it gets done."

``Please, Clay. No. You will be wanted for kidnapping by your own people. Let's just go to the reservation. There is no crime in that."

``There is, to my way of thinking, if I go without those two guys. I've gotta at least give it a try. If it looks too risky, I'll forget about it, okay?"

``Promise me you won't take any chances, Clay. Frank needs you. He doesn't know it yet, but he will."

155

``I'll be real careful." Clay avoided making the promise.

Late afternoon, July 22 --- The IBM parking lot, Tucson

Bruce was almost too easy. Clay simply waited for him to show up at his car after work in the large parking lot at the IBM plant. He had read the police report well.

Bruce had initially shown an inclination to run, but when Clay exposed the short-barreled Smith and Wesson under his newspaper, any thoughts of running disappeared from Bruce's mind. He quietly sat in the front seat of the GTO, Maria right behind him. Clay handed Maria his single-action Colt and asked her to guard Bruce as he drove for the hospital.

Dusk, July 22 --- Tucson Medical Center

When they arrived at the hospital, it was almost dark. The late afternoon cumulus clouds ripened with the dying sun, waiting for darkness to fall, sowing thoughts of rain in the last moments of light. Clay took it as a good sign.

He stepped inside the big hospital and walked casually down the hall, slowing to admire a row of paintings on the wall. He moved from painting to painting inexorably towards Charlie's private room. His hands began to shake and his heart to pound in his eardrums as the door to Charlie's room came into view.

As he drew nearer, he heard voices.

``...still don't see why the senator thinks anyone would want to harm his kid just over him shooting himself on the reservation. It don't make any sense to me."

A second male voice, this one deeper, said, ``Me either, but it doesn't really matter whether we watch him or the senator, we get paid the same."

``Yeah, but this seems kind of... "

Clay moved out of earshot. *Damn! Those guys sound like the Secret Service! What the hell are they doing here?*

He moved down a corridor until he found an orderly, who he

asked for directions to the laundry. Five minutes later, Clay came out of the laundry room wearing a bloodied green gown and surgical mask. Through the mask, the smell of the dried blood was unpleasantly pungent, bringing back unwanted memories.

He found an unattended gurney near a door and quickly pushed it around a corner and up the hallway towards Charlie's room, expecting someone to challenge him at any moment. His hands trembled as he approached the door to Charlie's room. He stopped and breathed deeply several times. *Come on, Clay. Don't fall out now.*

The two bodyguards snapped around when he entered the room. The one with the deep voice said, ``What are you doing here?''

Clay spoke through his mask. ``I've got orders to move Charlie here to another room.''

Deep Voice looked at his companion. ``The Senator say anything about this to you?''

The second man shook his head.

Deep Voice pulled his pistol. ``Put your hands on your head and don't move.'' He pointed the revolver at Clay's chest.

Shit! ``What's the matter with you guys? I'm going to report this.''

``Put your hands on your head, or you won't be reporting anything to anybody.''

Clay did as ordered. The second man pulled his mask down. ``Who the hell are you? And who sent you here?''

``Who the hell am *I*? Who the hell are you? I get orders to come in here and move a patient, and two nuts with guns threaten to kill me.''

``You got some I.D.?'' asked Deep Voice.

``Yeah, sure.'' He slowly dropped his left hand.

``Wait a minute.'' Deep Voice turned to the other man. ``Pat him down, Joe.''

Joe moved up to him. Clay winced as the bodyguard slapped the Smith and Wesson tucked into his belt.

``Well, well, what have we here?'' said Joe sarcastically as he pulled the pistol out from under the gown.

157

``It looks like a gun to me. Don't move – anybody."

Both men looked in the direction of the door – the direction of the voice.

``Who the hell are ..."

Clay brought his hand down hard on Deep Voice's wrist, just as he started to swing his pistol towards the door. The weapon clattered harmlessly to the floor.

``Give that gun very carefully to the gentleman in the hospital gown." Maria stood just inside the door, the big single-action Colt cocked and held firmly in her right hand.

``Are you people crazy? You can't get away with this." Deep Voice looked about the room as though he expected help from somewhere within the walls.

Clay snatched his revolver from Joe's hand, then moved quickly to the pistol on the floor. He picked it up, then returned to Joe and took the man's personal weapon from his belt. He said nothing to Maria. He panned the two bodyguards with his Smith. ``Back into that corner. One sound and I'll kill you both."

With the two men standing in the corner, Clay wheeled the gurney next to Charlie's bed and dragged him onto it. Charlie was so doped up on pain killers, he never stirred. Clay pulled the mask up over his face and spoke to the two bodyguards.

``You two push this gurney to the parking lot. If you make any attempt to warn anybody or do anything else stupid, I'll put a bullet in good ol' Charlie's head. The young lady will do the same for you. Any questions?"

They said nothing.

``Let's go, gents. Out the door and to your left."

Early evening, July 22 --- The desert east of Tucson

Clay finished tying the two bodyguards to a Palo Verde tree east of town. With a promise to notify the police of their location within two hours, he left their pistols next to them and ran back to the GTO. He slid behind the wheel and spoke to Maria for the first time since she had appeared at the hospital.

``Thanks. I was expecting to spend the rest of my life behind bars.''

She said nothing.

``When is old Bruce back there going to come around?''

``He will not wake up for a long time,'' said Maria.

``How can you be so sure? Oh no, Maria. You didn't...``

``Don't be foolish, Clay. This is very important. He's all right.''

Clay breathed a sigh of relief. He glanced at Charlie, unconscious in the back seat. Bruce was on the floorboard.

``You sure he's not going to wake up?''

Maria nodded. ``Not until morning.''

``Whew! That must be potent stuff you used, whatever it is.''

Maria smiled in the darkness.

Clay started the engine and drove south, towards the interstate. He pulled into a convenience market and placed a call to Teresa Chatla. She had given him her home phone number on their second meeting. He waited nervously as the phone rang for the fifth time.

``Hello?''

``Teresa?''

``Yes. Who's this?''

``Clay Price. I'm sorry to bother you at home, but I may have that big story we talked about. Did I wake you?''

``Heavens no. I was about to take a bath. That's what took me so long to get to the phone. Now what's this all about?''

``I'd recommend real strongly that you get yourself a mobile unit and get out to the reservation first thing in the morning.''

``What's going on?''

``First, I'll have to ask that this stays confidential until tomorrow night. Then you can do what you want with it.''

``I'll do what I can, Clay, but I have to tell my assignment editor something if I'm supposed to go to the reservation in the morning.''

``Okay, but keep it vague. There might be lives at stake. The story's too complicated to go into details right now, but I'll try to contact you later if you can't get there. The main thrust of the story is that the Apache are declaring themselves an independent nation. And the good senator Williams is having me followed and busting into my apartment."

``Are you serious, Clay?"

``I swear to you. Oh yeah, one more thing." He paused.

``Okay, go ahead."

``I've got Bruce Stinton and Charlie Williams, and I'm taking them back to the reservation for trial by the Apache."

``My God, Clay! Do you know what you're doing?"

``I'm doing the right thing, Teresa. I fight a war for my country. I lose my best friend. I mind my own business and I pay my taxes. For this I get followed around, my apartment is gone through, and the good senator is about to frame me for shooting his no-good son. If the Apache weren't declaring independence, I'd go somewhere else."

``They'll never pull it off, Clay."

``It won't be for lack of trying. I belong down there. I believe in those people. And I know they're gonna make it."

``How, Clay? How can they possibly make it?"

There was a smile in his voice. ``If they had a little good press, it sure wouldn't hurt their cause."

``I'm a reporter, Clay. I don't fabricate things, and I try not to skew my reporting."

``That's all they need; the facts, ma'am, nothing but the facts. Listen, I've got to go. If you decide to make the trip, ask for a guy named Frank Redhawk. He may have a big grizzly bear with him, but don't worry about it. I understand the bear hasn't bit anybody in a month of Sundays."

``Clay, have you been drinking?"

He glanced at Maria, sitting in the car. ``I wish women would quit asking me that. No. I'm serious. If you can't get ahold of Frank, try Oscar Gosheyun. He's the Fire Marshal out there.

``Oh, one more thing. Would you mind making a call to the sheriff? I left these two guys tied to a tree out east of..."

Evening, July 22 --- East of Tucson

He drove east on Interstate 10, exceeding the speed limit by no more than five miles per hour. In Texas Canyon, just east of Benson, the rain came. It was a hard rain, with drops the size of quarters. The windshield wipers were unable to handle the load, and Clay was forced to slow the car to forty miles per hour, still a dangerous speed with the almost zero visibility.

When Clay saw the roadblock, it was too late to turn around. He felt the single action Colt at his side. He had given Maria the smaller Smith and Wesson. ``We've had it, Maria. I can't shoot a cop. If they see those guys back there we're caught."

In the faint glimmer of the dash lights, Clay saw an expression of fear on her face. ``They cannot catch you, Clay. You will die in prison. They will never let you out."

``I can't shoot a cop, Maria, not even for you. I'll tell them I forced you to do it. You'll be okay."

``I'm not worried for myself, Clay."

He braked the car to a stop. A Highway Patrolman in a yellow slicker approached warily, his flashlight held away from his body and pointed into Clay's eyes. His other hand covered his holster, ready to draw the service weapon through the slit in the raincoat.

Clay tried to see beyond the bright beam of light. He could see two cars. There might be enough room on the outside of that one on the right. He cracked the window into the heavy rain.

``Evening, folks. Sorry for the inconvenience, but I'm going to have to ask you for your driver's license."

``Certainly, officer. What seems to be the problem?"

Clay saw the patrolman relax slightly and he depressed the accelerator pedal about halfway to the floor. He released the clutch evenly in order not to lose traction on the wet pavement. The GTO lunged forward. He heard the patrolman shout. A man stepped out of the squad car to his right front, a pistol in his hand. Clay ducked as the bullet penetrated the windshield slightly to the left of his face, sending fragments of glass into the interior. The flying glass was followed quickly by the report of the handgun.

Clay steered to the right, narrowly missing the rear bumper of the patrol car. His drive tires broke loose in the mud on the shoulder of the road and the rear of the car drifted outward. He corrected with the wheel and eased off the fuel pedal. He heard the heavy thunk of bullets striking his door as the GTO straightened. Gently he turned the wheel slightly left and felt the tires bite the wet asphalt as the car gained the roadway on the other side of the roadblock.

A lone shot thudded into his door. He felt a sharp pain in his left side and reached across his body to touch it with his right hand. He removed his bloody hand and shifted through the gears as the car picked up speed. The Highway Patrol cars faded rapidly in the mirror as the speedometer climbed to over a hundred miles an hour.

As Clay conquered his fear, he realized the foolishness of such speed in the rain. The old Pontiac floated dangerously from side to side on the freeway as the tires hydroplaned on a film of water. His side hurt and he was losing blood. He took his eyes from the road for the first time since breaking the roadblock.

``Maria, are you okay?''

``Yes. I'm okay. Are you?''

Wind and water gushed through the hole in the windshield to the left of the steering wheel. He leaned right to avoid the water and see the road ahead.

He started to tell her about his wound, but thought better of it. He would wait until they were on the reservation. She would probably want to stop and look at it. There was no time now and the reservation was only another thirty minutes away.

``I'm okay. Check those guys in back, will you? I'd hate to see them cheat us out of a trial after all of this.''

Maria twisted and leaned between the two bucket seats. ``They are okay,'' she said after a moment.

As she turned to sit forward in her seat, her arm brushed his. The instant they touched, she froze. ``You're hurt.''

162

Apache Tears

Clay slowed the car and looked into her eyes briefly. ``How did you know?''

``There are things I just know.''

``Well, it doesn't hurt much. I think I was just grazed a little above the waist on my left side.'' He almost missed the highway exit. The car slithered left and right for several yards as he turned too abruptly on the wet pavement. Maria lost her balance and fell into him. He held onto the wheel and maintained control. The smell of her hair in his face as she struggled to sit upright stirred him.

Once on the two-lane highway heading south, he said, ``Sorry about the turn. I didn't see the off-ramp.''

``That's okay.'' She moved from his lap. ``We must treat the wound. It's in a bad place. It could be dangerous if we don't attend to it soon.''

``We can't stop now, Maria. A few more minutes and we're home free.'' He checked the mirror. Nothing followed. The Highway Patrol had better sense than to attempt to overtake a vehicle traveling in excess of one hundred miles an hour in this kind of weather.

Maria faced him and stretched her right arm across his stomach. She lifted his shirt and placed her hand firmly over the wound. Clay jerked at the warm touch of her hand. He was uncomfortable. The wound bothered him less than her nearness.

``That's okay, Maria. Don't worry about it. We'll patch it up later.''

She didn't answer. He took his eyes from the road long enough to look at her face. Her eyes were closed tightly, so tightly he could see the wrinkles near the top of her nose and in the corners of her eyes. She seemed not to breathe. He looked up at the road long enough to get his bearings, then returned his gaze to her face.

``Maria, are you okay?''

She did not respond.

Her hand grew warmer and he felt the warmth in the wound. He glanced back at the road, searching for the turn-off to Om'nitche. It was near. He slowed to thirty miles an hour. His wound burned. It was

163

almost too hot to bear, but he was afraid to move her hand – afraid to break her trance. Perspiration rolled from her face.

He saw the road to Om'nitche just ahead on his left. He slowed the GTO and made a gentle turn, careful not to create excessive G forces and move Maria away from him. The heat on his side was too much. His shirt was soaked in perspiration. *What the hell is going on? Am I crazy? Is she a witch? I can't take much more.*

They were on the reservation. The rain slowed to a steady drizzle. Clay pulled off the road and parked the car under a large mesquite. He couldn't drive any further with the heat on his side. It felt about to burst into flames. He shut the engine off and sat silently, jaws clenched with pain, waiting for Maria to snap out of whatever she was in. There was no sound save the softness of the falling rain on the convertible top. The rain and the darkness engulfed them.

With his right hand, he touched her temple gently. Her skin emanated heat like a blast furnace. He sat for another five minutes, unmoving, unable to determine what kept Maria alive. He put his face as close to hers as the heat would allow. He detected no sign of breathing, and a sudden fear washed through him.

Suddenly, she fell away from him, into her own seat. She gasped for air. There was a raspy sound as the air cascaded into her lungs.

``Maria! Are you okay?"

``Outside...Get me...outside."

Forgetting his pain, he sprang from the car and rushed to her door. He flung the door open and pulled her into the cool desert air, dragging her into the mud as he slipped and fell. ``I'm sorry, Maria. Are you okay?"

``Water... Get me into...more water."

She had no strength. He struggled to his feet and pulled her by her hands from the cover of the mesquite and into the gently falling rain. She rolled face up. ``Clay...mud...cool mud."

``Mud? You want me to put mud on you?"

``Please...hurry."

He dug into the soil with his hands, ripping loose clumps of wet sod and slapping it onto Maria's body.

``Where do I put it?''

``All over. Please…hurry. I'm burning up.''

Frantically he packed mud on her neck and face, on her arms and legs, then over her clothing. He piled the mud right on top of her clothing. He put it in her hair.

She began to breathe more slowly and less deeply. The intensity of the rain increased. Large drops fell in waves, washing the mud from her skin. Clay dug more mud with his hands.

She touched his arm gently as he placed mud on her neck. ``No more. I am okay now.''

Clay collapsed next to her on the muddy ground. The rain slowed again to a drizzle. After a long moment, he turned face upward next to her. He closed his eyes to protect them from the light rain. ``Would you mind telling me what this was all about?''

``Have you any strength left?'' she asked.

``I'm not going ten rounds with the heavyweight champ, that's for sure.''

``I'm sorry. When you have your strength back, we better be going.''

``Oh, I can drive all right.''

``You will have to carry me to the car. I'm too weak to walk.''

Clay stood, then went to one knee next to her. ``Let's give it a try. I'm game if you are. Put your arms around my neck.''

Her hands felt cool as they touched his skin. He looked into her face, only inches from his. ``Are you sure you're okay?''

She smiled faintly. ``Oh yes, Mr. Clay Price. I'm fine.''

Late night, July 22 --- Oscar's residence

Oscar came through his front door at the sound of the Pontiac approaching. Clay stopped in front of the house and turned off the engine and lights. He bolted from the car to Maria's door. ``Oscar, help me get Maria inside. There's something wrong with her.'' He opened the door and picked Maria's limp form from the seat.

``Who the hell are those two guys in the back?'' asked Oscar.

``Those, my brother, are the two creeps that raped and shot Angela Stillwater.''

``Christ, Clay, are they alive?''

``Yeah, they're okay,'' he said as he carried Maria to the front door.

Oscar turned on the livingroom light as Clay carried Maria into the house. Clay placed her gently on the sofa.

``What happened?'' asked Oscar

Clay shook his head. ``I can't really say.''

``Has she been shot?'' Oscar worked over Maria as he talked. He lifted an eyelid and checked her pupil. He took her pulse and felt of her forehead.

``No, she wasn't shot.''

``Jeez! Her body temperature feels about ten or twenty degrees below normal.''

``Yeah, I know. What happened was, I got hit in the side with a bullet or a piece of the door or something, and Maria placed her hand over it. I thought she was trying to stop the bleeding, but all of a sudden, her hand got so hot I could barely stand it. She looked like she was in a trance and I didn't know what to do. She came out of it and I had to put her into the rain and put mud on her and...''

``Let me see the wound.''

``Sure, but what does that have to do with it?'' He lifted the tail of his shirt on the left side. ``It's right...'' Clay looked down at his left side. ``I swear to you, Oscar...there was a wound there. It didn't hurt much, but I was bleeding all over the place. All I see now is a little dot where the pain was. See that little scar? The one about the size of a thumbtack?'' He lifted his shirt on the right side, searching for a wound – anything that would confirm his sanity. ``I don't understand this, Oscar. I swear to you, man. Look at the blood on my shirt. Something weird is going on.''

Carla entered the room. She looked from Maria's muddy hair

and clothes to Clay, then to her husband. She knelt next to Maria put a hand on her forehead. After a moment, she stood and turned to Clay. ``Are you okay, Clay?''

``Yeah, Carla, except I don't know what's going on all of a sudden. Can you fill me in or what?''

``May I see your injury?''

``There isn't much to see anymore. I don't get it." he lifted the bloody tail of his shirt.

Carla stepped next to him and bent down to examine the small scar closely. After a moment she stood and looked into his eyes. She said nothing, but turned and knelt next to Maria. She held the sleeping woman's hand and placed her cheek on Maria's breast.

Clay turned to Oscar. ``Brother, please tell me what in the hell is going on here. What's happening? Is there something wrong with Maria?''

``I can't tell you, Clay. I don't know enough about the old ways. I'm not sure Carla knows enough to be positive about this one either.''

``Who does?''

Oscar nodded to Maria. ``Besides her, maybe half a dozen people on the reservation – my father, Henry Laughing Bird, a few others. And now, maybe Frank Redhawk.''

Clay stepped back a pace from Oscar. ``There's some mighty weird things going on out here, and I'm having a little trouble coming to grips with some of it. Take me to someone who will tell me what's going on.''

Oscar nodded. ``You have prisoners in your car.''

``Yeah, but Maria told me they wouldn't wake up until daylight, and after what I've just seen, I believe it.''

Oscar looked at his Blood Brother, a mixture of anger and love in his expression. ``Clay, I asked you to come back here to talk to Frank. Now, you not only come back, you kidnap two white men. This could mean big trouble for all of us.''

``Think back a few years, Oscar. Would The Brothers have let something like this go? Wouldn't we have ridden in like the Cisco Kid

167

and Poncho and saved the damsel in distress and brought the bad guys to justice?"

``This is the real world, Clay.''

``So it is, brother. And those are real people out there in the back of my car. Should we turn them over to the Tribal Police or what? We can't just leave 'em in the car.''

Oscar shook his head. ``Can't turn 'em over to the Tribal Police until things are more settled – after The Gathering.''

``The Gathering?''

``I'll explain later. Right now, we've got to hide those guys.''

``How about Elmer?''

``Perfect. He can take them up to his grandmother's place and she can keep an eye on that one guy's leg.''

``Is Elmer's grandmother still alive? She must be a hundred years old.''

``She gets around better than most people our age.''

``What about Maria?''

``I think she'll be okay.''

Oscar handled the transfer of prisoners, insisting Clay should rest. After several protestations that he was fine, Clay eventually agreed to lie down for a while. Exhaustion enfolded him like a warm quilt as he lay down, and sleep claimed him as his head hit the pillow.

CHAPTER EIGHT: THE PLANS

Morning, July 23 --- Oscar's residence

Clay awakened quickly. He found himself in Oscar's bed. His mind raced over the events of last night and early morning as he got up. He showered and dressed. The house seemed deserted. He found that strange. He glanced at his watch. If nothing else, the children should be playing somewhere nearby.

He peeked into Maria's room. She was awake but laying quietly, looking up at the ceiling. She noticed him peeking around the door and smiled. ``Come in, Clay. How are you this morning?''

Timidly he walked to her bedside. ``I'm fine. How do you feel?''

``Weak, but better.''

He knelt next to the bed and stared into her face. ``Maria, what's going on around here? What happened last night?''

``Important things are happening, Clay. Things you will understand in time.''

``What about last night?''

Her dark eyes bore into his. ``You were dying last night, Clay. I took a chance that you were Tinde. You are. I knew you were.''

``Not really, Maria. That was just a bunch of kids carrying out a ritual. I've got no Apache in me.''

169

She smiled weakly. ``Not in your blood maybe. But in your spirit and your thought, you are Tinde.''

``What makes you so sure?''

``If you were not Tinde, I would be dead now.''

``What are you talking about?''

``Clay!''

He spun around to see Carla standing at the door.

``You can't be in here. She has to rest completely.''

``It's okay, Carla. I feel better already,'' said Maria.

Carla stepped into the room and felt of Maria's forehead. ``It's true. You feel warmer.'' She looked at Clay. ``I'm sorry I shouted at you. I was worried about Maria. She used a dangerous power. It uses the body's strength – sometimes all of it.''

Clay stood slowly. He looked from Carla to Maria, then back to Carla. ``Carla, I want to know what's going on.''

Behind him, Maria said, ``You will know, Clay, but we can't teach you.''

He turned to her. ``Who then, Maria?''

``Henry Laughing Bird – or Frank Redhawk.''

Morning, July 23 --- Near Henry's cabin

``I am uneasy about the gathering tonight, uncle.''

Frank and Henry sat in the morning sunlight high in the red rock formation behind Henry's cabin.

``Riding back here yesterday afternoon, I was confident. Everything seemed to be going well. This morning something has changed.''

Henry did not speak for a few moments. He looked at Frank with that strange, intense, searching gaze which always made Frank feel somehow transparent. Suddenly Henry spat on the ground, then leaned towards Frank and blew sharply twice on the left side of this face and twice more on the right side. He stood and moved behind Frank, took him by the shoulders, and turned him until he was sitting facing west.

``What happened in your dreams last night?'' he asked.

``I was in the sacred place. There was a scorpion there, as big as a dog. Shadows of death danced all around it. I was frightened, but I could not run.''

``Did it speak?'' Henry had not yet taken his hands from Frank's shoulders, and Frank felt an urgency through the old man's fingers.

``Only my name.''

Henry squeezed Frank's shoulders, his hands like vices. ``Which name?''

``My spirit name.''

Everything happened at once.

The snarling growl of an attacking mountain lion erupted behind him. Henry's hands released his shoulders. Something hit him hard in the middle of his back and knocked him forward. A heavy weight pinned him to the ground. He could feel teeth on his neck, and a hot breath rattled loud in his ears. The teeth sank into his neck and he screamed. The scream was cut short by Henry's voice whispering urgently in his ear.

``Hurry! Into the cabin. Don't look back. Get a blanket. Put it over your head and sit in the chair by the table. Face west. Now. Go!''

The weight lifted off Frank's back and in an instant he was on his feet and leaping down the rocks faster than he thought possible. Adrenaline pounded through his body. There was a great roaring in his ears. His breath came in short, shallow gasps. His stomach churned. His bowels cramped. It took every ounce of self control he had to keep the fear from turning into blind panic.

He reached the base of the rock formation and sprinted to the cabin. He pushed through the half-open door and grabbed the blanket off the bunk. In two strides he was at the table and had to force himself to stop, to focus his entire attention on holding everything still for just long enough to remember which direction was west. He dragged a chair around the table, and threw the blanket over his head as he sat down.

He pulled his feet up onto the seat of the chair, knees tight against his chest, arms wrapped around them. He focused on trying to

171

control his fear, forced himself to take deeper breaths. His heartbeat slowed. . . then raced again as he heard footsteps coming into the cabin.

Someone sat in the chair across from him and lifted the front edge of the blanket. It was Henry. The old man pulled the edge of the blanket towards him and let it fall over his head and down his back as he leaned across the table towards Frank.

Frank opened his mouth but Henry shook his head emphatically.

``Absolute silence. Do not even think." The old man spoke in a barely audible whisper, but the fear evident in his voice re-triggered the adrenaline in Frank.

In the shadowy half-light under the blanket, neither Frank nor Henry moved. Frank did his best to suppress his thoughts. Time seemed to stand still. The tense silence stretched into eternity. The old man's face began to change as Frank watched. The left side faded, and reappeared. The right side faded into blackness. A flickering red-orange light like fire brought the right side back into focus. In the dancing light, small black shadows darted back and forth across the ageless features like insects.

The light flared, blinding Frank for an instant, then faded. Frank stared into the grinning face of a coyote no more than two feet in front of his own. The amber eyes glowed in the shadows and the hot, salty smell of fresh-killed rabbit filled the confined space under the blanket. The coyote lifted its muzzle and howled. Frank screamed, jumped backwards, knocked the chair over, and sprawled on the floor.

Henry erupted into peals of laughter. Frank looked up. The old man was standing next to the table, looking at him, holding his stomach, and stomping one foot on the floor as he laughed.

Frank looked around the cabin and back at his great uncle. He shook his head in confusion and the action brought a renewed burst of laughter from Henry. Frank pushed himself to a sitting position and looked around the cabin again. Everything seemed normal except for the overturned chair and the blanket in a heap on the floor next to him. He remembered the fear with which he had thrown the blanket over his head and a flicker of a smile came and went across his face. He looked back at Henry. The old man was getting his laughter under control. He walked over to Frank and offered his hand.

``I'm sorry," the old man said as Frank took the offered hand to pull himself up. ``But you were perfect." The last word exploded in a new burst of laughter and Frank barely made it to his feet before Henry turned away, holding his side and stomping his foot again as he laughed. The ludicrousness of the whole situation washed over Frank like a wave and he grinned.

Henry turned and pointed at him, tried to say something and couldn't, slapped his thigh and laughed harder. He pointed to Frank again, lifted his head and laughed at the roof like a coyote howling, jumped backwards and sprawled on the floor where he rolled back and forth holding his sides.

The imitation was so perfect Frank couldn't help himself. Laughter erupted out of him like he hadn't known since he was a small boy. He laughed until his sides ached, and tears came to his eyes. He collapsed into a sitting position on the floor and laughed with his great uncle. He laughed at the coyote, at the world, at himself, and at his fear. He laughed at his great uncle's laughter. He laughed because it felt good to laugh.

It was several minutes before the laughter subsided, and when it did, it was more from exhaustion than anything else. Frank got to his feet and went over and helped Henry up. He righted the chair and they sat at the table, grinning at each other.

``I was never so scared in my life," Frank said. ``I was absolutely certain I was going to die."

``You were," Henry answered, his grin still in place.

A shadow of the fear flickered through Frank and his smile wavered for a moment. He liked the laughter better. He shrugged. ``Well, it sure felt that way. I thought for a minute I was going to have to borrow a pair of your pants until I could get mine washed."

Henry's grin was replaced by a look of utter seriousness. There was no levity in his voice when he spoke. ``It felt that way because if

Apache Tears

Brother Coyote had not helped me, and if you had not followed my instructions exactly, you would have been dead before the rising of tomorrow's sun."

A chill went up Frank's back and the hairs on the nape of his neck and along his arms tingled. His smile disappeared. Questions raced through his mind but he was not certain he wanted to hear the answers to any of them.

``Someone did a scorpion healing last night."

``I have never heard of this," Frank said.

``It is not often practiced. It is a dangerous healing, one which is done only when a healer is certain that death will be the result otherwise."

Henry took out a tobacco pouch and rolled two cigarettes, giving one to Frank. ``Let us smoke to honor Brother Coyote while we talk."

Frank lit his great uncle's cigarette, then his own. They puffed four times quickly, blowing the smoke to each of the four directions.

``What is a scorpion healing?" Frank asked.

``A scorpion healing can only be done by one who has the power of the coyote. The coyote is the trickster. One of his tricks is shape changing. The scorpion is the Messenger of Death. When Death summons one of the Tinde, it is the scorpion who delivers the message. To do a scorpion healing, the healer must disguise the patient's identity by melding the patient's spirit to his own. The scorpion is then coaxed to return, and the healer must trick the scorpion into believing it has delivered Death's message to the wrong person. To do so, the healer must willingly accept the scorpion's sting and survive it.

``This is a healing which will only work if the patient has lived an honorable life and has accumulated great power, for the healer must use that power in concert with his own to survive. If the healing is not successful, both patient and healer die. If it is successful, both live, and the scorpion must search out someone else whose path leads them close to Death's wickiup.

``When it finds such a person, it waits. If the person's path

174

doesn't arrive at Death's wickiup within a single cycle of the sun, at the critical moment the scorpion nudges events in Death's direction and delivers Death's summons. The scorpion chose you in your dream last night. When you told me of the dream, I could see the scorpion nearby, waiting for the right moment."

``But I don't understand," Frank said. ``I heard a mountain lion, and felt its teeth on my neck."

Henry laughed. As he spoke, he wet his thumb and forefinger with spittle and put out his cigarette, tore open the paper, and put the last of the tobacco back into his pouch.

``We had to trick the scorpion into believing you had died. The path you are walking is dangerous and uncertain enough without the scorpion waiting to interfere."

``Then the mountain lion. . . you were. . ."

Henry laughed. ``Brother Coyote honors me with his power and wisdom."

Frank laughed a bit, too, but there was a nervous edge to it. ``It all seemed so real."

``It was. If you can change your shape to that of a mountain lion, you are no less a mountain lion because you can later change back to the shape of a man. Your fear, and your belief that you were dying, had to be real or the scorpion would not have been fooled."

Frank shook his head. ``I truly have much to learn, uncle. Under the blanket, then, the coyote. . .?"

Henry grinned. ``I apologize. But the opportunity was too good to pass up. And there was a powerful healer's lesson to be learned."

``I'm afraid I missed it," Frank said.

``You have encountered Death many times on your path, nephew, but always someone else's, never your own. And always as an adversary. Never as an ally. A healer must come face to face with his own death. You did so this morning. But this was only part of the lesson.

``For most men, death is the final mystery, the end of all things and the entrance to the unknown. It is something to be feared. But a

175

healer must learn to laugh at death, to draw power from it. A healer must recognize death is not the final mystery, to be feared, but the final joke Power plays on men. A healer must learn death is not just the end of all things, but the beginning of all things, too.

``Consider this truth well, nephew. A healer can not heal by treating death as an adversary. A healer can not heal unless he is willing to have his patient die. This is the way of things."

``But how can you heal if you don't care whether the patient lives or dies?" Frank protested.

``I said nothing about caring, nephew. I said the healer must be `willing' to have his patient die."

Henry pushed his chair away from the table and stood. ``Enough words. Visitors will be here soon, and the horses need to be fed and watered. There is much to be done before the gathering tonight."

Morning, July 23 --- Oscar's residence

Clay turned with a start as he heard a knocking at the front of the house. Carla left Maria's room and moved to the door. Clay held his breath and listened.

``Hi, Eddie. What brings you here? Oscar isn't home right now."

``Hi, Carla. Yeah, I know where Oscar is. It's Clay Price I want to talk to. Can I see him for a minute?"

Clay stepped into the room. ``What can I do for you, Chief Vasquez?"

He smiled. ``Eddie is plenty good enough. Chief Vasquez is too long." He paused. ``You wouldn't happen to know the whereabouts of those two men who assaulted Angela, would you?"

``Are you going to advise me of my rights or what?"

Eddie stiffened for a moment, then relaxed quickly. ``You haven't committed a crime on the reservation that I know of. I just wondered if you might know where those two were. A couple of Feds are hanging around and asking a lot of questions. I'd like to know how to react. I have an uncle who would give me council if I knew where

176

Stinton and Williams were."

Clay shrugged. ``I can't say for sure. But I have a brother named Elmer whose grandmother is supposed to be blessed with the sight. It's possible that one of them might be helpful."

``I guess I'll be visiting with Elmer and his grandmother. I'd like to find those two and bring them to Henry Laughing Bird before the Feds start getting heavy handed."

``I may see you at Henry's," said Clay.

``I look forward to it. See you, Carla. Say hello to Maria for me if you see her." Eddie turned and left the house.

``Your car, Clay."

Clay turned to see Maria standing by her bedroom door. ``Are you okay?"

``I'm fine. But your car is probably being looked for, too. Let's get it up to Henry's. Frank will be there, I'm sure."

Carla packed food supplies while Maria dressed. Clay stepped outside and surveyed the damage to his GTO. Except for the windshield, the damage didn't look as bad as he had expected it would. There were three bullet holes on the left side of the car, two of them in the driver's door. He shuddered as he tried to recall the officer's angle to him when the shots were fired. It looked like one of the bullets should have hit him directly in the side, unless it had been deflected.

Carla rushed outside, carrying a large basket of food, and jumped into the back seat. Maria followed with another basket, which she handed to Carla, then she sat in the seat next to Clay. The GTO's four-hundred-cubic-inch engine roared to life.

Late morning, July 23 --- Henry's cabin

Maria and Carla stood outside Henry's cabin when Frank and Henry returned from the corral. They exchanged greetings, and Henry started to invite them into the cabin. He stopped in mid-sentence and walked up to Maria. He held her by the shoulders and looked into her eyes for a long moment.

``It was you."

177

Maria nodded. ``It was necessary.''

``He is here?''

Maria gestured with her head towards the trail back to the road. ``He wanted to be certain he was welcome.''

``Who?'' Frank asked, moving closer to them.

``Clay.''

Frank looked at her for a long, hard moment. ``What is he doing here?'' The words had an edge to them.

Maria did not take her eyes from Frank's. ``I went to Tucson to tell him what was happening.''

Frank's jaw muscles clenched. His eyes narrowed. When he spoke, his words were measured and ominously quiet. ``We talked about this. I said I didn't want to put this obligation on him. We are Tinde. We don't rely on others for help.''

Maria's eyes flashed. ``He is part of this. His power is intertwined with yours. It was his decision to make, not yours.''

Frank struggled to control his anger. ``I need your help, Maria. Why do you oppose me in this?''

``I do not oppose you. I act as Power directs.''

Frank looked from Maria to Henry. The old man nodded almost imperceptibly. He turned back to Maria. ``Where is he?''

``Waiting in the trees by the trail.''

Frank walked across the small meadow towards the trail into the tree line. He was still angry, but the anger was under control now. There was a part of him which was glad Clay was here. Another part was angry, almost offended. The path he was walking was uncertain, and he felt death all around him, but it was an Apache path, and he was not sure any white man had a place on it. The uneasiness about the Gathering which had been bothering him since awakening was strong again in his consciousness. Something told him Clay's presence was at the heart of it.

He walked silently through the trees to one side of the trail. Without knowing why, he wanted to see Clay before he was seen. He continued another seventy-five yards and smelled the smoke from

178

Clay's cigarette before he spotted him. Clay was squatted on the side of the trail, leaned back against a tree, facing towards the cabin. Clay field stripped his cigarette as Frank watched.

A breeze moved through the trees and ruffled Clay's hair. Frank studied him for a long time. The warmth and closeness he had come to feel for the white man returned. There was something about him, something almost Apache about the patience with which Clay squatted under the tree – as though unaware of time. Still, Frank did not show himself. He waited, looking for something else, something which might relieve his doubts, quiet the uneasiness he felt, something which might explain why Maria had brought him here.

Frank waited a while longer and, just as he was ready to step out from behind the concealment of the trees, a slight movement, ten feet behind Clay and to his right, caught his eye.

Frank shifted his focus. A large Mexican Gray wolf sat on its haunches, staring at Clay. As soon as Frank saw it, the wolf turned its head slightly and looked into Frank's eyes. It got to its feet and turned, making a slight sound. Clay turned towards the sound and froze as the wolf walked slowly away.

Frank stepped out of the trees. ``You seem to have a friend."

Clay turned to face Frank. ``I'll take a friend wherever I can find him."

Frank walked up to the edge of the trail and stopped three or four feet from Clay. Clay stood.

``I owe you my life," said Frank, ``but you have come at a difficult time."

``Ten-four on the difficult time, Doc. And things could get worse."

The use of the nickname from Vietnam stirred a flash of memories. Frank pushed them aside. ``What do you mean?"

``I brought you a couple of uninvited guests. I'm not sure if I did the right thing, but it sure seemed like the thing to do at the time."

There was a sudden emptiness in Frank's stomach. ``Who?"

``You remember Charlie and Bruce?"

179

Anger filled the empty spot. ``What the hell did you bring them here for?''

``I don't know what you've been told about their release, but the whole thing is total bullshit. They were home free. There wasn't going to be any prosecution. Period. It was over as far as the U.S. Attorney was concerned. I didn't feel that way, and I didn't think you did either.''

``So you decided to bring them back here.'' It was a statement rather than a question.

``After Maria gave me a rough idea of what was going on out here, I figured since it happened in your new country, it came under your jurisdiction.''

``Goddamnit.'' Frank turned away, paced up the trail a few steps, then turned back around. ``I'm trying to do this thing without giving the government any reason to use force. What am I supposed to do now?'' Frank paused briefly. ``How many people know they're here?''

``Maria, Oscar, Eddie, Carla, Elmer and his grandmother. And, from what I heard from Eddie, I imagine maybe a few Feds got some kind of an idea. Who else would steal them? They aren't worth all that much as humans.''

``So it's not exactly a covert operation.''

``Not exactly. What the hell do you care? Are you an independent country or not? Is it all talk, or is it for real?''

Frank walked back towards Clay. ``Until the Gathering tonight, nothing is official. But that's beside the point. I'm walking around with the responsibility for eighty-five-hundred lives. There's a lot at stake.''

``A lot at stake? A lot at stake! You're telling me there's a lot at stake? Do you think the Feds aren't going to find out who kidnapped those assholes?'' Clay's eyes narrowed. ``Do you think they're gonna give me a medal for it? Do you think I'm looking back? I thought you were serious about this independence business. If you are, then do it right. Start out with some real justice, not the kind of bullshit the lawyers pass out in the States. It was my decision. If you're not serious, I'll take them back and face the music and to hell with you.'' Clay's face

180

grew red with anger as he spoke.

Somewhere off in the trees a wolf howled. Both men turned toward the sound. It seemed to go on forever. When it died, Frank stepped toward Clay and offered his hand.

``A man who can't recognize a friend dishonors both the friend and himself. I apologize if I sound critical. Things are happening so fast, it sometimes seems everything is going out of control."

``No offense taken." He accepted Frank's hand. ``I'm sorry I couldn't get the word to you. I tried. I had to make the decision on my own."

``When Maria first suggested I contact you and invite you back to the reservation, I said no. You fought a war for your country. Your presence here may mean you'll have to fight a war against it. I did not want to put you in that position."

``I don't want to fight a war against the U.S. but, if I have to, I won't be fighting against my country anymore. My country will be here, if you'll have me."

``You are here and you are welcome." Frank stepped to Clay and the two men embraced.

The smell of fresh-brewed coffee filled the clearing around Henry's cabin as Frank and Clay walked out of the trees. Henry, Maria and Carla were seated on the grass around the fire pit. They got to their feet as the two men approached. Carla filled two cups from the pot hanging over the small fire.

Frank walked up to Maria. He embraced her. "You have done well." He spoke softly. ``There is a wolf who watches over Clay."

They dropped the embrace, and Maria smiled. ``We heard."

Frank nodded, and turned to Clay. ``I want you to meet my great uncle, Henry Laughing Bird." Frank turned to the old man. ``This is Clay Price. He has chosen to join us."

Clay stuck out his hand. Henry ignored it, and took Clay by the shoulders. He looked Clay in the eyes for a long moment and then nodded once. ``Enju. It is good." He released Clay's shoulders and stepped aside so Carla could hand Clay a cup of coffee.

Clay accepted the cup a little uncertainly. ``I've heard a lot about you, Henry Laughing Bird. All of it good. I'm honored to meet you.''

Henry smiled. ``Perhaps there will be a time when what we know of each other will not be based on someone else's words. Maria has told me you passed near Death's wickiup on the way here last night. I am honored by your decision to join us.''

Frank accepted his cup of coffee and the group sat again on the grass.

After a few moments of comfortable silence, Clay spoke, his words directed to Henry. ``I know you have matters of great importance to discuss, but there's something I'd like to ask if you'll grant me the time.''

Henry nodded politely. ``The others will not be here for a while. If I can answer your question, I will do so.''

``Has Maria said anything to you about the healing she did on me last night?''

``She has spoken of it.''

``I'd like to know exactly what happened. I have almost no scar. According to what I know of weapons and wounds, that chunk of metal should have killed me. Except initially, I felt almost no pain, and Maria looked closer to death than I felt. Can you explain all that?''

Henry laughed. ``You do not ask simple questions, Clay Price. But the answer is simple – power.''

``I mean no disrespect, sir, but that's the same thing Maria has said. That doesn't tell me anything.''

``It tells you everything. It tells you the truth. Perhaps it is that you cannot yet hear what is being said.''

``But I want to know about this power. Who grants it? Who can use it? Can it be used at any time? Does it ever run out? Can it be used on anybody?''

Henry laughed. He indicated the world around him with a sweep of his arm. ``It comes from everywhere. It is not granted. It is

182

earned. Only those who have earned it can use it. It can only be used when the time is appropriate. It is always available if one lives in the proper manner. There are no limits on its use. Power is power, as the sun is the sun, and the moon is the moon."

``Oh, great. Now I understand everything." Clay looked at Frank. ``You got anything you'd like to add, Doc? You know, to kinda clear up anything that might still be a little muddy in my mind?"

Frank, Maria, and Henry all laughed, and Carla hid a grin behind her cup.

Henry reached out and touched Clay's arm. ``You have experienced power. You understand it. But your mind argues with you. It says you could not have experienced what you did. This creates a great confusion in a man. It would do no good for me to explain to your mind what you already know. There is another way, but not at this moment. Power works in its own time."

``Listen," Frank said, his head cocked to one side. He looked towards the trail to the road. The faint sounds of a car engine stopped abruptly.

``The others have arrived," Henry said.

Mid afternoon, July 23 --- Henry's cabin

``So, we are agreed," Frank said. ``Eddie and those of his men who choose to join us will close off the reservation at the appropriate time. Oscar and his smoke jumpers will consolidate supplies and see to our fuel needs. Elmer and some of Oscar's men will inventory and redistribute the available weapons and ammunition. He will also be in charge of gathering livestock from the southern range and driving it within reach of the Stronghold we have chosen. Carla will oversee the movement of women and children to the Stronghold, with whatever food, medical supplies, and clothing are available. After the Gathering tonight, Maria, Henry and I will work with whoever joins us to set up a provisional government. If we have to split the reservation, we will establish our headquarters at Portal, on the eastern side of the mountains." He paused and looked around the group. ``Is there

183

anything I've missed?"

Clay stood. ``Only about a million things."

Frank turned to Clay, suppressing a momentary irritation. ``I know we have much more to plan, but until we know how many are joining us, we can only cover the basics." He knew the irritation had been evident in his voice, and he smiled apologetically as he realized how they had left Clay out of the discussion for the most part. ``Are you concerned about something specific?"

``Yeah, the U. S. Army and Air Force. You plan on stopping them with Winchesters and shotguns?"

Frank shrugged. ``I hope we won't have to try to stop them. But if we do, we can only use what we have."

``Then let's get something more."

``With what?" Oscar asked.

``And from where?" Eddie added.

Clay studied the group. ``With what?" He pointed to Henry and Maria. ``Ask them with what. You have power, and you have medicinal plants that do amazing things when used properly. Any country in the world would be willing to pay well for these things, including Mexico, on our southern border."

``He's right," said Eddie. ``And I may have the contact we need. I have a second cousin, on my father's side, who works for the Minister of Health in Mexico City."

``Power cannot be bought or sold," Henry said quietly. ``But in some things, it can be taught. And there are many plants of value in these mountains. There may be merit in this idea."

``We could also take up a collection," said Carla. ``Once we've closed the reservation, American money will be useless ..."

``Not in Mexico," Clay interrupted. ``The almighty dollar is always good there."

Elmer let out a low whistle. ``That's not a bad idea! There are more than eight thousand of us on the reservation. If everybody kicked in only twenty bucks, that would be $160,000."

``That's a good start. But you're gonna need more if you want to convince the U.S. Army that you're serious," said Clay.

``That much money would feed our children for a long time. It seems sad to have to spend it on arms," said Frank.

``It's not as sad as having to bury about eight thousand people. You were over there, Doc. You know the reality. There are times when freedom depends on guns."

Frank nodded. ``You are right, but some truths rests heavy on my heart."

``This is the way of things for one who walks a healer's path," said Henry, quietly. ``Yours is not the warrior's way. That is a path which Clay walks."

``Can we ask this of him?"

``The decision is not ours to make."

``Who have you got better qualified?" Clay asked.

Elmer cleared his throat. ``Are you suggesting Clay be War Chief?"

Clay looked at Elmer. ``Would you follow my lead, brother?"

``I would. If it was agreed upon, everyone here would. But there are some on the reservation who would find it hard to follow a white man in a war against white men."

``I never even gave that a thought," answered Clay, surprise evident in his voice.

``Clay is Tinde in all but blood," said Maria. ``And his blood was mixed with yours, Oscar's and Billy's in his youth."

``Unfortunately, that doesn't show on the outside, and there are some on the reservation who can't see past the outside," said Eddie.

Clay addressed them as a group. ``Here I am, surrounded by people, and by a people that I love, and you guys are talking about my race. If changing my skin color is a prerequisite to being accepted, then I guess it's time for me to leave. That would be a tragedy, because I know what I can do. I'm offering my services because I want you to succeed, and I think your chances are better with me than without me. I offer you my life because I love you. I don't see what color your skin is. I love you for who you are and what you are. These things have nothing

185

to do with the color of skin."

``I do not believe anyone here intends to dishonor you with their words." Henry said. ``They speak only of their fears about what others may say or do. There was a time when any man who came among the Tinde was accepted as a friend until his actions proved him otherwise. But as a people we have lost much of the trust we once had. We have lost many of our ways. Part of what we are doing is attempting to recover that which we have lost."

``I can understand that," said Clay, ``but it doesn't change how I feel."

``Nor should it," Henry answered. ``If you are willing, nephew, there will be a way. At the Gathering tonight."

It was the first time any elder of the tribe had ever addressed him with the formal and familiar term `nephew'. The significance of this, and the acceptance it indicated, were not lost on Clay. He felt a tightness in his throat.

``What is this way?" he asked.

``I can not tell you yet. But you are part of this matter. You will be there tonight. Your path, like that of Billy Horse, is the path of the warrior. If war comes, we will need your leadership. These things are true. This is a matter of power. For truth, power always provides a way."

Oscar spoke through a grin that covered his face, ``So it's agreed? Paleface here is going to be our War Chief?"

``One more remark like that, and your job will be cleaning the corrals, brother. That'll give you an excuse for your red face," said Clay with a smile that matched Oscar's. He turned back to the group, serious again.

``Now, what are we going to do about the weapons?"

``Can you get what you need from Mexico?" asked Eddie.

``If nothing else, as long as we can establish some kind of trade, we can use Mexican Pesos to buy what we need from a third party I know," answered Clay.

``I can make the arrangements for a meeting in Mexico. If you think it appropriate, I will go," offered Eddie.

``Your presence here is too important. The men you command are the only organized armed force we have at the moment," said Frank.

``Then who?" asked Eddie.

``Maria and Clay."

All eyes turned to Henry.

``Whoever goes must go as an official emissary of the Tinde, and they must know the secrets of the plants. Maria is the logical choice."

``But I speak very little Spanish," said Maria.

Henry looked at Clay and smiled.

Clay studied Henry's smile. ``How do you know I speak Spanish?"

Henry made a short, musical whistling noise and was answered immediately by a mockingbird somewhere in the trees nearby. ``As I have heard it said, a little bird told me."

``Surely there's got to be somebody else on this reservation who speaks Spanish?" said Clay.

Henry nodded once, a grin on his face. ``Hundreds. Maybe more." He looked at Maria and smiled. ``But none I would trust with Maria's life, and none who knows weapons as you do."

``I appreciate your confidence in me, but I would rather stay here and prepare our defenses."

``When Power chooses the path we walk, personal desires must often be overlooked," said Henry. ``There is no one else who can do this as it must be done."

Clay experienced conflicting emotions as he thought of leaving the reservation to go to Mexico. Part of him was attracted to the idea of being able to spend so much time alone with Maria. He felt guilty, knowing that he would agree much easier to accompanying Maria than he would anyone else.

``We won't be able to put up much of a defense if we don't get any more weapons than what we have," Eddie said.

``We have something else we could trade," Elmer said. ``We

could spare some of the cattle on our southern range, couldn't we?"

``Maybe five hundred head,'' Eddie responded, ``but if they close our borders, how would we ever get them into Mexico?''

Clay jumped in. ``I know someone who could help us. He owns the ranch I grew up on, and it borders the reservation on the west. If we gave him permission, he could truck the cattle into Mexico through Douglas, legally. And, he can be trusted.''

``What are we looking at in terms of money?'' asked Carla.

Clay figured in his head. ``With the current market, I would say about $200 per head. That's $100,000. And while we're at it, I have $12,000 I've been saving up for a rainy day.''

Thunder rumbled somewhere in the mountains south of them.

``Sounds like rain to me,'' Oscar said, and a comfortable laughter spread through the group.

``This all sounds very good,'' Maria said. ``But there are a couple of questions we have not addressed. How are Clay and I going to get to Mexico City and back? And if we are successful, how are we going to get everything back to the reservation soon enough?''

``You remember Tubs, don't you?'' Clay asked.

``It would take many trips in those small planes,'' Maria protested.

``We could use his Beech Baron for the trip down and back. And for the transportation of supplies, he's got Daisy Mae,'' Clay answered. He addressed himself to the rest of the group. ``Tubs owns the crop dusting outfit I worked for until very recently. Daisy Mae is an old C-47 he has restored. It's his pride and joy. He'd probably love to put it to use in a good cause.''

``Our own air force,'' Oscar quipped.

``Not much on offense,'' Clay answered, ``but it'll do the job that needs to be done. And there's a landing strip on the ranch I was talking about. All we have to do is come up with a way to get the weapons and supplies from the ranch to where we want them.''

``That will work as long as the white eyes don't take over his ranch,'' Eddie said.

Clay smiled. ``They won't do it while he's alive. By the way, what ever happened to those Feds?"

Eddie laughed. ``They got tired of looking everywhere we suggested, and left. Some white eyes don't have much in the way of endurance. Present company excepted, of course."

A crackle of static came from the hand-held police radio on Eddie's belt. He took it out of his holster case as he stood up and moved away from the group. After a moment he turned back around. ``Well, it looks like things are starting to liven up. There's a woman reporter from a Tucson TV station down in Om'nitche. Says she was told something big was happening on the reservation tonight." Eddie looked at Clay. ``She claims you told her to ask for Frank."

Clay looked at Frank and grinned sheepishly. ``I knew there was something I forgot to tell you."

CHAPTER NINE: THE DECLARATION

Mid-afternoon, July 23 --- Henry's cabin

It was mid afternoon when the meeting at Henry's cabin broke up. Clay and Maria left for Oscar's where Clay could make his calls to Tubs and Mr. Foster, while Maria packed for the trip to Mexico.

Eddie took custody of the prisoners, who had been kept at Elmer's Grandmother's during the meeting. Two of his men would move them up into the draw east of the cottonwood grove at the Gathering site, and they would be kept there until after the event was over.

Everyone agreed it would be best to make as many preparations as possible before the Gathering. They would meet at the cottonwood grove an hour before sundown, then, if everything went the way they hoped it would, they could start implementing their plans immediately afterwards.

Only Frank and Henry remained in the small meadow in front of Henry's cabin. They sat in comfortable silence until the last sound of the departing vehicles had faded and the day was reclaimed by the afternoon breeze brushing through the pines and the indolent buzz of myriad insects going about the earth's business.

Finally, Frank spoke. ``I should go into Om'nitche and see that reporter. She's probably getting tired of being kept at the visitor center."

``What are you going to do with her?" Henry poured the last of the coffee onto the coals of the fire. A great cloud of steam rose around him.

``I'm not certain. My first instinct is to let her stay. She is Navajo. If she understands what we are doing and reports it honestly, she could be a blessing." Frank stood up and brushed off the seat of his pants. ``But if she's just another reporter, she could be a curse. And this possibility makes me want to have her escorted off the reservation instantly."

The two men gathered up the cups and walked to the cabin. ``Clay brought her to us," Henry said quietly.

``I know," Frank said, stepping aside to let the old man enter the cabin first. ``Just like he brought those two white eyes."

``What do you make of this?" Henry asked as he dipped water into a basin and set it on the table.

``I don't know." Frank set the cups beside the basin. He rinsed them and handed them to Henry, who put them in the apple crate cupboard. ``It frightens me, and that makes me angry. I don't want to give the white eyes any excuse to use force."

``Have they ever needed an excuse, nephew?"

``You speak the truth. But I think their world has changed. I don't think they can make up excuses quite so easily these days, especially since Vietnam. I think there are a large number within their population who would protest very strongly against any use of force."

``In the times of my grandfather, and of his father, there were whites who spoke the truth about the mistreatment of Indians, and who protested Washington policies. It made no difference." Henry put the last of the cups away and took the basin to the door to empty it.

``Their words lacked immediacy," Frank said, wiping the table. ``By the time their words reached a large circle of people, the events of which they spoke were weeks or months past. And for every one who spoke or wrote the truth, there were ten who wrote the accounts of events which they believed their readers wanted to hear. Very few people had the opportunity to see for themselves what was happening. Today, with television. . ."

Frank stopped suddenly as he remembered something. Henry waited patiently until Frank spoke again.

``A friend of mine, in Vietnam, worked in military intelligence. He told me that if the Viet Cong thought one of their headquarters was in danger, their first order of priority was to save the mimeograph machine.

``They thought it was the most important weapon they had because they could use it to communicate directly to Vietnamese people who lived and worked in areas controlled by the Americans or the South Vietnamese."

Henry went to his trunk by the door and began digging through its contents. ``As Clay was brought to us, so too have the reporter and the two white eyes been brought to us. It is not enough to say `if' the reporter understands, and `if' she reports truthfully. Power has brought her here. You must find a way to make certain she understands and reports truthfully."

Henry wrapped three or four items in a piece of buckskin and tucked the bundle inside his shirt. He turned back to Frank. ``It is the same with the prisoners. Power has put them here for a reason. You cannot afford to indulge yourself in fear, or worry about how the government in Washington will react. A moment will come, just as it did with the reporter, where you will understand Power's intention in bringing them here. That will be the time to act."

``And until then?" Frank asked.

``On an uncertain path, there is danger in looking too far ahead. It is better to keep all your attention on each step you take. The path will lead where Power intends it."

They got horses from the corral and rode into Om'nitche, taking their time, neither feeling a need to hurry. Outside the visitor center, they halted.

``I will join the old ones in their preparations at the grove," Henry said. ``I will wait for you at the mouth of the draw an hour before sunset."

``I will be there, uncle." Frank dismounted and tied his horse to the branch of a mesquite tree. Henry rode off down the street.

Frank walked up the path and into the visitor center. Two of Eddie's officers in khaki uniforms sat at a table drinking coffee. The receptionist at the counter smiled at Frank. He nodded and walked over to the officers.

``The reporter?"

One of the officers motioned with his head towards the hall beyond the reception counter. ``In the lounge. We offered her food and drink, but I don't think she appreciates our hospitality. We had to lock the door. Her cameraman's in their truck out back. Somebody's with him."

``The key."

The officer picked up a key wired to a wooden plaque with ``Visitor Center Lounge" painted on it. He handed it to Frank.

``You've done well," Frank said, accepting the key. ``I know you have a lot to do. You are free to go. Ask the man at the truck to remain until I relieve him."

One of the two officers spoke as they both got to their feet. ``Is it true you are going to split the reservation?"

Frank looked at them for a long moment before replying. ``Those who choose not to walk the Gahan's path for the Tinde must have somewhere to live. We will do what is necessary."

``What about Om'nitche?"

Frank motioned around him with his arm. ``It was built with white man's money. It should be left to those who wish to continue accepting such generosity."

The officer who had asked the question turned to his partner. ``It sounds like we have some packing to do."

They said their goodbyes and left. As Frank passed the reception counter, the young woman sitting behind it stopped him.

``I heard your words, uncle," she said nervously. ``Everyone else who works here is gone. We are normally open for another three hours." She hesitated. ``My mother is old. She will need help getting ready." She stopped again, as though uncertain how to proceed.

Frank nodded to her. ``Go," he said. ``Help your mother. I will lock the doors when I leave."

A smile broke across the young woman's face. ``Thank you, uncle. I was at the Gathering three nights ago. Your words spoke to my heart."

``Then we are the same, sister. It is good to have your strength beside me." Frank smiled.

The girl looked down, embarrassed and pleased by the equality Frank had granted her with the use of the term ``sister." ``My mother is also the same," she said shyly.

``The Tinde have always relied on the strength and courage of their women," Frank said. ``Go now. Make your preparations."

He turned and walked down the hall towards the lounge. He unlocked the door and opened it. Teresa Chatla stood across the room facing him, her back to the window. She was dressed in dark slacks and a gray western-cut man's shirt, open at the throat, a red scarf tied around her neck. She stood straight, arms at her sides. Anger sharpened the angles and flattened the planes of her face. Her nostrils flared slightly as she breathed. She stared at Frank in open challenge as he walked into the room.

Frank left the door open behind him. He stopped about six feet in front of her. Her gaze didn't waver.

``I am Frank Redhawk."

``And I am Teresa Chatla." Her words had an edge of defiance and pride.

``You are angry." Frank spoke quietly.

``No angrier than anyone would be, getting locked up and held against their will."

``You come to us at a critical time."

``So you take it upon yourself to have me arrested."

``No, Ms. Chatla. I asked them only to keep you isolated from anyone else on the reservation until I had talked to you. You could have left at any time. You would have been escorted off the reservation. Were you not told these things?"

``Yes,'' she answered, some of the indignation subsiding. ``But there is something going on out here. I'm a reporter. I talk to people. That's how I get my information. You have no right …''

``That's why I am here, Ms. Chatla. To talk. In critical times, balance is difficult. You might upset the balance. I can't allow that.''

``You? You can't allow that? Who the hell do you think you are?''

``After tonight, I may be chief of my people. For the moment, I am Frank Redhawk. Am I not the one you asked for?''

``That's beside the point.''

``What is the point, Ms. Chatla?''

``The point is you have no authority to restrict my movements, on or off the reservation. I've done my homework. You're a paramedic, not police. And you are not a member of the Tribal Council.''

``You are correct. I have no authority. But I had the responsibility to do as I did.''

Frank walked past her and stood looking out the window. There was already much about Teresa he could like. But there was still something, some barrier around her that was not her anger or insulted pride. It was something more fundamental, and Frank knew he had to get through it. He didn't know how.

He let his vision range beyond the buildings of Om'nitche to the mountains rising steeply to the southeast. Clouds piled up above the peaks, their flat bases a dark slate gray. Lightning flashed on a distant ridgeline. Frank waited, and the words came with the muted rumble of the thunder.

``As individuals, and as a people, we live our lives like a man alone in a canoe on a river no man has ever been down. That river is the river of time. Ahead of us on that river are all the possible futures we might ever encounter, each like a different current. They separate, come together, break apart differently, and perhaps never meet again. Alone in our canoes, we spend all our time and effort merely trying to keep the canoe from capsizing as we are pushed from obstacle to obstacle and current to current, forced into this channel or that, into whatever future fate decrees.

``But, sometimes, a man or woman is favored by the spirits and is lifted up high enough above the river to get of view of how it stretches ahead, how the channels line up, where the currents are strongest. When he is put back in his canoe he has a choice. He can attempt to steer towards the future which looks like it has the best chance of getting him through safely, or he can steer towards the future which holds the best hope of survival for his people.

``If they are the same routes, there is no choice to be made. If they are not. . .'' Frank turned around to face her.

``Three nights ago I made a choice and set in motion a series of events which might mean the life of every man, woman, and child on this reservation. That sequence of events can no more be stopped than the man in the canoe can go back up the river. They can only be guided. I take that responsibility very seriously.''

Teresa walked across to the coffee table in front of the sofa and picked up a tape recorder and microphone. ``Can I tape this?''

Frank shook his head negatively. ``Hear it. What I am saying is for you, not your public.''

Teresa crossed behind the table and sat on the couch. She crossed her knees and folded her arms across her chest. ``Okay,'' she said, ``I'm all ears. You had a vision. A pretty dangerous one, from the sounds of things. What did your vision tell you you have to do? How many white men do you have to kill to bring the animals back? How many virgins are you going to sacrifice to please the mountain gods?''

For a moment, something shifted in Frank's consciousness and he saw her with a different set of senses. He saw past the hostility and the fear, past the uncertainty, past the last defenses of pride, until he saw inside her. She was empty except for a huge machine and a wall of petrified pain around her heart.

``You are empty,'' he said.

She looked at him uncertainly.

196

``You've spent so much time looking at life through a camera lens; you see it that way all the time. There's always a frame around things. And inside you there's this big machine which takes what you see through this frame and translates it not into the reality which you want people to see, but into the reality you think your bosses want people to see.''

Teresa stared at him stonily, but did not respond. Her tension filled the room with a high-pitched energy.

``You're an Indian,'' Frank went on. ``You know they aren't interested in what *you* think the people should see. You're an Indian. They aren't interested in what *you* think is important. Your only hope is to give them what *they* think is important. Not just in your stories, but in your life. Look at you. Do you see any of the other television reporters wearing western shirts with scarves around their necks? Do you see the Hispanic reporters wearing serapes or sombreros, or the Orientals wearing kimonos and sandals? But you are an Indian. Indians are supposed to look like Indians.''

``Yes,'' she flared. ``I am Indian. Full-blooded Navajo. And I am proud of it.''

``Then why do you dance like a puppet on the white man's strings?''

``I dance on no man's strings!''

``Do you deny the truth of what I say?''

``Yes. . . no. . . yes, damnit, some of it I do deny. I am not empty inside.''

Frank turned back to the window. ``You are empty inside. You have cut yourself off from your mother. You have pride. And ambition. And determination. Even courage. But inside, behind all that, you are empty. And you dance on the white man's strings because you know you have no power of your own.''

Frank turned to face her again. Teresa paid no attention to the tears in her eyes as she held his gaze.

``Maybe you better keep your medicine man wisdom to yourself. Save it for your people. It sounds like they're going to need it."

``You still don't understand, do you?" Frank asked, his anger coming to life.

``I understand I like my life the way it is."

``Then why does your grief run down your face?" He reached across the coffee table and took her by the wrist. ``Come," he said. He led her out from behind the table and out of the room. He let go of her wrist and she followed him down the hall and out of the building. He led her away from the building a couple hundred feet, into the open desert.

``Look," he said, pointing to the northwest. Dark, jagged shadows of the Dragoon Mountains reached out towards them across the twenty-mile expanse of the Sulphur Spring Valley. Heat waves danced and undulated across the valley floor.

Frank turned her towards the Chiricahua peaks to the southeast. ``Look," he said. Thunderclouds towered above the peaks. Lightning danced. He swept his arm in a half-circle, indicating the desert around them. ``Look."

He leaned down and picked up a handful of dirt. He took her hand and held it in front of her, palm up. He put the dirt in her palm and curled her fingers closed around it.

``Feel that," he said. ``Look around you and see the land. That is your mother. I don't care if you live in a penthouse apartment in a fifty-story building, and never go outside except to get in a car, and out of the car only to go in another building. I don't care if you live in a space station in orbit. If you are human, this is your mother. This is where your life came from. This is what sustains you. There is no frame around her. Nothing is isolated. This earth you stand on is the same earth my ancestors walked over. The air you breath is the same air your ancestors breathed on the Long March to Bosque Redondo. That rain up there in those clouds is the same water that washed the blood and fluids from your great-great-grandmother's body at birth.

``Can't you feel it all around you? The power of life itself in every rock and bush, every tree and animal, every bird and insect, every stream and every stretch of empty sand? Don't you feel it in the earth in your hand? Don't you remember a time when that same power filled you inside? When you walked out of your Hogan at dawn on a summer morning and the wind whispered to you, and the bushes talked to you as you passed? When a distant coyote howled a short good morning and you knew it was meant especially for you?"

He took Teresa by the shoulders. ``Don't you remember how much easier it was to be proud, then?"

He stepped back and turned in a circle, his arm outstretched. ``This is our land. It is our mother. It is all we have ever had, and for seven hundred years it provided everything we needed. It is all we ever wanted. And we fought to protect it as you would fight to protect your family.

``This land received the blood and body of every Apache, every Spaniard, every Navajo, every Mexican, and every white that died here. There is a sorrow on her, still. The rivers no longer flow. The animals are gone. The summers get hotter. The air grows foul.

``In the end, the land was taken from us. Then we were given back a small bit of it. And even then we had to live on it as we were told. We had to use it as Washington instructed. We had to plunder it if they so decreed."

He stepped back up to Teresa and took her again by the shoulders. Tears continued to run down her face. ``No more," he said. ``The time has come when we must take back our freedom. We must take this small portion of the land they have given us and declare it wholly ours. Without restriction. We must defend it if necessary. And if we are successful, we must pray that it is not too late. We must pray that our mother can once more provide for us, will once more teach us to live."

They stood looking at one another in silence for a long time. Teresa made no attempt to stop the tears. Frank made no attempt to comfort her. He let her grief flow as he had learned he had to let the blood flow from some wounds. It was cleansing. When her grief had subsided, Frank dropped his hands from her shoulders.

She held her hand up in front of her and uncurled her fingers. She knelt and poured the dirt gently back onto the earth. She stood and faced him again.

``You may be crazy. What you are doing may cause trouble for Native Americans all over the country. But I think I understand something of why you are doing it. With your permission, I'd like to help. By telling your story as honestly as I know how."

``What if your station won't run it?"

``There's a computer in the truck. With the satellite link I can feed directly to the networks."

``Can you work alone?"

``I have a cameraman with me. I think he's with the truck."

``Can you work alone?"

Teresa hesitated. ``Well, in theory I know how to operate the equipment in the truck. I can handle the camera."

Frank nodded. ``There is a Great Gathering called for tonight. I will be going out there soon. I will take you. Once you are there you are free to talk to anyone who will talk with you. Take any pictures you want, but remember that every individual here has the right to their privacy, if they choose to exercise it. Record what you wish. I ask only that you tell me before you actually release anything."

``No final approval?"

``If you understand, you will not lie, and I have no desire to hide the truth. But when you release your story, things will happen fast. I'd like to know before hand."

She nodded. ``Agreed."

Frank motioned with his head and they turned and walked back towards the visitor center. ``You will work alone," Frank said. ``I will have your cameraman escorted off the reservation and provided with transportation to Tucson."

``It would sure be a lot easier ..." Teresa started, but Frank cut her off.

``You will work alone. If the world is going to witness these events, I want them witnessed through your eyes. No one else's. You said you can handle the equipment. If you need other kinds of help, let me know. Anything I can provide I will." He held the door of the center open for her and followed her in.

``I could use someone to carry the battery packs and tape recorder," she said. ``And maybe someone to pull cable and carry the camera when I'm not shooting."

They walked down the hall. ``You can handle everything else?"

``It looks like I'm going to have to," she said. ``Doesn't it?"

They re-entered the lounge, and Teresa picked up her tape recorder and purse. ``When do we leave?"

``As soon as I take care of your cameraman." He paused. ``You realize, I have no idea how any of this is going turn out?"

She nodded.

``It may get very ugly before it's over. You may find yourself in the middle of a blood bath. I may not be able to protect you."

She nodded again.

``Do you still want to stay?"

``I don't have any choice," she answered. ``It's an important story. I have to tell it."

Frank looked at her long and hard, then nodded and smiled slightly, ``You are welcome here, Teresa Chatla."

``I'm glad to be here, Frank Redhawk."

``Let's go out to the truck," Frank said.

Late afternoon, July 23 --- The Gathering site

Frank rode his horse to the cottonwood grove, while Teresa followed behind, driving the news truck. He had her park it on the southwest side, where the distance between the outer edge of the trees and the open area in the center was the shortest.

There were already several hundred people in the general area. Some sat in family groups on blankets, in shade provided by tarps stretched from the bed of a pickup to two poles. Others carried in loads of firewood for the fire pits scattered across the open area in the center of the grove. Others stood in small groups, talking. More pickups and

201

four-wheel drives and dusty sedans pulled in all the time.

Nowhere did Frank see any evidence of alcohol. That would come later, after dark, if at all.

Several picket lines had been strung up in the trees on the west side of the grove, and there were already fifty or sixty horses tied in the shade. Frank was aware of a faint tension in the air, a sense of building anticipation. Thunder rumbled in the distance, but here the late-afternoon sun still beat down hard and hot. The shadows were lengthening, but they were still stark and hard-edged against the light.

Teresa got out of the truck. Frank dismounted and looped the reins through the truck's door handle. He saw Danny Blue standing and talking with two other young men, about fifty yards into the trees. *Good,* he thought. *Let's make him a part of this. Keep him occupied.* He turned to Teresa. ``Come on. I want you to meet someone.''

They walked side by side through the shade under the big trees. The three men turned to face them as they approached.

Frank stopped, and nodded to Danny. ``Danny Blue,'' he nodded to Teresa. ``Teresa Chatla.''

Teresa stepped forward and offered her hand. Danny looked at it, hesitated, then accepted it. Teresa stepped back.

``She's a television reporter,'' Frank said. ``I'd like you to pass the word around for me. She's here with my permission. She's free to interview who she wants, tape what she wants, and photograph what she wants. But every person here has the right to chose not to be photographed, taped or interviewed. All they have to do is say no.''

``Sure,'' Danny said, a little uncertainly.

``And one other thing. She needs a couple of people to help her carry things. Can you see if you can find someone to give her a hand?''

``No problem,'' Danny said, his eyes on Teresa.

Frank nodded and turned to Teresa. ``Danny will get you oriented, introduce you around.''

``Where are you going?'' she asked.

``I have some final preparations of my own,'' he answered. ``We'll talk again after the Gathering.''

He turned and walked back to the truck. Remounting his horse, he rode towards the ridgeline to the north. He figured he still had half an hour before he had to meet Henry. He wanted to spend it alone.

Late afternoon, July 23 --- East of The Gathering site

When Frank arrived at the mouth of the draw, Henry, Clay and Maria were already there, sitting around a small fire. He dismounted and joined them. Oscar, Elmer and Eddie had all checked in and had gone on ahead to the grove. They had agreed to stay near the center of the clearing during the Gathering, in case they were needed, and to meet at Henry's cabin afterwards.

Clay squatted on his heels, his back to a large, flat-topped rock near the fire. ``What happened with Teresa?"

``I sent her cameraman back to Tucson. She's staying."

Clay nodded. ``She seemed pretty straight to me."

``The prisoners?" Frank asked.

``Up the draw three or four hundred yards. They're comfortable. Eddie's got a couple of his men with them. He's in radio contact."

``How is Charlie's leg?"

``I guess it was bothering him until Elmer's grandmother mixed up some kind of poultice and put it on. He's not complaining now, and he's not bleeding."

``Good. And your phone calls?"

Clay grinned. ``All set. Tubs sounded twenty years younger, and Mr. Foster just said he'd help any way he could. Well, he didn't actually say it that way. He said it was about time."

Frank smiled faintly.

``Eddie's got everything set up for the meeting in Mexico," Maria said. ``We can meet as early as tomorrow afternoon, if we can get there."

``We'll get there," said Clay.

``Perhaps we should begin," Henry said quietly. ``We want to arrive in the grove at sunset."

Late afternoon shadows filled the draw. Henry sat to the north of the fire, Frank to the east, Maria on the south, and Clay to the west. Distant thunder rumbled to them from the mountains.

Henry took some juniper from his medicine pouch. ``The smoke of the sacred juniper clears the mind and strengthens the heart,'' he said. ``It clarifies our prayers and carries them up to the gods.'' He threw the juniper on the fire. With his feather fan he wafted the smoke first over Frank, then Maria, then Clay, and finally over himself.

From the buckskin bundle inside his shirt, Henry removed some vials of pigment. He moved next to Frank and turned Frank's face towards him.

He put two horizontal stripes of black on his left cheek. ``The darkness comes out of the east. Out of the darkness each day is born. Out of each season of the white wind, when darkness is longest upon the land, a new cycle is born. We honor the east in the morning so that each day might be filled with new vision and understanding.''

He put two vertical stripes of blue from Frank's lower lip to the point of his chin. ``Blue is in the south, the long days of summer sun and open sky, when the earth is abundant and the people relax under the shade of trees high in the mountains. Blue is the time of rest and healing.''

He put two yellow horizontal stripes across Frank's right cheek. ``Yellow is in the west, when the year is in the time of the golden grass. It is the direction of endings, of hunting and war, of funerals and mourning. It is the direction of change, and the great mystery of death and regeneration.''

He put two vertical stripes of white down Frank's forehead, from his hairline to the bridge of his nose. ``The white wind blows from the north. This is the time of reflection, of many hours spent by the fire in the wickiup, contemplating the mysteries, learning the lessons of the summer and autumn. This is a time of understanding and clarity.''

Henry moved back around the fire to squat next to Clay. He turned Clay's face towards him. He put a single, slanting stripe of black down Clay's left cheek. ``Black is the death and mourning you bring upon your enemies. Out of each death something honorable must be born. This is the first wisdom of the warrior."

He put two horizontal blue stripes across Clay's chin. ``Blue is the color of the cleansing streams of tears that run on both sides of the warrior's path. This is the second wisdom of the warrior."

He put a single, slanting streak of yellow down Clay's right cheek. ``Yellow is the color of our father, the sun, who puts the fierce purpose and strength in the warrior's heart to guide his actions. It is the heat of battle and the blaze of courage. It is the will to endure. This is the third wisdom of the warrior."

He put a single white horizontal stripe across Clay's forehead. ``White is the color of the calm which settles on the warrior after the battle, like mist on a morning lake. It is the calm which allows him to see the battle as it was, without the heat of emotion. It is the calm in which he mourns his enemies. It is the calm in which he forgives himself. This is the highest wisdom of the warrior."

Henry took his place again to the north of the fire. He intoned a low, humming chant that went on for a while, and then faded away. A restless breeze stirred the embers of the fire, making them flame briefly.

``These are the four wisdoms of a warrior. If you are to lead us in battle, Clay Price, it is well you should know them."

Henry took out tobacco and papers and rolled a cigarette. He put a twig to the coals and, when it was burning, he used it to light the cigarette. He puffed it four times, once to each direction, then passed it to Frank who did the same. Maria and Clay repeated the steps, and then Clay handed the cigarette back to Henry. The old man wet his forefinger and thumb and put the cigarette out. He tore it open and put the tobacco back in his pouch. In the distance the constant whine and drone of engines told them that people were continuing to arrive.

``It is time to speak of certain things," he said. He turned to Clay. ``When you asked Billy Horse to enlist with you and go to Vietnam, he came to me and asked me to prepare him for war in the old ways. I did as he asked, for the Gahan had spoken to me of a war chief

205

who would come among us in the days when the circle of the Tinde was to be completed. Billy had much power, and used it wisely."

``He was the best fighting man I ever knew." Clay's voice was almost a whisper.

``You were with him when he died," Henry continued. ``When he saw his path would not lead him back to his people, he passed his power on to you."

A silence stretched out for a time before Clay spoke. ``Everybody keeps talking about me having power. I hate to disappoint you, but if I've got power I'm not aware of it. Sometimes I can feel Billy's spirit close to me, but even that's pretty tenuous."

``You have power," Henry repeated. ``Billy's spirit animal was the wolf."

Clay's whole body shook as a shiver passed through him. His fists clenched.

``You have power," Henry repeated. ``Hold out your left hand."

Clay did so, fingers still curled closed.

``Open your hand."

Clay did so. There was a scorpion on the palm of his hand. He jumped back against the rock behind him and shook his hand violently, flinging the scorpion to the sand near the fire. He shuddered and his whole body trembled briefly.

``The scorpion is the Messenger of Death," Henry said quietly. ``Billy knew the scorpion well. It was part of his preparation. A warrior must act as messenger of death to his enemies."

Henry paused. ``Pick the scorpion up in your right hand," he said quietly.

Clay looked at him sharply. Henry nodded. ``Do it," he said. ``Put your hand in front of him and let him crawl on."

Clay hesitated, then squatted again. He started to put his hand out, then drew it back. He looked at Frank. Frank nodded almost imperceptibly. He looked at Maria. Maria returned his gaze and said nothing. He looked again at Henry.

``The scorpion's power is the fear of death," Henry said.

``Overcome his power and the scorpion will go before you in battle, striking this fear into the hearts of your enemies.''

Clay took a deep breath. He looked back at the scorpion on the sand, tail arched up over its back, ready to strike. He put his hand down slowly onto the sand two or three inches in front of the scorpion. It did not move. He edged his hand closer. Still, the scorpion did not move. He edged his hand closer yet, and the scorpion darted forward suddenly, up onto his palm. Clay's whole body trembled in the struggle he waged to keep his hand still.

Suddenly he felt the sharp sting of the scorpion's tail as it struck in the center of his palm. His mind told his body to react, but his body failed him. His limbs weighed a ton. He felt beads of perspiration erupt on his forehead as he struggled to make his hand move and rid itself of the angry scorpion. He watched helplessly as the tail arched forward and struck again. He felt the pain again and watched unmoving as the menace in his hand seemed to relax.

It's waiting. It knows it got me good, and now it's waiting. Sonofabitch.

The sharp pain in the palm of his hand was gone, and in its place a ring of fire spread rapidly up his arm and to his shoulder and chest. Behind the ring was a numbness, not unlike the feeling left by Novocain. The numbness spread. Only his head moved. No other part of his body responded to his conscious efforts to make them move. He looked at Henry, then Frank, then Maria. They had all betrayed him. He was stupid for believing in that spirit business anyway. He deserved whatever he got.

He smelled perspiration from another body. It was beneath him. He was lying on top of it. He felt it move as it breathed irregularly.

``Clay.'' The voice was weak.

``I can't move, Billy. I can't get help. Oh, God, Billy. I'm so sorry. I don't know what's wrong. Nothing will move but my head.'' Clay looked skyward. ``What the hell is wrong?'' he shouted into the empty air.

``Clay. I'm . . . dyin', brother.''

Clay let his head fall onto Billy's chest, his nose touching the helmet covering the intestines. ``No, Billy. Godammit. No!''

``Not much . . . time. Listen. The power. The Tinde need you. You can . . . help. Take my power. It's yours. Stay alive, brother. Walk . . . with the . . . wolf. Oh! Damn!''

Clay felt Billy exhale and waited for his chest to rise again. It didn't happen. Unable to move, the bloody camouflaged helmet touching his nose, Clay felt the silent tears pour from his eyes.

One instant the scorpion was there, and in the next it had vanished. It didn't move. It simply disappeared. Tension drained visibly from Clay's body as he exhaled the breath he had been holding.

``Now think,'' Henry said. ``Think about the wolf. Billy must have given you a song with which to call it.''

Clay shook his head. ``He never taught me any songs. He talked about his wolf – sometimes – but I always thought he was dreaming.''

``Think,'' Henry said. ``Right at the end, just before he died.''

``I'm afraid I was unconscious when he died.''

``He would have found a way,'' Henry said with a quiet insistence.

Clay thought for a while longer, and shook his head again.

``Take out your medal,'' Henry said, ``and put it on.''

Clay looked at him quizzically. ``How ...''

``Put it on,'' Henry repeated.

Clay took the Medal of Honor from his pocket. He held it in his hand and looked at it. He glanced up at Henry.

``Put it on.''

Clay slipped it over his head, the medal, hanging by the light-blue ribbon with the white stars, in the center of his chest.

``Now sing,'' Henry said.

Clay was obviously uncomfortable. ``I'm not much of a singer,'' he said.

``Sing,'' Henry repeated. ``Growl, scream. Make whatever sounds are in your heart.''

In the long silence which followed, Clay took several deep

breaths, as though about to begin, but he made no sound. ``I'm sorry,''
he said.

``A warrior does not apologize. He does what he has to do.''
There was a hard edge of authority and urgency to Henry's words. ``Put
your attention on the coals of the fire. Hold Billy in your heart. Sing.''

Clay looked at the coals. They flared briefly into flame. The
shadows shifted around them and Clay was no longer on the
reservation. He was sitting outside a bunker in Vietnam. To his right
and above him, there was a soft, melodious whistling. He turned to
look. Billy sat in jungle camouflage on top of the rock behind him,
loading magazines for his M-14. He whistled the Marine Corps Hymn
softly to himself as he meticulously wiped each bullet with a cloth
before inserting it into the magazine. Billy looked up from his work and
into Clay's eyes.

``You should try it before battle sometime, brother. It gives you
an edge.'' He smiled, and the flames flared again, and he was gone.

Henry moved off into the shadows. ``Sing,'' he urged softly,
``sing.''

Clay began to whistle quietly. Soon the words were sounding in
his mind. . . ``First to fight for right and freedom, and to keep our honor
clean. . .'' Up the hill behind them, a single wolf howled once, then
again, closer.

``Keep singing,'' Henry whispered from further away.

Clay continued to whistle softly. The big Mexican Gray Wolf
Frank had seen watching Clay on the trail to Henry's cabin appeared on
the rock above Clay, where Billy had been.

Clay looked at Frank as the latter nodded his head, indicating a
position somewhere behind Clay.

Clay continued whistling as he turned and looked up at the
Wolf. It leaped down onto the sand beside him and sat with its head no
further than three feet from his. The whistling faded into silence as
Clay and the magnificent animal sat looking into one another's eyes.
The Wolf raised his head and howled, a long, plaintive, lonely cry.
Tears ran down Clay's face. The Wolf howled again, then stood. It

stepped forward to sniff at Clay's arm and shoulder. It looked at Clay for another long moment, then leapt back to the top of the rock behind Clay, turned, and disappeared.

A pocket of pitch exploded in the fire, sending up a shower of bright red sparks in the darkness.

``Enju," Henry said, walking back into the firelight. ``It is good. We are ready now."

Sunset, July 23 --- The Gathering Site

The last of the sun was slipping behind the crest of the Dragoon Range to the west as Frank approached the cottonwood grove, Henry, Clay, and Maria behind him. Great purple shadows covered the floor of the Sulphur Springs Valley with a blanket of mystery. The cloud build-ups over the Chiricahuas to the southeast had moved closer. They towered in mighty columns of orange and salmon pink – and blood red.

People were everywhere. They filled the grove and spread up onto the hillsides of the draw which flanked the grove on both sides. They stood in tight-knit groups far out onto the flatland to the west and southwest. There were vehicles as far as he could see. Small fires burned everywhere. Hundreds of horses snorted and stamped at the picket lines. From the center of the grove came the steady beat of the drums which had started as soon as the sun touched the western horizon. Voices accompanied the drums with the Gahan Chant, many more voices than four nights ago, Frank noted. He picked up the chant as he walked, and soon heard those behind him join in.

We are blessed in the Mountain Way.
The Gahan sing songs in our hearts.
We are strong in the Mountain Way.
The Gahan sing songs in our hearts.

He continued the chant as he reached the treeline, and again the crowd opened before him. Henry, Clay and Maria moved closer to him, and the crowd closed in behind. Again Frank moved towards the large fire at the center of the clearing. Again the circle of chanters, much larger this time, parted to make room for him and the others.

Apache Tears

The circle of chanters stood facing the fire and the drummers who sat around it. Their backs were to the crowd. After four repetitions of the chant, Frank stepped back out of the circle and walked around it facing the crowd. He continued to chant, and with gestures, he urged them to join in. ``Sing,'' he called to them. ``Honor the spirits we have neglected for too long. Honor yourselves and the source of your power. Sing.''

It started slowly, those nearest him joining in first, then it spread outward through the crowd like a seismic wave. First two, then three, then four thousand voices joining the chant. The power of the voices drowned out the drums. The rhythm of the chant pounded over the earth around them, echoed back off distant mountain sides, leapt up into the fading colors of dusk, continuing until it had chased the last light from the day and had ushered in the magical darkness all around them.

When the darkness was complete, the drums stopped. The chanting died away, and an intense silence descended around them. Far away, a single coyote raised his cry. The horses stamped nervously in the shadows under the trees. Frank stood to the east of the fire, Maria to the south, Henry to the north, and Clay to the west. No one moved.

His back to the fire, Frank looked out at individual faces in the crowd. On each, there was a quality he had not seen before. There was tension and excitement. On some there was fear. Yet on each there was something new. He saw it on the faces of the old ones, and on children. He saw it on the faces of young, unmarried men, and on the faces of mothers of large families. He looked until he recognized what he was seeing. It was hope. He was strengthened by his understanding.

Frank knelt down and put the palms of his hands to the earth. The crowd sat, the sound of their movements rushing out from the center of the grove. Frank let the power flow up into him, filling him, and when the words flew from his heart to his lips, he stood again and circled the fire as he spoke.

``Three nights ago, we gathered here in council to speak of matters of great importance to the Tinde. For three days I have traveled

211

our land speaking with you, individually and in groups. For three days you have discussed these matters among yourselves. We gather now once more in council to decide our fate as a people."

Frank knew he was being heard. He could feel a power from the earth surging up through his feet and legs to fill his heart and pass through his lips to carry his words to his people, even to those on the farthest edges of the massive gathering.

``There is great power at work in these matters. The Gahan have spoken. The sacred silver Bear has brought his power back to our land. The Wolf of our warrior chief ancestors has returned. It is well for us to begin our council by honoring those powers we have neglected for too long."

Frank felt a peace come over him. The words lifted him up and spoke themselves. He walked slowly around the circle, his step a hypnotic dance.

``The Gahan have spoken of a time in which the circle of the Tinde is to be completed. That time is now. Wisdom tells us that before we make our decision tonight to complete that circle, we should look once more at how that circle has been drawn."

Frank saw Teresa for the first time, crouching at the edge of the crowd in front of him, camera on her shoulder, backing up steadily in front of him to keep the camera on him as he spoke. A girl Frank recognized as a high school student crouched next to Teresa, moving backwards with her, holding a microphone out towards him. He turned his attention back to the crowd.

``In ancient days, our land was vast, stretching hundreds of miles in all directions. We lived in peace with the Pueblo Peoples and Buffalo Hunters to the north. We lived in peace with the Farming Peoples to the west, and the Pyramid Builders to the south. We lived in peace with the Basket Weavers and Pottery Makers to the east. We were a strong people. We spoke the truth among ourselves and to our neighbors. Many among us had been granted the power of the deer and the antelope, others the healing power of the beaver, and others the sacred vision of the eagle who flies close to the gods. We were honored by our neighbors as great hunters, and we traded with them for what we could not hunt or gather.

``In the hot days of the summer sun we followed the animals high into the mountains where we were cooled by the shade of the trees and refreshed by the clean water of the springs and streams. In the cold days of the white wind from the north, we moved back to the desert valleys where we were warmed by our father, the sun, and nourished by the game which filled the mesquite and cottonwood stands along the water ways. Always we honored our land and the power that filled it with life. We did not build our wickiups near water, for water belongs to all things, not just to the Tinde. When a deer gave itself to us for our nourishment, we did not eat just the choicest parts and leave the rest. We used all that we were given and we honored the spirit of the deer for its gift to us. We held our ceremonies at the proper times, celebrating our mother the earth, and our father the sun, honoring the Gahan, the great spirits of the mountains who guided us. We lived until our hair was white like the winter snow, and did not mourn the deaths among us, for we lived honorable lives and knew the spirits of those who died were returning to Ussen-the-Giver-of-All-Life. This was the way of things in ancient times."

Frank felt his anger kindle.

``Then, five-hundred years ago, the Spanish arrived, those of dark beards and metal shirts, and the men in long black. They spoke of peace and we greeted them like brothers and showed them the ways of our land so they would not lose themselves and die in the days of the summer sun.

``But they were not men of peace. They were men of domination. They did not respect the earth. They tried to own it. They made slaves of the Pueblo people and the Farmers, and turned them into moles burrowing into the earth in search of yellow metal. Those who ran were shot. Those who resisted were hung. The noise of their thundering muskets drove off all the animals."

Frank walked in silence for several paces, letting his anger grow and fill him with its purpose.

``We watched all of these things. And still, we let the Spanish come among us, to judge for ourselves. When we were not fooled, they tried to dominate us."

He let the anger rage.

``We rose up and drove them from the land!"

A wave of loud agreement swept out through the crowd. Frank let it die.

``We defended our land with an implacability of purpose because our land is our mother."

Another chorus of agreement rippled through the crowd.

``Our land was all we ever had. It was all we ever wanted. It was everything to us."

He made a full circuit around the fire without speaking. He looked at faces out in the crowd, felt their strength flowing to him, and the love of the Gahan flowing out to replenish them. He felt the bond being re-woven between them.

``For a time we were again at peace. But the Spanish returned, and continued to return. And we continued to drive them back to the south. It went this way for many years. Over time, the Spanish established their domination over other tribes around us, and turned them against us. When we would not submit, they cut off our trade and we became raiders to survive.

In the south, the Pyramid Builders accepted the Spanish as their conquerors, and Mexico came into being. When the Mexican people spread north, they came as dominators, like the Spanish, not as men of peace.

``We fought back. Though their numbers continually increased, we fought back. And as long as we fought hard and well on our borders, we kept them from the heart of our land."

Frank let the anger put edges on his words. ``When their government began paying fifty dollars for every Apache scalp brought in, still we fought back."

The chorus of support swelled.

``For more than two-hundred long, bloody years – we fought

214

back!"

The chorus became a cheer. Frank raised his hands to quiet them. ``We fought for our land, our mother. The land is all we have ever fought for.

``When the Whites came from the east and north, we heard that they, too, fought against the Mexicans. And we thought at first, this might be a group of men we could live in peace with. But they, too, were dominators. They wanted to lock us up in outdoor jails called reservations. They wanted us to live on whatever handouts they chose to provide. They wanted to lock us away so they could take and destroy our land."

Frank rode the rhythms of words and silences.

``We fought back."

The crowd answered him.

``For sixty more long, bloody years – we fought back."

The thunder of the crowd's united voices was answered by thunder from the southeast. ``Several times we tried peace with them. Every time they broke their word. You know the history of betrayals. We went on their reservation at Camp Grant. While our men were away hunting, they let a group of drunken townspeople on the reservation to slaughter our women and children."

Frank could hear the shrieks of pain and cries of terror- stricken children echoing in the darkness around him.

``So we fought back. We fought until there were too few of us left to fight."

Somewhere in the crowd an old man began a high, wailing chant of mourning. Frank walked towards him and the crowd moved aside to let him through.

The old man sat on the ground, head back, eyes closed, tears zig-zagging down through the maze of wrinkles on his ancient cheeks.

Frank touched the old man's shoulder. When he opened his eyes, Frank helped him to his feet and embraced him. Tears came to Frank's eyes. He stepped back and held the old man at arm's length, hands on his shoulders.

215

``I know your pain, grandfather. Your tears and mine are the same. But the Gahan have told us the time for mourning is past.''

The old man stood straighter. He took a deep breath, and like a mask, the pain on his face was replaced by a fierce, indifferent pride. ``Enju.''

Frank nodded, embraced the old man again, and then returned to the fire.

``In all those years of war, my brothers and sisters, in five-hundred years of almost continuous battle against invading peoples who wanted to dominate us and our land, we were never defeated. But in the end, the pain of our long years of war began to take its toll. In the end, we began to fight for revenge rather than out of love for our Mother, the land. In time, some among the Tinde began to be contaminated by contact with the white eyes. Their honor and integrity became brittle, like oak leaves in autumn. They adopted white ways and cut themselves off from their mother. As a people, we began to lose our access to power and our enemies multiplied like ants in the spring. Until finally, surrender was the only hope our leaders had for keeping a few of the Tinde alive.''

Frank let the silence stretch out.

``For a hundred years we have lived as prisoners of war, in outdoor prisons. We have lived under the domination of a people who have done everything in their power to erode our self-respect, to destroy our culture, to obliterate our religion. They have tried to force us to become like them, but have forbidden us the freedom they claim to worship.

``The white eyes pass laws guaranteeing us our rights, but they have never intended us to be free. They want tame Apaches, ones who follow white eye orders without protest, who accept their handouts with profuse thanks.

``They don't want free Apaches. Free Apaches are strong and proud!''

A wave of sound swelled in the night.

``Free Apaches live honorable lives!''

The swell rose.

``Free Apaches are in touch with the magic and mystery of power all around them in the world."

Still the volume of voices rose. Frank waited for it to recede.

``Free Apaches live in peace when it is possible. . . but free Apaches submit to no one!"

The roar of approval and stamping of feet shook the earth.

``When the Gahan spoke to me, they gave me the task of recovering the spirit of the Tinde. At first I did not even know what to look for, much less how to recover it. But power has opened my eyes, and I have seen the spirit of the Tinde. It is the spirit of independence and freedom."

His words began to take on a cadence. His pacing became again a dance.

``It is the spirit of pride and honor. It is the spirit of integrity. It is the spirit of reverence for our mother earth, and father sun, and all the spirits who look over us and guide us."

The crowd was responding now, to each declaration, and each response built on the last.

``It is a spirit of respect and great courage. It is a spirit capable of supreme determination. It is a spirit filled with love of family and kinsmen. It is a spirit which understands that living a life of honor and integrity is more important than death. . . It is a spirit which can not go on living in a state of captivity."

The cries erupted again, and then quieted.

``When I had been shown these things, I knew what had to be done. I knew. . . and I say to you tonight. . . if the spirit of the Tinde is to survive. . . we must be free!"

The night erupted with the cries of four thousand voices, cries which had not echoed off these mountains for a hundred years or more, the high, yipping, undulating, Tinde cries of joy and freedom. Lightning danced along the peaks to the south east. The drums began to sound. Frank stood in the east, and began to chant.

We are blessed in the Mountain Way.

Apache Tears

The Gahan sing songs in our hearts.
We are strong in the mountain way.
The Gahan sing songs in our hearts.

Others joined him and gradually the cries were replaced by the soothing rhythms of the healing chant. Frank stopped chanting and the drums were immediately stilled.

``We are gathered here tonight in council to decide our future as a people. Part of that future depends upon whether or not you want me as a leader." There were quick cries of approval, but he quieted them.

``Before you make your decision, you should know something of the path upon which I would lead you. The first step on that path is a commitment; I will live free, and I will defend my land. . . or I will die trying."

There were more cheers and he let them go on for longer this time before quieting them.

``What I propose is very simple. The Chiricahuas have always been our land. They have been the heart of our land. Even the whites gave them back to us. . . sort of. The way whites do most things."

Laughter rippled through the crowd.

``I propose simply, that we stop waiting for Washington to give us our rights to our land. I propose we tell them, in clear and certain terms, that this land is ours. Wholly and without restriction. That we claim it as a sovereign people. And that we will, without hesitation, exercise our native-born rights to protect it with arms if necessary. And that we are committed, every man woman and child of us, to die rather than continue living as we are."

Frank quieted the voices before they could rise. He paced in silence for a time. Lightning danced closer. Thunder rumbled loudly out of the southeast.

``That is part of the path upon which I would lead you. It will not be an easy path. Even if the army is not sent in, we will have much to learn and do in a short time. Things will be hard for a while. But we will survive. And we will prosper. If we respect the land, and honor it, it will provide for us.

Apache Tears

``Our government will be, like the old ways, founded on the principle that every one of us is free, and responsible for our own lives. And it will be based on the principal that voluntary cooperation must always be the basis of a community.

``Our laws will be few, simple, and easily understood. No stealing, no killing, no rape, no lying, no cheating, no child abuse, no physical assault. . . perhaps a handful more. They will be enforced fairly, but strictly. Any citizen of Chiricahua would be free to leave at any time. That is part of the path upon which I would lead you.

``One morning, perhaps six or seven months from now, you will awaken at dawn on a crisp spring day to the sounds of birds outside. You will get up and walk out into that magic pre-dawn light, onto this earth, and she will speak to you of her love for you. And you will be filled with joy and pride. This is something of the path upon which I would lead you.

``I would tell Washington that we have no desire to go to war. We wish to be left in peace. We have long-since drowned the cries for revenge which once filled our hearts in the tears of our hundred years as prisoners. I would tell them clearly that we are willing to talk about anything. . . except our freedom and our rights to the land. And I would caution them not to mistake our desire for peace for a reluctance to die in defense of our homeland.''

Frank let the cheers roll out through the night.

``There will be those among us who do not wish to take the first step on the path. It is their right, and they are not to be judged for exercising it. So that they might still have somewhere to live, I would propose splitting the reservation along an east-west line through the white-rock bend in Pinery Creek, eight miles south of Om'nitche. Those who wish to continue living as they are will have the reservation north of that line. South of that line will be Chiricahua. . . our homeland.''

``The Chiricahuas!'' A strong voice from the eastern edge of the crowd flung the words into the night like a triumphant prayer.

``Chiricahua!'' Other voices picked it up.

``Chiricahua!'' More voices joined in until it became a chant, the

219

drums accenting the rhythm – two short beats on ``Chir-i,'' the emphasis beat on ``-ca-,'' and a final short beat on ``-hua.''

``Chir-i-ca-hua! Chir-i-ca-hua! Chir-i-ca-hua! Chir-i-ca-hua!''

Frank let the chant go on for some time before he held up his hands to quiet the crowd.

``That is something of the path upon which I would lead you.'' He walked slowly around the circle, his eyes on the earth. What was coming next, he knew, was critical. But he had no choice. When he spoke, his voice was quieter and more powerful.

``If the worst happens. . . and we are forced to honor the commitment we have made to Chiricahua. . . If they send the Army, and we are forced to go to war. . . you will see terrible things.''

Images of Vietnam flashed around him and became images of his people trapped in the last high passes of the mountains.

``You will see a hillside covered with the bodies of young men. Your husband, or brother, or son, or cousin will be among them. The blood will be visible from far off, and the sharp, acrid smell of death will insult your nostrils.

``You will hear a monstrous thumping roar, and wickiups around you will burst into flame and the cries of those inside will haunt your dreams for many days.

``Your nights will be filled with songs of mourning and your days will be spent in constant fear. You will cradle your child in your arms as it dies of napalm burns. Your brother will scream when you cut off his arm to stop the gangrene, and scream longer and louder when you smear hot pine tar on the stump to seal it.

``Hate will grasp your heart with talons, and struggle to consume your soul. It must never be allowed to do so. There is no honor in fighting or dying in hatred. If we are to fight and die well, it must come always from our love for the land.

``These things, too, may be part of the path upon which I lead you.''

The silence on the earth was absolute. No breeze disturbed the trees. The horses were still. No one moved. No thunder echoed. No cricket sang. A tension built as the silence stretched out, communicating itself from one person to another, spreading out in a process of crystallization through the gathering, linking the people together, bonding them as independent entities into a unified whole.

``In the old days, in the time of the Spanish arrival, we adopted the ways of our brothers, the Navajo, and we had a Peace Chief, and a War Chief. After the Mexicans came, there were no longer any intervals of peace, and the War Chief became the one Chief. I would go back to the old ways. The path I would lead you on is uncertain. We would walk it seeking peace. But the possibility of war would be all around it. We must be prepared for both.''

Frank saw Eddie and stepped over to him.

``Have some of your men bring the prisoners down.''

``That's kind of risky, Frank.'' Eddie glanced at the crowd around them.

``Bring them down,'' Frank said. ``Hold them on the outer edge of the grove until I give you the signal. Then bring them here, to the fire.''

Eddie shrugged. ``You're the boss.''

Frank continued around the fire and stopped next to Clay, standing at his left shoulder.

``I am not a War Chief,'' Frank said. There were murmurs of protest but he stilled them. ``My path is that of a Healer. If I must fight, I will fight. But I am not a leader of men in war. I do not know a war leader's ways. But power has brought such a man among us.''

Henry moved around the circle onto Clay's right, and Maria moved around until she stood behind him.

``He fought long and well in Vietnam. He wears the scars of his wounds with pride. His courage was honored with his country's highest medal.''

They turned as a group, holding the same relative positions, and began walking around the fire slowly. Eddie nodded at Frank as they moved by. Frank nodded back and pointed at the earth next to him. Eddie raised his radio to his ear and spoke into it. Frank turned his attention back to the crowd.

``This man was born and raised in the foothills of the Chiricahuas. He roamed our mountains as a boy. He is Blood Brother to Oscar Gosheyun, and Elmer Pipestem. . . and Billy Horse. When Billy died, this man was there, carrying enemy bullets in his body, trying to save his brother. When I was wounded in Vietnam, and lay near death, this same man carried me to safety through intense enemy fire."

Frank continued on around to the west side of the fire and the group stopped and turned again to face the crowd.

``This is the man I would have as our War Chief. Clay Price." Frank lifted Clay's left arm into the air.

A confused murmur went out in the crowd. There were isolated cries of protest. There were a few calls of encouragement. Frank let go of Clay's arm and quieted the crowd. He could see a localized disturbance at the eastern side of the crowd, moving steadily towards him.

``This man was with me when the rape and shooting of Angela Stillwater occurred. He took the two white eyes prisoner by himself. For a second time, he saved my life."

Frank waited until Eddie's men reached the fire with the two prisoners. He had them put Charlie's stretcher down on the southwest side of the fire. Bruce was ordered to sit cross-legged next to it. Frank didn't know what he had expected to feel when he saw the two white men again. But what he felt was a cold, objective detachment. He noted the intense fear and uncertainty on their faces, and he was neither pleased nor distressed. Frank thanked Eddie's men and dismissed them. He moved back to Clay's side. He could feel eight thousand pairs of eyes on him. The tension hummed around him in the darkness.

``You know what happened when the two white men were turned over to the white eye courts. They were set free."

There was an ugly rumble from the crowd.

``Clay Price is an honorable man. He is Blood Brother to the Tinde. He could not stand by and allow this to happen. Last night, Clay

222

Price brought these two white men back to us to be tried for rape and murder."

There were cheers, but there was still an odd, uncertain edge to them.

``In doing this thing, Clay Price had to turn his back on the country for which he fought and bled. He stood on the edge, between the world of the white eyes and the world of the Tinde. Both bloods coursed in his veins. He chose the world of the Tinde. I claim him as my brother."

Whorls of confused reaction raced back and forth through the crowd. Henry leaned close to Clay's ear. ``Sing," he whispered. ``Hold Billy in your heart, and sing."

``I feel the uncertainty in your hearts." Frank spoke to the crowd. ``You do not know this man as I have come to know him. He is a stranger to you ..."

``We cannot be led in a war against the white eyes by a white War Chief!" The shout drew cries of support. The cries grew into a roar. For the first time, Frank's hand went to the shrapnel hanging on his chest.

Henry stepped away from Clay, out towards the crowd. He raised his arms to the heavens and let out a long, high-pitched, wavering cry. Lightning bolts slammed onto the hills around the grove. Explosive claps of thunder ripped through the night. Gusts of winds stirred the fires and flames leaped from glowing coals. Henry's cry seemed to go on forever, and when it faded, the crowd was silent.

``The Gahan have spoken." Henry's voice was full and deep and boomed like thunder itself through the night. ``They have spoken of a War Chief who would come among us in the time when our circle as a people is to be completed. Once, I thought Billy Horse would be that War Chief. He came to me, and I prepared him for war in the old way. The great Wolf who ran at the side of Cochise, and Nana, and Juh, came and stood at his side, and spoke to him of the ways of war.

``But Billy's path did not lead him back to his people. It lead him to a death in a place far from his homeland. And when he knew

223

this truth, he passed his power on to one he trusted to use it well for the Tinde. He passed it on to his Blood Brother. He passed it on to Clay Price."

Frank noted a confusion back under the trees on the west side of the grove. The horses snorted and stamped nervously. They milled around, tugging at the picket lines as men moved among them, quieting them.

``That was many years ago," Henry went on. ``But power acts in its own time. Power has brought this man among us, now, in the time that was foretold. His skin may be white, but in his heart he is Tinde. Thus have the Gahan spoken."

Lightning struck again, and again, four times around the grove. The light and noise assaulted the senses. When the last of the thunder had rumbled off into the distance, a single voice from the crowd, a child's voice, broke the silence.

``It's a Wolf!"

Frank looked and the big Wolf stood at Clay's right side, where Henry had been. Power surged through Frank. ``You now know something of the path upon which I would lead you, brothers and sisters. It is an uncertain path. It is not an easy path. But the Gahan have spoken that it is the only path left to us if we wish to survive as Tinde. Consider well. I ask you now. . . Will you have me as your leader?"

For one long, tense moment, the silence held, and then the old man who had earlier sung the chant of mourning, spoke.

``Enju! I will follow you, Walks-With-Bear."

As if a dam had broken, a roar of approval swept through the crowd. The high, yipping cries of freedom were started here and there. Others picked them up and they spread until the night pulsed with their sounds. The Wolf stood and answered the people's cries. Maria joined in, then Frank, then Clay.

After long minutes, Frank finally held up his hands for silence. The crowd quieted again.

``You have spoken," he said. ``And I am honored by what you

hold in your hearts." He motioned for Eddie, Elmer, Oscar, and Carla to join him in the circle. Clay and Maria moved in closer. ``These are the people who will help me lead. Their hearts, and your hearts, and my heart are the same. They will answer your questions and tell you what to do."

Teresa was still in front of him with the camera. Sweat poured off her and exhaustion smudged her features. Frank realized that she had never stopped taping. He looked at the crowd.

``You have spoken what is in your hearts." Frank looked directly into the camera lens for the first time. ``I say then, to the white world. . ." He looked back at the crowd. ``And I say to you. . . as of this moment. . . and for every cycle of the sun and moon to come. . . Chiricahua is ours! Chiricahua is free!"

``Chir-i-ca-hua! Chir-i-ca-hua! Chir-i-ca-hua!" The chant boomed again into the night. A terrible exhaustion came over Frank. He turned to Eddie, speaking just loudly enough to be heard. ``See that the prisoners and Teresa get to Henry's cabin, will you?" Eddie nodded.

The exhaustion turned to lassitude, and Frank felt the strength draining from his body. He turned to Clay. He did not need to speak. Clay motioned to Oscar and they helped him out of the grove, the great Wolf following silently behind.

CHAPTER TEN: THE TRIAL

Night, July 23 --- The Gathering site

Frank struggled to walk, but he knew without Oscar and Clay on either side of him, he would collapse. He could feel Maria's presence behind him, and the touch of her hand on his right shoulder. The lassitude was heavy on him. The Bear called to him from a steep, rocky slope on the side of a distant peak. He wanted desperately to join it. He drifted off, and stumbled, and jerked back to his body. He did not want his people to see him collapse.

He needed the support of those who walked close to him, their bodies against his, their arms around him. With it he managed to put one foot in front of the other. His eyelids drooped and he looked down at the earth. It became a steep, rocky slope on the side of a distant peak and the Bear paused in its climb and looked back over its shoulder at him.

``Come, Walks-With-Bear.''

Frank drifted.

``Not yet.'' Frank heard his great uncle's voice from far away. ``Not yet, Walks-With-Bear.'' Frank drifted further. He stumbled, and jerked back into his body. He concentrated on moving his legs. They

226

got heavier with each step.

As they neared the remains of Henry's fire in the mouth of the draw east of the grove, his legs would no longer move. They drug behind him and he knew he was being carried. He became aware of Maria's hand on his shoulder. His head lolled forward. The earth passed below him, and he soared high above a steep, rocky slope on the side of a distant peak. The Bear looked up at him from below.

``You fly with Grandmother Eagle, Walks-With-Bear.''

Frank turned his attention up and behind him. A huge golden Eagle, with a fifteen-foot wing span, soared easily on the air currents. Frank realized he was being carried in the great bird's talons.

``That is good,'' the Bear called. ``She has many lessons to teach, and great gifts of power to bestow.''

``Put him here, beside the fire.'' Frank heard Henry's voice. It had a hollow, timeless echo to it. He felt his body being lowered to the sandy earth. He lost consciousness.

``What's wrong with him?'' Clay asked. He squatted beside Frank, watching Henry gather the last of the dry twigs.

Henry shook his head, concentrating on his work. He blew on the coals gently. The cooler, insulating top layer of ash swirled away. He blew again and the coals glowed. He arranged the twigs carefully and blew again. The coals glowed brighter. Henry blew a fourth time and the twigs burst into flame.

The old man moved back around to the east side of the fire and sat on the ground next to Frank, Clay to his left. Maria positioned herself north of the fire and sat with her eyes closed. Oscar went back to the grove to see to his family's preparations.

Henry looked down into Frank's face for a long moment.

Suddenly Henry blew twice sharply on each side of Frank's head. He turned to Clay. ``Gather some wood. I will explain soon.''

Clay stood. He walked into the shadows, and suddenly the Wolf was back, sitting in the moonlight only a few feet away. The Wolf met his gaze impassively. It did not move, but something passed between them. Clay couldn't identify what it was. He was worried about Frank. He couldn't seem to find the time to think about things. He walked up the draw a ways, staying to the rocky part of the flood channel.

He moved without effort. Every sound was magnified. Time slowed, then stopped. The dry, broken branches of driftwood glowed silvery-blue in the moonlight. They seemed to put themselves in his arms. *I'm in a trance. I've got to be. This can't be happening.* He felt the rough, barky weight of the branches on his arms. They got heavier as he concentrated on them. They no longer glowed. He made his way back to the fire.

Henry had collected some stones and arranged them around the fire in a large circle. Frank lay inside the circle. Maria sat outside. Henry sat next to Frank and sprinkled pollen on him in a spiral pattern from his head to his feet. When he had finished, the old man looked up at Clay.

``Put the wood here, next to me. Sit next to Maria."

Clay put the wood down, crossed to the base of the rock and squatted on his heels.

``Sit," the old man said. ``It is good to sit on the earth when dealing with power."

Clay sat, and a burst of energy raced up his arms, into his chest, and spread out through his body. The wood he had gathered glowed again. He looked at Maria and her features grew faint in the uncertain light. They faded, reappeared, faded again and the face of an eagle stared back at Clay. It, too, danced in the light and faded. Maria opened her eyes and looked at him. She closed them again. Clay shook his head. Henry began a low, soothing chant.

Clay looked to the fire. Multi-colored, scintillating blankets of transparent energy floated over Frank as he lay stretched out in the sand. The energies surged, flashed and flared as Henry wafted sage smoke through them with his feather fan. Henry worked from within a transparent wickiup of cool blue energies. Hundreds of thin blades of green energy rose like spring grasses from the earth around Frank's body. They grew up and over him, weaving themselves into a

228

transparent, pulsing mat, embracing him, anchoring him gently to the earth. Clay could only watch. He couldn't think.

He did not resist what he saw. He let it flow through him. The experience carried shadows of every emotion, yet was not emotion. It felt like every energy he had ever experienced, but it was not energy. It produced a near-frightening clarity of vision, but suspended his ability to think. It bolstered his strengths and magnified his weaknesses.

Clay looked around. The bushes and trees glowed with a blue-green luminescence as they danced in the gentle wind currents which rippled the moonlight as it fell to the earth in slow waves. He looked back into the fire – and knew he was experiencing the nature of Power.

Henry stopped chanting. Clay looked at him. The energies were gone. The old man nodded. ``All is well,'' he said.

Maria moved and opened her eyes. Clay looked at her and she smiled slightly. He looked back at Henry.

The old man smiled. Clay felt a warmth coming from him even before he spoke.

``It is said in the old way, if you tell a man something, he forgets. If you show him, he remembers. But only experience brings understanding.''

Clay contemplated the words. ``Power.''

The old man nodded. ``Power.''

``What about Frank?''

``The Power of the Gahan is immense. When one uses it, the body is stretched to its limits. Reserves of physical strength are quickly drained. The Bear was calling him. We had to anchor his body here, to the earth, and protect it, so he could answer the call. He will sleep until the darkness pales, and will awaken restored.''

Clay looked at Frank laying by the fire, then into the shadows where the Wolf had been, then back to Henry.

``It is best not to talk about these things too soon. Too many words stop up the ears and cloud the eyes. Perhaps we will talk after you have returned from Mexico. When will you leave?''

Clay struggled for a moment to adjust. The phone calls to Tubs and Mr. Foster seemed to have happened long ago, in another reality. He shook his head. His sense of sequential time returned. He looked automatically at his watch. The hands glowed in the dark, indicating 11:45.

``Tubs is flying the Baron onto the strip at the Bar-X at dawn. We'll refuel and take off from there. We should be in Mexico City in six or seven hours."

``You have time for rest. Will you sleep here?"

Clay looked at Maria. She gave no sign. He looked back to Henry. ``As much as I'd like to stay – maybe I could convince you my ears could hold a lot more words without getting stopped up – I guess I'd feel better bedding down somewhere closer to the strip. It's a couple hours by horseback. I don't think it'd be real smart to use the roads. I don't want any delays after Tubs gets there tomorrow. The less time the Baron is on the ground near the reservation, the less chance of somebody deciding to check it out."

Henry nodded. ``Enju. I will stay with Frank until he awakens. Power accompanies you on your journey, Clay Price. Use it wisely. Remember your song. It is for times of need."

Frank felt the great talons release their grip and he fell through a tense moment of fear before he felt the lift of a thermal under his wings. He let the thermal carry him effortlessly up until he gazed down on grandmother Eagle flying below and in front of him. Everything stood out in a shocking clarity of detail – every feather on her wings, every leaf and twig and blade of grass, every rock and crevice on the ground a thousand feet below.

He matched the great Eagle's actions, trimming the feathers on the tips and trailing edges of his wings and tail to follow her into a level, banking turn to the right, another to the left, then back to the right in a gentle spiraling climb – fifty feet, a hundred, two hundred feet.

Suddenly she folded her great wings back against her body and dropped into a steep, sleek dive towards a rocky ridge far below. Without thought, Frank followed suit. He was intoxicated by the sensation of the swift, arrow-like descent, delicate, instinctive adjustments of his tail feathers keeping him from going into an uncontrollable spinning and tumbling fall. The euphoria vanished in an instant. The details of the craggy ridge raced towards him at an alarming rate. Uneasiness edged towards fear.

At the last moment grandmother Eagle spread her enormous wings as great, perfectly designed and controlled air brakes, and pivoted her body around them to settle gracefully and gently onto a spur of rock right on the edge of the near-vertical face of the ridge, dropping away to the valley floor two thousand feet below.

Frank tried to wait. The rocky spur leaped up at him. Fear surged through him and he spread his wings, gasping at the sudden, powerful breaking effect. He tried to pivot his body around the wings but he was still ten feet above the spur. The lift went out from under his wings and he began to fall. He flapped his wings desperately, trying to regain lift. The effort carried him beyond the spur. He brushed the rock with a wing tip and fluttered desperately as he tumbled towards the valley floor. Suddenly his wings caught air and Frank pulled down hard against it. He soared out away from the cliff face. His fear was replaced by exhilaration. He reached up and pulled hard against the air again, chest muscles flexing. He surged forward and up. He banked gently to the right as he pulled again and felt the lift of a thermal. He rode it up, above the spur. He circled back over the mountain and completed his turn, gliding back at a gentle angle to flare his wings and settle onto the rocky perch next to grandmother Eagle.

She turned her head to look at him. ``Do not spread your wings too soon, Walks-With-Bear. Freedom and flying are alike. Timing and balance are everything." She thrust herself away from her perch and glided out over the valley below. Four thrusts of her great wings carried her up in a widening spiral ascent. She caught a thermal and soared. He watched until she became a tiny dark spot in an infinite blue vista, and finally disappeared.

Frank heard a rock fall behind him. He looked. Bear stood fifteen feet from the base of the spur upon which Frank sat. Frank turned around and climbed down. He felt momentarily strange – heavy and awkward – in human form. He walked up to Bear, affection for the great creature filling him.

``You have done well, Walks-With-Bear. The healing is begun. Come.''

Bear led Frank down across a talus slope to a hummock filled with aspen and a few pines. With its great claws, Bear created a large hollow in the moist, clean-scented earth.

``Rest,'' Bear said. ``The Mother will replenish your strength. There is much still to be done.''

Frank lay down in the hollow Bear had scooped out. The cool earth embraced him. He looked up at Bear.

``I will be here,'' Bear said.

Dawn, July 24 --- East of the Gathering site

Frank awakened slowly, becoming aware of the sandy soil of the dry wash against his cheek. For a moment he was suspended in a timeless state, and simultaneously remembered everything from the day and night before – physical and spiritual, waking and dreaming – with equal clarity. There was no qualitative difference in the reality of the experiences as he recalled them. He opened his eyes.

It was early dawn. The songs of birds filled the clear light with sound. Frank was laying on his side with a blanket over him. Henry sat across the fire from him with his back to the flat-topped rock. The old man smiled.

``It is good. You have rested.''

Frank sat up and put the blanket around his shoulders. He returned Henry's smile.

``I am rested. But there is a part of me that doesn't seem to have slept at all.''

``It is the way of power.''

He passed Frank a canteen. As Frank sipped the cool water, he considered the day ahead. ``There is much to be done,'' he said, handing the canteen back to Henry.

The old man nodded.

Frank took the blanket off his shoulders and folded it. Henry stood up, showing no signs of fatigue or stiffness as he moved to his saddle.

``Maria left two horses for us in the trees up the draw.''

``I'll get them,'' Frank said. He got to his feet and started up the draw. After ten steps, he stopped and turned back to Henry.

``About last night, uncle – I thank you. My strength failed me at the end.''

``You are the hope of the Tinde, nephew. My power is yours.''

They broke camp and rode back to Henry's cabin in silence. Teresa appeared in the doorway of the cabin as they dismounted. In spite of the obvious lines of fatigue on her face, Frank sensed a new vibrancy in her, an aliveness that lit up her eyes from within and glowed around her with a faint luminescence.

She stepped out of the doorway towards Frank as Henry led the horses to the corral. ``Are you all right?'' she asked.

Frank nodded. ``I'm fine. Did you get what you wanted on tape.''

She reached out and touched him. A wave of pleasure radiated out through Frank. ``It's fantastic,'' she said. ``I taught Danny to use the second camera. He's a natural. He got a lot of good crowd footage. I stayed up all night editing everything. It's incredibly powerful. I'd like for you to see it.'' She stopped herself, and took her hand away. ``If you're interested, I mean, and have the time.''

Frank saw her uncertainty return, accenting the fatigue lines, dimming the luminescence. He wanted to reach out and hold her. ``Of course I'm interested. And we'll make the time. I just have to get a little planning done, first.''

Henry returned from the corral. ``I will make food,'' he said.

``Please,'' Teresa said, ``Let me help.''

Henry smiled. ``Thank you. I am honored by your offer. But I am an old man, and set in my ways. I have my routines. It will not take long.'' He entered the cabin.

``Are you alone?'' Frank asked.

``Rebecca, the girl who helped me last night, is still asleep inside.''

``Did Eddie bring you up here?''

She nodded. ``He left shortly after we got here.''

``Did he say anything about his plans?''

``No, but he left your truck parked down by the road. He said you could reach him on the radio if you needed him.''

``Good,'' Frank said. ``I'm going to run down and check in with him. We'll talk more when I get back.''

Mid-morning, July 24 --- Henry's cabin

Frank, Henry, Teresa and Rebecca finished their breakfast of cornmeal cakes, boiled venison jerky, and coffee in silence. Frank noted the adoration in Rebecca's eyes as she followed Teresa's every movement. He could understand it. He was finding it increasingly difficult to look anywhere except at Teresa, himself. When they had finished, Rebecca took the plates, pans and utensils to the stream to clean them.

``What is the news?'' Henry asked.

The meal had been ready and waiting when Frank had returned, and Frank had not yet filled them in on what he had learned from Eddie.

``So far, everything seems to be going okay. Eddie has his road blocks out, but a couple of BIA people are the only ones he's had to turn away. They weren't told anything except that part of the reservation was closed.

``They've already moved the radio base-stations and everything else of value from the fire and police buildings in Om'nitche. They've got them set up and running off generators, one of them up high, near the Stronghold, as a repeater, the other at the Botanical Research Station in Cave Creek Canyon.

``He says people started moving out of Om'nitche last night, right after the gathering. Most of them are out now, but the road is still

234

pretty busy in places. For the moment, most people are being directed to the Stronghold. He's got a few people out in Portal, but he's setting up his main headquarters at the Research Station. He says the canyon makes it a lot more defensible.

``Oscar is with him, and said not to worry about the medical supplies. He went to the hospital last night and Dr. Hardesty showed him what we would most likely need, and it's all been moved. Elmer already has the fuel stockpiled, and he and a group of his friends have gone after the cattle. Carla's at the Stronghold, organizing things there.'' Frank stopped and thought for a moment. ``That's it, I guess. He's got the prisoners under guard at the Research Station. He said to let him know when we leave, and he'll meet us there.''

``I hope Danny got some of that on tape,'' Teresa said. ``I left a camera and a couple battery packs with him.''

``We'll find out when we get over there,'' Frank said. He turned his attention to his great uncle. ``Since I no longer have to go into Om'nitche, we can leave whenever you are ready.''

``Do not wait for me, nephew. You and Teresa both have trucks to move. Go now. I will pack a few things and lead the horses to the Stronghold. We will meet there.''

``Good,'' Frank said and started to get up. Teresa stopped him.

``Frank, before we go – '' she hesitated, uncertain. ``When. . . how soon do you think I can release what I have on tape?''

Frank looked at her carefully. ``I did not say you had to wait for my permission to release anything,'' he said. ``I asked only that you tell me before you did. It is your decision.''

``I know,'' she answered. ``But this is important. It isn't about freedom of the press. It's about freedom of people. I just – I just don't want to mess anything up. I'd really prefer to wait for your okay.''

Frank looked at her and thought. He wanted the world to know what had occurred last night, but he knew things would happen very quickly once they did. For a moment he was perched on a rocky spur, high in the mountains, and grandmother Eagle turned her head towards him. ``*Do not spread your wings too soon, Walks-With-Bear. Freedom*

235

and flying are alike. Timing and balance are everything."

While the transition seemed to be going well, he knew it was not yet time.

``Does your release contain footage of the white-eye prisoners?'' She nodded.

Frank made a decision. ``They will be tried tomorrow at dawn. I think it would be good for you to tape it, and include it as part of your first release. Then the world will know exactly what happened, and how we intend to operate in the future.''

He saw the disappointment at the delay in her eyes.

``We need a little more time,'' he said. ``To make certain we are ready. You can release any time you choose after the trial.''

He saw her wrestle with the disappointment and banish it. She smiled tiredly. ``Why not? I guess I don't really have to worry much about somebody scooping me on this story, do I?''

Late Afternoon, July 24 --- The Research Station

Frank walked into the room where Charlie and Bruce lay on bunks, handcuffed to the metal bed frames.

``Well, if it ain't Geronimo himself,'' Charlie snarled.

Frank stopped and looked at him. He turned his attention to Bruce. ``Are you being fed?''

``Yes, sir,'' Bruce answered. There seemed to be a genuine eagerness to please in his voice. ``They're takin' good care of us.''

Frank nodded. He turned to Charlie. ``How's your leg?''

``Screw you, chief. I'll dance one-legged on your grave when my ol' man gets through with you.''

Frank held up two small packages. ``Morphine. For the pain if it gets too bad.'' He walked to Charlie's bedside table. Charlie raised himself on his elbows and spat in Frank's face. Frank slowly closed his eyes. The spittle burned darkly into his flesh, filling his nostrils with the stench of hate and death. A great sadness rose up in him. He opened his eyes. Charlie had laid back on the pillow. Frank put the morphine on the table. He took a tissue and wiped his face. The black energies of the insult pulsed in the tissue in his hand. He put the tissue in the ashtray and lit it with his lighter. When the flame went out he crushed the ashes. He took another tissue and emptied the ashes into it. He folded it up and put it in his shirt pocket, then turned and walked towards the door.

``You go on trial tomorrow at dawn."

He walked out and closed the door. He stood for a few moments, eyes on the floor, letting the sadness find its own level. He did not try to suppress it, or force it away. He sought only a balance with it. When he had achieved it, he sighed, looked up, straightened his back, and walked to the front door of the Research Station.

From the porch he could see Teresa talking with Danny Blue under a tall sycamore tree near the road. Frank had led Teresa to the Stronghold and had put some of the people there to work camouflaging her truck and a generator set up nearby. When he told her he was going down to the Research Station, she had asked to come along.

``So what do you think, Frank? Are we crazy, or is there really some hope for pulling this off?" Eddie spoke quietly from where he sat on the porch; his chair leaned back against the wall.

Frank looked at him. ``There's always hope. Even Charlie in there has hope. He hopes his daddy can find some way to get him out of this."

``Do you think he can?"

Frank shook his head slowly. His hand went to the tissue of ashes in his pocket. ``But I think he'll try. Once the government knows for sure we have them. They'll have to try."

``How long do you figure we have?"

``I want to try them at sunrise tomorrow." He looked out towards Teresa. ``I've told her she can tape it. She can broadcast anytime after that."

Eddie tipped forward in his chair. ``You got any idea how long it will take Clay and Maria in Mexico?"

``I think it will happen quickly if it is going to happen at all. A few days, if we're lucky. A couple of weeks at most. Why?"

``We've gathered up and redistributed most of the extra weapons. We've got quite a few rifles. A few pistols and shotguns. But we're real short on ammunition, Frank. You know how it is. Nobody keeps more than a box or two of shells.''

``Any re-loading outfits? Powder?''

``A couple. About a hundred and twenty pounds of powder. They're set up at the Stronghold. I gave orders for no unnecessary shooting, and to pick up and save all the empty casings, if possible. But we still can't afford to fight any prolonged battles. If the white eyes try something big, we're going to have to scatter to stay alive. It'll be hard on the old people and kids.''

``You saying you think I should delay the broadcast?''

Eddie got up and stood with his hands on the railing of the porch, looking out through the long shadows of the afternoon. ``I guess I'm saying, the longer we keep the white eyes in the dark about what's happening, the better chance we have to be ready for whatever they do when they do find out.''

Frank walked to the railing and stood next to Eddie. ``You could be right,'' he said. ``But they've got to know by now that Clay snatched those two in there. And that he was the one that ran the roadblock. There have already been a couple of Feds out here nosing around. So I've got to figure they're already planning something, and the longer we delay broadcast, the more time we give them to get their story established about kidnapping, and drunken riots on the reservation. I don't want to let that image get established.'' He watched Teresa talking with Danny. ``We can never hope to win this thing militarily, Eddie. For the same reason Cochise couldn't win. There are just too many of them.''

``Doesn't sound real hopeful to me,'' Eddie said. ``Why send Clay and Maria after weapons at all?''

``Because there's just a chance, this time, that we might win the battle for the hearts of the American public. We have to be able to survive long enough to do that.''

``Seems like it would be a little difficult to win the hearts of a

238

country you're fighting against."

Frank looked at Eddie and smiled. ``The VC did a pretty good job with the American public. And they were ten thousand miles away."

Eddie sighed. ``Yeah, but that war lasted eight years anyway."

Frank shrugged. ``I guess we'll have to hope that all those slow learners learned their Vietnam lessons well. Maybe they won't wait so long this time."

``You've spent more time with the whites than I have, Frank, but it seems like a pretty slim hope to me."

Frank turned to face his friend and put his hand on Eddie's shoulder. ``It probably looks slimmer to me than to you. But does it really matter? Could we have gone on the way we were?"

Eddie shook his head. ``It was all coming apart, Frank. Nobody cared about anything any more."

``Do you remember the Gahan Chant?"

Eddie nodded.

``When the hope gets to looking too slim, sing it to yourself," Frank said. ``These mountains around us really do love us."

``I know," Eddie answered quietly. ``I felt it last night at the gathering. And today, driving back and forth through them, getting everybody over here. Every time I would get to thinking that this whole thing was crazy, I'd feel it, and it stabilized me somehow."

Frank patted him on the shoulder and turned back to the railing. ``You've done well."

``A lot of people helped."

``I know, but it took a leader to keep it organized." Frank paused. ``I've got something else I'd like you to do for me."

``Name it."

``At the trial tomorrow morning, I need someone to speak for Angela, to present the case against Charlie and Bruce. Clay left an affidavit. I saw Oscar at the Stronghold and he said Hardesty had written something up, and that there is a Tinde nurse who came with us who says Angela identified the two men to her the night we brought them in."

``I'm no prosecuting attorney, but I can lay out the facts, I guess."

``Thanks. That's all I need. I'll handle the rest."

``Where do you want to hold the trial?"

Frank pointed. ``Across the road, there, under those trees. There's no sense moving Charlie around any more than necessary."

``You want me to pick the old ones?"

``I'll ask Henry to do that. He knows the ones that speak English. But you can make the arrangements to get them down here from the Stronghold. Let's try to be ready to go by sunrise."

``Everything will be ready."

Frank pushed himself away from the railing. ``Thanks, Eddie. If you need any help, let me know. I'm going to head back up to the Stronghold. I'll have somebody standing by the radio in the truck, if you need me."

``Go ahead. I think I can handle everything."

They embraced.

``Remember what I said about the chant," Frank said, stepping back. ``It helps."

Eddie smiled. ``I'll keep it in mind."

Frank walked off the porch and towards the sycamore tree under which Teresa and Danny were still talking. As he approached he sensed something that bothered him, but he could not identify it. He let it go as he walked up to them.

``Danny." He nodded to him, then turned to Teresa. ``Did you get what you wanted?"

``I won't know for certain until I view the tapes in the truck, but it sounds like it."

``Good. I'm heading back up to the Stronghold. If you want to, you can come along. Now might be a good time to take a look at what you have ready for broadcast."

A sudden smile lit up Teresa's face. ``I'd love to. I really want to know what you think."

Frank looked back at Danny. Danny's posture had stiffened, his eyes had narrowed slightly, and there was visible tension in his jaw muscles. There was hidden challenge in the way he met Frank's gaze. Frank spoke carefully.

``You've done well."

``I could be doing more out on one of the road blocks."

``I know you'd rather be carrying a rifle than a camera, Danny. But what you are doing is more important than you know. If it becomes a matter of rifles only, we can never hope to win in the long run. If Teresa is successful with her camera, we have a chance. I'd like you to continue helping her."

Danny paused before answering. ``I'll do as you ask because I've accepted you as my leader. But I don't have to agree with your thinking. My ancestors never relied on their women to win their battles for them."

``True," Frank said. ``Nor did mine. Perhaps, however, if they had listened to their women more closely, they might not have lost the war. Still," Frank smiled, ``you're right. You don't have to agree with my thinking. Sometimes, I even have doubts about it myself."

``Doubts can be a dangerous thing in a leader."

``Lack of them can be even more dangerous," Frank answered evenly. ``The coyote teaches us that we are most at risk when we are most certain of our rightness."

``I'll do as you ask. But if the white eyes come, I fight."

Frank nodded. ``If they come we will need your courage. Until then, what you are doing is valuable to me, even if it's not to you. I thank you for it."

Danny didn't respond and Frank turned to Teresa. ``The trial will be held here, at sunrise. Will you need help taping it?"

She nodded and turned to Danny. ``If you would."

``I'll be there."

Frank noted the softening of Danny's face and tone of voice.

``Good," Teresa said. ``I'll be here early. I'll have fresh battery packs and extra tape."

``Do you want the camera now?'' Danny asked.

``Keep it,'' Teresa said. ``You still have some tape, and time left on your batteries. You might see something tonight worth shooting. If you can be here a little early, we can talk about how to shoot the trial.''

``I'll be here,'' Danny said again.

``Thanks.'' Teresa turned to Frank. ``Shall we go? I'm really anxious to show you what I put together.''

Frank had watched the changes in Danny when Teresa had asked for his help. Now, he noted the instant reversal of those changes. The stiffness came back into Danny's posture, the tension back into the face. Frank knew now what had bothered him as he approached. It was more complex than Danny wanting to be on roadblock with a rifle. He also knew it was not the right time to try to do anything about it.

``Sure, let's go,'' he said to Teresa. He nodded to Danny. ``Sleep well, friend. I'll see you in the morning.'' As he turned towards his truck, Frank noted how Danny's eyes followed Teresa. He sighed. As if things weren't already complicated enough, he thought.

Evening, July 24 --- The Stronghold

Frank and Teresa climbed slowly through the shadow-fractured moonlight under the pines towards a rock outcrop on the hillside above them overlooking the Stronghold. They had just finished watching the tape Teresa had prepared of the Great Gathering. Except for Frank asking her to walk with him, neither had spoken since she had switched off the equipment.

They reached the outcrop and found a spot to sit with their backs against the rock. Thousands of small fires, lanterns, and flashlights flickered across the floor of the high mountain valley they had chosen as a Stronghold.

Protected by near-vertical ridges of rock reaching up several hundred feet on the north, west, and south, the pine and aspen-filled valley narrowed and sloped away to the east towards its only easy entrance, a passage no more than three hundred feet wide between two rock walls. A road had been cut through the opening into the valley, and a stream, born of two springs in the southern end of the valley, flowed out through the opening.

When Frank had arrived earlier in the day he had found people already at work building a dam across the creek to create a small reservoir to handle their water needs.

Here and there he could see clusters of lights and though he couldn't see the activity associated with them, he knew people were still at work, digging latrines, constructing stone-lined storage caves for food and supplies, and cutting and stockpiling firewood.

The lights of heavily laden pick-up trucks occasionally flashed across the rock walls on either side of the entrance as they entered the valley. Frank knew that while some of them were late arrivers, others were loaded with hastily gathered firewood, foodstuffs, and feed for the livestock. Hundreds of horses, a few milk cows, and a few sheep had been penned up in temporary rope corrals near the Stronghold entrance.

He had moved among the people in the Stronghold after he had arrived. He had never seen so much energy, enthusiasm, cooperation and hope among the Tinde. He had been proud of his people, even a little proud of himself.

But that had been in the afternoon. Now, he had watched the tapes. He knew how the world would see their actions. From where he sat, under the impassive moon and with the immensity of the universe stretched out overhead, the Stronghold seemed somehow very fragile and transitory to Frank, and his pride a foolish thing.

Charlie had given him a scent of death that afternoon and Frank had not been able to get it out of his nostrils. His hand went to the tissue in his shirt pocket.

``Was it that bad?'' Teresa asked quietly.

Frank faced her. He studied the angles and planes of her face in the moonlight. He looked into her eyes and felt an impulse to reach out and hold her. He shook his head.

``No, it was not bad,'' he said gently. ``You have honored me, Teresa Chatla. You have honored my people with your work.''

He reached out and put the tips of his fingers lightly on her

243

cheek. ``You have told the truth. In order to do so, you must have heard it with your heart. I could ask no more.''

He saw tears come to her eyes and run silently down her cheeks. He could no longer keep his distance. He reached for her and she moved to him. He held her gently, her head cradled in the hollow of his shoulder and neck.

He looked out over the Stronghold and realized for the first time the full depth of the commitment he had asked his people to make. The thought of Teresa's death filled Frank with the beginnings of a horror he had never known. He knew now his own decision had been easy. He had only to make the commitment for himself. He thought of the mothers and fathers, the husbands and wives, the brothers and sisters and lovers among those who labored into the night in the valley below, building a dream from the materials the earth provided. He knew for the first time what the commitments had cost them, and his own silent tears rose with the outpouring of love he felt for them.

Teresa looked up at him. ``It's good not to feel empty inside,'' she whispered.

A few nights ago, the Gahan had taught Frank he was not alone. For the first time he knew what that meant. He kissed her gently. ``I know,'' he whispered.

Pre-Dawn, July 25 --- The Stronghold

Frank awakened to Henry's touch on his shoulder. He lay on his side, knees up, Teresa tucked up against him, her back to his chest. The pine-scented smell of her hair thrilled him through the vestiges of his sleep.

``I have coffee prepared,'' Henry said quietly. ``Near the truck. I'll wait for you there.''

Frank nodded. He eased his arm from under Teresa's neck, trying not to wake her. He slipped out from under the blanket that covered them, and tucked it in again around her back. They had not set up a shelter, choosing instead to spread Frank's sleeping bag as a mattress and sleep with only a blanket between them and the stars.

Teresa murmured something inaudible, turned over and pulled the blanket tight under her chin. After a moment, she opened her eyes.

Frank touched her cheek. ``It is nearly dawn,'' he said. ``Henry has coffee ready over by the truck.''

She smiled. ``You go ahead. I'll be along in a few minutes.''

Frank pulled his shirt on. He got fresh socks from his pack and put on his boots. He leaned over and kissed Teresa on the forehead before standing and walking over to the fire where Henry sat.

``Don't you ever sleep?'' Frank asked, as he poured himself a cup of coffee.

Henry laughed. ``Gray heads sleep lightly on the pillow, nephew. Especially in times of great change. I awakened about an hour ago, when the moon disappeared.''

Frank sipped at his coffee. ``Have all of the old ones been awakened?''

Henry nodded. ``Eddie has drivers standing by to take them down to the site.'' Henry looked at Frank for a long moment. ``Are you prepared?''

``I honestly don't know, uncle. I don't like judging people, or handing out punishments. When I think of Charlie and Bruce, I find myself remembering all the things I've done which I wish I had not. I become very aware of my own weaknesses and failings.''

``It is good you feel this way. It is why we have always allowed the old ones to judge guilt or innocence. It brings the mercy of experience to bear on the matter.''

Frank sighed. ``It's not an easy thing.''

``It is part of the path, nephew.''

``It is part of the path,'' Frank answered. He finished his coffee and set the cup on a rock next to the fire-ring. ``I think I will take a horse and ride down alone. I need the time to think. Will you see to it that Teresa gets there?''

Henry nodded. ``I will have one of Eddie's drivers take her.''

Frank stood. He looked down at his great uncle, sitting cross-legged on the earth, the maze of wrinkles on his ancient face like a map of his life. For the first time Frank realized there would come a day when Henry would no longer be there for him. The thought triggered an instant and near-overwhelming grief.

Henry looked up at him and smiled. ``It is the way of things, nephew."

Sunrise, July 25 --- The Research Station

Eight old men and eight old women sat on the ground on folded blankets in a large circle under the stand of sycamore trees across the road from the Research Station, women on the east side, men on the west. Four egg-size stones were on the ground in front of each of them, two white and two black.

Frank sat at the northern apex of the circle, Eddie to the south. A large crowd of spectators sat around the outside of the circle. Teresa and Danny sat with cameras ready in their laps, across from one another.

Despite the crowd, a heavy stillness filled the morning. Occasionally, off up the creek which ran behind the Research Station, a solitary bird broke the silence with its song, but in the grove, there was no sound. No one spoke. No one moved. The leaves hung motionless on the trees.

As the first rays of the sun broke over the ridge to the east, the door to the Research Station opened and two of Eddie's men carried Charlie out on a stretcher. Behind them, two others walked out on either side of Bruce.

Teresa and Danny both brought their cameras up as the two white men were brought to a clear area on the west side of the circle. Frank noted Bruce was trembling as he sat down. Even Charlie was subdued, and Frank could see uncertainty in his eyes as his stretcher was placed on the ground. The four guards remained standing behind the two men.

Frank looked back to the circle. He reached up with his left hand and clasped the shrapnel at his breast as he spoke.

``We are gathered here to resolve the matter of the shooting, rape and death of Angela Stillwater." He looked around the circle at each person in turn. ``As is our way, no friend or relative of Angela sits in the Circle of Judgment. We have prayed for clear minds, and quiet hearts. Passion has no place in judgment."

He pointed to Charlie and Bruce. ``Two men, Charlie Williams and Bruce Stinton, are accused of these crimes." He pointed to Eddie. ``Eddie Vasquez will speak for Angela. Jack Stillwater, her uncle and her only relative, chose not to join us, and has remained in Om'nitche."

Frank paused, and the silence re-established itself in the grove. Again, he looked around the circle slowly.

``These are serious matters. This Circle of Judgment is one of our first official acts as a newly free and independent people. There is not one among us who has not suffered in some way at the hands of the whites. These hurts must be put away. We must not judge the accused as white men. We must judge them as men. May the spirits grant us the wisdom to do so."

Frank put the palms of his hands to the earth and sat for a moment in silence before continuing.

``I was present at the time these crimes occurred, but you have chosen me as your chief. As such, if these men are found guilty, decisions as to punishment must be mine. Therefore, I do not feel it is appropriate that I should speak for Angela. I have asked Eddie Vasquez to do so. When he is finished, I will speak of what I saw and heard. If we are in agreement," he paused, and looked around the circle quickly, ``we will begin." He nodded at Eddie.

``Clay Price, who is now one of us, was also present the night Angela was raped and shot." Eddie picked up some papers. ``Since he knew he was going to have to be away on other matters, he left a written description of what occurred. I will begin by reading that statement."

Frank quickly lost track of Eddie's words as he moved back through his own memories of the incident. He was pleased to find little emotion in them beyond sadness.

He looked at the faces of the old ones sitting in the circle and

247

felt pride at the quiet dignity and patience with which they sat and listened. Eddie finished with Clay's statement. He put the papers down and picked up another set.

``Dr. John Hardesty was called into the hospital the night Angela was brought in. He also treated the leg wound of Charlie Williams the same night. The doctor, too, has written a statement. In it he claims Angela saw and identified Charlie Williams as her attacker. I will read it."

Again, Frank ignored the words. He looked at his people, the old ones in the circle, and those outside. Frank had been struggling with two fears about the trial. The first was that the unexpressed anger and resentment against whites, which he knew lay just below the surface with most of those present, might erupt. He was pleased. Even among the spectators, there was attention, there was solemnity, but there was no anger.

The second fear was more personal. It had to do with his responsibilities for deciding punishments. As much as he tried to hold any final conclusions in abeyance, he had been there. He knew what had happened. And he knew what the punishment must be. He pulled his attention away from the fear again. Something might happen. Something might change.

Eddie called the nurse into the circle to speak. *She's not much older than Angela*, Frank thought. Her nervousness was apparent, but so was her pride and courage.

``I was on duty the night Angela was brought in. I worked double shifts the next two days to be able to spend time with her. I was raped when I was seventeen, at the Indian School in Phoenix. After it happened, I needed another woman, a Tinde woman, to talk to. It helped me, so I tried to get Angela to talk about it. She finally did. She told me she had been hitchhiking from Om'nitche to her uncle's place, when those men there," she pointed at Charlie and Bruce, looking them in the eye, ``picked her up. I recognize them now because I saw them when they were brought into the hospital that night. She said that one, with the amputated leg, drove her to a spot out along Pinery Creek, and

248

forced her into the back of the truck at gunpoint. She said she yelled and fought, and that when she got the opportunity, she bit him, hard, on the hand."

Eddie stopped her momentarily. He nodded to his men and two of them picked up Charlie's stretcher and carried it into the circle. As they carried the stretcher around in front of each of the old ones, another of Eddie's officers walked beside it, holding out Charlie's hand, displaying deep bruises still recognizable as bite marks. When they had completed the circle, they returned Charlie to his place, and Eddie nodded for the nurse to continue.

``There's not much else. Angela said that after she bit him, he shot her." She started to walk out of the circle, and then stopped. ``There is one other thing. I was with Angela when she overheard two men talking in the hall outside her room about the charges being dropped against these men. She closed her eyes and would not speak to me anymore. She did not speak or open her eyes again." The nurse looked at Eddie, and when he nodded, she left the circle.

Eddie then gave his account of events after the men had been brought back to Om'nitche. When he had finished, Frank spoke.

``When I arrived at the campsite, Bruce was the only one visible. Charlie and Angela were in the back of the truck. I heard her cry for help. Bruce ran for the rifles and I fought with him, knocking him down. While I was doing so, I heard Charlie scream in pain, and then about three seconds later a shot. I grabbed a rifle and ran to the camper door. As I was reaching for the handle, Charlie slammed it open into me. He shot at me, and I fought with him until Bruce kicked me in the face. While Bruce was getting rope to tie me up, I heard Charlie tell him that he had shot Angela because she bit him. That is what I know of this matter. That is what I saw and heard."

Frank closed his eyes and sat in silence for a moment. There was an inevitability to what was happening which tore at him. He wanted it to be over. He opened his eyes.

``It is our way to allow those accused of a crime to speak in their own defense, and to call on anyone they wish to speak on their

249

behalf. We will begin with Bruce Stinton."

Frank waited until Bruce had been moved to the center of the circle and seated. Fear rolled off Bruce in waves.

``Our ways in the Circle of Judgment have been explained to you," Frank said. ``Is there anyone you wish to call to speak on your behalf?"

Bruce shook his head mutely.

``Do you wish to speak to the circle?"

``Please." Bruce's voice cracked and he cleared his throat.

Frank nodded to him.

``What I did was wrong," he started. He cleared his throat again. ``I didn't do anything with the girl, and I didn't shoot her. But I knew what was happening and I was wrong because I didn't try to stop it. It wasn't my idea. I don't know if I would have done anything with her – I mean if nobody had showed up. I might have. I was pretty drunk. And I've always been pretty easily influenced by other people. I'm really sorry she died. I never wanted that. I never would have shot her. I'm really sorry. . ." He stopped for a moment and struggled to get the tears out of his voice. ``I wish I could bring her back. I wish I could do something to make up for everything. But I don't know how." His voice trailed off and he sat looking at the ground in front of him, hunched over, shoulders rounded, his whole body trembling.

Frank let him sit that way for a time before speaking.

``Is there anything else you wish to say?"

Bruce shook his head, and Frank nodded to Eddie's officer who led Bruce back out of the circle. Two other officers carried Charlie's stretcher into the circle and set it down. Frank noted Charlie's usual look of angry defiance back on his face. Only his eyes betrayed him. They darted around the circle like a trapped animal's.

Frank spoke formally. ``Our ways in the Circle of Judgment have been explained to you. Is there anyone you wish to call to speak on your behalf?"

Charlie propped himself up on his elbows. ``The whole god damn U. S. Army's going to speak on my behalf, Geronimo. My old man's gonna hang every one of you bastards."

``Do you wish to speak on your own behalf?"

Charlie tried to laugh but it came out sounding forced and strangled. ``You call this a trial? You people are all crazy. Every one of you. You're all gonna die. You got no jurisdiction over me. I know my rights. You can't prove shit."

Beads of sweat stood out on Charlie's forehead as he lay back on the stretcher.

``Is there anything else you want to say?"

Charlie twisted his head around to look at Frank. ``Yeah. Screw you. Screw all of you damn drunken Indians."

Frank nodded to the officers and they picked up Charlie's stretcher and carried him out of the circle.

Frank spoke quietly, struggling with his own dread. ``The matter is before you. Are there any in the circle who wish to speak before the decision?"

Frank waited. He looked at each face in the circle in turn. There was no response.

``Then, I ask for your judgment. Is Charlie Williams guilty in the matter of the death of Angela Stillwater?"

One by one, sixteen black stones were picked up and thrown into the center of the circle. The dread surged up in Frank, but he controlled it. His head ached and he felt an immense weariness.

``Is Bruce Stinton guilty in the matter of the death of Angela Stillwater?"

Again the judgment was unanimous, sixteen black stones. Frank sighed. It was over now. He could do nothing but walk it through.

``Bruce Stinton and Charlie Williams, you have been judged guilty in this matter. As chief of the Tinde, it is my duty to decide your punishments." Frank got to his feet and walked to the center of the circle, facing the white men.

``Bruce Stinton, you have shown some evidence of remorse, and a willingness to speak truthfully about your part in the matter. While you did not shoot Angela, you have admitted your part in

251

creating the situation in which she was shot. And you have admitted you knew you were wrong in doing nothing to stop Charlie." Frank paused, waiting for the words to come. ``We have no jails or prisons. Therefore, you will perform labor for the benefit of the Tinde, under guard during the day and restrained at night, for five years. When that time is up you will be expelled from our land. This will be your punishment."

Frank saw the wave of relief go through Bruce, and tears come to his eyes. He nodded at Frank.

``Charlie Williams," Frank hesitated. He took a deep breath. ``Your punishment is death. You have four days to prepare yourself. You will die at sunset four days from today."

``You're outta your mind, man!"

``This Circle of Judgment is ended," Frank said. He wanted to cry. He wanted to run, far up into the mountains. He wanted to be alone to nurse the pain that tore at his heart. He watched Eddie's men pick up Charlie's stretcher and start towards the Research Station with it.

``You're dead, man," Charlie screamed. ``You hear me? You're all dead meat!"

Mid-Morning, July 25 --- The Secret Place

Frank dismounted and led his horse to the stream below the beaver dam and let him drink. After the trial, Frank had spoken briefly with Teresa who was going back to the Stronghold to edit the trial footage. He had agreed to meet her there later. He had then borrowed a radio from Eddie so he could be reached if necessary, and had ridden to the Secret Place alone.

When the horse finished drinking, Frank led him away from the stream, hobbled him, and turned him loose to graze on the lush summer grasses.

Frank returned to the stream and sat cross-legged on the bank. He closed his eyes and waited. The aftereffects of the trial still churned in him. Pronouncing the death sentence on Charlie had been the hardest thing he had ever done.

Apache Tears

All the truths he had learned in Vietnam, everything he had experienced in the past week, everything he had ever learned from his great uncle, everything he had ever read which echoed with that special resonance of truth, all of it shared a common core – life was sacred. All life. Even the life of someone like Charlie Williams.

For just a moment, when Charlie had spit in his face, Frank had seen the white man through the eyes of the Eagle, had seen him with the eyes of power. It was not a visual seeing, as it had been with Teresa when he first met her. It was as though for a brief time he had shared Charlie's consciousness in a state of near co-existence.

He had found his mind filled with intense and confused images of revenge and death. He had felt the maelstroms of terror and rage, a thousand times worse than his own fear and anger had ever been, tearing Charlie apart inside. He had gagged on the hate that fueled a compulsive lust for violence, and had burned with the corrosive acids of evil intent behind all Charlie's actions.

When that moment was over, Frank understood what made Charlie the way he was, knew the terror of believing the whole world was trying to destroy him and that his only hope lay in destroying it first, knew the sense of utter inadequacy that lay as a foundation below the terror, knew the horrors of physical and sexual abuse he had suffered as a child at the hands of his father – and Frank knew Charlie was beyond any healing he could do.

As much as he fought against the implacability of the reasoning, Frank knew Charlie had to die. He had considered sending him back to the white world to let them deal with him, but he knew in his heart that if he did so, Charlie would rape or kill again before anything was done. Frank knew those events, if they occurred, would be his responsibility. Just as he knew that if Charlie had to die, he alone could take the responsibility for Charlie's execution.

Frank had killed once, in self-defense, and the burden had been almost too heavy to bear. Without Henry's help, he didn't know what he would have done. But this would be different. He would have to pick up a rifle, aim it, and pull the trigger, killing Charlie in cold blood. The image filled Frank with horror. He tried to look at it like killing a leech in Vietnam, or the black widow spider he once found in his bed, but it wasn't like that. The horror remained, and it had driven him here to the Sacred Place.

Without willing it, he felt his Bear Song start deep in his chest. The vibration of the sounds spread out through his body, easing the tension a bit. He continued the song, letting it drive away some of the confusion of his thoughts.

He felt the Bear's approach and opened his eyes. He let his song trail off as the Bear ambled towards him from the south. The immense creature lowered itself to the ground five feet to Frank's right. Frank turned to face it, glad of the reassuring comfort of its presence.

``You are troubled, Walks-With-Bear.''

``I am, grandfather. It is the matter of Charlie Williams. And his execution.''

The great Bear shifted to a more comfortable position. ``You have done what was necessary.''

``It is not so much what I have done, as what I still must do. The thought of it fills me with a horror I am not certain I can live with.''

``Good,'' the Bear answered. ``You have learned the first part of the lesson.''

``Life is sacred.''

``Life is sacred,'' the Bear answered.

``But I am a healer. How can I intentionally take a man's life without leaving the healer's path?''

Frank took the tissue of ashes out of his pocket and set it on the ground before him. ``I know the wounds that gave birth to the evil which consumes him. And I know I cannot heal those wounds. Can you not do so? Or the Gahan?''

``All wounds can be healed. But would it change matters, Walks-With-Bear?''

The question stopped Frank. He had not considered it. He had wanted so much to see some sign of remorse from Charlie, some signal of change which might have justified a less harsh punishment, but he

254

had not considered what he would do if he had seen such a change. He knew at some level he had never expected it.

``Is it not true, Walks-With-Bear, that if you see gangrene in a wound, you must cut it out?"

Frank nodded.

``And is it not true that there are living cells which you will kill in the process?"

Again, Frank nodded.

``Healing sometimes involves death, then, does it not?"

``Forgive me grandfather, but a cell is only a cell," Frank protested. ``He is a man."

``Of all the forms of life Ussen has put in the world around us, Walks-With-Bear, only man is capable of evil intentions. Charlie Williams is such a man. He is a wound gone rotten, a gangrene which must be cut out."

``But if he could be healed. . ." Frank started. A growl from the Bear cut him off.

Confusion plagued Frank. ``I still do not understand."

``It is the only healing left for him, to be returned to Ussen to be cleansed. It is as you have seen. The father's evil has been visited upon the son. But there are many who experience such evil, and do not become evil themselves. This man did so, and in the evil of his actions, he has infected himself beyond healing in this life."

The Bear lifted his muzzle to sniff the light breezes moving through the morning. ``Is it not true, Walks-With-Bear, that you have seen the beginning of a healing in the other white man? Did you not see his relief when you pronounced his punishment?"

Frank scanned back through his memories of the trial. ``Yes," he said, after a moment. ``But I thought it was because he had been afraid he would be sentenced to die."

``It was because you gave him a chance to continue the healing which had already started. You gave him a chance to atone for some of the damage he had done. Had you set him free, as the whites did, the torment of his guilt would have led him to take his life within the year.

But you gave him a chance to atone for his crime, to help those he had injured.

``With the other man, what punishment short of death would provide such a chance for atonement? After being wounded by his father's evil, he had a choice. He could fight the effects of the evil, or embrace them. He chose to embrace them by walking the path of violence and destruction. Up to a certain point, he could have reversed himself, and taken another path. He did not do so. After a certain point, his every action was driven by the intention to continue his destruction until someone destroyed him, because he knew that death alone would be adequate atonement. Only in death would he find peace."

``It sounds as though you are saying the only way I can heal him is by killing him."

The Bear growled again, louder this time, its massive head swinging from side to side. ``Your arrogance clouds your mind and stops up your ears, Walks-With-Bear. Neither you, nor I can heal any man who does not wish to be healed. This man has walked a path to the only atonement possible for him – death. Only then, only after giving his life in atonement, will he feel worthy of healing. Only then can Ussen cleanse and heal his spirit.

``Evil carries with it its own power, Walks-With-Bear. This man sought you out to act as the instrument of his atonement. He chose to come here to commit his crime. He chose to be in the spot where you found him in the act of his crime. It would not be so if you did not have the strength to do what must be done."

The Bear's words finally brought to Frank a clarity and a calm. Though the idea of the execution was still not easy to accept, he knew he could do it and still live with himself afterwards. The horror was gone, and in its place there was a deep, quiet sadness.

``It is not an easy thing," Frank said.

``The healer's path is not an easy path, Walks-With-Bear." The Bear reached out a huge forepaw and dug its claws into the sod between them, turning it over and leaving a hole where it had been.

``Put the ashes here, Walks-With-Bear. The Mother will take

them and transform them back into life, as Ussen will do with the white man's spirit."

Frank placed the tissue in the depression, and replaced the sod over it. He felt a weight come off him as he did so, but the relief was temporary as he remembered what still lay ahead. He sighed deeply.

``So much is still in doubt," he said.

``Great forces are still at work, Walks-With-Bear. At such times, there can be no certainty beyond the moment. It is the way of things."

``It is the way of things," Frank answered.

Early Afternoon, July 25 --- The Stronghold

Teresa was waiting outside the truck when Frank returned to the Stronghold. He dismounted and walked over to her.

``Are you all right?" The depth of her concern was evident in her voice.

``Was it that obvious?"

``To me, it was. Henry probably saw it. No one else seemed to notice anything."

Frank nodded. ``I'm fine," he said. ``I just had to work some things out."

Teresa put her hand on his arm. ``What are you going to do?"

``What I have to."

Teresa touched his cheek lightly. ``I love you."

Frank smiled, and put his hand over hers. ``I know. I love you, too. I just don't know what it all means yet."

``Maybe that's all it means, that we love each other. It's enough for me, for now at least."

Frank drew her towards him and put his arms around her. He held her gently. ``It's more than I've ever had, Teresa Chatla. For now, at least, it is enough for me too."

Teresa stepped back and took his hand. ``Come on, there's fresh coffee on the fire, and food if you want it. Then you can look at the trial footage. It's ready for release."

Frank declined the food, but accepted a cup of coffee. As they walked back towards the truck, he struggled to find the right words to say what he wanted to say.

``I don't want you to misinterpret this, Teresa, but I don't want to look at the trial footage. It's not that I don't care about what you've done. I do. It's just too soon for me to go back through it. If it was anybody else, I'd have to, but I have seen your work. I trust you.''

He saw a brief look of disappointment cross her face, but by the time she spoke, it was gone.

``There was very little editing, just splicing together the shots from the two cameras, and putting my intro on it. The whole trial is there.''

``Will they use it all?''

``There's no way to know. The whole tape is very visual, and pretty dramatic – what my bosses like to call `perfect television news.' But they probably won't use it all immediately. They probably won't see it as a big enough story at first to warrant it. What they do later depends on how events develop. But by releasing this way, they'll have all the footage on hand if they want to do a special broadcast of the whole thing.''

They sat on the steps of the trailer. ``Are you ready?'' Frank asked.

``I think so. I went back through the manuals. I think it will work.''

``Where, exactly, is it going?''

``There's a computer in the truck that can talk to a computer onboard the satellite. I've got a log in the truck of all the network feed numbers, as well as some of the cable news services. I'll punch those ID numbers in, and then send the signal to the satellite. It will automatically download it to all those ID numbers.'' She hesitated. ``I'd like to download to my station, too. It will be the only local station. But they might use most of what I send them.''

Frank thought for a moment. ``Could you set up a live link between the Stronghold here, and the networks?''

``I'm not sure about the networks, but I could with my local station, and they could patch to the networks. Do you want to do something live?"

Frank shook his head. ``Not yet. But there may be a time for it. If we did set it up, could the government jam it?"

``Not legally," Teresa answered. ``Technically, they probably could. It's a real-time link, so it would give them plenty of time."

``What about the release of taped footage, like you've got now?"

``Probably not. It's a high speed transfer, to save satellite time. The only way to block it would be to take the entire satellite off the air, and that would shut down the networks. I don't think they could get away with it."

``Are you restricted to a single satellite?"

``It looks like there are two I could use. But I won't know until I try."

Frank sat in silence for a long time, thinking it all through again. He listened again to Eddie's arguments about the advantages of keeping the government in the dark about what was going on for as long as possible. But he knew it was a short-term advantage at best. There were too many of the people who were at the Great Gathering who had stayed behind. While he didn't expect any intentional betrayals, he knew it was inevitable that the word would get out soon. He went through all the reasoning again, and when he had finished he knew that their only hope lay in walking this thing through before as many eyes as possible. It was a gamble, a long-shot gamble at that, but it was the only one which offered any hope of final victory.

He turned to Teresa and kissed her gently. ``Go ahead and send it," he said.

CHAPTER ELEVEN: THE RACE FOR ARMS

Late night, July 24 --- A large plantation, north of Mexico City

Clay lay awake under the mosquito net and smiled. It was going much better than he had dared hope. The flight down from the Bar-X had been uneventful, and he and Maria had spent the afternoon and evening with General Estavan Villasenor of the Mexican Army, and Dr. Alejandro Rodriguez, representing the Minister of Health. By the end of a formal dinner, all the fundamental agreements had been worked out.

The sound of a board creaking outside pulled Clay from his thoughts. It was probably just the cooler night temperature causing the boards on the covered walkway outside to contract, but he decided to take no chances. He slipped out of bed and put on his trousers. He left his room bare chested and without shoes and stepped onto the veranda that ran the length of the north side of the house.

Maria's room was next to his. The louvered doors onto the veranda appeared shut, but when he tried them, they swung open at his touch. In the dim silver light of the moon, a man stood over Maria, his face in shadows.

``No!'' screamed Clay. He charged, catching the man in the

chest with his shoulder. They went down in a tangle of arms and legs.

``Maria!'' Clay shouted as he flailed, trying to get a firm hold on the man. He felt the man's perspiration and smelled his breath as their faces brushed in the darkness.

Clay managed to get a hammer-lock on his opponent, but before he could secure it, an elbow caught him in the solar plexus, knocking the wind out of him. The man twisted away, and by the time Clay could breathe again, he had escaped back through the doors, over the veranda railing, and into the deep shadows of the tropical garden.

Clay moved to Maria's bedside. He pulled the lamp chain next to the headboard and squinted as light flooded the room. A large golden eagle perched on the headboard, wings partially unfurled. Maria had vanished.

``Jesus!'' Clay gasped. He closed his eyes tightly and shook his head.

``Are you okay, Clay?''

Clay opened his eyes. Maria was laying in bed, the sheets drawn up to her chin. ``Me? Forget about me, what about you?''

Maria sat up. ``I'm fine. Did you see who it was?''

Clay shook his head. ``It happened too fast.''

``What do we do,'' Maria asked. ``Wake the General?''

Again Clay shook his head. ``Let's play this close to the vest. I don't want anything to mess up the negotiations.''

He moved towards the veranda doors. ``I'll be right back,'' he said.

He returned moments later with his Colt .44, and put it on the bedside table. ``I seem to remember you being pretty competent with this. I'll sit guard next door until morning, but keep this handy just in case.''

``Clay, do you have any idea what's going on?''

``Nope. But I expect we're going to be learning a lot in the next few days.''

``You don't think it's them, do you? The Mexicans, after the money?''

``I seriously doubt it. If that's what they wanted, we'd just disappear.''

He checked to make sure the door to the interior hallway was locked, then crossed back to the bed. ``I think it's going to be OK now, but lock the veranda doors after I leave, and don't open them for anybody but me. OK?''

Maria looked up at him and nodded. Her eyes narrowed at the outside corners and sparkled as she smiled. ``Sit,'' she said, patting the bed beside her.

Clay hesitated.

``Please.''

Clay moved to the bed and sat gingerly on the edge, careful not to touch her.

``Kiss me, Clay.''

``What?'' His discomfort increased.

She looked at him innocently. ``Don't you want to kiss me?''

``I don't believe this. You've just been through a trauma, Maria.'' He wanted to kiss her so badly he could scarcely contain himself. ``I don't take advantage of damsels in distress.'' He managed a weak smile.

``Why are you afraid to kiss me?''

``I'm not afraid. I just don't think this is the. . .''

``You love me, Clay. Why do you fight it?''

She unnerved him. He couldn't make himself deny it – he wasn't certain himself – and yet he couldn't just sit there and do nothing. He leaned towards her and pecked her quickly on the lips. She dropped the covers and let them fall to her waist as she put her arms around his neck and drew him to her.

Clay closed his eyes and took in the moistness of her kiss. He felt the warmth of her breasts against his bare chest. He put his arms around her and pulled her tightly to him as he savored the tingling sensation that ran the length of his body. The feel of the skin on her back was the feel of pure silk. Warm silk. Their tongues danced together – a short embrace, a gentle touch, then a deep searching. Their bodies quivered and trembled. As one, they relaxed their embrace.

Their tongues retreated but their lips remained lightly touching. He felt the warmth of her breath as it mixed with his own.

Slowly he pulled away from her until he sat upright on the edge of the bed. His eyes went to her firm breasts, nipples hard and erect. He pulled the covers to her neckline and stroked her hair at her temple as he stared into her ebony eyes. They danced, pulled at him, and reached deep into his soul. He felt his own gaze about to waver. She reached up and held his hand – the one stroking her hair.

``Your hand is shaking, Clay Price."

She's mocking me. She's controlling me with her power. ``So you kiss good." He tried to sound casual.

``You aren't alone, Clay. I too am afraid."

``You? Of what? Me?"

She released his hand and displayed her own. It trembled almost imperceptibly, but it trembled. ``No, Clay, I'm not afraid of you, but of something inside you, something that will not let you love."

``Just because that was the sexiest kiss I've ever experienced, that doesn't mean we're in love," said Clay unconvincingly.

She took his hand again. Her eyes seemed to deepen. He couldn't find the bottom of them. She communicated without words. He felt a thought from her pass into him, but he couldn't understand it. *God, she's beautiful! I can't walk away this time.*

He pulled his hand from hers. ``Maria, I'd better go. I'll wake you for breakfast." He took two steps towards the door and stopped. He turned to look at her.

``What are you smiling at?" he asked.

``I was right, you know. You do love me."

``Any man would love you, Maria. Many would die for the privilege."

Maria shook her head slowly. ``I don't know why you're afraid to acknowledge it now, but that's okay. You will come to terms with it in your own way."

Clay tried to smile lightly and knew the attempt was not entirely successful. ``I've gotta admit, you sure are positive about things." He turned and left the room. The incomplete smile on the outside masking the turbulence within.

Late afternoon, July 25, 1979 --- The plantation

Clay stepped into the foyer of the large plantation house. He felt good about his visit to the armory in Mexico City. The weapons were exactly what he wanted and the price was at least fair. As an unexpected bonus, the General had assured him supplementary air transport would be available if he needed it.

On the short trip back to the plantation in the Baron, Clay had wrestled for a while with all the unanswered questions about the intruder the night before, but he had learned nothing new, and with no new data his speculations had just run in circles. To free himself he had begun a detailed check of his gauges, radio settings, and position relative to his maps. Flying almost always made him feel better.

Maria greeted him at the door, and after a quick embrace, guided him to a large room with several leather chairs facing a large television set.

Dr. Rodriguez stood just inside the door of the room. ``Please sit down, Clay. There is a news broadcast of interest being presented at any moment now."

The commercial on the screen ended, and the face of a familiar network anchorman appeared.

ANNOUNCER: A story which sounds like it might have come out of the 1800's is unfolding today on the Chiricahua Apache Indian Reservation in Southeastern Arizona.

Charlie Williams, 23-year-old son of U.S. Senator Edward Williams from Arizona, and Bruce Stinton, 20-year-old son of Arizona rancher Clarence Stinton, are being held prisoner on the reservation, where they were tried on charges of rape and murder yesterday in what Senator Williams called ``a barbaric and grotesque kangaroo court proceeding."

Both men were found guilty in the trial, and while Stinton was sentenced to five years of labor, Williams was sentenced to death.

Clay watched the screen intently, unconsciously leaning forward in his chair as the camera moved in for a close-up of Frank as he pronounced the sentences. The screen flashed back to the announcer.

This action follows a mass meeting held three days ago on the reservation, during which the Apache declared their independence from the United States, and established their reservation as the new Apache nation of Chiricahua.

Clay glanced at Maria as images of the Gathering were projected from the screen. At the end of the brief clip, the announcer again appeared.

FBI agents and Federal Marshals who went to the reservation today to take custody of Williams and Stinton were turned away by heavily armed Apache men at roadblocks set up on the borders of the reservation.

According to an FBI spokesman, no shots were fired. Federal agents and U.S. Marshals, aided by Arizona Department of Public Safety Officers and Sheriff's Deputies from Cochise, Santa Cruz, and Pima counties, have set up a cordon around the reservation to ensure Williams and Stinton are not moved to a new location.

Teresa Chatla, a Navajo and a reporter for television station KDWI in Tucson, is apparently on the reservation, and released the video tape you saw a moment ago. Here is her background report.

Clay watched and listened as Teresa recounted the sequence of events: the shooting, the release of the suspects, and the declaration of independence by the Apache. He found himself remembering the day he first met Teresa in the restaurant in Tucson. It seemed a long time ago. He returned his attention to the screen. The announcer was back.

How Williams and Stinton got back on the reservation is still something of a mystery, but authorities believe Clayton Price, an ex-Marine and Medal of Honor winner in Vietnam, may be involved. Alan Larson, of station KDWI in Tucson, has this report.

Clay watched stoically as Larson reported on the disappearance of Bruce, the kidnapping of Charlie, the two bodyguards found in the desert west of town, and the running of the roadblock.

In Washington, correspondent Judy Blakesly talked this morning with Senator Williams at his office.

JUDY: Senator is it true that the Apache Tribal Police had filed charges of rape and assault with a deadly weapon against your son and his friend, and that the federal government dropped the charges against them?

WILLIAMS: Yes, it is true. I have talked with the U.S. Attorney who handled the matter, and he assured me that there was no evidence to support those charges. I'm limited in what I can say right now, but it appears that the man who kidnapped my son at gunpoint from the hospital where he was recovering from a serious hunting accident, may have actually been responsible for those crimes. "

JUDY: Do you believe the Indians actually intend to carry out the death sentence they imposed on your son?

WILLIAMS: As you know, I have been very active in Native American affairs during my years in the Senate, and have consulted regularly with the President on Indian matters. He has assured me that no effort will be spared to gain my son's release.

ANNOUNCER: In Washington, unidentified White House sources say the President is analyzing the situation and reviewing options, but that he is confident the matter can be resolved peacefully. In other news. . .

Dr. Rodriguez turned off the TV set. ``I have our people taping the rest of the broadcast. They will notify us if something of interest surfaces."

``Thank you, doctor. May I make a call to the States?" asked Clay.

``Of course. You may use the library for privacy. Please. follow me."

After thirty minutes of transfers and number switching, Clay heard the familiar voice on the other end of the line.

``General Purvis."

``Bill, this is Clay.''

``Clay! What the hell are you doing, calling here? Don't you watch spy movies? This line is probably bugged.''

``Are they planning a military action against the Apache?''

``Damnit, Clay. You know that a military action is always planned, even if it's never used. We have to be ready in the event we're called in.''

``Don't let 'em do it, Bill.''

``I'm not on the Joint Chiefs. I can't do much about their decision.''

``We don't want a fight, Bill. Let's talk it out.''

``Your people are set to kill the senator's boy in two days. Something will have to be done to put a hold on that, or this thing is gonna blow sky high, Clay. Can you do anything?''

``I don't know, Bill. Let me give it a try.''

``Call me at that other number.''

``Okay. Thanks.'' He hung up the phone and dialed Oscar's number on the reservation. An operator's voice came on the line. ``I'm sorry, service has been temporarily interrupted in the area you have dialed. Please check with your local customer services office for further details. Thank you.''

Late morning, July 26 --- Near the plantation

Clay slowly walked the worn path in the thick tropical forest surrounding the plantation. The previous night had been uneventful, and the first of the weapons had arrived at the plantation that morning. He had decided to take a walk while waiting for the next batch to arrive.

He tried to concentrate on the training schedule he would have to set up when he got back, but – as they had been doing all morning – his thoughts drifted back to Maria.

She had said she loved him; of course she had said he loved her too. He felt her touch as his thoughts went to her kiss. Involuntarily, he shivered in the hot morning sun.

Apache Tears

Since returning from Vietnam, he had held back, waiting for the perfect woman. But with every woman, he had been disappointed in one way or another. They weren't always major disappointments, but it didn't matter. He used whatever excuse he could find to justify the termination of a relationship when he began to feel trapped. He felt trapped now with Maria. It was almost like she could read his mind. Maybe she had cast some kind of spell on him.

He shook his head and re-focused his attention on the training schedule, but it wouldn't stay focused there. Random images of Maria drifted through his consciousness; Maria holding a gun on two men in a hospital, Maria finding him drunk – passed-out and helpless, not once, but twice. He saw her smile as she tickled his face with a mesquite branch. He felt her hand on his side, and saw her burning with fever as she called upon a mysterious power to heal his wound. He felt her moist mouth and her silken touch.

He looked up at the canopy of trees overhead. *Here I am, right in the middle of one the most significant events in the history of the Apache and the United States, and all I can think of is a woman. What's the matter with me?* The trees overhead gave no answer. He picked up his pace a bit, deciding to return to the house. Tubs should be landing at the airstrip soon.

He had covered little more than a couple hundred yards when the sound of rushing water ahead told him he had a large stream to cross. *Probably a footbridge.* He hated footbridges, especially footbridges over jungle streams. He always felt so exposed. Old training dies hard. He touched the .357 magnum tucked into his waistband. *This is stupid*, he thought. But he couldn't ignore his intuition. He left the trail and moved downstream in the thick vegetation.

His heart pounded in his ears as he waded across the water and moved upstream, the sounds of his movements hidden by the sounds of rushing water. He didn't know what caused his fear, nor why he had left the trail. As he neared the trail again, he slowed his progress and searched for the source of his fear. He felt Billy at his side.

Apache Tears

He stopped and let his eyes search those areas he thought conducive to the ambush of someone approaching the stream on the trail. His chest constricted as he spotted a man sighting down a rifle, nestled in the fork of a tree, watching the trail's approach to the bridge. The man was dressed in camouflage dungarees and cap. His face was covered with camouflage paint, and even his rifle was painted varying shades of greens, browns and grays. Only his blond hair, sticking from beneath the cap, had given him away.

You should have painted your hair too, buster.

Clay moved cautiously to his right in an attempt to move in on the man from the rear. He made no sounds not drowned out by the rushing water. He was a mere fifteen feet from the man's back when he said in Spanish, ``Do not move, or you are a dead man."

The man remained frozen in place.

``Very slowly, take your hands away from the rifle."

The man did as ordered.

``Now, put your hands on your head. Lock your fingers together and back up to my voice. Don't turn around."

``How do I know you have a weapon?" The man spoke Castilian Spanish.

``Take my word for it or try your luck. I don't care which you chose, but chose quickly."

The man backed up slowly.

Clay searched him hurriedly but carefully. When he finished, he studied the collection of weapons found in the man's possession: a garrote, one fragmentation hand grenade, one yellow smoke grenade, a sheath knife, and a Walther PPK pistol. He examined the garrote with its professionally constructed handles at each end of the fine wire. He looked from the garrote to his prisoner, who squatted fifteen feet away.

``You plan on using this on Maria last night?"

The prisoner said nothing, showed no emotion.

``Who are you working for?"

Still no response.

``Look, I'm not crazy about someone hiding in the brush with a

269

rifle and pistol and all this other stuff, waiting for me – but involving Maria takes me a step beyond that.''

``She's not involved,'' the blond said in English.

``Then what were you doing in her room?''

``Looking for you.''

Clay cocked the hammer on his .357. ``Who are you working for?''

Except for a single eye blink, the blond's expression didn't change.

``You're not going to kill me.'' He spoke softly but with confidence.

``What makes you so sure?''

``Executions aren't your style, Price.'' He paused. ``I'm going to do you a favor because of the Medal. Don't go back to the States.''

``Who wants me dead?'' Clay's heart beat in his ears.

``If you're gonna play grown-up games, Price, you better grow up.''

Clay shoved the pistol under the man's chin. ``You're starting to piss me off, asshole. I asked you a question. Who wants me dead?''

``It's not the Apache. Who does that leave?''

``You're lyin'.''

``Then you tell me who. The Mexicans have nothing to gain by killing you. Use the process of elimination, man. It's real simple. A Medal of Honor winner joining up with a bunch of rebel Indians makes real bad press. If you disappear in Mexico, the U. S. Government doesn't have to deal with the issue.''

Clay felt weak at the knees. ``Who the hell are you?''

``Sorry.'' The blond shook his head negatively. ``And I won't repeat what I said to the Mexican officials, either. The only reason I said anything, was because of the Medal. I was over there in '69. I didn't want this job in the first place when they told me who the target was. I got respect for you, Price. But the plain and simple truth is, you've been sold out again, my friend.''

Clay looked into the man's deep blue eyes. ``Where you from

270

originally?''

``Colorado. And I won't repeat that for your Mexican friends either.''

``Get the hell outa here.''

``What?''

``You hard of hearing or something? I said get the hell outa here. And here, take this smoke grenade with you. I imagine you'll have a helicopter looking for it.'' Clay tossed the smoke grenade carelessly to him.

The would-be assassin caught the grenade. ``I'll have to come back.''

They held each other's gaze for a moment.

``If not you, it would be somebody else. I'll be ready. Now get out of here before I change my mind.''

The blond held out his hand. ``I'm sorry, Price.''

Clay accepted the hand, his pistol held firmly in his left. ``Don't be. I'm not dead yet.''

``Either way it goes.''

``Yeah, I guess you're right.''

The blond turned and walked slowly away, his hands kept carefully in plain sight as he moved down the trail.

Clay gathered the weapons into his arms. His body trembled with hurt and rage as he thought of his government paying for his assassination. He didn't want to believe it. *That stuff was for the movies, not for real people. The United States didn't do things like that.* He thought of Vietnam. *Anybody who could do what they did over there can do anything.* It took a conscious effort to suppress the tears as he walked back to the plantation house.

Night, July 26 --- The plantation

Clay sat on the veranda with Maria, Tubs, Dr. Rodriguez and General Villasenor. Tubs had arrived in the late afternoon and the first ten percent of the arms destined for the new nation of Chiricahua was already safely aboard his old C-47. Three privately owned C-54 cargo planes, chartered through General Villasenor, stood on the grass next to the C-47, loaded with the remainder of the shipment.

Dr. Rodriguez stood and lifted his glass to Maria. ``To your health, Señorita. And to your success. We have worked well together. The herbal healing remedies you have brought us show great promise. I find this a very exciting partnership we have developed. I wish you and the Apache well. You have a very difficult time ahead of you."

Clay translated for Maria. She nodded and thanked the doctor. As they drank the toast, one of the house staff approached Dr. Rodriguez and whispered into his ear. The doctor turned to Clay and Maria. ``Perhaps we should retire to the lounge. A special news broadcast is airing in a few moments. It pertains to your new country."

Once inside the house, they walked briskly to the lounge and sat down. The broadcast began almost immediately.

ANNOUNCER: Tensions continued to build today around the Chiricahua Apache Indian Reservation in Southeastern Arizona, as the President ordered elements of the Army's 82nd Airborne Division from Ft. Bragg, North Carolina, into positions around the reservation to supplement law enforcement officials already in place.

In a prepared statement released today at the White House, the President said the Army troops were moved into position for the purpose of stabilizing the situation and to maintain order. He said the government has no intention of using force to resolve the crisis.

The Soviet news agency Tass was critical of the troop deployment, pointing out America's history of mistreatment of the Indians.

Four days ago, the Apache tribe broke from the U.S., declaring their independence, closing off the reservation, and claiming sovereignty as the Apache nation of Chiricahua.

The situation is further complicated by the fact that the Apache are holding the son of U.S. Senator Edward Williams and a friend. The two were tried in a traditional Apache Circle of Judgment yesterday for rape and murder. The senator's son was sentenced to death, the

272

execution to be at sunset, the day after tomorrow.

Public demonstrations in support of the Apache were held today on eight college and university campuses around the country. The largest crowd, at the University of California at Berkeley, was estimated at twelve thousand people. Demonstrations also took place on many Indian reservations around the country, and numerous tribes offered the Apache whatever help they could provide.

Hollywood celebrities Marlon Brando and Martin Sheen have each donated fifty thousand dollars to start a fund-raising drive to provide humanitarian aid to the Apache.

Late this afternoon, government sources reported they had cut phone and power lines to the reservation in an effort to pressure the Apache into turning over the two white men to U.S. authorities.

Just prior to the phone lines being shut down, we got this short telephone interview with Frank Redhawk, chief of the Apache separatists.

ANNOUNCER: Mr. Redhawk, the U.S. government has indicated that if you will just turn over the two white men to the authorities, they are willing to negotiate any demands you may have. Do you plan to take them up on this offer?

FRANK: No. We do not. In 100 years, no white man has ever been convicted and punished for raping an Apache woman. And that is not because such rapes never happened. This crime occurred on our lands. The white men were there illegally. We turned them over to U.S. authorities once, and they were set free."

ANNOUNCER: Are your people responsible for kidnapping them and taking them back to the reservation?

FRANK: No. They were delivered back to us. I am responsible for the decision to keep them and put them on trial. I sentenced them. And when the time comes, I will be responsible for carrying out those sentences.

ANNOUNCER: What about the government's offer of negotiation?

FRANK: We have been negotiating with the U.S. government

273

for one hundred and fifty years. Check the history. The Apache have never failed to live up to their part of negotiated settlements. The U.S. government has nearly always failed to do so. Nonetheless, we are willing to continue negotiating – except on two issues. Our independence and sovereignty are non-negotiable, and the two prisoners will not be released."

ANNOUNCER: What else is there to negotiate?"

FRANK: That's for the U.S. Government to decide. Historically, the Chiricahuas have been the heart of the Apache homeland. When the U.S. government moved west, all its actions relative to Native Americans were based on the European political tradition of ``might makes right." If a Christian, European nation ``discovered" a new land, and was strong enough to exterminate or control the native peoples who lived there, they considered themselves to have the ``divine right" to do so, and usurp the land to their own benefit.

We dispute that self-assumed right, and have exercised our own rights to our homeland. White men believe they have a divine right to divide the land up, buy it and sell it, pollute it, exploit it, and plunder it. We believe we have a divine right and a divine duty to protect our land, because we know it is our mother, as it is the mother of all things on it. We respect our land, we listen to it, we seek its wisdom, our spirits are strengthened by the love we feel for it, and we pray she might show us new ways to live in balance. Who's rights would you say are more ``divine?"

ANNOUNCER: What do you say to those who claim what you have done, and are doing, is a form of terrorism?

FRANK: You've seen the video tapes. Let the rest of the world see them. Let every individual person who cares enough to watch make their own decision about what we are doing. We are hiding nothing. Can your government say the same?

ANNOUNCER: If the government decides to use force, do you really believe you can win such a war?"

FRANK: It is my sincere hope and prayer that they do not make such a decision. It is unnecessary. We have no desire for a war with the

U.S. But if they invade our land, we will defend it. We may not be able to win militarily. But I assure you, every Apache who chose to join us in our independence is firmly committed to die rather than surrender. So, if the U.S. makes the decision to use force, they will have to kill every one of the seven thousand men, women, and children who are citizens of Chiricahua.

We may die in defense of our land, but if we do, the ideals of freedom and human rights the U.S. so loftily proclaims will die along with us. And the U.S. will be forever identified with the worst hypocritical, genocidal, totalitarian regimes of history. I repeat, we want only to be left in peace, and. . .

ANNOUNCER: The interruption of phone service to the reservation ended the interview there. Following this broadcast, we will air a special three-hour broadcast of the full video tape of the mass meeting leading up to the Apache declaration of independence, and the full trial of the two white men, Charlie Williams and Bruce Stinton.

Late night, July 26 --- The plantation

The mood was subdued as everyone said their good-nights after the special broadcast. Clay and Maria walked along the dark veranda towards their rooms.

``Things are happening too fast, Maria," Clay said finally. The knot in his stomach from the news of the arrival of airborne troops had not gone away.

Maria reached out to him and put her hand on his arm. ``You are doing all you can do."

``I guess you're right. We better get some sleep. No telling what we'll run into when we get back."

They paused outside Maria's room. She opened the door. ``Come inside, Clay."

He hesitated, then followed her into the room and closed the door behind him.

Maria didn't say a word. She turned, hands at her sides, and kissed him softly. He responded to the kiss in the same manner, his hands at his side. It was a long kiss. Their mouths opened slightly and it became a soft, moist kiss. Still their hands did not move.

Clay held his eyes closed and experienced a multitude of feelings, all of them good. He felt no weight to his body. He drifted in a vastness that was peaceful and euphoric. There was no time and no space – only being. The touch of Maria's lips and tongue fired needles of excitement through every molecule of his body. His flesh did a slow burn that began at the top of his head and flowed to his toes. A wisp of her hair touched his cheek. The scent of her plunged him deeper into the vastness that surrounded him. Slowly, softly, she broke the kiss, their lips lingering together as they pulled apart.

Clay breathed heavily. ``Maria. I don't . . .''

She put an index finger to his lips. ``Don't talk, Clay.''

She removed her dress and undergarments and stood naked before him in the dim light cast by the bedside lamp. Clay stood, mesmerized by her movements.

``You're so beautiful ...''

Again she put her finger to his lips. She undressed him slowly and gently. Clay tried to help, but his help seemed a hindrance. She looked at his naked body and he became aware of his scars from Vietnam. They seemed disfiguring next to the perfection of her body. She reached towards him and gently drew him to her. His ears rang and his heart raced. They touched the length of their bodies and Clay became lost in a world he never knew existed. They fell onto the bed in slow motion.

Dawn, July 27, 1979 --- The plantation airstrip

Clay watched from the grass as Tubs led off with his C-47. The three C-54s followed closely behind. After the news of the Federal troops arriving, Clay knew it would be too risky to land at the Bar-X. General Villasenor had made arrangements to land the planes at a dirt airstrip near Douglas, just south of the Mexican border. The cargo would be unloaded and staged until Clay could get the Apache to move south into Mexico, under the cover of darkness, and transport it safely back to Chiricahua.

He and Maria would follow a few hours later in the Beechcraft, after finalizing and signing the formal trade agreements.

When the last of the transports lifted off, Clay turned and walked back to the plantation house with Maria at his side.

In the library, he waited while the phone rang in the receiver. Maria sat in a chair nearby. Purvis answered, ``324."

Clay responded. ``Sir. 324 Zulu." Clay could hear the tension and fatigue in his old commanding officer's voice.

``Reference the data you requested. Several items of note. Particulars enroute to your bird handler's location. Should arrive late today."

``Yes, sir." Clay hung up the phone and turned to Maria.

``We have something on the senator."

CHAPTER TWELVE: THE TRANSFORMATION

Late Night, July 27 --- Mexico, just south of Douglas, Arizona
Clay tied the Beechcraft to the eye-bolts near the small hanger on the private airstrip. He stepped around the plane to the rear and met Tubs, who had just finished tying down the other wing. A bare lamp hanging over the hanger door cast a harsh light on Tubs' features. The older man smiled.

``That's one mighty fine lady you got there, Clay."

Maria had just left the plane to bring the horses Tubs had secured for them. They were tied behind the hanger. ``You don't have to tell me that, you old rascal."

``Maybe not, but I felt like saying it anyway. How was the flight?"

``Routine. I hope the ride across the border goes the same. You get four horses?"

``The best American money can buy." Tubs grinned from ear to ear.

``You're startin' to enjoy this too much, Tubs. Must be something wrong. Maybe you oughta see a doctor."

``If there was anything wrong with me, you couldn't get your

278

job done. Shorty gave me those papers that came in from Washington. He drove straight down to Agua Prieta as soon as Federal Express dropped 'em off."

``Where are they?"

``In `Betsy'. Where else?"

Clay put his arm over Tubs' shoulders. ``C'mon, old man. Let's get that envelope. Maria and I have a long way to go before daylight, and we've still gotta load the rifles on the pack horses."

Pre-Dawn, July 28 --- The Research Station

Frank leaned over the map on the table as Eddie pointed out the locations of the Apache defense forces.

``It's a pretty thin line, Frank, with no ammo reserves at all. I've tried to give everyone clean lines of retreat. If the Feds move in, our defenses are all going to have to be hit and run."

Though well under control, Frank could hear the tension in Eddie's voice. Frank understood it. He had been gripped by the same tension himself, ever since the U.S. had moved units of the 1st Air Cav into positions around the reservation, early the day before. Combined with the elements of the 82nd Airborne, and the law enforcement personnel already in place, Frank estimated that Chiricahua was now surrounded by more than 8,000 thousand heavily-armed troops.

He and Teresa had been monitoring the news broadcasts and he felt his gamble might be paying off. Public support was building, and there was mounting criticism of the use of the military, coming both from the media and from Congress. Indians all over the country were gathering weapons, ammunition, and supplies, and starting in convoys towards Chiricahua.

Frank hoped the federal troops had been moved in to prevent those reinforcements from getting through, and not as a prelude to an attack. But his knowledge of history, and his experiences in Vietnam, kept him from putting much stock in the President's promise not to use force.

All day and night, helicopters had clattered back and forth

overhead, and while none had attempted to land, Frank knew they were picking their spots, and doing their best to pinpoint Apache defenses. In an effort to counter the effectiveness of the aerial reconnaissance, Eddie had waited until dark and then moved all the defense forces to new positions.

``Excuse me, Frank.'' One of Eddie's officers stuck his head through the doorway from the next room. ``Teresa's on the radio. She says she needs you up at the Stronghold, fast. Say's it's important, and she can't talk about it on the radio.''

A jolt of fear went through Frank. He didn't know what was wrong, but he knew it had to be serious.

``Tell her I'm on my way.'' Frank turned to Eddie. ``I'll get word to you as soon as I can. I'll take my truck. If the Feds move and you can't reach me, do what you have to do.''

``I'll handle it.''

Frank wheeled the pickup through the narrow entrance to the Stronghold and drove as quickly as he dared to his campsite near the TV truck. Teresa was waiting for him.

``It's Danny,'' she said. ``He's taken six of his friends and they're headed for the Sun Sites Power Station. They're going to blow it up.''

``Goddamnit!'' Frank clamped down hard on the fear and anger Teresa's words triggered.

``How long ago did they leave?''

``About half an hour. On horseback.''

Frank took a deep breath and let it out slowly. ``Okay, tell me everything.''

``He showed up about forty-five minutes ago, asking for blank tape cassettes. Said he was going to get me some pictures of how real Apaches fight. He had the camera tied to his saddle. He's convinced the government is going to attack us. He said Apaches never sat back and waited to be massacred before, and he wasn't going to do it now. Apparently one of his friends worked at the government powder plant, near Benson. He'd stolen some explosives and hidden them somewhere on the west side of the reservation. They're going after them now."

Frank's emotions quieted as Teresa spoke. An icy calm settled in their place.

``You did well not to say anything over the radio. Use a runner to get word to Eddie. Tell him I've gone after them, to stop it."

``You can't go alone," Teresa said, fear in her voice.

Frank pulled her into his arms and held her. ``Taking somebody else would just slow me down." He hugged her tightly, then stepped back. ``After you get word to Eddie, find Henry. Tell him what's going on."

``What can he do?"

Frank's hand went to the shrapnel at his breast. ``Pray for me," he said.

Dawn, July 28 --- The Stronghold

In the gray of early morning, before the sun broke the horizon, Clay and Maria stood under a large pine tree facing Henry. Oscar and Elmer stood nearby. The rugged hills around them, covered in aspen and evergreen, stood out in sharp detail in the clear morning air.

Teresa greeted Clay as she approached the group. ``Clay! Am I ever glad you're back."

Clay rubbed the stubble on his chin. His eyes were red and watery from the strain of last night's journey. ``I'm not unhappy about it myself, Teresa. But, what are you doin' hanging around here?"

She smiled at him. ``You asked me to come. Remember?"

``Yeah, but that was only so you could get your story and report it as fairly as you could. I saw the tape in Mexico, and you did a helluva job, but I figured you'd be gone by now. Things have changed. There could be trouble. Big trouble."

He saw Teresa's glance at the stack of M-1s.

``Clay, you don't really think you can win a war against the United States, do you?"

``Teresa, I hate to do this, but I'm gonna have to ask you to leave Chiricahua."

``You have no right to make those kinds of demands." Her smile disappeared.

``As War Chief, I have the right to restrict the movement of the press in any area I feel might endanger the chances of our success."

Teresa softened. ``Clay, I'm not asking for any military secrets. I give you my word. I would never reveal something like that to the rest of the world."

Clay felt Maria's hand on his arm. ``Let me think about it a minute." *Why did I say that?* He turned to Henry.

``Where's Frank?"

Henry looked at Teresa, then back to Clay. ``He has gone to stop Danny Blue from destroying the power station."

``Destroying a power station? With what? Is he crazy? Who gave him the order to do that?"

``He has explosives. One of his friends stole them from the government powder plant, near Benson. They hid them in the mountains on the west side of our land until this morning. Danny took it upon himself to make the move." There was no emotion in Henry's answer.

``How did Frank find out?"

Henry smiled slightly. ``Danny told Teresa of his plans. She told Frank."

``And you didn't broadcast any of that information?" Clay asked Teresa.

She shook her head silently.

Clay turned to the stack of M-1s and picked one. He said nothing as he moved to an ammo canister and pulled out a bandoleer of ammunition. He felt Henry's hand upon his shoulder.

``You have other responsibilities now. The people await your orders."

``But, Henry. If Danny blows up the power station, he's starting a war. And Frank's alone."

``Frank is not without power."

``But ..."

``If a warrior turns away from an enemy before him, to face a new threat from another direction, he cuts himself in half. In matters of power, things must be dealt with in their own time." Henry's voice was strong and stern.

Clay wavered, then made his decision. *Henry's right. For the moment, at least.* He looked at Elmer and Oscar. ``Can you guys gather up the people? I want to speak to them in five minutes. Everybody in the Stronghold – men, women and children."

Oscar smiled. ``They've been waiting. They'll be ready in three." He and Elmer moved off at a dead run.

Clay looked into Henry's face and saw his almost imperceptible nod of approval. He felt stronger. He turned to Teresa. ``I reserve the right to restrict your movement, and to confiscate any of your material I think might compromise us militarily."

Teresa smiled.

``Film what you want of this," Clay went on, ``but hold it in your archives. My people will guard it until such time as I feel it can safely be released."

``Thanks, Clay. And, uh, Frank's already got a couple of guards on the truck, under his orders." She smiled.

Clay looked at her sharply, sensing a challenge. She didn't respond. Clay glanced at Maria, who merely looked back at him, a faint smile on her lips.

Clay looked back at Teresa, held her gaze for a moment, and then grinned. ``Okay. If Frank trusts you, I trust you. No limits. But remember, we're dealing with a lot of lives here."

``You won't be sorry, Clay."

``I know that." He looked at Maria and smiled. ``An angel told me so."

Clay loaded the M-1 as he walked towards the west end of the Stronghold which sloped up towards the peak that formed its western wall. He climbed the slope and up onto a large, flat rock formation. More than two thousand people filled the basin stretching down and away from him.

Clay's eyes roved the crowd. He didn't look for any faces yet. He was overwhelmed by the size of the throng. Many were women and children, but the women could fight like men, and many of the children could be useful in non-combat roles if it came to war.

An image of Oscar's son, Billy-Clay, dying in defense of his homeland passed through Clay's mind. He shook it off. He took two steps forward on the rock. The murmuring of the crowd ceased. They waited for him to speak.

``Greetings to all of you." His voice boomed into the morning, carrying far beyond the last of the Tinde.

``The decision has been made to claim this land as ours and declare it a sovereign nation. As a sovereign nation, we have the right and the duty to defend our country if we are invaded by a foreign power."

The crowd responded with subdued cheers.

``You have accepted me as your War Chief. I am honored by this. I know there are those among you who do not agree with this decision, and to you I say: If you can lead us better, then step forth. I want only success for our cause, and I will gladly step down if it will increase chances for that success."

Clay let the silence stretch for a time before he continued.

``Good. The time for doubt is over. We must now learn how to defend ourselves." He held the rifle above his head, in both hands. ``I have with me a case of M-1 Garand rifles and some ammunition."

The crowd cheered. He dropped the rifle to his side and held it loosely in his right hand.

``We have many more rifles, cartridge belts and munitions in Mexico, just south of Douglas. By tomorrow morning, we will have them here, if we work quickly, and with stealth. The federal government of the United States has troops along much of our border. We will have to use the skills of Cochise, Mangas Coloradas, and Juh to get these materials here safely. I cannot overemphasize this point. We must have these weapons.

``Not one of you will be forced to fight, but if you choose to

284

stay and fight with us, you will follow the orders of those in charge. I have appointed several other leaders to assist me in the conduct of war, in the event we must fight. All of these men are known to you. Oscar Gosheyun, Eddie Vasquez, Elmer Pipestem and Will Stonebreaker will be my leaders. They will assign others to command smaller units.

``Let us understand. If we fight, it is a fight we cannot lose. We must win or die. The commitment is total. So I ask you to be sure you are committed to a battle to the death before you make your decision.

``The spirits have spoken to Henry Laughing Bird and Frank Redhawk and have told them that the circle is complete. Now is the time for the Apache to reclaim the freedom that is theirs by birthright."

The canyon roared with cheers. Clay raised his hands. The crowd fell silent immediately.

``We cannot defend all the land we have claimed as ours, if we are invaded. That is why most of us are here in the Stronghold. We have made our capital in Portal, but it is too vulnerable to defend if we are attacked. Where we stand now is where the last of us will die if we are unsuccessful in the lowlands.

``We will keep a token force in Portal to maintain our government in modern facilities until such time as we are victims of aggression. We will have one thousand men stationed near the Research Station as our second line of defense. It will act as our military headquarters until we can no longer defend the position. If we are forced to withdraw, those of us who make it, will meet here with our main force. If and when the time comes, we will show the whites that we have neither forgotten how to fight or to die honorably. "

The crowd cheered wildly.

``Starting today, the leaders will give instruction on the use of the M-1 rifle. They will also make recommendations as to who should be given special weapons or assignments. If you have any military skills, please tell your leaders. We must use every skill we have to its maximum potential. Each Apache must be equal to ten Federal soldiers if we expect to win.

``Remember the old ways, and use the land to your advantage.

We know the firepower of the Federal Army, but they do not know our land as we do. They do not know our ways.

``Keep your Winchesters and Marlins. We will need everything we have. If you have old pots and pans, bring them to a collection point. Nails, old batteries – anything we can use to make fragmentation devices and bullets would be of great help to our cause.

``We have no time to waste. I will speak to my leaders after this meeting, and we will make arrangements to transport our arms into Chiricahua from Mexico. We will assign each of you to a small, seven-person unit. Each such unit will be part of a larger unit. Please go to your staging areas and wait for more information. I have much to do. I would like to see the leaders. May the spirits be with all of you."

Clay turned from the gathering of people and motioned to Oscar.

Oscar ran to his side. ``What do you need, brother?"

``Do you know how to handle an M-1?"

Oscar smiled. ``Hell, you know I was in the Army National Guard."

``Give a class to the other leaders. Have them pick their leaders and give them classes. Have those leaders give their men classes. Eddie will handle getting the rest of the weapons up here. I've got to go somewhere. I'll be back in an hour or two."

``Consider it done." Oscar turned and shouted for Elmer. Clay headed back to Henry's camp.

Henry sat with Maria under the big pine tree. Clay noticed Teresa off to his left, filming his every move. He sat between Henry and Maria, still holding the M-1 rifle. ``I've got to go after Frank, Henry."

Henry nodded slowly. ``But the Tinde also need you. Hold this thought in your heart as you do whatever you must do."

``I can't let Frank go up against Danny and his guys by himself. Not to mention the people at the power station."

``There is great danger there for you," said Henry.

Maria touched Clay's arm. ``Don't go, Clay. Send Oscar or one of the others."

Clay shook his head. ``They've got their hands full.'' He stood and slung the rifle on his right shoulder.

``I'm going with you.''

``Not this time, Maria.''

``We are one, Clay Price. I'm going.''

Clay looked over to Henry for help. He knew Henry's wisdom was not a thing to trifle with.

``Clay must go alone, Maria. Any help we can offer, we can offer from here.''

Clay turned to his horse, tethered twenty feet from where he stood. ``Can I get a fresh horse? Mine had a workout last night.''

Early Morning, July 28 --- A ridgeline on the northwest side of Chiricahua

Frank sat on a sandstone formation, using binoculars to carefully scan the flat expanse of the Sulphur Springs valley stretched out to the west in the early morning sunlight. He searched every dry wash and draw between his position and the Sun Sites Power Station which stood halfway across the valley, then scanned the detachment of U.S. forces spread out around the perimeter of the power plant. When he was finished, he breathed a sigh of relief. There was no sign of Danny and his friends, and that meant they had not yet crossed the Chiricahua border.

Frank brought the glasses back to his eyes and looked over the disposition of Federal troops ringing the reservation. There were not as many here, on the west side of the mountains, but they covered all the natural exits from Chiricahua. Even if he didn't spot Danny soon enough to stop him, the possibilities of him reaching the power station looked slim. But it would make no difference. If Danny and his friends were killed or captured outside the borders of Chiricahua, with explosives in their possession, the intended target would be obvious, and U.S. would have all the excuse it needed to invade.

Frank set the glasses on the ground next to him, and rubbed his eyes. The lack of sleep and tension of the last three days were beginning to take their toll. Adrenaline had kept him going in his ride to his current location. As he realized he'd made his first objective in time, the adrenaline receded and the fatigue settled on him again.

He placed the palms of his hands on the sandstone and let the energy flow up into him. He knew he didn't dare relax yet. He had to figure out his next move.

Leaving the Stronghold, he had known his options were limited. Even the most expert trackers among the people would have found it next to impossible to pick out Danny's tracks from the profusion of tracks leading in all directions just outside the entrance to the Stronghold. Since he couldn't track them as they went after their explosives, he knew his only hope was to try to cut them off before they could cross the Chiricahua border.

He had figured Danny would want to stay to the safety of the mountains as long as possible, before trying to cross the open expanses of Sulphur Springs Valley. From his current location, Frank could watch most of the logical routes out of the mountains. With luck, he would see Danny's group in time to stop them.

What he did not yet know was how he was going to stop them. Teresa had tried to get him to take a rifle, but he had refused. Something would not let him even consider using a weapon against one of his own people. Now he was questioning the wisdom of his decision. He worried at the problem for a time, and then heard again the Bear's words from the day before. ``There can be no certainty beyond the moment.''

Frank smiled ruefully. *Getting ahead of myself again*, he thought. *I've got to find them first.* He picked up the binoculars, turned to the east, and began searching the draws and canyons leading down out of the mountains.

After twenty minutes with no luck, Frank began to get worried again. Maybe he had underestimated Danny. Maybe Danny had considered this too obvious a place to leave Chiricahua, and had decided to cross the valley somewhere further south and attack the power plant from the Dragoons, to the west.

He started to turn back towards the valley, to search it again, then stopped himself. If Danny was coming out this way, every minute that passed increased the possibilities of Frank seeing them. If he was looking at the valley, he might miss them until it was too late to stop them. The confusion weakened him and he clamped down hard on it. His intuition had not failed him yet. He couldn't allow himself to start doubting it now. He started the Gahan chant softly as he turned back to the east and picked up the glasses again.

Before he could get them to his eyes, a movement in the sky above one of the canyons leading down past his position caught his attention. He raised the glasses. A large golden eagle glided in lazy circles. As Frank watched, the large bird banked out of the circle and with great, powerful thrusts of its wings, flew straight towards Frank. Halfway to him, it banked into a one hundred and eighty degree turn and flew back to the oak and juniper-filled canyon and began circling again.

With the binoculars, Frank searched the canyon. Almost immediately, he spotted Danny and his group slowly picking their way on horseback down through the heavy vegetation. A wave of relief rolled through him. He lowered the glasses. *Thank you, grandmother.* As if in response, the great bird broke out of its circle and soared off to the east. Frank watched until it swooped down and disappeared behind a distant ridge.

He raised the glasses again. Danny and his friends were still nearly three-quarters of a mile away. He scanned the canyon as it came down towards his position. There were a couple spots he couldn't see, but about a quarter-mile from where he was, he found what he was looking for.

Two side draws came into the canyon from the south, and the canyon narrowed and passed between sandstone walls on either side. At that spot the canyon was no more than seventy-five feet wide, and for nearly two hundred feet the violence of regular flash floods had kept the bottom swept clean of vegetation.

Frank got to his feet and put the glasses back in their case. He climbed down from his vantage point to where his horse was tied, hung the glasses from the saddle horn, and mounted. He didn't know yet how he would stop Danny, but he knew where he would try.

Frank covered the distance to the narrow canyon passage quickly. He tied the horse well away from the north canyon rim and walked west to the spot where the canyon widened out again. He found a split in the sandstone where run-off had created a narrow, natural stair halfway down the face of the rock, ending in a small, bowl-like depression about fifteen feet above the sandy canyon floor.

Frank made his way down to the bowl. It was just deep enough that if he lay in it he would be hidden, yet still be able to observe anyone moving through the narrow passage, from the time they entered, until they were right under his position. He stretched out on his stomach and waited.

The tension built with each moment that passed. Frank found himself trying to slow time down, to delay Danny's appearance, because he still didn't know what to do. He could call out to them, and order them to turn around and go back to the Stronghold, but he knew Danny's hatred of whites, and his desire to impress Teresa, would never allow him to obey such an order without a fight.

Frank heard them before he saw them, the rustlings of the horses through the manzanita and oak, an occasional murmur of soft voices, the strike of a horseshoe against exposed rock. Danny came into view first, followed closely by the others. The last man in line led a pack horse loaded with what Frank had to assume were the explosives.

Adrenaline pounded through Frank. He waited for the right words and they would not come. Danny threaded his way through the boulders, staying to the sandy bottom of the passage. Frank fought the fear that tried to rise in him. He began his Bear song, the rumbling, growling sounds echoing eerily off the canyon walls.

Danny reined his horse to a stop, holding up his hand. He pulled his rifle from its scabbard. Frank continued to sing. The other men drew their weapons. The horses danced skittishly on the sand.

``Come on out, Frank,'' Danny yelled. ``You're not going to spook me with that spirit way stuff.''

Suddenly the canyon was filled with the awesome roar of an angry grizzly's rage. The horses shied in terror, bucking and fighting the reins that kept them from racing back east and out of the canyon. Danny got off a wild shot before his horse reared violently, falling backwards against a sandstone boulder. Danny and three of the others were thrown. The Bear roared again. Two of the men raised their rifles. Danny had dropped his rifle in his fall and he ran towards it just as the others fired. Frank saw one of the slugs catch Danny in the back and slam him forward onto his face. Three more shots rang out at an invisible target. Once more a bellow of rage echoed in the canyon. Those still mounted turned and rode hard to the east, the men on foot following as fast as possible through the deep sand.

Frank stood up. He started to yell for the men to stop, then decided to let them go. He looked back to Danny. The young man lay unmoving in the sand. Frank looked around for a quick way down to the canyon floor. There was none. He stepped to the edge of the rock and jumped.

Frank rolled as he hit the sand, and ran to Danny's side. He dropped to his knees, his fingers automatically seeking a pulse in Danny's neck. He could feel nothing. The bullet had entered the left side of Danny's back, just below his shoulder blade. Gently, Frank turned Danny over onto his back. The young man looked up at him. Shock and pain contorted his features and glazed his eyes. Blood soaked the front of his shirt around the fist-sized hole in his chest. He tried to speak but no sounds came out. He tried again and Frank leaned down closer to listen. The sound, when it came, was a raspy croak, filled with hate. ``White eyes. . .''

A wrenching grief tore at Frank. He took the young man's hand. ``I'm sorry, Danny. . .''

Danny stared up at Frank, blinked once, exhaled a long, burbling breath, and died.

Frank could not contain his pain. He closed his eyes, threw back his head, and screamed a long, wavering wordless cry into the silence of the morning.

``Frank! Frank, are you okay?'' The shouted words echoed off the canyon walls.

Frank opened his eyes. Clay sat on horseback on the south rim of the canyon, near the eastern end of the narrow passage. Before he could sort out his confusion at Clay's sudden appearance, a blast of wind whipped around Frank, filling the air with swirling dust and sand. It was gone as quickly as it came, and as Frank blinked his eyes to clear them, he saw the dust devil leap from the canyon floor to the south rim of the canyon. It raced east towards Clay, growing larger as it moved.

Terror slammed through Frank. ``Clay, look out!'' he screamed. ``Run!''

Clay looked down at Frank, who seemed to be pointing to Clay's left. He looked left and saw nothing but a dust devil, expanding and gaining strength as it approached his position. He looked back down at Frank.

``Run!'' Frank shouted again.

From what? He looked again to his left, just as the dust devil engulfed him. The wind slammed small pebbles and twigs into his body, creating sharp, stinging sensations. Suddenly, the left side of his body began to go numb. Deep within him, he sensed a foreign presence. An alien hatred, so deep and dark that it frightened him, passed through his consciousness. His horse reared, frightened by the sudden onslaught of the wind. Clay groped for the saddle horn. He tried to grip the horse's barrel with his legs, but had no control over the left side of his body. He felt himself falling, felt the impact as he hit the earth, and lost consciousness.

Frank was on his feet, running for the east end of the narrow passage when he saw Clay go down. He raced towards a cleft leading up to the rim, and clawed his way up the narrow crevice. Clay lay fifteen feet from the edge of the rim, on his back, his left arm twisted under him. By the time Frank reached him, Clay was coming around.

``Don't try to stop me, man." Clay's speech was slightly slurred.

Frank dropped to his knees next to Clay. ``Take it easy. Let me check you out." He straightened Clay's left arm.

``Take your stinkin' hands off me!" The slur was still there but there was no mistaking the hatred behind the words.

``Goddamnit, Clay, I told you to run." Frank checked Clay's pulse. It was strong and steady.

``Hey, Doc. I can't feel anything in my left side. What's goin' on?"

Frank looked at his friend for a long moment. ``You want the truth, or an answer that makes sense?"

``What the hell kind of a question is that? I want the truth."

Frank paused. ``You just got caught in a Ghost Wind."

``What the hell is that?"

``Danny Blue just died down there. His spirit was full of hate. He's taken over the left side of your body."

``You're full of shit. You just want her for yourself."

``I warned you. The doctors on the reservations call it wind-induced stroke. Somebody gets caught in a dust devil, and they lose control over half their bodies."

``So who's controlling the other half, and how can they do it?"

Frank shook his head. ``I don't know how. But we do know that dust devils, or Ghost Winds as we call them, are dangerous. When someone dies, if they have not lived honorably, and the proper ceremonies are not performed, their spirits do not return to Ussen. They wander the land, often in the form of whirlwinds. When someone is caught in one, that spirit grabs half of the person's body. Danny got yours."

``Sounds like superstitious bullshit to me."

``Like the Wolf?"

``The Wolf is a myth, like all the rest of the old spirit way crap. The only ones that believe in it are old and feeble Apache and white liberals."

293

Frank shook his head. ``Are you listening to yourself? Are you hearing what's coming out of your mouth?''

``You're no better than the white eyes you're pretending to fight. You don't even know how to make it a real fight.''

Frank clapped his hands once, sharply, just in front of Clay's eyes, then blew forcefully on both sides of his face. Clay blinked rapidly several times.

``Hey, Doc. What's wrong with me? Why am I talking like this? Why am I saying these things?''

``You're not. It's Danny talking.''

``This ain't gonna work, Doc. Get me some help. Get me to a doctor.''

``I can get you to one, but doctors claim there's no treatment for wind-induced stroke.''

``What about Henry?''

``I don't know. He's the one who told me about it, but I don't know if he can treat it.''

``We gotta do something, Doc. I can't function like this.''

``C'mon,'' Frank leaned over and got an arm under Clay's back. ``Let's get you over into some shade. I'll get my horse, load Danny's body on him, and try to chase down yours. We can double up on him.'' He lifted Clay into a sitting position.

Frank returned with the horses and Danny's body twenty minutes later. Clay was sitting where Frank had left him, with his back against a rock ledge. Frank dismounted and walked towards him.

``We might have to tie you in the saddle. . .''

Frank saw Clay's right hand move across his body and draw the pistol from its holster. He stopped as Clay pointed the gun at him.

``You think you've got her all to yourself. But if I can't have her, neither will you.''

Frank feinted to Clay's right and dove to his left, rolling towards a cluster of rocks. The shot rang out just as he reached cover. He heard Clay struggle to get to his feet and fall back to the earth.

Frank probed out towards Clay with his mind, trying to reach him, to help him regain control. Without intending it, Frank found himself whistling the Marine Corps Hymn. He raised his head just above the rocks. Clay snapped off another shot in his direction which went wide of its mark, whining off into the canyon. Frank ducked back behind the rocks. He continued to whistle. He heard the Wolf howl from somewhere beyond the rock ledge against which Clay sat.

``Help me, Doc.''

Frank raised his head and looked over the rocks again. The Wolf walked around the edge of the rock ledge and stood next to Clay. Clay tossed the pistol away from him, towards Frank.

``Take the pistol, Doc. Keep it away from me. Get me to Henry.'' Frank could hear the fear in Clay's voice.

Early Afternoon, July 28 --- The Stronghold

Frank untied the ropes holding Clay in the saddle and eased him off the horse. With Henry's help they half-carried Clay into Henry's tent, set up well away from anyone else in the Stronghold. They laid him on a cot. Maria and Teresa followed them inside. Maria knelt on the left side of the cot.

``Maria, please don't stay here. Weird things are happening. I could turn into a demon at any second. I don't want you to be here if that happens.''

``You're not going to turn into a demon. As long as you can manage your fear, Danny won't be able to take control.''

``I still don't feel like a whole man. I don't want you to see me like this.''

``I've seen you in worse shape, if you'll recall.'' She leaned over and kissed him. ``But I understand.'' She rose and took Teresa by the hand. ``There is nothing we can do here.'' Teresa looked at Frank.

He nodded. ``It's best,'' he said.

Teresa and Maria left the tent. Henry turned and started to follow them out.

Fear surged up in Clay at the thought of Henry's leaving. ``Henry, where are you going?''

The old man turned back to Clay and smiled. ``To make food. It is past lunch time."

``Food? Henry, what the hell are you talking about? I need some help here."

Henry shrugged. ``I have never done this healing before. It is a dangerous thing to attempt. My power is greatest after dark. I dare not attempt it until then. For the moment, I am an old man, and I am hungry. You are in no immediate danger, so I am going to make food. Would you like me to bring you something?"

Clay shook his head in exasperation, then thought for a moment. ``I don't feel much like eating, but there is something. Maria has a manila envelope we brought back from Mexico. Will you bring it to me?"

Frank opened the envelope General Purvis had forwarded to Clay. He pulled out the documents inside. One by one he read them aloud to Clay, his hope growing with each new piece of data. When he had finished, he slipped the papers back into the envelope and tossed it on the floor. He smiled.

``With Teresa's access to the networks, we may have everything we need here to get the President to call off the troops."

``And we may not," Clay answered. ``You read what Bill said. He's violated all kinds of regulations to get this data for us. If we release it and it doesn't work, we've ruined the career and destroyed the reputation of one of the finest men I've ever known."

``It would have to work," Frank said. ``What he's got there proves Williams has hidden-ownership in companies that have stolen tens of millions of dollars from Indian tribes all over the country. It also proves he's been in the middle of a massive conflict of interest for at least the past ten years, going back to when he was head of the BIA."

``Yeah, and it also exposes his unofficial advisor status with the President on this whole thing. And the fact that he used his position on the Senate Intelligence Oversight Committee to illegally send a CIA assassin after Maria and me in Mexico." Clay paused. He looked into

Frank's eyes. ``But remember, Bill said he was trying to get this data through channels to the President. He asked us not to disclose it except as a last resort. Now, he's trusting our judgment. Let's at least be worthy of that trust.''

Frank sighed. ``Okay, you're right. We can't release it yet. But when the time comes. . .'' Frank let it trail off.

``If, and when the time comes, we release it. Bill wouldn't have sent it if there were any absolute prohibitions against release.''

Frank smiled. ``Fair enough. Now what's this about a CIA assassin in Mexico?''

The afternoon passed quickly as Frank and Clay talked, filling each other in on everything that had happened since they had seen each other last. When the news and business were exhausted, they talked about themselves, their lives, their experiences, their fears.

At sunset, Eddie called from the Research Station headquarters with an update on the training activities, and with a couple questions about where to place the mortars when they arrived. Clay answered the questions and signed off. He looked at his watch, impatience obvious in the gesture.

``It's damn near dark outside. Where's Henry?''

``He'll be here soon. I know you want this thing over and done with, but power moves at its own pace. Everything will work out.''

Clay looked at Frank. His expression softened. ``I sure hope you're right about that, Doc. If it doesn't, I'm gonna miss your sorry ass.''

Frank crossed the tent and sat on the floor next to Clay's cot. ``You're a better friend than I ever thought I might deserve, Clay. Whatever happens, this much I know. Our awareness doesn't end with death, and for my part, neither will our friendship.''

Frank pulled out his pocket knife and opened the blade. He held up his right hand and made a small cut on the web between the second and third fingers, deep enough so that blood flowed. He looked at Clay. Clay held up his hand, and Frank made a similar cut. They placed the two cuts together, their bloods mingling, and Frank clasped the joined hands with his left hand, holding them tightly.

Tears ran down both men's cheeks. After a moment, Frank released the grip with his left hand and their hands parted. With his right hand Frank reached out and touched the tears on Clay's face.

``Apache tears, brother.''

``Apache tears,'' Clay answered.

Four candles, one on each side of the tent, provided the only illumination as Clay watched Henry finish laying out a circle of quartz crystals on the floor around his cot. Except for asking Frank to leave, Henry had not spoken since re-entering the tent. He had dragged Clay's cot to the center of the tent and aligned it so Clay's head was to the west. He had lit and placed the candles, turned off the kerosene lantern, and smudged the interior of the tent with sage smoke.

He put the last crystal in place, then sat on a folded blanket on the floor on Clay's right, inside the circle of crystals.

Henry sat quietly, looking at Clay intently, his eyes roving up and down Clay's body. The silence made Clay uneasy. Henry's eyes seemed to penetrate deep inside him, leaving him feeling naked, defenseless, and somehow inadequate.

``Henry, I apologize if I seem impatient, but can we get started on this?''

``Your impatience is part of who you are, nephew. It is the drive of the warrior's Sun power. To apologize for who you are is to give away your power.''

``I just didn't want to seem disrespectful.''

``Disrespect is a matter of intention, not words.'' Henry smiled slightly. ``But to answer your question, we have begun. Before we can go further, there are some things you must understand.''

``That would be nice.'' Clay tried to smile and felt a momentary resurgence of the repugnance and fear he felt each time he was reminded he could neither feel nor control any part of the left side of his body. ``There sure have been a lot of things going on that I don't understand.''

``You are like many of the younger Tinde, Clay Price, a Tinde spirit raised in the reality of the white world. That reality is one of the mind, of analytical thought, and one of it's central laws is that it is the only reality, as they believe their God to be the only God, and their way of worship and belief, the only way. You have lived as an outsider in that reality, because as a Tinde spirit you know there are other realities, you know there are many Gods and Spirits, and you know there are many ways to worship.

``The Tinde give precedence to neither the reality of the mind, nor the reality of the spirit. To us, they are both parts of a larger reality which includes all possibilities. We seek to find in our lives a balance between the two, and that requires that we learn to operate in both.

``Everywhere you turn in the white world, you find agreements about the reality of the mind, the reality of logic, and denial of the spirit world everywhere except within narrow and restrictive limits. It is very difficult to maintain your awareness of, and ability to operate in, the world of the spirit when you live alone in a reality which denies its existence.

``Now you have come among the Tinde, and have become one of us. You find access to the spirit world, and its realms of power, opening to you. You are strengthened by the agreement of those around you about the validity and importance of the spirit world. Yet still, you find your experiences strange, and even frightening, because you have no foundation for them. This is the first thing you must understand."

Clay understood what Henry was saying, but couldn't understand what it had to do with healing the effects of the stroke.

``Henry, the night of the Great Gathering, I didn't understand totally what was happening. But I knew I felt like I'd come home after a long time away. I promise, I'm not fighting against any of these experiences just because I find them a little strange. I want to understand them. I just can't seem to get anyone to give me a straight explanation that I can grasp."

``That is because words are part of the reality of the mind, nephew. Power is part of the reality of the spirit. You cannot teach

299

someone about the reality of the spirit with words. You can only learn about it by living in it. That's what makes what we are doing tonight so dangerous. . .for both of us."

``What are we going to do?"

``Traditionally, this healing is a four-day process."

``Four days! Henry, I haven't got four days. In four days we could all be dead."

Henry nodded. ``I have consulted with brother Coyote about the matter. He says there is a way to do it in a matter of hours."

``Then let's get to it."

Henry grinned. ``Unfortunately, with brother Coyote, things are seldom straightforward. He also says this is possible only if one condition is met. You must be capable of operating independently in the spirit world."

``Why? I thought you were going to do the healing. I don't understand."

Henry reached up and put his hand gently on Clay's shoulder. ``If, as a healer, I do not have the time to do what is required; if I do not have the four days, I cannot do the healing. I can only guide, protect and support you while you heal yourself."

Clay was stunned. Fear raced through him. ``Look, I don't even know what the hell happened. All I know is that I've lost all feeling and control over the left side of my body, and there seems to be somebody in here with me that keeps taking over my mind and mouth, and even my body. I tried to shoot Frank, for Chrissake."

Henry smiled, and squeezed Clay's shoulder. ``But, you see, you do know what happened. There is somebody in your body with you. Danny Blue."

``But Danny's dead."

``Danny's body is dead, nephew. The spirit cannot be killed."

Clay shook his head in frustration. ``I just don't. . ."

``Close your eyes!" Henry's words were a sharp command that cut off Clay's protest. He closed his eyes.

``Now make a picture in your mind of the pinto horse you gave to Elmer."

Clay had no problem picturing the horse. He nodded.

``You closed your body's eyes. The body can die. The picture you are looking at is in your mind. But who is looking at the picture of the horse, nephew?"

Clay opened his eyes. ``I am."

Henry nodded. ``You – that is who you are. Not your body. Not your mind. You. Consciousness. Spirit. Awareness. Life, sent by Ussen to occupy the tiny body growing in your mother's womb, to animate it. You. You do not die, nephew. Danny Blue did not die. He is with you now, in your body, and you are going to have to get him to leave. It is the only way."

Clay sighed. ``Okay, I'll give it a try. But how? What do I do?"

Henry picked up a small bowl he had brought in with him, and held it out to Clay. ``You begin by drinking this."

Clay managed to prop himself up on his right elbow and looked into the bowl. It was filled with a watery, pale-green liquid like a Vietnamese peasant tea. Clay looked up at Henry.

``This isn't some of that peyote stuff, or something, is it?"

``Does it matter what it is, nephew? It will open the doors of the spirit world to you. Once you have passed through them, I can guide you, support you, even advise you, but whatever must be done, you will have to do."

Clay struggled into a sitting position and took the bowl in his hand. He looked at Henry. ``You said this was dangerous. Okay, I can handle that. But it might be easier if I had some idea of what kind of dangerous."

``Several kinds. As we leave this reality to enter the reality of the spirit world, we leave our bodies behind. They are vulnerable. They are like empty houses waiting for someone to move in."

``Oh, great, I get rid of Danny and come back to find somebody else in his place."

Henry nodded. ``It is one of the dangers. That is what the crystal circle is for. Protection. But it is not absolute. In Danny, we are

301

dealing with a spirit filled with pain and hate. He is like a wounded animal, tormented and striking out at anyone who approaches. He is an Apache spirit who has denied the reality of the spirit world, his own reality. He has been twisted by the results of the denial. He is trapped here by his rage.

``You are a warrior, trained in the harsh experiences of war. You instinctively respond to aggression with a stronger aggression." Henry took Clay's right hand and wrapped it around a crystal. ``Hear my words well, nephew. If you do that while in the spirit world, if you engage in a struggle, or contest of wills, you run the very real risk of being trapped there, as Danny is trapped by his rage."

``And if that happens?"

Henry shrugged. ``Your body dies. Or is taken over. When you engage in a struggle, the energies generated disrupt the harmony, and therefore the protection, of the crystal circle."

Clay nodded slowly. He took a deep breath and let it out slowly. ``Okay. What do I do if I encounter aggression?"

``I can't tell you that. Only you will know, in the moment of encounter, what is the right thing to do."

``How am I supposed to just know this? This is a pretty serious risk we're runnin' here, to be relying on faith."

``You do it by clarifying your intentions before entering the spirit world, and using your will while you are there only to hold those intentions in place. If your intentions are honorable, and in harmony with the intentions of the spirits who watch over us, then you will know what is right at any given moment. It will be the choice which maintains the balance, which maintains the harmony. The only faith you need is in yourself."

``Okay, let's start there. What should my intentions be? I'm pretty strong-willed when it comes to doin', once I've decided what has to be done."

``Only you can answer that question. What are your intentions towards Danny?"

``To do whatever it takes to get him the hell out of my body."

``And if he resists?''

``I said, whatever it. . .'' Clay stopped and grinned sheepishly at Henry. ``I guess I won't know what to do until he does it.''

Henry nodded his approval. ``And what about after he is out? What are your intentions towards him then?''

Clay thought about it for a moment. He hadn't considered it before. ``I don't know. I guess he's on his own.''

``To take over someone else's body, or maybe even yours again?''

``Look, I'm no healer. I don't know what to do to fix him.''

``I didn't ask you to fix him, nephew. I asked you what your intentions were towards him. Would you want him fixed, as you say? Would you want him healed?''

``After what he tried to do, I. . . well, yeah, of course I'd want him healed. I mean, I don't have much respect for what he did, but if he stuck around and took over somebody else, I'd feel pretty bad. I'd rather have him healed than have that happen.''

Henry laughed. ``You retain a hard warrior's edge, Clay Price. That is good. But you understand what I am telling you?''

Clay nodded. ``I think so.''

``There is only one other matter, then. The only way Danny was able to take over part of your body, was because you have a weakness, nephew.'' Henry shook his head. ``No, I don't know what it is. But it is something in you, in your experiences, in your emotions, so similar to the pain and hate and rage driving Danny, that he was able to latch onto it. You must find that part of yourself, and heal it. When you have done so, Danny will no longer have any way to hold himself in place. He will be gone.''

``And then? I mean Danny.''

``With the support of your intentions I will do what is necessary to return him to Ussen.''

Clay looked down at the bowl in his hand, then back at Henry.

``Do you have any other questions before we begin?''

``Just one. I'm willing to risk my own life doing this. I've got

303

nothing to lose. But you said this was dangerous for you, too."

Henry nodded. ``Should you end up in a struggle with Danny, I could not stand by and watch you both remain trapped. I would have to do something, and doing anything would mean risking getting trapped in the struggle myself."

Defeat flashed briefly but brightly in Clay's mind. ``I can't ask you to take that risk, Uncle."

Henry laughed. ``You are right, nephew, you can not. But I can choose to take it. You are important to the Tinde. If we are successful, the Tinde have a chance to survive, to heal, to grow. If we are not, the time of the Tinde will have ended. It is no risk. It is an opportunity."

Clay smiled, and nodded. ``Fair enough." He started to raise the bowl to his lips. Henry stopped him.

``Just for a moment, close your eyes. . . reach out and find the Wolf's presence. . .clarify your intentions well. . . now drink."

Clay kept his eyes closed as he raised the bowl to his lips. His heartbeat speeded up. He tipped the bowl and filled his mouth. The liquid was incredibly bitter, but he swallowed, and swallowed again, and once more to drain the bowl. He opened his eyes and tried not to grimace at the aftertaste. He handed the bowl to Henry.

``Hold your crystal," Henry said softly.

Clay picked it up off the cot.

``Lay back and relax."

Clay did so.

``Now, join me in the Gahan Chant. . .

``We are blessed in the Mountain Way,
The Gahan sing songs in our hearts.
We are strong in the Mountain Way,
The Gahan sing songs in our hearts."

Clay joined in as wave after wave of energy broke over his body, racing through him. The rhythms of the chant merged with the rhythms of the energy waves, and he rode those rhythms, letting his voice carry him. The tent and everything in it glowed with a faint luminescence, like the night of the Great Gathering.

Clay looked at Henry. He was surrounded by a field of blue, green, and white energies. His face changed. Years fell away, and a strong, mature, powerful Henry in the prime of life looked back at Clay.

``The doorway is behind you, nephew. The Wolf will show you the way." Henry's words had a strange, echoing quality to them. Clay felt as though he were hearing them with his body instead of his ears.

He turned around, and realized he was no longer in his body. The Wolf stood next to him. Before him was a huge tree, stretching hundreds of feet into the air. At its base, nearly hidden amongst the massive snarls of roots, there was an opening. The Wolf started towards it and Clay followed.

Clay stepped through and found himself in a long tunnel. The Wolf loped ahead, and the instant Clay intended it, he was alongside the Wolf and keeping pace. He saw an opening ahead. The Wolf didn't pause, and Clay followed him through.

The staccato sound of AK-47 automatic rifles erupted from the jungle to his right front. Someone tossed a grenade. It exploded harmlessly in the dense vegetation. The branches over Clay's head fell to the ground as the enemy fired a burst blindly at them from somewhere in the jungle.

Clay found an M-60 in his hands. He dove to his left, rolling behind a fallen tree. He put the machine gun to his shoulder and brought it up over the log, aimed in the general direction of the enemy. He started to pull the trigger and something jerked his hand away from the gun. The Wolf stood directly in front of the muzzle. From somewhere in the jungle nearby, he heard Henry call to him over the noise of the battle. ``Your intentions. Your intentions! Look at where you are."

Clay lowered the gun and turned around, laying on his back behind the log. He looked around. There was an air of familiarity to everything. He saw faces he recognized, Worm, Shooter, Brown, running, shouting, fighting, falling. Clay called out but they couldn't seem to hear him. Fear began to grow in Clay. Explosions continued to rock the jungle around him.

The Wolf nosed at Clay's shoulder. Clay looked at the wolf and it walked a few feet away, and then stopped and looked back over its shoulder. After a moment, the Wolf broke off his gaze and continued walking. Clay got to his feet and followed in a crouch, flinching at each explosion and scream of pain.

The Wolf led him into an open area, and the jungle in front of Clay erupted with small arms fire. He dove to the ground, his cheek to the dirt. Terror raced through him. He knew where he was. He tried to get up, to run.

``Do not struggle, nephew, it is your healing."

Clay ached with fear. Bullets continued to churn the ground around him.

``Clay! Are you all right?"

Billy stepped out of the shadows of the jungle into the clearing. Clay watched, horrified, as bullets from an AK-47 on full automatic ripped into Billy's stomach. Billy squeezed off one round from his M-14 as he fell.

``No!" Clay screamed and charged towards Billy. The Wolf leaped on him from behind, pinning him to the earth. Clay watched himself run, firing his M-60 in the general direction of the VC. He watched the VC bullets strike his arm and chest, then his side. He watched himself hold onto the machine-gun and felt the rage keeping his body upright. *I'm dead. So this is how it feels to die. I'm not going out alone. Jesus, just let me get some more.*

``Listen to yourself," Henry called, from somewhere far away. ``Listen to your heart."

He recoiled from the rage he felt as he watched himself fire the M-60 in the direction of the enemy. He choked on the hate that gave life to his determination to kill more VC before he died. A movement in the jungle drew a twenty-round burst from his gun. He watched the body fall to earth and shuddered at the momentary savage exaltation which surged through him, doing nothing to soothe the pain behind the hate.

306

Another enemy bullet struck him. He dropped to his knees, strength leaving his body. All firing ceased. *Where the hell is everybody?*

``Your crystal." Henry's voice called to him from somewhere nearby, an urgency to the words. ``Focus your attention on your crystal."

Clay looked down at the crystal in his hand. The world collapsed around it and he was alone with the crystal, floating in a timeless flux of multi-colored energies. Henry appeared before him.

``If a warrior fights, and kills, in defense of his mother, the land of his birth, if he fights out of love for that land, this is an honorable thing. There is great power in it, much wisdom to learn. Towards the end of our long war, we ceased fighting out of love for the land. The pain of many years of suffering had grown so great, we fought out of rage, and hatred. We fought for revenge. This is not an honorable thing, and we lost our power."

Clay saw it all at once. He knew why this one battle, of all his experiences in Vietnam, stayed with him with such freshness and clarity of detail. He knew why he had fought so hard, for so long, not to remember it. Not to talk about it. Not to think about it. He knew why he had stayed away from the reservation for so long. He was ashamed.

It wasn't that his carelessness in triggering the ambush, or his inability to get help, had resulted in Billy's death, something he had blamed himself for many times. It was how he had fought after seeing Billy shot. He had given in to hatred and a blood rage. He had exalted in killing those VC. He had tried to burn away his pain in the fires of a bloody and savage revenge. His memories of the event were void of any of the sense of sadness and remorse that permeated all his other memories of death in Vietnam.

Maria floated in front of him for a moment, and he knew he loved her desperately, and knew why he could not acknowledge it. He was not worthy of her love. He did not deserve it. He had killed in hatred and savored the bloody taste of revenge. Her image disappeared, and an overpowering grief filled him.

Apache Tears

He was back in Vietnam, staring at his body sprawled over Billy's.

He had been dazed, hurt, and exhausted. He didn't remember looking at any of the VC he had killed in detail, yet they surrounded him now. He knew it was them, bodies still freshly bloodied and torn, faces still contorted in shock, surprise, and pain. They silently approached him from all sides, moving slowly, inexorably closer, their hands raised to him, palm up, in supplication. Suddenly Clay became aware of Danny among them. Still they closed on him reaching out of their pain, until one by one they grasped a ring of dark, murky energy that circled Clay's chest. Clay recoiled from their need, from their pressing closeness, from their demands. He tried to shrink into himself away from them.

The Wolf appeared in front of Clay, lifted its muzzle in a long, wavering, mournful wail so filled with grief Clay felt something break inside. He knew the Wolf was crying for the pain of everything it had ever had to kill.

A tide of remorse and grief rose in Clay, and he wept. He wept for the pain of those he had killed. He wept in shame for those VC around him whom he had dishonored with his hate. He wept for the years he had held them in bondage to his secret shame. He wept because they were warriors, too, and he loved them. He forgave them for what they had done to Billy. He forgave Danny for what he had tried to do, and for taking over his body. He asked them for their forgiveness. Finally, understanding fully at last, he forgave himself.

The energy around his chest began to glow. It lightened to a purple, a violet, and then a pale, transparent blue. One by one, the VC let go and drifted away. A different kind of strength seemed to pour into Clay's body through an energy vortex in the center of his chest, a gentler, more resilient strength, a strength of balance instead of a strength of will. Clay looked into Danny's eyes. Danny blinked once, then let go and drifted away.

Clay floated alone in a timeless realm. A warm and gently pulsing energy filled him. The Wolf appeared before him. He knew he should follow it. It led him back through the jungle, silent now and deserted, to the entrance to the tunnel. He stepped through and felt a sudden sinking sensation as he flew through the tunnel and out the other end.

His body jerked on the cot, lay still, and then jerked again. He moved the fingers on his right hand, squeezing against the reassuring solidity of the quartz crystal. He moved his right foot. He took a deep breath and let it out slowly. He moved his left foot. He moved his left leg, and then his left hand. He probed with his awareness and knew he was alone in his body. He opened his eyes. Henry was standing over him, looking down. Clay smiled tiredly.

Henry returned the smile. ``Enju. You now have your spirit name. You have done well, Wolf Brother. Now sleep. You will need all your strength soon."

Clay closed his eyes, the peaceful smile still on his face. The Wolf licked at the last of the tears on his face like a pack adult cleaning a pup. Clay slept.

CHAPTER THIRTEEN: FIRST CONTACT

Pre-Dawn, July 29 --- The Stronghold

Clay awakened to the soft touch of Maria's hands and her soothing voice. ``You have much to do, my love. How do you feel?'' She kissed him on the cheek lightly.

Clay opened his eyes. It was still dark. Last night swirled around him like a dream, one in which he couldn't remember all of the details, but which he knew had changed him in some profound way. ``What time is it?''

``Almost four o'clock. The weapons are here. You are needed.''

Clay sat up and swung his legs over the edge of the cot. ``They're here already?''

He could see Maria's smile in the dim light cast by a candle in a corner of the tent.

``Isn't that what you ordered?''

He returned her smile. ``Yeah. I almost forgot.''

She held out a steaming tin cup. ``Would you like some coffee?''

He took the cup. ``Remind me to marry you the first chance I get.'' He took a sip of the hot coffee, burning the end of his tongue

310

slightly.

Maria's smile broadened. ``Was that a proposal?"

Clay shook his head, momentarily confused, then grinned. ``I guess it was."

``Does that mean you love me, or are you just making early morning small talk?"

He put the coffee on the floor next to his cot and reached up to pull her down towards him. He kissed her and held her head cradled against his chest.

``I love you more than I ever thought it was possible to love, Maria."

She sat up and smiled down at him, tears in the corners of her eyes. ``In that case, I accept your proposal. Welcome home, Clay Price."

When Clay was fully dressed, he and Maria moved out of the tent to the small fire she had going. He sipped his coffee and stared into the fire.

``Are you feeling okay, Clay?"

He looked up from the fire. ``Yeah, physically I feel pretty good. But there are a few things running through my mind that need a little clarification. It was like a dream. A really weird dream. And yet it was so real. I know it happened. There's no doubt in my mind. But how?" He shook his head slowly.

``You will understand how when it's time. For now, I'm happy you're back."

Clay was on his second cup of coffee when Frank and Teresa arrived. They sat on the ground and accepted coffee from Maria.

Clay became aware that Frank was gazing at him intently.

``Will you stop that? It's bad enough when Henry does it."

Frank laughed. ``Sorry. Henry told me about last night. I thought I'd take a look at the results myself."

``Well?"

``Well, what?"

``Do you like what you see?"

Frank grinned. ``Not a bad patch job. Especially for an ex-jarhead who used to throw his battle dressings away to make room to carry extra ammunition.''

``If there weren't ladies present, you'd get a properly improper response to that remark.''

Frank laughed. ``It's good to know the changes aren't too profound. Seriously, though, are you feeling okay?''

Clay nodded. ``A little light-headed. And everything I look at has a sort of glow around it. But other than that, I never felt better.''

Frank smiled. ``I'm really pleased.''

``No more pleased than I am, Doc, believe me.''

Frank finished his coffee and put his cup down. ``So what's on the agenda for today?''

``I've got to get down to the Research Station and see how the training is going. Then I've got to get the troops and weapons deployed. By that time,'' Clay shrugged, ``I'll have ten times more things to do than there will be time for.''

``I have a hunch that's the way it's going to be for a while, no matter what happens. I'm going to hang around the TV truck for a while. Try to catch the early morning news broadcasts. See what's going on out there since they moved in the 1st Air Cav.''

Clay nodded. ``We'll keep in touch by radio.''

``With your permission, Clay, I'd like to tape some of the training and deployment.''

Clay looked at Teresa sharply and she held up a hand and smiled. ``Just for the archives.''

Clay grinned. ``Sure. Maria's going down with me to help set up the casualty triage center at the Research Station. You can ride with us.''

Dawn, July 29 --- The southern ridge, overlooking the Research Station

Clay sat next to an M-60 machine-gun. He looked around and realized that sunrise was not far off. He reached over and turned off the

Coleman lantern. With him were Oscar, Elmer, Eddie, Will, and several others. In the pale pre-dawn light, he was just finishing his advanced class on the care, cleaning and operation of the M-60 machine-gun. Teresa's presence with the camera had made him uneasy at first, but the feeling had quickly passed. He looked up at the group. Each man sat cross-legged, part of a semi-circle around the gun.

``Any questions?"

No one spoke.

Clay looked down at the Research Station in the gray of the early morning, then back to the group. ``I know you've each got some men in your teams with military experience. Use them to train the others. Use every resource you have."

He turned to Eddie. ``Have all of those men in your team with mortar experience learn both guns – the 60 and the 81."

Eddie nodded.

Clay faced Elmer. ``I want the men assigned to the 3.5 rocket launchers and mines to assemble up the canyon east of the Research Station in thirty minutes."

Elmer nodded.

``Oscar, get your heavy machine-gun teams assembled with them. There are some important differences between the M-60 and the fifty-caliber gun that we've gotta cover."

Without waiting for a reply from Oscar, he turned to Will. ``I want to talk to you about your guerrilla teams. Let's take a hike. We can plan as we walk." Clay turned to Teresa. ``You want to tag along?"

``Sure."

Clay took one last look at the group. ``That's it, gentlemen. Unless you have questions."

They stood as one and moved in separate directions, solemn and businesslike, not a man speaking. Clay and Will turned and walked slowly east along the ridge line, Teresa just behind them.

``Will, I want to be sure we have no misunderstanding about your unit's function. The rest of the forces will fight semi-conventionally until we get pushed back into the stronghold – if it goes

313

that far. Your unit will use only guerrilla tactics unless I have to call you in to bail us out. If that happens, the men using longbows and crossbows should pick up an M-1 for as long as it takes to provide the needed reinforcement. Other than that, if the terrain or the tactics in any given fight are not right, you stay out of it. Understood?"

Will nodded. His experience in Vietnam with the 101st Airborne made him an ideal choice as the leader of their guerrilla unit. Will didn't talk much. He didn't have to. He had been there. He knew what was expected. And Clay knew he knew what was expected.

Clay stopped at a spot on the ridge which gave a clear view back up the canyon which ran from the west to the Research Station, as well as clear views on down the canyon to the east, towards Portal, and north up the road to the Stronghold.

``You want us to set up here?"

Clay nodded. ``Your command center, at least. The terrain's right for your kind of fighting. You've got lots of cover, so you can move in any direction. And you can see every approach to the Research Station. For the moment, protecting it is your prime mission. Nobody said you had to dig foxholes, or set up a defined perimeter. Handle it your way. I've got confidence in you."

``We'll get set up right away," Will said.

``Good. One other thing. I'd like you to let Teresa stay with you. Let her film your training and deployment. Just make sure any would-be TV stars keep their minds on what you're telling them and not on what she's doing."

Will looked from Clay to Teresa, and back again. He shrugged. ``Whatever you say."

``Thanks, Will. I'll check back with you later." Clay turned to Teresa. ``You need anything?"

She smiled and shook her head. ``Got it all with me."

Clay nodded. ``Then, I'll see you later. If you do need anything, Will's got a radio."

Clay started back down towards the Research Station. Behind him he could hear Will on the radio, calling his units to assemble.

314

Early morning, July 29 --- Cathedral Rock, two miles southwest of Portal, three miles east of the Research Station

Clay sat with his 7x50 field glasses and searched the hills for the Apache positions. He could see some of them, but that was only because he knew where they were. They formed a line high on the ridges southeast and northwest of the road running through the canyon below and northwest of Cathedral Rock, where he sat.

He moved his glasses to the road and searched each end of the canyon where the men were planting explosives on the hills on both sides of the road. The stream paralleling the road on the southeast presented a logistical problem, but it was minor. If the Federals sent tanks onto the reservation, there were some places where they might escape to the south, through the stream, and up the steep banks and onto the ridgeline. Clay watched as his men placed anti-tank mines in the suspect areas. He lowered the glasses and moved down the hill.

Fifteen minutes later he mounted his roan tied near the stream and followed the road west, back towards the Research Station. He was five hundred yards from the station when the distinctive sounds of M-16's triggered an adrenaline rush through his body. He stopped the horse, picked up the small, hand-held PRC-6 radio draped over the saddlehorn and listened.

``Red Leader One, Red Leader One. This is Blue Leader One. Over." It was Will.

Clay keyed up. ``Go ahead, Blue Leader."

``We've got contact in that draw about three-quarters of a mile south of the station. There are casualties. Over."

Will was breathing heavily into the radio.

``What is the estimated size of the enemy unit? Over."

``Ten or fifteen men. Looks like a special unit. Green Beret or Delta Force type. Over."

Damn. I put Teresa right in the middle of our first firefight.

``Do you need help? Over."

``Negative. We have medical help with us, and we have several

315

prisoners. It looks like two or three got away. They're fighting a running battle up the draw to the south. We'll get them. Over"

Clay smiled. ``Roger. I'll be at your position in a few minutes. Keep me advised. Over."

``Roger. Out."

Clay nudged the roan into a lope as he called the radio operator at the Research Station and told him to contact Frank with news of the fight.

When he arrived at Will's position, he was impressed by the professionalism displayed by the ex-airborne leader's men. The Federal troops were assembled in groups of two or three, each group guarded by two Apache. Clay counted nine Federal prisoners squatting, their hands clasped on the back of their heads. Teresa was off to one side, by herself, loading another cassette, and changing battery packs on the camera.

Will walked over to him. Clay pointed to three men laying in the shade under a cedar.

``Wounded. One of ours. Two of theirs. None of 'em are hit too bad."

``Good. We'll get 'em down to the station as soon as possible."

Will nodded. He pointed to three bodies, uncovered, laying in the shade of another cedar. ``They weren't so lucky."

Clay walked to the dead men. He looked down into the blank faces of two Federals and one Apache. The Apache was a young man in his late teens. Clay had seen him, but didn't know his name. He looked at the camouflaged faces of the Federals and felt the gut-wrenching pain of Vietnam. *They could have been in my old outfit. We could have been on the same side a few years ago. Killing is so stupid. There has to be another way.*

``You okay, Chief?"

Clay looked up at Will. He shook his head. ``I'm never okay when I look at a dead man – no matter whose side he's on."

``There are a few of 'em got away. Up there." Will nodded up the draw to the south. ``Our men are waiting." He nodded back at the

Federal prisoners. ``Judging from the looks of this outfit, I'd say they were sent in to grab the senator's son and his buddy. They sure aren't armed for long-term battle."

Clay walked to the stack of weapons. He picked up one of the M-16's. The serial number had been ground off. He checked another. Its number, too, was obliterated. He handed the rifle to Will. ``Spread them out among your men. But remember, we don't have any extra ammo for those M-16s."

``Got it."

Clay moved to the nearest group of three prisoners. He addressed the oldest of the group, the one who looked like a leader. ``This wasn't necessary."

The man remained silent, staring at him, eyes shooting darts of defiance.

``I appreciate your loyalty to your country, and I understand the training you've gone through regarding the code of conduct of a prisoner of war. You'll be treated fairly and humanely. But it's important that we know certain information. It is all information you are permitted to give. All I need are your names, ranks, and serial numbers." He panned the prisoners. No one spoke. They glared at him.

``My hat's off to you, gentlemen. You are well disciplined." He turned back to the man he had been addressing. ``Now, let's start over. What's your name, rank and serial number?"

The man glared into Clay's eyes. Clay leaned down close to him. ``Let me see your dog tags."

The man didn't move.

``I said, let me see your dog tags."

Still, the man failed to respond to Clay's request.

Clay turned to Will. ``Strip-search this guy."

Will turned and motioned to two of his men.

Clay looked at the next nearest group of prisoners. He saw something which made him hold up his hand.

``Wait a minute," said Clay. ``Just get them down to the Research Station. I'll talk to them there."

317

The sound of gunfire drifted down to them from up the draw. It was sporadic at first, then intense. Then there was silence. The PRC-6 radio in Will's hand crackled. He spoke into it briefly, then turned to Clay.

``It's over. We've got the last three of the Feds. Two of 'em are dead, the other wounded. One of our men was hit in the arm. It's minor.''

Clay clenched his fists. ``Damn!'' He turned back to the prisoners. ``This was such a waste. I know you men are soldiers of sorts, and just following orders, but damnit, this is insane.''

``Do you want me to get them down to the station?'' asked Will.

Still looking at the prisoners, Clay said, ``Yeah. Blindfold 'em.'' He moved to his horse, mounted and rode down the draw, towards the research station.

Morning, July 29 --- The Research Station

Frank and Clay stood at the window of the main room of the Research Station, looking out at the Federal prisoners sitting around under the Sycamore trees where the trial had been held. Four armed Apaches stood guard over them.

``That one,'' Clay pointed. ``The one with the blond hair.''

``Are you sure?'' Frank asked. ``He's got a lot of camo paint on his face.''

``It's him,'' Clay said. ``He had camo paint on his face in Mexico, too.''

``Have you said anything to him?''

Clay shook his head. ``I don't know if he'll tell us anything. But if he does, I wanted you to hear it.''

``Let's bring him in. We'll have Teresa come in and tape it.''

``We've got to do it right. He might talk to me, because he feels like he owes me, but not if he thinks he could get hung for betraying his unit. ``

``What are you going to do?''

``I'll have a guard bring the prisoners in one at a time. We'll

318

make him number four. I'll spend some time with each of them. Ask their names, ranks and serial numbers. I doubt anybody will tell us anything. This unit is under deep cover. Even the serial numbers are missing from their weapons. But I'll have to do it alone. You and Teresa can be in the next room. We'll leave the door ajar and she can film through there." Clay turned towards Teresa. ``If this guy's superiors recognize him, he's a dead man. Those are the rules the spooks play by. Can you disguise his voice, and distort his features somehow?"

``The features are no problem. Probably the best way to do the voice is to record some white noise, or static, over it ," Teresa said. ``It would be like a bad radio transmission, understandable, but with enough of the print missing from random places that the print couldn't be matched."

``Let's go for it," Clay said.

Frank and Teresa left the room and Clay had the first prisoner brought in. He asked a series of standard questions, got no response, and sent him back out. He went through the same routine twice more, and then had the fourth man brought in.

The guard turned and went back out on the porch, leaving a tall man with straw-blond hair standing alone across the desk from Clay.

Clay looked at him for a long moment. ``You know," he said finally, ``you're beginning to irritate me, Colorado."

The man Clay addressed as Colorado smiled slightly.

Clay indicated a chair in front of the desk. ``Sit," he said. He pulled out a pack of smokes, lit one, then offered the pack to Colorado. ``This group isn't even worth keeping as hostages, is it?"

Colorado took a cigarette from the pack and shook his head. Clay lit the cigarette. ``I didn't think so. The government is going to deny they have any knowledge of this whole operation, right?"

Colorado shrugged.

``So you guys must be working for some unknown power without the approval of the U.S. government, or so they're gonna say, right?"

Colorado shrugged again.

``Damned convenient.'' They smoked, and stared quietly at each other for a time. Clay broke the silence. ``I've gotta know, Colorado. How did you find me in Mexico?''

Colorado looked at his cigarette and back to Clay. He thought for a moment, then shrugged. ``A man's got to pay his debts, I guess. Radar. We followed you off that ranch from the installation at Fort Huachuca. An AWAC picked you up when you got out of Huachuca's range.''

``How did you know to look there?''

Colorado smiled. ``A good friend of yours, a senator, has a dossier on you about this thick.'' He held his thumb and forefinger out, about four inches apart.

``The good senator, huh?''

Colorado nodded.

``Was it really a sanctioned operation?''

Colorado shook his head. ``From what I hear, my boss owed the senator a couple of favors.''

``Is he behind this one too?''

``This operation is on U. S. soil. It took a higher authority.''

Clay put his cigarette out and stared into the blond man's eyes. ``The president?''

Colorado nodded confirmation. ``Of course, you'll never hear me say it. Personally, I think the whole thing stinks. I thought it was a bad idea from the start. But I'm a soldier, just like you. I follow orders.

``They thought we could sneak in here, pull off a successful snatch, and be out without any trouble. Just in case it didn't work,'' he looked around him, ``none of us has any I.D. We can't be tied to any official agency. We're just a group of patriotic Americans, trying to see that justice is done, funded by a wealthy philanthropist.''

Clay smiled. ``Thanks, Colorado. I'm going to put you back with the others now. You've been supremely unhelpful, as always. Guard!''

The guard stuck his head in the door. ``Take this man back.

Send in the next."

It took almost half an hour for Clay to finish seeing each of the nine unwounded prisoners. When the guard came in to escort the last man back out, Clay stopped him.

``When you get this guy back, contact Will. Have him get a team down here to search all of these guys. Make a record of all their personal possessions, if there are any. Get me an inventory of what you find. Then take their boots and socks, blindfold them, and get them up to the Stronghold. Put them in a cave with a couple guards on them. Make sure they have adequate food and water, but there's no need to overdo the traditional Apache hospitality bit. We're not the Hilton, and our supplies are limited. Any questions?"

``No, sir. I'll take care of it."

The guard left, taking the last prisoner with him. When he had closed the door behind him, Frank and Teresa came back into the room and sat down across from Clay.

``You get it on tape?" Clay asked.

Teresa nodded. ``I never got a clear shot of his face, but I got everything he said, and enough to tell he's the one saying it."

``What do you think?" Frank asked.

``He's got no reason I can see to lie."

``Do you think you could get him to repeat it on a live linkup with the networks?"

Clay shook his head. ``I let him go in Mexico. He figures he's repaying the debt by tellin' me what we're up against. But we won't get anything else out of him."

``It might be worth a try," Frank said. ``He sounds like he thinks the government's way off base here."

``He probably does," Clay answered. ``But agree or disagree, he's a professional. He's said his piece. I mean, if you want me to try. . ."

Frank shook his head. ``Leave it. You're probably right."

``Can you use what you've got?" Clay asked.

Frank thought for a moment. ``I'm sure going to try. Teresa got

321

some tape of the battle. She say's Will gave them plenty of warning, and that they opened fire first. I think we'll head back up to the truck and see if we can put it together with this stuff. I don't see any advantage in not releasing it right away."

``The networks will snap this stuff up," Teresa said.

``How so?" Clay asked.

``The President promised he wouldn't use force. This tape proves he broke his word. The networks love to be able to turn up the heat on the White House."

``That tape doesn't prove anything," Clay said. ``It might strongly suggest it, but we've got nothing but Colorado's word tying these guys to the President."

``With the networks, a strong suggestion will do just fine," Teresa said. ``They leave the proof to the courts."

``And we've got the Purvis data confirming the Mexican connection," Frank said.

Clay looked at him sharply.

``I'm not suggesting we release it yet," Frank said. ``Just pointing out we do have it, if and when the time comes."

Clay sighed and rubbed at his face with his hands. ``Let's hope what you've got is enough. When you get it put together, if it looks weak, let me know. We'll talk about the Purvis data."

Frank looked at Clay closely. ``You okay?"

Clay nodded. ``Just tired of the killing and pain, Doc. Maybe I'm gettin' old or something. I looked at those bodies up there, and it just all seemed so goddamn senseless and unnecessary. We don't want a war. Do we?"

Frank shook his head. ``No, brother, we don't want a war. But like you said. Freedom doesn't come easy or cheap."

Clay smiled tiredly. ``You'd think we'd learn, wouldn't you? You'd think after all the deaths, and all the bloodshed, and all the agony, that we'd learn."

Frank tried to lighten his friend's mood. ``Maybe it's better that we don't. All you war chiefs would be out of work."

Clay looked at him seriously. ``I'm beginning to think that might not be such a bad idea. You pick up any encouraging news this morning?''

``Some,'' Frank said. ``There's more demonstrations, and they're getting bigger. And not just on college campuses and reservations, either. There were close to seventy thousand people on the mall in Washington last night. And nearly as many in Los Angeles and New York.

``Four other reservations have kicked all the BIA people off and have closed their borders, but nobody else has declared independence yet. The President's taking heat from Congress about moving the 1st Air Cav in. His `maintaining public order' excuse is wearing thin.

``Ever since the networks did their special broadcasts of the whole tape, support has been building. The government has backed off the kidnapping and terrorist angle, and William's has been `unavailable' for comment.''

Clay nodded and sighed again. ``Encouraging, but a long way from conclusive.'' He put the palms of his hands flat on the desktop and pushed himself up. ``I guess while you go fan the flames of public outrage, I'd best get back to looking after our defenses.'' Clay paused. ``And don't worry about putting me out of work. I need a vacation anyway.''

Mid-Day, July 29 --- *The Stronghold*

Frank was checking on the conditions of the Apache and Federal wounded when he saw Teresa running towards him from the TV truck. He met her halfway.

``It's Perkins. The head of the BIA. He wants to talk to you. I was finishing the editing when he was patched through by my station in Tucson.''

Frank nodded and thought for a moment as they walked back towards the truck. The government probably knew by now that their rescue attempt had failed. Even if the rescue force had not managed to get radio word out, they would have been long overdue by this time.

Maybe this was a first step in trying to open negotiations. But it was the wrong first step.

``Tell them I said we have nothing to discuss with the Bureau of Indian Affairs. Tell them, if they want to talk to me as the leader of the nation of Chiricahua, I'd be happy to speak with an authorized representative of the State Department."

Teresa looked surprised.

``If we can force them to negotiate with us through the State Department, we've forced them into dealing with us as an independent nation. If we let them try to handle it through the BIA, they continue dealing with us as a bunch of renegade Indians rebelling against the great white father in Washington."

``But, if it would save lives," Teresa started. Frank cut her off.

``You were at the Gathering. You know the commitment."

She nodded. ``I guess I hoped it wouldn't come to that."

``So did I," Frank said. ``I still do. But that commitment is the best weapon we have. Our only real hope is that the American people will not allow their government to massacre seven thousand men, women, and children rather than give us our freedom."

Frank saw the pain in Teresa's eyes. Across the Stronghold, the mother of the Apache youth slain in the early morning raid raised her voice in a keening wail of mourning. Frank put his arms around Teresa and held her. ``Tell them what I said. Then tell your bosses at the station to keep the link open for another release. Tell them I'll have a live statement immediately afterwards." He kissed her gently. ``Go on."

Frank waited next to the door outside the truck, listening to the conversation. When she was done, Teresa turned to him.

``They're standing by."

``Have you got the tape ready to go?"

She nodded.

``Good. Go ahead and release it. Then get your camera and I'll make my statement."

Ten minutes later Frank stood in front of the camera, holding a microphone. Teresa signaled him when the live link was operative.

Apache Tears

``I am Frank Redhawk, Chief of the Chiricahua nation. For days now, the President of your United States has been telling you he would not use force in dealing with our move to independence. This morning he sent a heavily armed force of sixteen men into our land. They were sent in without identification, and with the serial numbers removed from their weapons, so that if they failed in their mission, the President could deny any responsibility."

Frank held up one of the rifles. Teresa focused the camera on the area where the serial number had been ground away.

``When that invading force was spotted and challenged, and given the opportunity to surrender, they chose to fight. Four died. Three were wounded. Nine were taken prisoner. One seventeen-year-old Apache man was killed defending his land. Three were wounded.

``These deaths and injuries were absolutely senseless and totally unnecessary. We seek no war with the United States. We seek no revenge or retribution for past wrongs. Hear me. We want nothing except to be left alone to live our lives in our own way.

``The footage you have just seen is a graphic illustration of the way the U.S. Government has dealt with Native Americans all over the country for the past two hundred years; one set of benevolent and humanitarian words, promises, and proclamations for public consumption, and another hidden agenda formulated and carried out with no regard whatsoever for the lives or rights of Native Americans.

``Now, each and every one of you, as individual American citizens, must make a choice. You must decide if you are going to go on tolerating a government of hypocrisy and lies, or demand a government of open, honest men who will do their best to live up to the ideals expressed in the Constitution and Bill of Rights upon which your country was founded.

``No one else can make that choice for you. And it is not necessarily an easy choice. If you decide you have had enough, your conscience will demand you do something to back up that decision, to make it meaningful. If you decide liars and hypocrites are the kind of leaders you want, you will have to learn to live with that unpleasant

325

truth about yourselves.

``There is little more I can say. We do not want war. But I assure you, no matter what size armed force the U.S. sends across our borders, we will fight. There will be more deaths, more injuries, more suffering. On both sides. We have made our choice – to be free, or die in defense of our freedom and our land. Whether we live or die is a choice that is now in your hands. You can still stop your government. Or you can stand by and watch a blood bath. May the spirits help you live with the results of your choice."

Frank lowered the microphone and Teresa switched the camera off, set it on the ground, and re-entered the truck. Frank coiled up the microphone cord and laid it next to the camera.

He sat cross-legged on the ground, elbows on his knees, his head in his hands. His first thought on awakening that morning had been of Charlie. His execution was scheduled for sundown. The thought had instantly filled Frank with dread. For a time, the firefight and broadcast had driven thoughts of the execution from his mind. Now they were back, and the day seemed to stretch endlessly before him. He wanted sundown never to come, and he wanted it to be now, to have it over with.

Teresa came back out of the trailer and sat down next to him, putting her arm around his shoulders.

``They loved it," she said. ``They're going to use all of it, and they're preparing it for feed to the networks and wire services right now."

Frank looked up at her and tried to smile. He knew it never reached his eyes. Teresa looked into them for a long time.

``Isn't there any other way?" she asked gently.

Frank shook his head. ``I sentenced him. It's my responsibility to carry it out."

``Could you change the sentence?" Teresa asked. ``I've been thinking about it. The networks have run the tape of the trial. Everybody knows he is guilty. If you turned him over to them now, they would have to put him on trial."

``On trial, yes," Frank said. ``But imprison or execute him? A U.S. Senator's son? You know how the justice system works as well as I do." Frank shook his head. ``If there's another way, power has not yet revealed it to. . ."

Frank looked up as one of Eddie's men, who had been standing radio watch by Frank's paramedic truck, came running up.

``Henry just called. He's down at the Research Station. He said you'd better get down there as soon as possible."

Adrenaline flooded through Frank. ``Are the Federal troops moving in?"

``No. He said it's something with that senator's son."

Early Afternoon, July 29 --- The Research Station

``Please, Daddy, don't hurt me. . . please, don't. . . I love you, Daddy, please don't. . . it hurts. . . I promise. . . please don't hurt me."

Charlie groveled on the floor in the corner of the room, his face smeared with tears and mucous from his nose, his voice that of a child, filled with pain and terror, eyes staring into space as he cringed away from someone only he could see.

Frank turned away from the door, shuddering as a wave of horror passed through him. The guard closed the door to Charlie's room, and Henry took Frank by the shoulder and led him out of the Research Station and across the road to sit on the earth under the Sycamore trees.

``His spirit has been pulled back in time by his pain and fear," Henry said softly. ``It is trapped there. Only his emotions remain."

Frank shuddered again. ``Your words are like knives in my heart, uncle. If I execute him now, he will remain trapped."

Henry nodded.

``His spirit would be forever cut off from Ussen."

Henry nodded again. ``He would become one of the dark ones."

``Could we reach him?" Frank asked. ``Bring him back?"

``All things are possible, nephew. But why do you wrestle with power?"

Frank thought about the question. He heard the Bear again. *In matters of power, Walks-With-Bear, there is no certainty beyond the moment itself.* He knew what he had to do.

``I want to call an emergency council, uncle. Here. As quickly as possible."

Mid-Afternoon, July 29 --- Sycamore grove near the Research Station

Clay, Maria, Elmer, Oscar, Eddie, Carla, and Henry sat with Frank in a circle, Frank in the west. Teresa stood outside the circle with her camera ready.

``You have all seen Charlie. You all know he has been sentenced to die at sunset tonight. You all know it is my responsibility to carry out the sentence."

Frank paused and looked around the circle. ``If I do so, now, while his spirit is trapped back in the pain and fear of his childhood, it will remain trapped there, forever lost in time. He will become one of the dark ones of the spirit world. I am not willing to take the responsibility for doing that to someone."

``What difference does it make what kind of crazy he is?" Clay asked. ``He was never very sane to begin with."

``It's not a matter of crazy or sane, Clay. When he raped and shot Angela, when he screamed obscenities at the old ones in the Circle of Judgment, he was present, his spirit was present, choosing those actions. If he were executed with his spirit present, we could do the necessary ceremonies to ensure that he returns to Ussen to be cleansed and healed. But he is not here now. He is trapped back in time. If he dies now, he remains trapped there forever. I can't do that."

``How can you be so sure he's not fakin' it? He's the kind of creep that will do anything to keep from dying when the chips are down. Even if it means degrading himself to the level he's at now," said Clay.

Frank looked into Clay's eyes. ``You have seen him. Do you think he's faking?"

Clay shrugged. ``I'm not sure."

``If there is a doubt in your mind, then he must not be executed," said Frank.

Clay said nothing.

Frank looked around the circle again. ``It is your right, under these circumstances, to replace me as your chief. If you choose not to replace me, I intend to have Charlie Williams taken to our border at sunset tonight, and released to U.S. military representatives. I propose to give his father, who inflicted the pain and fear which now hold Charlie trapped, the responsibility for deciding his fate."

Again, Frank looked slowly around the circle. ``I ask you, then. Do you wish me to step aside?"

The songs of the birds overhead, and a distant rumble of thunder, were the only sounds in the grove. Frank let the silence stretch out a long time before he broke it.

``Let's get it done, then." Frank turned to Eddie. ``We'll put him in the back of a pickup. A fast one. I'll need three men, a driver and two men to unload the stretcher at the border."

``No problem."

Frank looked at Clay. Before he could speak, Clay grinned. ``I'll have our best marksmen in position to cover them. And a few pre-plotted mortar settings."

``Nothing outside our border," Frank said.

Clay shrugged. ``I can guarantee you no explosions outside our border. But I can't control where the shrapnel goes."

``Fair enough. I'm going to head up to the Stronghold and have Teresa patch me through to her station. I'll let them know what's happening. I'm going to restrict them to three men and an open vehicle. Can you think of anything else?"

``A half-mile buffer zone," Clay said. ``One vehicle and three men. If anybody else comes closer than a half-mile, we will consider them to have hostile intent."

Frank nodded, and looked quickly around the circle. ``We don't have time for a full gathering of the people. I need the rest of you to make sure that a full and accurate account of this decision is communicated to them. Tell anyone who has serious questions or problems to come to me directly. And please see to it that they do so. We don't need any rumors."

The council broke up and Frank and Clay walked together towards the creek where Clay's horse was tied. Neither spoke until they reached the horse. Clay untied the reins and stood with them in his hand.

``It's a good thing I got that transfer to the Navy and corpsman school," Frank said, scuffing at the ground with the toe of his boot. ``I guess I wouldn't have made much of a marine, would I?"

Clay looked at Frank for a long time, and then grinned. ``Doc, I swear I never thought I'd be saying it about a swabby, but in my book, you'd have made an outstanding marine."

Frank smiled. ``Thanks, brother, for everything."

Clay swung up into the saddle. ``It ain't over till it's over, Doc. But until it is, you can count on me."

He rode off towards Portal.

Evening, July 29 --- The Stronghold
The transfer of Charlie Williams took place without a hitch. Clay, Maria, Henry, Teresa and Frank were all packed into the TV truck, watching the network news special which had become a nightly event.

With the news of the first actual fighting and casualties, demonstrations had doubled in size and number across the U.S. Reports were coming in of smoke-jumper teams from reservations as far away as the Mohawks, in northern New York, arming themselves, packing equipment and supplies, and planning to parachute into Chiricahua as reinforcements. Indians were leaving active-duty military posts and returning to their reservations. Some were reportedly heading for Chiricahua.

Criticism was mounting fast in congress and impeachment talk was being heard. Fundraisers were stockpiling food and supplies and trying to figure out how to get deliveries through the Army blockade.

Apache Tears

There was coverage of Charlie's release, pictures of the military picking Charlie up, bringing him back, and transferring him to an ambulance. Then the tape Teresa had made. Pictures and sounds of Charlie cringing in the corner, crying, begging Daddy not to hurt him. Frank watched his own image and listened to his own words.

``Daddy is Senator Edward Williams. Listen to his son. ``Please don't hurt me, Daddy." Daddy is an Indian expert. He's the former head of the Bureau of Indian Affairs. Listen to his son. ``Daddy, please don't hurt me anymore." Daddy is working behind the scenes advising your president on how to handle the matter of our independence. Listen to his son. I think you'll find Daddy has lots of skeletons in his closet."*

The broadcast switched live to Washington, where a reporter asked the president, ``Now that they've shown their good faith by releasing the senator's son, Mr. President, are you ready to withdraw the troops?"

The president did not hesitate in his answer.

``There is still another American citizen being held hostage on the reservation. If he were released, then I think it might be time to pull back some units while we work things out. At that point, Chief Redhawk would be welcome to come to Washington to sit down with congressional leaders and the people from the Bureau of Indian Affairs, and I'm certain some peaceful solution could be worked out."

A mixture of adrenaline and fear surged through Frank at the words. He reached out and switched the set off.

``They're coming," he said. ``Tonight. Or first thing in the morning. They're coming in force."

331

CHAPTER FOURTEEN: OPEN CONFLICT

Dawn, July 30 --- A ridge, west and south of Portal.
Clay watched as Eddie moved toward him in a crouch. The ex-tribal policeman stopped and squatted next to Clay who sat behind a fallen tree trunk, watching the approach to the Research Station.

``It's done,'' said Eddie. ``The wire is right behind me. Elmer and one of the guys from Oscar's unit are stringing it.''

Clay nodded and looked down at the small plunger on the ground near his right knee. He looked back up at Eddie. ``Have the rest of the men fall back to their assigned positions.''

Eddie hesitated. ``Clay, I can set these charges off. You're awfully exposed out here.''

Clay sighed. ``Thanks, Eddie, but I'll handle it. I hope it won't be necessary, but if it is, I've gotta be the one. I want to try to trap as many as possible. If I let someone else do it and it goes wrong, I wouldn't know whose fault it was. This way, I know who to blame.''

``But you're too close to the road. I think we should run more wire – up into the hills behind us.''

``We've gotta save as much of that wire as we can.'' Clay smiled. ``We don't have the same budget as our worthy opponents.'' His

332

smile faded. ``Besides, I can see both ends of our trap real good from right here."

``Then let me and one of my teams stay here with you."

Clay looked deeply into Eddie's eyes. ``I appreciate what you're saying, Eddie. But it only takes one man to push the plunger down. We're not going to fight the way they fight. Each man has got to be his own army. Take your men to your positions and be ready."

Elmer puffed his way to their position. He and another man crouched low on either side of a large roll of det-wire, unwinding it from the spool as they duck-walked along the steep slope of the hill. They stopped next to Eddie and Clay, and set the half-empty spool on the ground.

``Damn, brother, it didn't look that far up to here," puffed Elmer.

Clay smiled. ``You're gettin' old, Elmer. Cut it there and see if you can drag yourself and what's left of the spool up the hill and take your position."

``Old?" Elmer displayed a mock look of injured pride. ``I'll show you what old is after we've whipped the cavalry." He cut the wire, turned and moved quickly up the hill in a low crouch, the second man following.

Eddie shook his head. ``I still can't believe the change in Elmer."

``Quit stallin', Eddie. Take your position," said Clay as he stripped the ends of the wire and wrapped them around the metal posts on the plunger. He tightened the thumb-screws.

A serious look came over Eddie's face. ``Be careful, Clay." He turned and moved up the hill.

Clay watched him go until he was hidden in the pinions, then turned his attention to the road winding its way through the narrow canyon. He put his 7x50 field glasses to his eyes and searched the east end of the canyon, where it opened to the flat land around Portal. He glanced skyward and took note of the build-up of heavy cumulus clouds.

He saw the Apache evacuating the town. Everything of value to the provisional government had been removed last night. But a token force had been left behind to claim the town until it became obvious the U.S. intended to use force. The movement below and to the east of his position told Clay the U. S. armored column he had seen staging during a pre-dawn reconnaissance was moving in on Portal.

He shifted his glasses to the east of the town and saw the thick clouds of dust, turned a rosy pink by the early morning sun. Adrenaline pumped through his veins. He felt the shaky, heavy thumping in his chest. On the leading edge of the dust, he picked out the first vehicle in the column. *A tank! I guess they mean business this time.* He moved the glasses back to the convoy of pickup trucks evacuating the last of the Tinde out of Portal and tried to pick out Frank. The distance was too great for positive identification.

Why in the hell did he have to go to Portal? He should have stayed at the Research Station.

He glanced again to the armored column, and saw dark specks, five hundred feet in the air, emerging from the thick clouds of dust. *Helicopters!*

He searched the sky for fixed-wing aircraft but found none. *They're so confident we'll roll over and play dead they aren't bringing in the jets. Yet.*

Clay removed the glasses from his eyes and glanced down at the 3.5 rocket launcher leaned against the tree trunk. *Maybe I should have let Eddie stay, just in case. Sure would be a lot quicker loadin' that thing with an assistant gunner.*

He picked up the small PRC-6 radio near his knee. ``They lead with an iron horse. They have hawks to guide them. Teams six and seven come into play." He unkeyed the mike.

``Roger. Copy teams six and seven." The radio went silent.

Clay looked through his glasses again. The last Apache vehicle passed the first set of explosive charges. The armored column advanced through Portal and continued west on the road, in pursuit of the fleeing Apache.

Apache Tears

They're not going to stop in town! Clay felt the thumping in his chest grow stronger. He looked to the early morning sky. *Don't let this happen. This is suicide.* He reached up and held the Medal with his right hand. *Those are Americans out there. Kids, like Billy and I were when we went to Vietnam. We don't want to kill them. We just want to be left in peace.*

He looked back at the column. It continued to advance. He scanned the hills on the north side of the canyon. His heart thumped heavily in his chest when he picked out Teresa operating her camera from just below the crest of the ridgeline. He held tightly to the Medal and softly whistled the Marine Corps Hymn. Despite his recent experiences, he felt unnatural in the act, and yet it was comforting.

Clay's position was only a little west of the center of the two explosive charges, and four hundred yards up onto the ridgeline south of the road and stream. He watched as the last of the Apache vehicles moved west of his hiding place. The armored column continued the advance, trailing the Apache by no more than a mile and a half, stretching out for almost half a mile from the leading tank to the jeep in the rear. Clay continued to whistle.

He felt the presence of the Wolf behind him. He turned and stared into the green, emotionless eyes, only a foot from his own. ``Damnit. Stop doing that.''

The wolf remained motionless.

``There's got to be a way to stop this thing without killing those guys out there.''

``You must do what you must do, Wolf Brother.''

``I thought you were supposed to help me out a little bit.''

``What is it you wish?''

``I want to win this thing and not have to kill any Americans.''

``I understand it bothers you to kill, Wolf Brother. This is one of the reasons you were chosen to lead the Tinde. A warrior never kills unnecessarily, but a warrior does what he must do. You will do what is right.''

``Begging your pardon, but that's not a bunch of help right

335

about now."

Clay again glanced back at the advancing column. When he turned again, the Wolf was gone.

``Damnit!" He pounded his fist on the fallen tree trunk. The leading tank passed the first set of charges in the canyon. Clay held his breath as the clanking machine rolled west on the road, slowing as it moved further into the canyon, causing the vehicles behind to bunch up. He ducked low in his foxhole to avoid detection by any of the five helicopters.

With his heart in his throat, Clay watched and waited until the last vehicle had passed the first set of charges. When they were in the trap, Clay pushed down on the plunger. The explosive charge at the west end of the canyon blasted tons of rock and soil from the steep ridgelines on either side of the road. Clay watched without the aid of his field glasses as the earth shot skyward, narrowly missing the leading helicopter. The Huey banked sharply to the left and swooped up and over the ridgeline behind Clay. The earth cascaded onto the road below, a mere hundred feet to the front of the leading tank.

The tank stopped suddenly and turned to the left, making for the large stream to the south. It struck one of the mines, planted during the night. Clay watched the track peel off the left side of the tank. When the wheels reached the end of the track, the big machine turned helplessly in a counter-clockwise direction through 120 degrees of rotation, then stopped. *I hope nobody got hurt.*

He turned his attention to the eastern end of the trap. The charges had not ignited! In a panic, he lifted the plunger and pushed it down again. There was no response from the explosives planted on either side of the canyon. The vehicles in the rear of the column were turning – backing up and turning – moving forward and turning the other way – backing up and turning again. Clay was thankful the rear units were not tanks. They would have simply spun around and moved back to the east.

The helicopters were spread out and firing at the hillsides – in all directions. Clay heard the Apache return fire. The M-60s rattled almost in unison as they reached for a target in the sky.

Panic swelled in Clay's chest as he fought the urge to pick up the M-1 at his side and charge into the column single-handedly. Those were no longer Americans down there. They were his enemy. And they were about to escape the trap.

Clay grabbed at the Medal on his chest. He squeezed it tightly. ``I need your help, Wolf, real bad.''

He saw a man in uniform down by the stream. Clay squinted. It was an American uniform, but an older style. The helmet had the green camouflage canvas cover used by the Marines since World War Two. Clay put the field glasses to his eyes.

``Jesus! It can't be!'' Clay took the glasses from his eyes and stood. He waved his arms and shouted. ``Billy! Get the hell outa there!''

Billy turned and waved, then made an unmistakable signal that Clay should push the plunger again.

``No! Get out of there!''

Billy repeated the gesture, more emphatically.

Clay fell to his knees and raised the plunger to the upright position. Quickly, he pushed it down until it bottomed-out. Again the charges failed to fire.

He raised his head above the tree trunk. Billy raised his hands to the sky, his head tilted back.

A bolt of lightning flashed from a dark, heavy cumulus cloud. Time slowed. Clay gasped as the bolt split only a hundred yards above the earth and struck both sets of charges. The eastern end of the canyon disappeared in a turbulent cloud of dust as the surrounding ridgelines erupted and crashed down onto the road, closing off escape for the armored column. Billy disappeared under the tons of earth.

Clay stood and screamed. ``No!'' His voice was drowned out by the thunder of the landslide.

A tank in the center of the column turned to the left and ploughed into the stream, water splashing up over the gun turret. On the south side of the stream, it took the steep bank at full speed, nearly flipping over on its back. It righted itself and managed to escape the

337

confines of the water. The tank closed rapidly on Clay's position. Others fell in behind.

Clay picked up the loaded 3.5 rocket launcher and brought it to his shoulder. He aimed and squeezed the trigger. He watched helplessly as the rocket missed the tank by fifteen yards. Before he could take the launcher from his shoulder and pick up another round, he felt the added weight of a second round as it was inserted into the tube. He didn't take his eye from the sight. He felt the tap on the top of his head, telling him the round was in place and ready to fire.

``I told you to take your position, Eddie. . . but thanks anyway." He squeezed the trigger mechanism. His ears rang with the detonation of the rocket as it left the tube and sped towards the target. Clay watched as it struck the leading tank in the track on the left side. The big machine spun helplessly in a counter-clockwise circle and stopped. The tank immediately behind the disabled unit veered to the right and struck a land mine, blocking the trailing units in a tight group.

Clay put his glasses to his eyes and searched through the clearing dust to the east. He pulled the glasses from his eyes and turned to offer them to Eddie. ``Would you take a look at that? They were so confident, they left their infantry to secure the town. We've got. . ." He stared at Frank as the latter accepted the field glasses.

``Frank! What are you doing here?"

Frank put the glasses to his eyes and searched the east. ``There will be injured. They'll need treatment."

``Frank, put those glasses down and get the hell out of here!"

The ridge behind them shook. Debris filled the air as a 105 millimeter shell exploded seventy-five yards from where they sat. Clay pulled Frank down and into the small foxhole behind the tree trunk. Metal fragments whizzed overhead. Sod and pieces of shredded vegetation fell to earth all around them.

Clay heard the heavy reports of the Apache .50 cal. machine-gun as it raked the trapped column on the road. He raised from the foxhole and watched the gun turrets on the tanks swing from side to side, searching for the origin of the machine-gun fire. Clay smiled.

338

They had removed the tracers from the ammo belt. The tanks would have to guess at the gunner's location. The whoosh-whoosh of 81 mm mortar rounds falling to earth caused Clay to drop back into the foxhole.

The Apache mortar barrage hit. The ground shook and rumbled as the twenty-round barrage fell among the column. Clay looked into Frank's eyes. ``Can you stay here until some of the shootin's died down?" He stood and picked up his rifle, not waiting for an answer, and charged down the slope towards the trapped Federal column.

Clay concentrated his thoughts on the mission. This was different than it had been in Vietnam. They had a real mission – one that all of his men knew and felt. *This is our land. We can't lose – can we?* He looked for the Wolf. He saw only the geysers of earth tossed into the sky by the exploding mortar rounds.

Apaches from both sides of the canyon rushed to the road under the cover of the mortar barrage. A helicopter exploded overhead, the burning fragments of its epitaph drifting downward in tight spirals of black smoke. When the last mortar round exploded, the nearest Apaches were only fifty yards from the column. They poured in among the vehicles.

The helicopters could offer no support to the men of the 1st Air Calvary while the Apaches were in the midst of the column. They moved east, to Portal and hovered, out of accurate range of the Apache guns. There were sporadic shots fired by both sides on the ground, but the end came swiftly for the Federal force. Under the threat of high explosives and flame throwers, the column commander surrendered his unit.

Clay walked among the tanks, armored personnel carriers, trucks and jeeps of the column, marking the units that would be taken into the hills by the Apache. Eddie's men followed behind him, two men jumping into each unit Clay marked, starting them up and moving to the western edge of the trap. There were only two men on the reservation who knew how to operate a tank, and for this reason, only two of the tanks were taken.

A third set of charges were set off to open an escape route to the west, back towards the Research Station. Before the dust settled, the Apache drove the captured units swiftly through the opening.

Oscar found Clay kneeling next to a Federal soldier. The man's arm was severed at the elbow. Clay worked feverishly, tying off the stump with the wounded man's web belt. He looked up at Oscar. ``Where are all of our healers, brother?''

Oscar looked tired. ``They're pretty busy.'' He glanced at the young soldier. ``I'll get you someone right away.''

As he turned to leave, Frank ran up. Without a word, he knelt and took over the wounded man's treatment. Clay stood and continued his walk through the remnants of the armored column, glad to be away from the suffering of the young soldier.

``Clay. You okay?''

Clay turned to Oscar's voice. ``I'm okay. Get me a casualty report as soon as you can. I want ours first. Then I want the dead, wounded, and captured for the Federals.''

``You're the boss,'' said Oscar. He turned and shouted orders to his men as Clay stepped up to a jeep.

Clay picked up the handset to the field radio on the passenger seat and keyed up. ``Any station this net, this is the commander of the Apache forces. Over.''

The radio crackled and fell silent for a moment. A crisp voice broke the stillness. ``This is the commander of the U.S. forces. Over.''

``Give me a name and rank. Over,'' said Clay.

Again the pause. ``This is Colonel Ronald P. Hardcastle, U.S. Army. Who are you? Over.''

Clay squinted into the morning sun. ``My regards, colonel. My name is Clay Price. We have captured your unit, most of it intact. I will contact you with the names of those killed and wounded as soon as we get the information together. It appears that the final number of casualties will be substantial. Do you understand? Over.''

``I understand you, Mr. Price. Over.''

``One more thing, Colonel. Keep in mind that we are not a party

340

to the Geneva Accord. Your men will receive humane treatment, so long as none of your aircraft violate our airspace. Do I make myself clear? Over."

``You cannot win this foolish war, Mr. Price. Don't shed anymore blood in a losing cause. Over."

``We didn't want any blood shed. It was your choice. We may lose, but it will cost you. And, colonel, it will cost you your career if you remain in command. The Federal government needs its scapegoat, you know. Think about it. I repeat. If I get any reports of Federal aircraft violating Chiricahua airspace, ten of your men will be executed for every occurrence. Do you understand? Over."

``I understand. Over."

``I'll get back to you when I have the information I promised. Out." He switched off the radio to conserve the battery.

Elmer stood at his side. ``Would you really do that?"

Clay looked at him. ``We're defenseless against their air power. You ever seen what napalm does to women and children? How bad do you want to win?"

``Bad. But I never thought of doing it that way."

Clay looked grim. ``Me neither. Let's hope they don't force the issue." He took one last look around at the remaining Federal vehicles, then back at Elmer, managing a smile. ``I always wanted my own jeep. Let's take this one with the radio." He jumped into the driver's seat. Elmer sat beside him.

10:14 A.M. July 30 --- The Research Station

Clay watched Maria, Carla and the others as they moved from one wounded man to the next, treating each quickly. The room was filled with the chants of the old ones, as Frank's healers made their rounds.

Clay approached Frank. ``Have we got a final tally on the casualties, Doc?"

Frank looked up from his work. ``Wait one." He turned his attention back to the Federal soldier he was working on and finished removing the pieces of shrapnel from his back. When he was done he motioned Carla over. ``Would you finish up?''

She nodded and knelt next to the man as Frank stood and wiped his hands. He turned to Clay.

``The loss of even one man makes our casualties heavy. But under the circumstances, we did well.''

``Put that in numbers for me, Doc.''

Frank motioned Clay to follow as he stepped through the door onto the porch. Clay followed.

Outside, they walked to the corner of the building. ``This isn't Nam, Clay. Haven't you had enough `body count' to last you the rest of your life?''

Clay was surprised by Frank's statement. ``Take it easy, Doc. I don't care about their losses. I'm worried about ours. We have a finite number to work with. Remember?'' He pulled a pack of cigarettes from his pocket and offered it to Frank.

Frank accepted one and rolled the end of it between his thumb and forefinger until a bit of tobacco fell into his hand. He threw the tobacco into the slight breeze and put the cigarette to his lips. He waited for Clay to light it, took a deep drag, then said, ``I'm sorry. I guess I just took what you said the wrong way.''

Clay smiled. ``No sweat, Doc.'' He glanced at his pack of cigarettes before returning it to his pocket. ``Sure hope this little war doesn't last too long. I'm getting low on smokes.''

``I don't think you'll have to worry about that. If the President can't be convinced to call off the troops real soon, our days are numbered in single digits.''

``What are you talking about, Doc? We can hide in these hills for a hundred years and teach 'em what they didn't learn in Vietnam.''

Frank took a deep drag from his cigarette and looked at the hills surrounding the Research Station. He looked back at Clay. ``You're a good man, Clay. With you leading us, we could hold out for a long time. But if the Army breaks through, we're moving back to the Stronghold. That's where we'll make our stand.''

Clay smiled weakly. ``I heard you say that once before. But I thought it was for the benefit of the camera. You don't really expect to stand toe-to-toe with the U.S. Army and win. do you?"

``No," Frank said quietly. ``I don't."

``You're talkin' crazy, Doc. That's suicide. Let's take to the hills and show 'em what. . ."

Frank cut him off. ``What would you do with the women and children, and the old and feeble?"

``The women can fight with us; some of the kids too. The others, we'll hide."

``Too many before us have tried. The result is always death and suffering. Think of the great leaders and what the people endured. Juh, Mangas Coloradas. Remember old Nana? Remember his twelve-hundred mile running battle down into Mexico and back? Remember how, time after time, he won the fights, only to see his people die of hunger?"

``But this is different, Doc. We don't have to run all over the country. We can stay here."

Frank shook his head. ``We can't beat the white eyes with guns, Clay. Any more than my ancestors could trust their treaties. Our only path is freedom or death. All we can do is hold out as long as we can, and hope public pressure forces the government to leave us in peace. Our only hope is that the American public won't let their government massacre all of us."

Clay thought of Maria. ``Damnit, Doc. I've never been one for committing suicide. And I think being a martyr is even dumber."

``I'm sorry," said Frank. ``I know this isn't your fight. It's an Apache path we are walking. I never should have. . ."

Clay hit Frank in the jaw with a quick and powerful left hook, knocking him to the ground. Clay stood over him menacingly.

``Get up, goddamnit. Get up and tell me again how it's a goddamn Apache matter. And tell me again how it's none of my concern. You think you got some kind of goddamn monopoly on justice and freedom or something?"

343

Frank propped himself up on an elbow as he rubbed his jaw with his free hand. He looked up into Clay's eyes. ``Helluva punch for a white man.'' He smiled.

Clay's anger cooled at the sight of Frank's smile. ``Yeah, well, I was holdin' back so I wouldn't hurt you.'' He barely managed to suppress the smile that wanted to surface.

``I deserved that,'' Frank said. ``I'm sorry. Now, are you gonna let me up, or do I have to have you arrested?''

The smile broke through. Clay reached out a hand to help Frank to his feet. ``I owed you one anyway – the fish, remember?''

Frank took Clay's hand and pulled himself to his feet, rubbing his jaw again. ``I'm glad you held back.'' He leaned over and picked up his cigarette while Clay retrieved his.

Clay puffed on his smoke and looked at Frank. ``I'm sorry, Doc.''

``Forget it. I was out of line.''

Clay shrugged. ``So we try to hold 'em as long as we can. Then we fight a rear-guard action and get 'em up to the stronghold. If you've got any last-minute details you want to put in your will, you better get it done today.'' He offered his hand with a smile on his face.

Frank took the offered hand and pulled Clay into an embrace.

A communications runner rushed through the door. ``Clay! Oscar's on the radio. The Federal Army is moving west from Portal. And he says he's spotted four C-47's flying in low from north of Harris Mountain.

Clay looked at Frank and arched an eyebrow. ``C-47's? Not even the Marine Corps is using them anymore.''

The droning sound of the old piston-driven engines of the planes broke the stillness. Clay grabbed his rifle from against the building wall and ran to the clearing to the west of the buildings, Frank and the runner right behind. They stopped and looked into the sky.

The planes approached the Research Station at an altitude of less than five hundred feet.

``Jesus! The cargo doors are open. I think they've got airborne

344

on board." Clay turned to the runner. ``Get Will on the radio and tell him what's happening. Tell him to have his men surround them if they jump. No shooting unless they shoot first."

The runner nodded and ran for the building. Frank and Clay moved further into the clearing and watched as men poured from the cargo doors of the lumbering old machines. Chutes opened quickly and the men drifted downwards.

``They're not in uniform," Frank said.

``Maybe not," Clay answered, ``but they're armed."

Will's men began to appear on the edges of the clearing.

``They're Indian," Frank said suddenly.

``So were the scouts that led General Crook to Geronimo's Stronghold," Clay answered.

When the first man touched down, Clay stood only twenty feet from him. ``Hands on your head," Clay ordered, when the man had unbuckled his parachute harness. ``One quick move and you're dead."

The man quickly complied with Clay's order. ``Seems like a helluva way to treat volunteer reinforcements," he said.

``Reinforcements? What the hell are you talkin' about?" With his peripheral vision, Clay saw Will's men surrounding the others as they landed, disarming them. No shots were fired.

``I'm Lyle MacDonald. Team leader for a Navajo smoke-jumper unit. We thought you guys might want some help."

Clay leaned forward. ``Are you for real?"

MacDonald looked around him. ``We had more planes, but most of them got turned back, it looks like. But don't worry, those who didn't jump in, will join the ones infiltrating on the ground."

Clay stepped up to MacDonald and relieved him of his lever action .30-.30. Clay turned to Frank, handing him MacDonald's rifle. ``Would you have Will hold these guys until I can find out what's happening with the Feds?"

Frank accepted the rifle and nodded. ``Be careful."

``Careful as a porcupine in matin' season."

Clay started for his jeep.

345

Elmer looked up at his approach. He had remained by the radio as ordered. ``I guess you heard?''

Clay nodded. ``Let's get down there. Is your unit in position?''

Elmer grinned. ``Who do you think you're talking to?''

Clay slid behind the wheel. ``Sorry. I lost my head there for a minute.'' He started the jeep and put it into gear.

``Who are the paratroopers?''

``I'm not sure. They claim to be Navajo smoke jumpers. We'll find out when we get this situation with the Feds straightened out.''

11:35 A.M., July 30 --- Eastern end of the blocked canyon

Clay knelt next to a large boulder, blown from the ridgeline earlier in the day by the explosive charges. He looked through his field glasses at the slow-moving troops. They moved in a large skirmish line, spread out on line for a half-mile on each side of the point unit in the center.

``How many you figure? Two or three thousand?''

Clay brought the field glasses to his waist and looked briefly at Elmer. ``Looks like a regiment to me. They've got armor coming up from behind. I think that's why they're moving so slow – they're waiting for the tanks to catch up.''

Elmer turned and looked at the remnants of the first armored column to enter their land. He looked back to Clay. ``How damn many tanks they got?''

Clay smiled a wry smile. ``More than we can ever hope to destroy. They must have had those other guys south of here.'' He looked at the disabled tanks behind him. ``Move your men up onto the ridgeline, Elmer. Leave two teams with me and the two guys with tank experience. If the Feds keep coming, have your fifties open up at one mile, the M-60s at about twelve hundred yards, and your best riflemen at a thousand. Tell the rest to hold their fire until the enemy is within five hundred yards. When the rest of your men open up, have the fifties, M-60s, and your sharpshooters fall back to your next position. When they're in position, open up and allow the rest of your men to fall back. You know the drill, right?"

Elmer nodded. He stepped away from Clay and passed the orders down the line. Clay moved to the nearest tank and waited for Elmer's men to assemble with him. In less than two minutes, fourteen men stood nervously around the disabled tank. Clay panned them briefly with his eyes and waved at the tank.

``What you have here, gentlemen is not a tank anymore. But that don't mean we can't use it. It is now an artillery piece. And a damn good one at that." He paused and looked at the group. ``Where are the two of you with tank experience?"

Quickly, two men stepped forward. One was young, in his early twenties, the other much older. Clay looked at the older man. ``Where did you get your experience?"

``The Battle of the Bulge," answered the old man quickly.

``In a Sherman?"

The older man nodded.

Clay smiled. ``I guess you can show 'em how to aim this thing, right?"

A toothless grin appeared on the man's face. ``You bet!"

``Take half of the men and give'em a two-minute class." He turned to the younger man. ``You, take the rest to another tank and give 'em the same class. I want rounds on the way in three minutes. Fire everything you can fire in four minutes, then get the hell out of here and up into the hills. It's gonna get a little hot in this area as soon as they figure out what we're doin'. Now, go to it."

Clay moved back to his observation post as the men separated into the two groups. He was alone, except for his young radio operator.

``Chief Redhawk wants to talk to you." He offered Clay the radio handset.

Clay took the handset and keyed up. ``Main Base, Main Base. This is Red Leader. Over."

He heard Frank's voice. ``Red Leader, this is Main Base. Have you established contact? Over."

``Negative, Main Base, but we've got a lot of folks headed for the party. They'll be at our front door in a few minutes. They're bringing more of their heavy friends. Over."

``Those recent arrivals are for real. You want some help out there? Over."

Clay smiled. ``Negative. Not yet anyway. Over."

``Roger. Keep me posted. Over."

``Roger. Red Leader out."

Clay gave the handset back to the young man at his side and put the field glasses to his eyes. ``Call in a fire mission to our mortars."

The young man keyed up the radio. ``Whiskey Red. Whiskey Red. Fire mission. Over."

Clay unfolded the contour map from his pocket and spread it on the ground in front of him. He studied it briefly, then turned to his radio operator. ``Fire mission. Troops in open with armored support. One round Willie Peter. Will adjust. Gun-target line. 653291. Fire when ready."

The radio operator repeated the fire mission. They waited. Clay saw the young man tense up as he received a call. He looked up at Clay and said. ``On the way."

Clay brought the glasses to his eyes. ``Roger, on the way. Wait." He searched the area in front of the leading element at the center of the skirmish line. He saw the men scatter as they heard the falling mortar round, and he watched as the white phosphorus shell exploded into a fountain of white burning death, with a deep red-orange blossom at its center.

He turned to his radio operator. ``Ten rounds of H.E. per gun. Search and traverse. Search up fifty. Search right fifty. Repeat elevation. Fire when ready."

When the young man had completed the message, he looked up at Clay and said. ``On the way Whiskey."

``Roger on the way Whiskey. Wait."

The first shot from one of the captured tanks thundered out of the canyon. Clay dove for cover at the unexpected sound. He glanced up at his radio operator who sat against a large boulder, his eyes large and round with fear.

Clay pulled himself back into the kneeling position and dusted off his clothing. ``Habit."

The radio operator smiled. Clay flinched as more of the captured tanks joined the action. The flinching was involuntary, and uncontrollable. He looked at the tanks below his position and saw the smoke and movement of the big gun before he heard the report. He knew the loud boom was coming, but his knowledge did him no good. His body flinched and twitched involuntarily as the sound of the round passed overhead.

He picked up his field glasses and watched as the mortar and tank rounds smashed into the Army to the east. He turned back to his radio operator. ``Tell the mortars, cease fire. End of mission."

The radio operator complied with Clay's order.

``Now leave that radio and get back up on the ridgeline to the south, with Oscar's men."

``But what about you, Chief?"

Clay couldn't get used to being called `Chief.' ``Don't worry about me. Leave that radio and get to Oscar's team. Now!"

He watched as the young man ran and stumbled over the debris that had once been on the northern side of the canyon, and which now formed a barricade against the oncoming First Air Cav. He breathed a sigh of relief when the boy's figure disappeared into the trees on the south ridge of the canyon. He looked down at the captured tanks. Elmer's men were retreating to the north ridge. He turned his attention back to the First Air Cav.

There were casualties, many casualties. But the line was reformed and seemed to be continuing the advance. Clay could see medics running from place to place, treating the wounded. A solitary jeep burned under an umbrella of black smoke. The skirmish line seemed to come to a halt. Why?

Clay heard the artillery shell whiz overhead and looked down at the vehicles trapped below him just in time to see the explosion. Now he knew why. He moved down the slope of the landslide. Suddenly, the ground shook and rumbled all around him. Large chunks of earth blasted skyward. The world at his feet turned fluid as the heavy Federal shells smashed into the landslide and the land below and behind him. He hung onto the PRC-25 radio and dove to the ocean of dirt at his feet. The sounds of flying metal fragments were almost drowned out by the heavier sounds of the explosions. He clutched his rifle tightly in his left hand.

How in the hell did I ever let this happen? These guys are serious. I've gotta get outta here. I've gotta get back to Maria. We won't have much time left together now. They've started the big push. His thoughts drifted to the Navajo. *Those poor guys. It wasn't even their fight.* He thought of Frank and their argument outside the Research Station. *Yeah, I guess it was, too.*

A 155 howitzer shell exploded only thirty yards from where he lay. He felt his body picked up by the concussion and slammed back to the rocky soil. ``Oomph!'' Air was mashed from his lungs. He gasped for breath as the heavy shells continued to land on target. When he could breathe again, he brushed the dirt from his hair and face and crawled down the landslide, towards the trapped vehicles, ignoring the falling shells, hoping only that none would land on top of him. The PRC-25 radio bounced along at his side as he made his way to the nearest vehicle.

He spit dirt from between his teeth and cursed the foul smell of the cordite in the air. Near a burnt-out tank he stopped and placed his back against trackless wheels. He keyed up the radio. It was dead. He looked down at the backpack and saw the shrapnel holes in the battery and radio. *Damn!*

He threw the handset to the ground and clutched his M-1 in both hands. He stared skyward at the heavy gathering of cumulus clouds. The Federal barrage lifted. The air was silent.

Clay looked about him and assessed the damage of the barrage. Most of the vehicles were ablaze from the Federal shelling. A scattered explosion here and there broke the stillness as ammunition caught fire and reached the flash point.

Apache Tears

A heavy rain began to fall.

Clay faced the sky and let the rain wash his eyes clear of dirt. He wondered if the infantry was still advancing, and how many of the Federal tanks were still operational. He made it to his feet, and was fifty yards up the southern ridge when the Federal shells struck again. They hit the trapped armored vehicles, the landslides, and the ridgelines north and south of the canyon. Clay fell prone and clawed his way upward.

A shell exploded fifty yards above his position, exposing what looked like the opening to a small cave. Clay crawled for it. Ten yards from the opening, a shell exploded almost on top of him. He felt his body falling through space. Fear clutched at his guts.

Clay awakened to the muffled sounds of explosions above him. He searched his body with his hands. Nothing appeared broken. A shaft of light from the opening in the ground thirty feet above illuminated the interior of the cave.

Astonishment momentarily drove the battle from his mind. The cave walls were lined with massive, water-clear quartz crystals, the floor pocketed with clusters of wide, stubby amethyst crystals, two to four inches in height. Further back in the cavern, champagne topaz lay on the floor in large mats, three feet or more in diameter. Scattered randomly throughout the quartz on the walls, tourmaline glittered and flashed in blue, green and deep pink, the bright colors coming from crystal columns that measured anywhere from one to twenty-four inches tall. It was the most beautiful sight Clay had ever seen.

A heavy explosion near the opening overhead rained dirt and debris into the cavern and brought the battle back to the front of Clay's thoughts. Slowly, he stood and moved about the perimeter of the large cavern. *I've got to get out of here.* He guessed the cave to be about a hundred to a hundred and twenty feet across. He found several openings in the walls, but beyond the main room, the darkness was total. If he lived, he would come back with lights and explore.

He moved back to the center of the cavern and stared up at the sky above the hole. Rain continued to fall heavily to the floor through the opening. He searched for some way to climb up, but even if he could scale the walls on the crystal formations, he knew there was no way to reach the small opening near the center of the ceiling. Depression worked its way into his mind.

``Don't give up so easy, brother."

Clay spun around at the sound of the voice. Billy sat on a rounded rock, next to a large cluster of amethyst crystals, the Wolf on his haunches at his side.

Clay closed his eyes and shook his head. He opened them again. Billy and the Wolf were still there.

Clay went down on one knee, only three feet from where Billy sat. He stared into Billy's face. He looked closely at the uniform. It was the same one he wore the day he was killed. The utility blouse was torn open at the stomach and covered with dried blood. An M-14 lay against the small rock upon which he sat, the safety off and ready to fire.

``Billy? What's goin' on, brother?"

``Looks to me like one helluva war up topside. What are you doin' down here?"

It was Billy's voice. It had the same warmth and laughter it always had. Clay stopped breathing and stared. A full minute passed.

``Billy. Will you still be here if we touch?"

Billy stood and opened his arms. Clay jumped to his feet and hugged him, tears coming to his eyes as they touched. ``Billy. Oh, Billy. Does this mean I'm dead? Is this what it's like to die?"

Billy squeezed him hard and laughed. He pushed Clay back far enough so they could see into one another's eyes in the dim light. ``What kind of a question is that? Hell no, you're not dead. I just thought I'd drop in for a visit.

``I understand from confidential sources that you aren't exactly the most reverent person in the world. But you at least have a quality about you that indicates there is hope."

Clay looked at the Wolf, then back to Billy. ``How can we do this? I know you're real. I can feel you." He squeezed Billy's arm. ``I can hear you. How can you still have that rifle and that uniform?

What's going on? Am I crazy? Is this a dream? Tell me, Billy, while we still have time together. I tried for so many years to reach you in my mind."

Billy nodded. ``I know, brother. You came close a lot of times."

``But why now?"

``You have learned enough of the old ways to reach me." Again, he glanced at the Wolf. ``Though there are those who say you still have a long way to go." Billy smiled. The Wolf sat passively, unmoving.

``Can it be like it was before? You know. . . when we were both alive?"

``Not exactly, but we can meet from time to time as you learn more."

Clay stepped forward and hugged Billy again. After a moment, Billy stepped back, holding Clay by the shoulders at arms length.

``As much as I'd like to continue this visit, brother, you've still got a whole lot of work ahead of you."

Once more, Clay became aware of the artillery barrage which continued to pound the Apache positions. The thought of the death and pain being inflicted by the exploding shells filled Clay with a momentary bitter grief. ``I didn't think they'd attack again so soon, Billy, with all of the political pressure that's supposedly being put on the President not to use force. I figured once they saw we were serious, they'd parlay for awhile – maybe negotiate a settlement – at least give us a day or two to think things over. We can't take this kind of pounding very long."

``You hurt their pride," Billy grinned. ``The army never did much take to the idea of gettin' their butts kicked by a bunch of rag-tag Indians."

Clay found Billy's familiar grin infectious, and the bitterness vanished. ``I guess you've got a point there."

``And don't worry much about the Tinde. Those who aren't safely dug in have pulled back to wait it out. They'll move up again when the barrage lifts."

``That sounds familiar," said Clay, remembering his experiences in Vietnam. ``You'd think they would have learned by now.''

Billy laughed. ``Unlimited resources have a negative affect on military minds. They start substituting firepower for common sense.''

``You got that right,'' said Clay. Another explosion overhead dumped more debris down through the opening. Clay looked at Billy. ``Is any of this going to work? I mean, do we even have a snowball's chance?''

Billy shrugged. ``It will be difficult. The Gahan haven't guaranteed a victory. They've just said that if ever there was a time, it's now. It may be that it was never meant to happen. If not, then now is the time for the Tinde to perish forever.''

``Great.'' Clay's shoulders slumped.

``You can't give up,'' said Billy, quietly. ``You can do anything you believe you can do.''

Clay looked into Billy's eyes. ``Who said anything about givin' up?'' He turned to the Wolf. The Wolf stared into his eyes and Clay felt power flowing into him, easing his fatigue, lightening the burden of his doubts.

``Everything you do,'' Billy went on, ``Every decision you make, every decision Frank makes, affects the outcome.'' Billy grinned. ``But then I seem to recall you were always saying that if you were makin' the decisions, the war would be over in a matter of weeks.''

Clay returned Billy's smile. ``You don't know how good it is to see that crazy smile of yours, brother.''

``I think I do. I feel the same way about yours.''

``I guess if I'm going to get on with this thing, I'd better figure a way to get out of here.'' Clay looked at the opening thirty feet above him. ``How do I do that?''

``There is another entrance to the cave, Cathedral Rock.''

``Maybe you guys can see in the dark, but unless I'm dead, I don't have infra-red vision.''

``Pick up your weapon and follow me.''

Clay looked at the Wolf. He bent down and retrieved his M-1. ``You're the boss.''

354

The Wolf led off, moving to a corridor in the northeast corner of the cavern, Clay on his heels. The blackness of the cave disappeared and was replaced with a soft green glow. The glow moved with them. Clay knew the eyes of the Wolf were the source of the light. The light bobbed up and down slightly with each step of the magnificent animal.

They traveled through small passages and large caverns, sometimes veering south or west, but always turning back to the east. They traveled two or three miles underground, but their straight-line distance measured only slightly more than half a mile.

When Clay crawled into the daylight, only a few seconds behind the Wolf, the big animal was nowhere to be seen. He turned back to the small entrance of the cave and waited for Billy. He put his head into the darkness and called. He was answered by silence.

The rain continued to fall, but it was much lighter than before. The Feds had lifted their barrage. Clay moved quickly south and west, in search of Oscar's unit. As he moved up the ridge, he got a clear view to the east, towards the Federal forces. *I'll be damned. They've pulled back again. We might win this thing yet.*

3:22 P.M., July 30 --- Research Station edit

Clay approached the Research Station on foot. He had made contact with some of Oscar's men and learned that, after lifting the artillery barrage, the Feds had made a final push towards the Apache positions and had been beaten back. The Feds then withdrew to their positions near Portal, out of range of the Apache mortars.

The door of the main building of the Research Station opened and Maria stepped outside. Clay stopped under a large sycamore and watched her as she moved away from the door about fifty feet and dumped a pan of bloody water onto the grass. A tuft of her dark hair fell over one eye. Her cotton dress was soiled with blood, and her face had a look of sadness so deep, Clay almost cried to see it.

As he stood under the tree watching her, his chest hurt with the love he felt inside. Her sadness was his. He stepped towards her.

Her back was to him as he approached. Suddenly, her body

went tense. She dropped the pan and turned quickly around. When she saw Clay, she put her hands to her face. Clay rushed the last few steps. He cradled her in his arms and brushed the hair from her face.

``Maria. What's wrong?''

She put her arms around his neck and smiled as tears ran over her high cheekbones. ``Oh, Clay. They told me you were dead.''

``Dead? Me? Who told you that?''

``Never mind. It isn't important anymore.'' She pulled his head down to hers and kissed him on the lips. ``I love you more than I love myself, Clay Price. It was difficult to remember why we were fighting when I thought you were dead.''

He held onto her tightly. ``Maria, I don't think we're gonna have a whole lot of time left together. The Feds have withdrawn for the moment, but they'll be back. They aren't going to wait to negotiate anything. How many wounded are left to be treated?''

``Most are treated. Maybe only a half-dozen left. And their wounds are minor.''

He held onto her forearm and started for the main building of the Center. ``I've gotta talk to Frank.'' She stopped to pick up the fallen basin, stretching out his arm, slowing him, then followed him to the building.

Clay held onto Maria's arm as they walked to the far end of the large treatment room and approached Frank. Frank turned and faced them. His face registered a look of surprise.

``Hey, Doc. We gotta discuss a few things. Quick.''

Frank smiled. ``You sure you're not half cat? You've gotta be on life six or so.'' Frank embraced his war chief.

``What are you talking about? What's going on around here?''

``Never mind. You're here. Let's go outside.''

Clay looked at the large numbers of wounded, mostly Federals. He looked at Frank. ``Yeah, maybe we better.''

They stood under a large sycamore tree, Clay's arm around Maria's waist.

``Where do we stand?'' asked Frank.

Clay kept his arm around Maria's waist. ``On mighty shaky ground, Doc. We did okay today, but it didn't come cheap. I think we'd better get rid of most of the prisoners. Especially the wounded. They're too big a drain on our resources."

Frank nodded. ``Can you set it up?"

``We've got Federal radios and frequencies. Let's get on the air ask for a cease-fire until dawn. Tell them we're sending most of the prisoners back as a show of good faith. We'll keep a few of them as insurance against aircraft. We can let Teresa film it. If they agree, it gives us a little breathing room to regroup. I've gotta get some forces shifted around."

``How so?"

Clay pulled his map out and spread it on the ground. They knelt around it.

``They've been hittin' us here." He pointed to the mouth of Cave Creek Canyon, south and west of Portal. ``They won't try that again for awhile. The road is blocked and the terrain is too steep and rough for armor if they can't use the road."

``Where do you figure they'll come next?" asked Frank.

``Here." Clay pointed. ``The two roads leading into Paradise from the north and the east. The terrain's harder to block, especially on the north road. We've got to get into position and get some traps set."

``Can you hold them there?" Frank asked.

Clay met Frank's gaze. ``Not long. A day. Maybe."

Frank stood. ``Let's do it."

Clay pulled Maria's hip to his in a quick hug, then removed his arm from around her waist and headed to the radio room.

7:15 P.M., July 30 --- On the Portal side of the eastern landslide

The top of the sun hung just above the tips of the highest peaks in the Chiricahuas, painting the undersides of the dark cumulus clouds hovering overhead various shades of pink, orange and gold. The shadows of the mountains hid the smaller shadows of the men laboring on the road near the stream.

Apache Tears

Clay could see Teresa with her camera on the northeast ridge. He turned to Colonel Hardcastle. ``That just about does it, Colonel. I hope we don't have to meet again under these circumstances.''

Hardcastle's face displayed a hardened look of sadness, guarded and contained by years of military training. ``You don't have a chance, Mr. Price. Surrender your forces. I have been given the authority to grant you and your men amnesty.''

Clay looked into the strong face of his military foe. ``Amnesty? Isn't that what they give draft-dodgers and terrorists?'' Clay shook his head. ``Thanks, but no thanks, Colonel. We're in this for the duration.''

``The governor of your state is willing to drop criminal charges against you if you capitulate now, Mr. Price.''

``It used to be my state. Until it secedes from the union and joins Chiricahua, it's part of the country I'm fightin' against. Nothing more.'' Clay looked hard into the eyes of his opponent. ``You're missing the whole point, Colonel. We're tired of deals. We're tired of the laws under which we've had to live, laws that are used and abused by those in power, laws that have no real meaning, laws that restrict freedom, laws that impose the will of those who control the vote, laws, laws, laws. Too many laws, Colonel.''

Hardcastle shook his head. ``You and your men are going to die up in those hills, Mr. Price.''

``Don't forget the women and children, Colonel. They'll be with us.''

``It's unnecessary.''

``For who?''

``I have my orders.''

Clay sighed. ``Well, then I guess you'd better follow them. Just remember – no aircraft over Chiricahua or the prisoners die.''

``Why haven't you threatened to kill them if we attack by land?''

``I would like to, believe me, but stronger voices than mine have restricted me to the limited threat against airpower. And, I promise you, if so much as one Piper Cub overflies our airspace, I'll kill the first man myself.''

Apache Tears

``I believe you, Mr. Price."

``Trust your judgment, Colonel." Clay glanced up at the small column of personnel carriers. The prisoners were all aboard. He looked back at the Colonel. ``Your men are boarded, sir. I suggest you leave Apache land before the shadows hit the stream."

The colonel hesitated. ``Mr. Price. . .I just wanted you to know that I. . . I have the highest respect for your bravery and your previous service record." He stared at the Medal, hung around Clay's neck. Briskly he snapped to attention and saluted the battle-scarred decoration. Clay returned the salute. The colonel spun about and stepped briskly to his waiting jeep.

CHAPTER FIFTEEN: FADING HOPE

5:09 am, July 31 --- Hill 6281, Northeast Chiricahua

The first hint of gray broke the darkness as Clay studied the terrain below and north of his position on the top of Hill 6281. He watched the lead elements of the 82nd Airborne move south on the road to Paradise, a small community in the northeastern area of Chiricahua. He turned his glasses east. Armored units from the 1st Air Cav moved slowly up the road from Portal. He pulled the glasses from his eyes and spoke to the two men with him.

``You guys sure you want to do this? Bein' a forward observer ain't all it's cracked up to be sometimes."

Both nodded.

``OK. Jacob, you take the road coming in from the north. Arturo, you got the one from the east."

Again, neither man said anything. They both nodded.

``If they get past the base of this hill and link up, destroy your radios and get out of here. If just one of the units breaks through, remain in position as long as you can. We may be able to mount a counter-attack. You don't have to be heroes. Just do what you've gotta do. Do you both understand how to call in your information?"

360

Jacob nodded. Arturo said. ``Clay, if we do well, will Frank let us go without a trial?''

Clay studied the young man. They had both been with Danny Blue when he had attempted to blow up the powerplant. Both were in their early twenties, young, and full of energy. They were basically good young men, and had volunteered for the dangerous forward observer duty. ``I don't know, Arturo. I'll do what I can for you and Jake, but I can't make you any promises.''

``That's fair enough, Clay,'' said Arturo.

``Okay then, let's get to it. Get to your sides of the hill. You've got to be able to see them when they get into the canyons.''

5:32 A.M., July 31 --- Paradise, northeast Chiricahua

Clay ordered his only two functional tanks to take up their positions, one to cover the roadblock north of town, the other to move to the cemetery on the road coming into the town from the east and hold there until ordered to move forward into the enemy. When he completed issuing his orders, he climbed aboard the tank destined for the Paradise Cemetery and rode in front of the turret as the tank lumbered up the dirt road.

At the cemetery, he dismounted the tank and met with his infantry leaders. Oscar and Elmer smiled as he approached.

``Good morning, brother,'' said Elmer.

Clay looked skyward, then back to Elmer. ``It's a mite early for me to be sure about it bein' a good one, but let's do our best to see it turns out that way.''

``We will,'' said Oscar.

He looked at both of them, then put his arms on their shoulders. ``We've got the toughest positions to hold. I gave Eddie and his men the blocked canyon and one of the fifties. Will and his men are south of us. They're in a position to reinforce either side of Silver Peak. I left the other two fifties just outside the stronghold. If it gets that far, we want to have something big left to fight with. You guys still feel up to it?''

``What about the Navajo and the others?'' asked Oscar.

``I have them in reserve, behind Will's men. If it looks like we need 'em to turn the tide, we'll use 'em. Otherwise, they stay in reserve.''

``It's good to have so much support from other tribes, even ones we don't normally get along with,'' said Oscar.

``I know what you mean,'' said Clay. He looked up to the top of Hill 6281. ``We better get in position. We surprised them yesterday. They'll be more than ready today.''

Elmer looked into Clay's eyes. ``Brother, they can't kill me. I was already dead when you came along. You gave me life. Only you can take it away again.''

Clay forced a smile. ``You keep your own life. I've got enough problems with the one I have.''

``Walk in power, Brother,'' said Oscar.

``And both of you. Keep your radio operators nearby.'' He looked at Oscar. ``I'll be with Elmer most of the time, unless something I don't expect develops. You better be gettin' on that north road with your men. Uncle's on his way in.''

Oscar nodded. He mounted his horse and rode quickly towards Paradise.

Clay turned back to Elmer. ``Where's my radio operator?''

Elmer pointed to the slope south and a little east of the cemetery.

``Let's get going.''

6:21 A.M., July 31 --- North side of Silver Peak, overlooking the Silver Creek roadblock, east of Paradise

Clay squatted next to a large pinon tree, his radio operator at his side. He watched through his field glasses as one of Elmer's rocket teams fired at the leading Federal tank. The tank disappeared in the boiling smoke of the explosion, and when the smoke cleared, it sat disabled and burning, blocking the road. *Perfect! Couldn't have done it better myself.*

There was enough room on the north side of the burning hulk, the side away from the stream, for another tracked unit to squeeze through, but it would slow them down considerably.

Clay watched with his heart in his throat as the rocket teams remained in position for another shot at the advancing armor. The rocks and crevices in which they hid exploded as the tanks fired point-blank into the hillside. Through his glasses, amid the clouds of blasted rock and earth, Clay saw bodies, and pieces of bodies, thrown into the air.

He reached for his radio. The young radio operator was ready, holding the handset at arm's length. Clay put the handset to his mouth and keyed up.

``Black Leader, Black Leader, this is Red Leader. Get your people out of there. Over."

Clay's radio crackled loudly. He heard the explosions first through the radio, then, two or three seconds later, his ears picked up what was left of the sound as it traveled up the mountainside. Elmer's voice broke through the static.

``Roger, Red Leader. On our way after one more shot. Over."

``Negative, Black Leader. Get them out now. Over."

Clay heard the explosions in his radio again, then Elmer's voice. ``Sorry, Red Leader. Can't hear you with all of this noise. Over."

Clay handed the handset back to his radio operator and brought his field glasses to his eyes. A second tank, threading its way through the narrow gap, exploded next to the first. *All right, damnit, so I'd have done the same thing. Now get out of there.*

Clay swung his glasses up the hill and sighed with relief as he saw Elmer's men pulling back into the trees below him, south of the stream.

The Federal tanks behind the disabled units continued to pour out heavy 105mm explosive shells. Trees fell like matchsticks. Mountain became rock. Rock became dirt. And dirt became opaque air. Clay lost visual contact with Elmer's men below.

Clay's radio crackled. ``Red Leader, this is Soup Can Two. Should I move forward now? Over."

Clay grinned at the clumsy radio transmission. *This is about the most impossible war that's ever been fought.* ``Soup Can Two, this is

Red Leader. Do not ask when to move, nor in which direction. You will be given orders per your briefing. Do you understand? Over?"

There was a short pause, then Soup Can Two keyed up. ``Yes, sir. Over."

``Stay off the air unless absolutely necessary. Red Leader out."

Clay turned his attention back to the Silver Creek roadblock below his position. Federal infantry moved through the rows of tanks, toward the small canyon. The blocked column of tanks split up behind the two still-burning hulks, some swinging onto the slope north of the road, some to the south. Their engines screamed as they slithered across the loose rocky soil, slamming into trees, uprooting smaller ones, backing up and crashing again into the larger ones, desperately seeking a way through to their objective.

Small arms fire broke out from the Apache in the trees on the side of the mountain south of the roadblock. The Federal troops opened up with their M-16's. Stray bullets whizzed all over the north side of Silver Peak, breaking small limbs from trees and bushes. The air was filled with a chorus of flat thumps as bullets buried themselves in the larger tree trunks. Clay's radio operator held out the handset. ``Sir. Oscar says the 82nd Airborne has breached the roadblock and is moving on Paradise."

Clay grabbed the handset and keyed up. ``Green Leader, Green Leader. Red Leader. Over."

``Go ahead Red Leader."

``Can you hold? Over?"

Clay could almost hear Oscar's smile over the radio. ``They're right where we want 'em. You need help over there? I can spare a short team. Over."

``Negative. Use what you've got. We'll manage. Out."

The 1st Air Cav below was spreading out, moving into the trees, firing at the Apache on the high ground. Elmer's rifle teams held their ground. The leading elements of the Federal troops were decimated as the Apache triggered a simultaneous blast of multiple claymore mines set in contour eighty or ninety feet up the side of the hill.

The charge slowed as the soldiers had to crawl over and around their dead and wounded. Medics rushed from man to man. An Apache mortar barrage fell on the Federal troops and their armor. Clay smiled grimly. *Good man, Arturo.*

For five minutes, the assault remained stalled, then the Federals broke through the center of the Apache line. They were getting closer. Clay could hear shouting voices. The bullets in the air around him increased in number. The heavier sound of the Apache M-1s drew back up the hill. Federal soldiers poured past the destroyed tanks in the canyon below, rushing west on the road to Paradise.

Clay grabbed the radio handset and keyed up. ``Soup Can Two, this is Red Leader. Now is the time. Over.''

``Yessir. We're on the way. Over.''

``Gray Leader, follow Soup Can Two. Over''

``Roger, Red Leader. Over.'' Clay called in his reserve unit, more than five hundred men from tribes all over the country.

``Brown leader, follow Gray leader. You know your mission. Over.''

He didn't know the commander of the reserve unit personally, but he knew he was Navajo, and that he had been a Captain in a 173rd Separate Airborne unit. He was the man Clay had held at gunpoint near the Research Station when he had parachuted onto their land. He was probably the most experienced infantry commander on their side.

``Roger, Red Leader. Brown Leader, out.''

Clay watched the Apache tank roll into view from the west on the road below. Elements of Will's command moved on foot, behind and on each flank of the tank. When the Apache tank turned at the small bend in the road, giving it a clear view of the blockage ahead and the advancing Federal troops, it loosed a shell into the men pouring through the jammed pass. Will's men moved forward, bayonets fixed, chanting and shouting as they ran to meet their enemy.

Clay keyed up his radio. ``Black leaders. Assault down the hill! Counter-attack! Gray Leader is moving up the canyon. Let's give 'em a hand. I'll see you all at the stream. Let's move!"

Clay gave the handset back to his radio operator and picked up his M-1. He pulled the bayonet from the scabbard on his belt and snapped it firmly in place on the barrel of his rifle. He glanced up at his young radio operator. ``Stay behind me as far as you can and still be there when I need you. Stay as low as you can."

Clay charged down the hill, into the advancing 1st Air Cav, passing his men, shouting words of encouragement, urging them on, rallying them to take back control of the pass, and to push the Federals east.

As he ran down the hill towards the melee on the road below, a young soldier from the 1st Air Cav suddenly appeared from behind a tree, right in front of Clay. He fell, groaning as Clay withdrew his bayonet from his chest. Clay rushed on, his well-honed instincts in control, his attention focused on the enemy below, his will implacably fixed on his intention to drive the Federals back, back, and back forever off his land.

He reached the south bank of the stream. Hundreds of men swirled and thrust, dodged and ducked, in a vicious hand-to-hand dance of death. Clay leaped into the fray at a dead run.

9:45 A.M., July 31 --- Paradise Cemetery

Clay stood in the center of the cemetery, his denim shirt torn across the chest. One of the sleeves was missing at the shoulder stitch. His clothes, his arms, his face were all smeared with blood and dirt. One knee in his trousers was ripped open, exposing his untanned skin. He looked around as the work details brought in more dead and wounded.

They had beaten the Federals, but the cost had been high. Though Federal losses had been much higher, they could more easily afford them. There were no replacements for the Apache dead and wounded.

Clay walked slowly through the cemetery, searching for familiar faces, hoping he would see none. He ached at the sight of each dead body, Federal and Apache. Seeing the wounded was worse, for he could feel their pain and fear.

His healers treated both sides, those in the worst condition first. Of those with minor wounds, the Apaches were treated first. Clay needed them to return to their units if possible. The sooner the better.

``Clay."

He turned toward the sound of the voice. Will Stonebreaker hobbled to him.

``How bad are you hit, Will?"

``Just a scratch." He handed Clay a piece of dirty paper. ``Casualty report for my units."

Clay took the paper and glanced at the numbers. Dead: 22. Wounded: 156. Missing: 1. Clay looked up at Will. ``It's little consolation to know there's more to come. How about the mixed unit?"

Will handed him another piece of paper. This one was made out a little differently:

Chief Price,

Due to the nature of our struggle, and the significance it will someday have in history, I have taken the liberty to list my casualties as you see. Their peoples will honor their deaths in ceremonies when they hear the news.

Lyle Ma cdonald
5th Mobile Team, Army of Chiricahua

Navajo: Kia 6; Wia 2; Mia 0.   Sioux: Kia 1; Wia 1; Mia 0.   Yaqui: Kia 1; Wia 2; Mia 0.
Mohawk: Kia 1; Wia 1; Mia 0.   Papago: Kia 2; Wia 1; Mia 0.   Ute: Kia 0; Wia 2; Mia 0
Cherokee: Kia 1; Wia 3; Mia 0.   Crow: Kia 0; Wia 1; Mia 0.   Totals: Kia 12; Wia 13; Mia 0.

Clay felt a kinship for these men and their tribes, and for the many men and tribes not on Macdonald's list. The losses hurt, but he

367

was thankful the list was no longer. He stuffed both pieces of paper into his pocket.

Eddie Vasquez reported his casualties in code. He had suffered only two wounded. His men had used the many caves along the creek to their advantage. The Federals had only lunged at the blocked road and quickly withdrawn. The main thrust had been at Paradise, just as Clay had guessed. They would change their tactics now.

``What're you thinking so hard about, brother?''

Elmer stood next to Will. Clay had been looking right at him and had not seen him. ``Too many things, brother. Too many things. How did you do?''

Elmer shook his head. ``Not so good. We beat 'em. But we sure couldn't afford to beat 'em too many times.'' He handed Clay his casualty list. Dead: 97. Wounded: 152. Missing 0.

Clay looked at the two men standing with him. ``Will, take your unit and relieve Elmer's men.''

``But, Clay ...``

``I don't want to hear it, Elmer. You've been cut up too bad. Your unit is too under-strength for that position. Bring your men back down into the canyon and collect the weapons. They left us plenty of M-16s and ammo. Too bad we didn't get more tanks. We'll use their big guns tonight for H & I missions. Oh, yeah, relieve Macdonald's men on the prisoner watch. I want all of his men held back in ready reserve. Now, go on, get it done. Those Feds out there might have had enough for today, and then again, they may be preparing another attack. Get movin'.''

Elmer quickly turned about and moved towards the hill, not speaking to Clay as he left.

``Is there anything else, Clay?'' asked Will.

``No. Just get it done as quickly as you can. I'll relieve your unit and get you back to guerrilla duties as soon as I can figure out how to do it. Maybe when we get straightened out with our casualties, some of those men that have been arriving from the other tribes can bring Elmer back up to strength.''

``Yes sir." He turned and limped away.

Clay's radio operator decoded Oscar's report from the northern road. He had routed the 82nd Airborne, and had even pursued them to the base of Harris mountain. It angered Clay that Oscar had allowed his men to pursue beyond the boundaries of Chiricahua, even if it was less than a mile. There was no guarantee the Army helicopters wouldn't join the fight once it left Chiricahua. Oscar had taken a foolish chance. Clay would talk to him about that. Despite the victory, Oscar's casualties were low, eleven dead and twenty-one wounded. Clay turned to his radio operator.

``Verify the casualty list for me."

``Yessir."

In two minutes, the casualty list was confirmed. *I guess the Great Spirit was with Oscar this morning. How in the hell do you rout a battalion of airborne troops and suffer a total of thirty-two casualties?* Clay turned from his radio operator and continued his search through the cemetery, feeling the pain of each wound, seeing darkness, then light with each death. The moans of the wounded faded as he walked towards Paradise, his radio operator thirty yards behind him.

10:35 A.M., July 31 --- Paradise

Clay studied the map on the small table before him. He looked at the contour lines representing the canyon the Apache had only so recently held. He thought of the young man in the tank and drew a large X on the map where he had discovered the tank's burned-out hull after the battle. The crew had perished instantly when a Federal tank scored a direct hit. Clay fought back the grief he felt well up in him. He was not entirely successful.

I'm so tired of the killin' and the pain. Why are we so stupid? Why can't we learn to let our fellow men alone? Why does somebody always think they know what's best for the other guy?

Oscar reported the 82nd appeared to be in the process of withdrawing to the south and east, towards Portal. *What are they up to now?*

A short time later, Eddie reported the 82nd was digging in on the eastern edge of the blocked canyon, near Cave Creek. Clay smiled. *So. They didn't do their job this morning, and now they've been assigned to guard against an Apache assault on the main road to Portal. An assault the Federal commanders know will never come.*

Oscar called in again. The Federals were moving in reinforcements, including heavy artillery, just west of Harris Mountain. Clay shook his head. *They have almost unlimited resources. Frank may not like this, but, what the hell. Might as well make it as expensive as possible.* He turned to his radio operator.

``Notify the weapons team to get two of the eighty-ones in range of Harris Mountain. Have 'em drop ten rounds per gun on the enemy positions, then move their location and drop ten more. I want it done five times until they have expended fifty rounds per gun. Then have 'em pull back to their assigned positions."

Clay put his head back against the old plaster wall and leaned against it. He knew their time was getting short.

He thought of Maria. *What a laugh. That's real funny. I finally meet the right one, and we don't even have a chance. I'll be lucky to see her before this is over. Why?*

He turned back to his radio operator, who had just completed relaying his instructions to the weapons team. ``Get Chief Redhawk on the radio. Tell him I'm on my way to his position."

Clay stood and left the house. He mounted his roan tied out front and rode quickly south towards the Research Station. He had gone a mere three hundred yards when the Federal artillery barrage struck Paradise. He turned in time to see the old house he had been using as a headquarters explode into the atmosphere.

Noon, July 31 --- Southwest Research Station

The Research Station buzzed with activity when Clay reined in his horse and dismounted. Scores of wounded men lay on the ground under the sycamore trees all around the station. Apache women and old men moved among them, treating when they could, comforting when they could not. An endless stream of pickups carried the dead and the wounded who had received preliminary treatment back to the Stronghold.

Apache wails of mourning formed a backdrop to the cries of those in pain as Clay stepped through the double door into the main treatment room. He spotted Frank and approached him at a fast walk. He was still three strides away when he said, ``Doc, we gotta talk.''

Frank motioned with his head and led Clay down a hallway to a small office. He closed the door and poured two cups of coffee from a pot on a hot plate. He handed one to Clay.

``You look like hell. Sit down.'' He indicated a chair. ``How bad is it?''

Clay sipped at the coffee. ``It ain't good. The Feds are sending in reinforcements by the bushel. They're not waitin' around for public opinion to stop them, Frank. You gotta do something.''

``Maybe we can slow them down. Teresa's been monitoring the news. The President is saying he ordered this morning's attack as a limited use of force to rescue the rest of the American soldiers we captured yesterday. I guess he's afraid we're going to burn them at the stake or something. You took more prisoners today, right?''

Clay nodded.

``Let's release them,'' Frank said. ``All of them.''

``So they can bring in the gunships and the jets? I don't think that's such a good idea, Doc.''

``We can keep the eleven CIA people.''

``Then he'll still have his excuse, won't he?''

``Damnit, Clay, I don't have all the answers. But at least it would show the American public that we're trying to act in good faith.''

``Yeah, well right about now I'm rapidly losin' faith in the good old American public.'' Clay sighed, and rubbed the stubble on his face. ``But you're probably right. I could use the guards, anyway. I need every man I can get.''

Frank nodded. ``See if you can set up a cease fire. Tell them

371

what we want to do. I'll find Teresa and have her tape it and we'll get it out on the air."

Clay finished his coffee, put the cup on the desk and stood. ``There's one other thing."

``What's that?"

``Let's release the Purvis stuff on the senator. It's the only hope we've got now. With what we're gonna be up against by dark, a division of marines couldn't hold those two canyons north and east of Paradise."

Frank nodded. ``Teresa's got it all ready to go. But it's still going to take some time for them to verify the data. How long can we hold?"

Clay shrugged. ``I'm calling all the men on the western perimeter in after dark. I want them in the Stronghold by daylight tomorrow. I think the push is coming from our side, through Paradise. If we're lucky, we'll be alive at noon tomorrow. Anything past that is wishful thinking."

5:15 P.M., July 31 --- The Stronghold

A cease fire had been agreed upon, to last until sunset, and the prisoner release had taken place without incident. Teresa was sending the edited tape to her station and the networks. Frank watched the images on the monitor in the TV truck as the disarmed American soldiers marched down the road from the Apache positions, through the half-mile buffer zone, towards the waiting U.S. Army units. Teresa's voice narrated over the images.

``At 3:30 p.m. today, Mountain Standard Time, leaders of the Chiricahua nation released more than one hundred and fifty United States Army soldiers captured today in battle, following the initial U.S. invasion of Chiricahua yesterday. It is the second prisoner release voluntarily offered by the Apache leaders. Frank Redhawk, Chief of the Chiricahua nation, said the release had been ordered as a humanitarian gesture of good faith. After the release had been completed, Redhawk issued the following statement."

Frank looked at his own image on the monitor. He was shocked by the fatigue and tension evident on his face. He couldn't remember the last time he had managed more than three or four hours sleep at a stretch. He was pleased he had managed to keep that exhaustion out of his voice.

``Three hundred and thirty-one Apache men and women suffered moderate to critical wounds today defending their land against an invading army, the United States Army. One hundred and thirty-one Apache men and women died. The oldest was seventy-two. The youngest, twelve.

``While I do not have an exact count of U.S. casualties, we believe them to be considerably higher than our own. As our dead and wounded are to us, these men were your sons, your husbands, your fathers, your friends, your uncles, your nephews, and your brothers.

``As with our casualties, some lost arms. Some lost legs. Some were blinded. Others were ripped apart by explosions. Too many died."

The tears that had come to Frank's eyes as he spoke were evident on the monitor image.

``Every Apache in Chiricahua shares your grief for your dead and wounded. We pray you share ours. It did not have to be this way. It does not have to go on.

``Your president, this morning, said he had ordered the action to rescue American prisoners taken in yesterday's battle, when we stopped the first attempt by the U.S. Army to invade our land. But he never asked us for their release. Instead, he ordered the attack.

``Two days ago, the U.S. government tried to contact us through the head of the Bureau of Indian Affairs. I told them we had nothing to discuss with the BIA. And I also told them I would be happy to talk with any authorized representative of the U.S. State Department. Yesterday's attack was the president's response. In a statement I released last night, after we had driven the invading forces back off our land, I reiterated my willingness to talk with someone from the State Department. Today's attack was the response we got to that second offer.

``This afternoon, we released all the U.S. prisoners in our

373

custody, with the exception of the following: Bruce Stinton, who will be released when he has served out his sentence, and the eleven surviving Americans of the initial sixteen-man U.S. force sent in to try to take custody of Charlie Williams and Bruce Stinton.

``These men are being held as security against the U.S. use of air power against us. These men, too, will be released – when all U.S. Army units are withdrawn beyond striking range of our borders, and when we have a signed document from the State Department stipulating that the U.S. will not again resort to the use of force against us.

``If you are wondering, as we have, why your president would take these actions, we think we may have an answer. In a moment Teresa Chatla will present a special report detailing that answer.

``In brief, we do not believe your president to be an evil or uncaring man. But we believe he has a friend, and unofficial advisor, who is – Senator Edward Williams.

``Going back more than ten years, to his days as a congressman, and then as head of the BIA, and today, as a senator, Williams has been systematically stealing tens of millions of dollars from Native American tribes and reservations all over the United States, through fraudulent and unethical business dealings.

``He abused his power as Chairman of the Senate Intelligence Oversight Committee to illegally send a government-paid-and-trained assassin into a foreign country to kill Medal of Honor-winner Clay Price, in a desperate effort to hide his son's involvement in the rape and shooting of Angela Stillwater, and to prevent disclosure of his own criminal activities.

``I expect there will be many of you who will find it difficult to believe that a man honored by his fellow citizens with the rank and privilege of a U.S. senator would be capable of such actions. I assure you, it is the case.

``Listen to the evidence. Decide for yourselves. And then, I ask each of you, in the name of all you hold sacred, demand that your president stop this senseless violence. Too many have already suffered.

Too many have died. It doesn't have to go on."

Frank turned away from the monitor and left the truck. Teresa followed him. He looked across the Stronghold at the ten crude outdoor hospitals he had set up, canvas tarps spread between trees to provide protection from the sun and rain, a network of ditches dug to channel rainwater away from the pine bough pallets which served as beds. All ten were already filled to overflowing, and the last of the day's casualties were only now reaching the Stronghold.

To the west end of the Stronghold, the dead had been laid out in neat rows and covered with blankets. Henry and some of the other old ones moved among the bodies, sprinkling pollen, wafting sage smoke, ritually assisting those spirits still trapped in the confusion and violence of their deaths. The soil in the Stronghold was too rocky, and space too limited, to make burial possible. When conditions permitted, the bodies would be moved to the meadow outside the entrance to the Stronghold where yesterday's dead had been buried.

Teresa took his hand, and he looked at her. The exhaustion and strain had etched lines at the corners of her eyes and mouth.

``At least they died with honor," she said quietly.

Frank nodded. It was little consolation, but he held onto it tightly. It was all he had.

Inside the truck the muffled cadences of Teresa's voice stopped as the equipment automatically shut down after completing the transmission.

``Clay thinks tomorrow will be the last day," Frank said quietly. ``There's nothing we can do now but wait." He squeezed her hand. ``But there's still plenty of time to get you out of here safely."

Teresa took her hand from Frank's and shook her head slowly. She knelt down on one knee and put her hand to the earth. ``I will die before I am driven from this land." She looked up at Frank. ``By anyone."

Frank looked at her for a long time, and then nodded once. ``I love you."

Teresa stood and they embraced. Frank held her gently, filled with wonder at the joy her touch brought him. He used the joy to hold his fear at bay.

``I have to talk to Henry,'' he said after a time. ``If no attack comes, I am calling a Gathering of those in the Stronghold tonight. There are ceremonies which should be performed. We may not have another chance.''

9:15 p.m., July 31 --- The Stronghold

Frank and Clay sat off to one side, watching the activities in the large fire-lit circle of people gathered on the slope at the west end of the Stronghold.

Frank had spoken to the gathering briefly, praising their courage, and doing his best to console their grief without giving false hopes. They needed no appraisal of the situation they were in. News of the battle, and news of events in the outside world, had circulated freely and with surprising accuracy through the Stronghold all day. He had led them in the Gahan Chant, asking them to send their prayers on the rhythms of the chant to all the Tinde and their allies outside the Stronghold. And he had then turned the gathering over to Henry and the other old ones.

There had been ceremonies of mourning and grief. There had been ceremonies to guide the spirits of the dead back to Ussen - the-Giver-of-All-Life. There had been songs honoring Mother Earth and Father Sun, songs asking for courage, songs seeking wisdom, and songs asking for the healing of the wounded.

At a signal from Henry, everyone in the circle stood and faced the west. Henry started a song which the others soon joined, the drums pulsing in the night, echoing off the walls of the Stronghold, the crowd swaying from side to side with the rhythm of the chant.

Though the chant was in Apache, Clay recognized the names of Cochise, Nana, and Juh. ``What are they singing now?'' he asked.

``It is the song of our ancestors,'' Frank answered. ``The Tinde are asking for their help and guidance. It will go on all night now, until dawn.''

``It's too bad there isn't some kind of chant you could do for re-enforcements,'' Clay said.

Frank started to reply, then turned as he heard someone approaching from their left. He recognized one of the women who had been assigned to guard the prisoner cave.

``My apologies for interrupting,'' she said, ``but I think you should come. The blond prisoner and Stinton wish to speak with you.''

Frank and Clay looked at each other, and got to their feet. They followed the woman along the slope of the Stronghold to the prisoner cave in the north wall.

Colorado and Bruce Stinton stood just inside the cave entrance. Frank and Clay stopped on the slope just outside.

``Clay.'' Colorado nodded.

Clay returned the nod.

``I been sittin' up here all day, watchin' and listenin' to what's goin' on. Been doin' a lot of thinking. I might be able to help.''

``Why would you want to?'' Clay asked, suspicion in his voice.

Colorado shrugged. ``Like I said before. I thought the whole operation was a bad idea in the first place. It's gettin' worse all the time.''

``What are you offerin'?'' Clay asked.

``I know about the TV truck. I'm willing to make a statement. On the record. About the Mexican assassination assignment and about the rescue orders. You can tape it and release it.''

Clay looked at him long and hard. ``You know you're a dead man if you do something like that.''

``Well, I've been thinkin' about that, too. I've gotta hunch that if it went out over the networks, if anything happened to me there would be too many questions. I might get kicked out of the company, but I'm gettin' too old for this kinda stuff, anyway.''

``I'd like to make a statement, too,'' Bruce said timidly.

Frank and Clay both looked at him, and Bruce seemed to flinch from the sudden attention.

``If it would help, I mean.'' He glanced at them and looked

377

down quickly.

``What kind of statement?'' Frank asked.

``Just tell my dad, and everybody, that I don't want to leave here. I want to stay and do what's right. I don't want to be rescued. I mean, if it would help, I could do that.''

Frank and Clay looked at each other.

``Couldn't hurt,'' Frank said quietly.

``We sure as hell don't have a lot to lose,'' Clay answered.

11:15 p.m., July 31 --- The Stronghold

Clay and Frank squatted at a fire near the TV truck, sipping coffee. Colorado and Bruce sat across from them, two Apache women with rifles standing behind them. Duties had pulled many of the people away from the gathering at the west end of the Stronghold, but nearly a hundred of the Tinde remained, tirelessly intoning the ancestor chant that echoed and pulsed through the night around them.

Teresa exited the TV truck and walked over to the fire.

``It's sent,'' she said, sitting on the ground next to Frank.

``It's more than we'd hoped for,'' Frank said.

``Now, let's just hope it's enough,'' said Clay.

``Do you want the prisoners returned to the cave now?'' one of the women guards asked.

Clay looked at Colorado, then at Frank. ``What do you think?'' he asked.

``Seems fair enough,'' Frank said.

Clay turned back to Colorado. ``You ready for a little hike?''

``Depends,'' the blond man answered cautiously.

``I don't know what it is about you, Colorado.'' Clay grinned. ``I'm going to have you escorted to our forward position and turn you loose.''

``I appreciate the offer,'' Colorado responded. ``But, if it's all the same to you, I'd kinda like to stick around to see how this thing comes out. If you can see your way clear to give me a weapon, I might be able to lend a hand somewhere.''

Clay studied him. ``You serious?''

``I'm serious as a heart attack. I think you guys have a legitimate right to your freedom. If I'm going to be forced into retirement, I wouldn't mind one last fight in a good cause.''

Clay looked at Frank.

``It's your call,'' Frank said.

Clay turned back to Colorado. ``I'm going to take you at your word. If I'm wrong, do me a favor. If you take me out, don't let me know it's you. I don't like the idea of dying, but I hate the idea of being wrong.''

Colorado laughed. ``I'll keep that in mind.''

``I'm going back out in a bit. I'll have one of Will Stonebreaker's team leaders come get you and set you up.''

Colorado nodded in silent assent.

Frank looked across the fire at Bruce. ``What about you? You want to be escorted out and released?''

Bruce shook his head. ``I meant what I said on the tape.''

1:10 A.M., August 1 --- Hill 6281

Clay and Elmer sat in the forward observer's position and watched the muzzle flashes of the Federal artillery, three and a half miles east. Clay cringed inside each time one of the heavy shells exploded among his men scattered in the hills around him.

His own forces had long ago expended the ammunition in the captured tanks. The afternoon and night had been long and tense, waiting for the Federals to launch another attack. Both sides had night patrols operating, and so far, the Federals seemed content to let it go at that. Clay knew they would come. He was saving what was left of his mortars for the expected big push. It could come at any time.

Will Stonebreaker's guerrilla teams moved silently through the trees on the hill, searching for Federal probes. Some of his men had moved southeast, down the saddle between Hill 6281 and the larger mountain on the up-side of the saddle. Clay knew Will's men were operating all over Hill 6483. He heard nothing from that direction, but

379

many of Will's men were armed with bows and arrows. Elmer's unit was once again positioned on Silver Peak. The return of many of his wounded, and the influx of numerous infiltrators from other reservations put him almost back to full strength.

Clay dropped down behind a rock and cupped his hands while he lit a cigarette. He turned to Elmer, who had insisted on accompanying him to the forward observation point. Clay knew the Feds would probe the hill, check out its defenses. He laughed inside. *If only they knew.* Clay was worried about the lack of protection on the hill, but the heavy losses earlier in the day forced him to the decision to leave the hill unprotected by conventional means. If he stationed Will's men and the Navajo unit on 6281, he would have no reserves with which to counter a heavy assault in another location.

Small units of Will's men would roam the hill during the night to fend off probes, but if the Federals took the hill during the night, the Apache would have to meet them in force west of the road. The Research Station would probably be cut off from a safe retreat into the Stronghold. And to top it all off, thick patches of ground fog rose from the damp ground and hovered five to six feet above the surface. It would help to hide the Federals if they advanced on the hill in the darkness. *What a damn mess.*

CHAPTER SIXTEEN: THE FINAL BATTLE

Dawn, August 1 --- Hill 6281

At dawn, the Federals opened up on Hill 6281 with an artillery barrage designed to cover every square inch of the mountain. Clay had given the order to evacuate the hill only ten minutes earlier.

Elmer's men held Silver Peak to the south of 6281 as the Federals advanced up the smaller hill following their barrage.

The fighting north of Paradise was intensive, and it was soon apparent the Apache could not hold. Oscar gave the order to fall back as previously planned. He moved half his unit to the rear. They took up new positions and provided covering fire while the other half moved back to positions beyond the first group, where the procedure was repeated.

By noon, Elmer's unit was forced off the mountain east of Paradise and back to the junction of the road with Turkey Creek. Clay called up Will's unit and Macdonald's men to reinforce that position until the evacuation of the Research Station could be completed. Eddie was still holding Cave Creek against heavy assault.

Clay had pulled the teams assigned to the western borders of Chiricahua back to the mountain and ridge lines west of the Stronghold where they were dug in. There were only about a hundred of them, and none were over eighteen years old, but the Federals showed no signs of moving across the rugged expanse from the west to reach the Stronghold through the mountains.

Clay ordered Eddie to fight a delaying action as he fell back west towards the Research Station, and then take up new positions within a half mile of the Station, and hold until the evacuation was complete.

From his position south of Paradise, Clay radioed Frank at the Research Station. When he had Frank personally, he spoke the agreed upon code. ``Time to go to the house, Doc.''

``Grandmother isn't feeling well. It'll take a little while to make her travel arrangements.''

Clay looked north, at the retreating Apache line. He keyed up his radio. ``You may have to leave some of her things behind. The train could arrive early, and you don't want to miss it.''

Clay thought he detected a sigh of resignation in Frank's voice. ``I guess we'll have to do the best we can. See you at the house.'' The radio fell silent.

The sounds of battle to the north of Clay's position and the rattle of gunfire from the east and south told him the two contingents of Federal forces were continuing their inexorable advances. Clay knew they would link up soon.

12:10 P.M., August 1 --- The Research Station

Frank put down the radio handset and turned to the three Apache women in the room with him. ``We're evacuating the Research Center. Now. Get the drivers ready and start loading the wounded, the most serious first.''

``What about the radio equipment?'' one of the women asked.

``Leave it until last. If there's time and room, take it. If not, leave it where it is.''

``Shouldn't we destroy it?'' asked the youngest of the women.

Frank shook his head. ``Just leave it. We'll switch all the

frequencies. At this point, a few more radios in Federal hands isn't going to make any difference to us. The explosives needed to destroy it might."

The women left hurriedly, and Frank walked quickly down into the main treatment room. A confused babble of tense voices, pleas for help, and moans assaulted Frank as he opened the door. Twenty of the most badly wounded men lay on the floor, teams of healers moving back and forth among them, doing the best they could with limited training and few supplies.

``Okay, listen up for a minute," Frank said, and the noise level instantly dropped. ``We're evacuating back to the Stronghold immediately. If what you are doing right now is absolutely necessary to save a life, continue. If not, get the most seriously wounded on the trucks first."

He looked around the room until he spotted Carla. ``Would you see to getting all the supplies on the first couple trucks? Fill the cabs. Leave the beds for the patients."

Carla nodded her understanding and left the room.

``The rest of you, start getting your patients ready. Remember, litters are in short supply. Save them for the neck and head injuries, and fractures – where you're going to have to immobilize the patient for transport. I'll get some help in here."

Twenty minutes later Frank was supervising the loading of the last two trucks of patients. The sounds of the fighting had come progressively closer. As Frank was closing the tailgate on the last pickup, a runner from Eddie arrived.

``My uncle, Eddie Vasquez says to tell you he is taking heavy casualties. But he said to tell you he will not fall back until the evacuation is complete."

He can't be over twelve, Frank thought. His first impulse was to pick him up and put him in the truck, but the fierce pride on the boy's face, the will with which he controlled his breathing after running flat out for over half a mile, the fierce light of determination that animated his eyes – all these things caused Frank to resist that initial impulse.

``You have spoken well, brother. Your courage is great to bring me this message. Go back now to your uncle and tell him the evacuation is complete. Tell him I will see him in the Stronghold."

``I will do as you say, uncle." The young man turned and dashed off towards the fighting, running with the elegant, bounding grace of a deer. Frank watched for a moment, and then leaned into the cab of the last truck.

``Go ahead," Frank said. ``My horse is tied behind the station."

The truck left and Frank re-entered the Research Station. He turned to the radio and contacted Eddie.

``I've sent your runner back to you to tell you grandmother's gone. Try not to let on that you already know when he gets back. But I thought I'd better call to save some time." Frank paused, not sure he really wanted to know the answer to the question he was about to ask. ``How bad is it, Eddie?"

``We're getting hurt pretty bad every time we try to hold someplace. As long as we can keep moving, we can keep them slowed up without taking many casualties."

``Can I be of any help out there with the wounded?"

``Negative. You're too important to be out here. We'll take care of things. As soon as I get disengaged, I'll send the wounded back to the. . . this isn't exactly proper radio protocol. Everything's under control. I'll see you back at the house. Over."

``At the house, my friend. May the spirits guide you safely. Out."

Frank put down the handset and turned the equipment off. He reached up and twisted the frequency knob. He was sure the Federals had discovered their frequency, but just in case they hadn't, he didn't want to give it to them. He exited the building and ran to his horse. He could hear the distant shouts and cries of Eddie's men now as they moved back down the rocky, tree-filled canyon towards the Research Station. Doubt began to gnaw at him. He knew what was happening out there. What right did he have to set something like this in motion?

He clamped down viciously on the doubts as he mounted and

384

urged the horse through the trees and into a lope up the road towards the Stronghold.

3:35 P.M., August 1 --- The Stronghold

Great towering billows of cumulus clouds built to the southeast as Frank rode through the entrance to the Stronghold. The air was electric, charged with pain, tension, fear, grief, courage, pride, and a stark implacability of purpose.

To his left, as he entered the Stronghold, the animals in the rope corrals milled in a constant, slow, bumping and brushing dance, as though the touching provided a sense of reassurance.

To his left front, on the gently sloping grassy meadow, the Apache dead were laid out side by side, in neat rows, heads to the west, the direction of death and rebirth. To the west of the last row, eight of the old ones sat in a circle, drumming and chanting the old songs of mourning and reunion with Ussen.

As Frank rode past the bodies, he saw faces he recognized, young and old, men and women, and he was filled with a profoundly melancholy love for them.

He loved them for their courage, and for their proud commitment to the defense of their land. He loved them for the strength with which they had so willingly attempted the impossible, and for the pain they had endured in the attempt. And their loss filled him with an immense, muffling sadness.

He knew the numbers would grow. All along the road back to the Stronghold, he had ridden past men and women and children, helping and carrying wounded and dead back to the Stronghold. Twice he had stopped to treat wounds that he knew were near fatal. Both times he had felt power flowing up through him from the earth, blending with his skills, and he had been successful. He knew the Gahan were speaking to him, reassuring him, helping him drive the doubts away.

Beyond the rows of dead, activity was intense. The makeshift hospital tents had long since filled, and more were being put up, the ditches being dug. Every available tent and wickiup had its contingent of wounded. The less-seriously injured lay or sat in the shade of the aspen groves. Children moved among them with food and water.

Old healers moved through the hospitals, singing the healing songs, as others worked on the physical wounds, cleansing, suturing, splinting – and amputating when that was the only alternative to death.

Higher up on the talus slopes which ringed the Stronghold just below the base of the towering, protective rock walls, work continued on the defensive positions for the final stand. When the attack reached the outside of the entrance to the Stronghold, everyone would be moved up behind the rock walls being built. They would fight their final battle from those positions.

Frank reined his horse to the right a bit, heading for the TV truck. He wanted to know if there had been any reaction yet to the release of the Purvis data, and the two statements from Colorado and Bruce. He dismounted and tied his horse to the picket line they had set up, in reach of water and feed. He was halfway to the truck when Teresa stepped out and ran to him. They embraced for a long, silent time, drawing new strength somehow from their closeness.

Finally, Teresa stepped back, excitement displacing some of the exhaustion evident on her features. ``Frank, I think it's working. The networks just finished a major update. People are outraged. There are demonstrations everywhere.''

She steered Frank to the fire pit where they sat down. She poured them both coffee while she talked.

``But, more importantly, the demonstrations are having an effect. The Senate has started impeachment proceedings against Williams, and they are voting tonight on whether to start impeachment against the President. The President has fired Jenkins, the head of the BIA, and has called a top level meeting of his advisors, Williams not among them.''

``What is he saying about Williams?'' Frank asked.

``Nothing. He says it's inappropriate for him to comment until he sees the evidence himself.''

Frank nodded. ``Nothing about withdrawing the troops?" he asked, after a moment.

``Not specifically. He says this meeting is to review the situation and determine the proper next step. But the House has passed a measure making the use of Federal armed forces on Indian reservations illegal, without prior majority approval from Congress. The Senate is voting on it tonight. Both the House and Senate are staying in session around the clock."

A faint hope began to grow in Frank. ``If the Senate passes it, he'd have to withdraw the troops, wouldn't he?"

Teresa shook her head. ``Not immediately. He could veto it and they would have to override. Then the President could challenge it in court on the grounds of unconstitutional infringement of executive power."

The hope waned. ``Politics," Frank said, the word coming out like a curse. He spat onto the coals of the campfire. ``They posture for votes while we die."

Teresa put her arm around Frank's shoulders. ``I listened to interviews with some of them. I think they are sincere. The majority of Congress wants the troops off our land. It may be because of pressures from voters. But that's what we've been trying to do. I think they are doing all they can. I think what we're doing is working."

The sound of distant thunder rumbled through the Stronghold. Frank sighed. He drew strength from Teresa's touch, if not her words. He smiled tiredly. ``Let's hope it works on the President."

He finished his coffee and put the cup down. ``I've got to find Henry and Maria and get a status report."

``I'll come with you," Teresa said.

Frank stood and helped her to her feet. ``Somebody has to monitor the news," he said. ``I trust your judgment. You might see the importance of something which somebody else would miss. Please."

She nodded.

``I'll be back as soon as I can."

She hugged him and he put his arms around her gently.

``I've been scared a lot the last few days," she said quietly. ``But there's only one fear I haven't been able to beat."

``What's that?" he asked.

``The fear that I'll never again feel your arms around me, holding me."

Frank tightened his arms around her, pulling her close as he pushed back tears. ``I'll be back," he whispered.

Frank wandered through the hospital tents, looking for Maria and Henry. The agony and pain he encountered were nearly overwhelming. When he finally found them, Henry led them to a spot alongside the small reservoir the people had created. They sat and looked silently at one another.

``It does not look good," Frank said finally.

``It is as it is, nephew," Henry answered quietly.

``There is so much suffering," Frank said.

``There is no more suffering, nephew, only a different kind of suffering – one honorably chosen, instead of one imposed upon the Tinde, which they felt powerless against."

A silence settled on them again as Frank considered his great uncle's words. They touched his heart with the reassurance of truth. Thunder rumbled again, closer now. The cloud towers had continued to build until the upper atmosphere winds tore off their tops, streaming them to the northwest like giant pennants atop the towers. The bases of the clouds had flattened and were darkening quickly.

``We will have rain soon," Frank said. ``Are we prepared?"

``As much as we can be," Maria answered. ``We still have plenty of tarps and rope. We'll keep putting up shelters until the wounded stop coming in."

``Is there anything else we can do?" Frank asked.

``Several people have told me they found the ancestor chants last night comforting," Maria said. ``Even some of today's wounded, who said they could hear them out in the defensive positions."

``We will begin them again at sunset," Henry said. ``The Gahan chant and the ancestors songs."

The late afternoon light began to fail as the massive cloud formations edged over the southeast rim of the Stronghold. Frank heard footsteps and turned towards the sound as Teresa ran up to them. She dropped to her knees next to Frank, trying to catch her breath.

``They just announced it," she said. ``Senator Williams is dead. He killed his son, and then shot himself in the head. They found him at his home."

The rain began to fall in heavy, cold drops.

Late afternoon, August 1 --- Junction of Turkey Creek with the dirt road.

Clay looked at his leaders. With the exception of Oscar, they were all present under the cottonwood tree near the creek. Clay pointed to the map he had spread on the ground before them.

``This is it. I'll pull Oscar's unit into the Stronghold first. Most of the units he was facing have joined up and are to our front, right here." He pointed to a position on the map with his finger. ``When Oscar is in position, his men will move into the fortifications on the south side of the Stronghold. He'll have that one tank with him, so I guess we'll leave it outside, just north of the Stronghold entrance where it can cover the road in.

``Mac, when Oscar is in position, I want you to take your men into the Stronghold and set up along the eastern perimeter.

``Eddie, you and Elmer have your men hold conventionally as long as you can. Elmer's unit on the north flank, yours on the south. When it gets too tough, let me know and we'll pull you back with the rest of them. Be careful of Will's men." He looked over to Will.

``Will, your unit will fight a delaying action here." He pointed to a draw leading towards the entrance to the Stronghold from the southeast. ``You probably won't get anything but small unit probes up there, but if the concentration of troops gets too heavy, pack it up and get 'em home right away."

Will nodded.

Clay let his eyes search the group. Thunder boomed nearby.

389

``We're going to get rain pretty quick. It will help cover our withdrawal. Under no circumstances do we want any unit outside the Stronghold after dark tonight, except those defending the approaches to the Stronghold. If we can hold the Feds until dark, we want to be in place for a dawn fight tomorrow at the Stronghold. If they're going to beat us, we want Teresa to get it on tape to show the world what they've done. Any questions?''

Elmer said, ``Where are you gonna be, brother?''

``From here, I'll head up to the Stronghold. I'll see you all up there before dark.'' He looked at Eddie. ``Don't forget that fifty caliber gun we've got set up on the ridge south of Turkey Creek near the Stronghold entrance. You can slow up the advance of a lot of troops with that thing.''

Eddie nodded.

Clay picked up Elmer's radio handset and called Oscar with the order to begin his withdrawal and to station the tank in a position to cover the mountain road leading into the Stronghold from the north. Oscar acknowledged Clay's transmission and signed off.

Clay turned to the others. ``I'll be near my radio at all times.'' He mounted his roan tied nearby and waited for his radio operator to get onto his horse. When both were mounted, he let the roan have his head as he picked his way upstream towards the Stronghold, two miles distant.

The sounds of the battle, still raging to the east, followed him up the draw. Mortar and artillery explosions echoed the thunder which cracked and boomed again, closer. Large, heavy drops of rain began to fall.

Sunset, August 1 --- The Stronghold

Clay walked among the women and children in the Stronghold. There was activity everywhere. Those not attending to the needs of the wounded prepared meals or dug trenches. Most carried lever-action rifles or placed them nearby their work.

Suddenly Oscar's son, Billy-Clay, appeared out of the crowd

and rushed to Clay, his Model 94 Winchester clutched in his hands.

``Uncle Clay! Uncle Clay! I can fight too!'' He brandished the Winchester proudly.

Clay tousled the young boy's hair and knelt before him. ``Billy-Clay, now I know you have a job you're supposed to be doin'. You get on back to it. You'll be told when your rifle is needed. I have a lot of things to do. We'll have time to talk later.''

Billy-Clay's eyes clearly showed his disappointment. ``I'm sorry, uncle. I just wanted to help.''

``You can help. By doin' what you've been told to do. A good soldier always follows orders.''

``Yessir!'' Billy snapped to his best imitation of attention and saluted smartly. Clay returned the salute.

``I'm going now. But I'm not a soldier. I'm a warrior.''

A lump grew in Clay's throat as he watched the boy disappear back into the crowd at a dead run.

He stood and moved on through the Stronghold, stopping periodically to raise his binoculars and scan the progress of the work being done up the talus slopes, checking and re-checking the defenses. He looked for Maria, but in the confusion of activity and crowds, he couldn't find her.

His radio operator, who continued to follow at a distance, approached with the handset held at arm's length before him. ``It's Eddie, sir.''

Clay accepted the handset and listened to Eddie describe the battle conditions at the junction of Turkey Creek and the dirt road. The Federal forces were linked up and the Apache were seriously outnumbered and outgunned. Losses were heavy.

Clay's heartbeat quickened. His mouth was dry. He keyed up the handset. ``Bring 'em home, Eddie. Red Leader out.''

He passed the handset back to his radio operator and moved east, toward the Stronghold entrance. They moved through the short, narrow passage between sheer rock walls and out onto the aspen-and-pine-covered ridge that formed the south flank of the Turkey Creek draw. The ridge ran down and away to the east towards the dirt road two miles distant. The sounds of small arms fire drifted up the draw towards him. About a mile down the draw, Apaches were dug in on both the north and south ridges. Clay heard them open up, laying down a covering fire while their brothers moved back up the draw to new positions.

Clay put his binoculars to his eyes and scanned the southern ridge. His adrenaline started pumping as he realized Oscar's men were not yet in position. He turned to his radio operator and took the handset.

He keyed up and called for Oscar. Relief washed through him when Oscar responded. His anger wasn't far behind.

``Where the hell are you, man? There's some important homework that isn't getting done, and time is getting short. Over."

``Sorry, Red Leader," Oscar said. ``We saw them split off a column of armor and head them north up the road. They'd have been knocking on our front door real quick. I figured I'd better blow the road. Over."

``Roger that. But be advised that you have important homework. I want it done as soon as possible. Do you understand? Over."

Clay could tell by Oscar's voice that his Blood Brother knew he was angry. ``Roger. I'm on the way. Should arrive in about fifteen. Over."

``Red Leader out." Clay gave the handset back to his radio operator. ``Damn!" Oscar's men were supposed to be in position on the south ridge to cover Eddie and Elmer as they moved into the Stronghold. He considered calling Will's men over to reinforce the ridge, then discarded the idea. That southeast draw had to be protected, too.

It began to rain again. Just a few big drops at first, but it quickly became a downpour. Clay and his radio operator sought shelter under a large pine tree, the radio operator answering a call on the run. He signed off as they stepped under the protective boughs.

``Sir. The fifty-caliber machine-gun on the southern ridge is out.

Eddie says they took a direct hit from an M-79. They don't answer their radio, and the gun is silent. Eddie says his men can't get to it from where they are. The White Eyes are moving on it now. He wants to know if we can move down the ridge from the Stronghold."

``Tell him we're on the way.'' Clay ran back to the Stronghold entrance and rounded up seven of the guards there, and then ran back east, down the ridge. Even muffled by the hissing rush of the rain, the sounds of the small arms fire and exploding grenades increased in volume as they dodged their way down through the aspen and pine.

Federal troops were breaching the parapet of the machine-gun pit when Clay and his men burst upon the scene. The point-blank exchange of gunfire was intense as the opposing factions fell into hand-to-hand combat.

Clay fired into the chest of one soldier, then spun and smashed another one in the face with a horizontal butt-stroke of his M-1.

The fight was short but brutal. When it was over, only two men remained alive. Clay knelt near the stock of the fifty-caliber machine-gun. He held onto it to keep himself from falling face down onto the muddy ground. Water ran down his face as the rain intensified. One of his men crouched nearby. The Apache spoke quietly. ``You're hit pretty bad, Chief.''

Clay removed a bloody hand from low on the left side of his chest. ``I damn sure ain't hit pretty good.'' He tasted blood in his mouth.

``Can you make it back up the ridge?''

Clay shook his head. He wiped water from his eyes and sighted down the barrel of the machine-gun at a squad of Federal troops barely visible through the downpour as they moved up the ridgeline on the other side of Turkey Creek. He pushed the trigger in short bursts as he swung the barrel from side to side and watched the bodies fall. Those of the enemy not injured or killed took cover and waited.

Blood ran from the corner of Clay's mouth. He coughed, spewing more blood onto the machine-gun. He turned to his man. ``I can gun it by myself for awhile. Get back to the Stronghold and get some help down here.''

The man nodded. ``I'll be back as fast as I can.'' He charged back up the ridge.

Clay sank back on his haunches as he watched the Apache run up the slope, and grimaced as a concentration of small-arms fire cut the man down. He pushed away the grief. *I guess I'll have to hold it myself.*

He turned and examined the muddy machine-gun pit. It was littered with the bodies of both sides. His radio operator lay grotesquely sprawled west of the sandbags a few feet. His eyes stared into the sky, unaffected by the rain falling in them, unseeing.

Clay held his right hand to his chest. It slowed the bleeding externally, but did little for the internal blood loss. *Damn! I wanted to be with Maria when this happened. Damn!* He peered over the sandbags, through the rain, at the terrain below. Thunder cracked and boomed. Clay saw the helmets of the advancing Federals. A wave of dizziness overtook him. He wavered, at the brink of unconsciousness. He shook his head and put his hand on the trigger mechanism of the gun. He fired a long burst.

Just after sunset, August 1 --- The Stronghold
Maria worked feverishly on the leg wound. She had just completed suturing when she felt the sharp pain low in her chest. She doubled up as she fell to the pine needles at her feet.

Carla, working on another of the wounded nearby, saw her fall and ran to her, kneeling as she arrived. ``Maria! What's wrong?'' She lifted Maria's head and cradled it in her lap.

``It's Clay. He's been wounded. He's dying, Carla.'' Maria struggled, trying to get to her feet, then fell back to the ground, clutching at the lower left side of her chest. ``He's alone out on the ridge. I've got to help him.'' Her voice was filled with desperation.

Carla called one of the nearest women over to stay with Maria while she went in search of Frank.

Just after sunset, August 1 --- The fifty caliber machine-gun pit
Clay heard the Federals open up from below, their bullets

striking well behind him, higher on the ridge. He pushed himself up towards the gun and felt himself falling into a vast emptiness. The fall became a floating sensation and far away in front of him, a small but brilliant light flared into view. He felt himself drawn towards it until a burst from his own machine-gun jarred him to consciousness. He opened his eyes to see Billy firing at the enemy. Billy released the trigger and turned to face him in the rapidly fading light.

``You gotta be more careful, brother. The white eyes were gettin' too close."

Despite his fears, Clay smiled. `Billy. Get us some help, brother." He coughed up more blood.

Billy's face saddened. ``I can't do it, Clay. I'm under orders, this time. I can't do anything except hold this position until more of the Tinde get here to take over. I'm sorry, brother."

Exhaustion washed through Clay. He closed his eyes and laid his head back against the sandbags behind him. An eagle flew silently overhead, beneath a puffy white cloud.

Just after sunset, August 1 --- The Stronghold

Oscar and two of his lieutenants stepped out of the rain under the protection of the hospital tent tarp, and waited as Frank finished suturing closed a scalp wound on an unconscious patient.

``Have you seen Clay?" Oscar asked when Frank was finished.

Frank stood and joined the three men, shaking his head. ``I haven't talked to him since he ordered the evacuation of the Research Station."

``He should have been here a long time ago," Oscar said. ``I've . . ."

Frank held up a hand to stop Oscar. He heard someone calling his name and looked around in the heavy rain until he spotted Carla waving as she ran towards him.

``Frank, I've been looking all over for you," she called. ``It's Maria. She says Clay is wounded and is alone out on the ridge somewhere."

``He's got to be hurt," Oscar said. ``He ordered everybody inside the Stronghold before dark."

An old, familiar rage began to burn in Frank. He took Oscar by the shoulders. ``Think. Where would he go?"

Oscar tried to remember what Clay had told them of his plans. ``He said something about a fifty-caliber machine gun position on the south ridge outside the entrance to the Stronghold. If Clay was needed, he would have gone where he could bring the most firepower into play."

Frank reached out and took the rifle from the hands of one of Oscar's men. He motioned for the cartridge belt, which the man gave him wordlessly. Frank buckled it around his waist, then turned to Oscar, his features grim.

``Let's go get him."

Ten minutes later, on the south ridge outside the entrance to the Stronghold

Frank's Bear song rumbled in his chest as he ran, stoking the fires of his anger and filling him with a strength which carried him easily down the uneven, heavily forested ridge line in the uncertain light. Oscar ran beside him. The rain was letting up as the light failed, and a ground fog rose silently from the wet earth.

Three Federal troops appeared before them in the mist and Frank and Oscar fired simultaneously as they ran. Frank pulled the trigger again and again until he heard the ping of the empty clip being ejected by the M-1. The three men fell and disappeared into the rising fog. Oscar veered off to the right.

``This way," said Oscar.

Frank followed, reloading as he ran. They broke through the treeline and Frank saw the machine-gun pit sixty yards ahead, Clay's body slumped behind the gun.

He sprinted to the parapet and dived into the pit. Oscar followed. Bullets ripped the air over their heads. Frank pulled Clay back away from the gun and laid him out on the muddy bottom of the pit. He ripped Clay's shirt open, feeling for a pulse as Oscar opened up with the heavy machine-gun.

Relief engulfed him as he detected a faint heartbeat. The ground fog rolled down the ridge over them, and Oscar ceased firing. The sounds of the battle slowed. Oscar squatted next to Frank.

``Is he. . .''

Frank cut him off with a shake of his head. The fighting slowed to a sporadic staccato as the ground fog thickened.

``He's alive. But he's hurt too badly to move. I'll have to work on him here.''

``I'll stand watch.''

Frank shook his head.

``Then I'll go back up and get some reinforcements down here. That way when you're ready to move him you'll have the man power to do it gently.''

Again, Frank shook his head. ``Go back to the Stronghold, but once you're there, stay.''

Oscar started to protest, but Frank cut him off. ``I can't do anything back there tonight. You and Eddie and Elmer have to see to the defenses for morning. If I can stabilize Clay, I'll bring him back in. If not,'' Frank shrugged. ``I'll see it through with him here.''

Oscar looked at Frank a long time before finally nodding. ``If you're not back by morning, we're coming back after you.''

Frank nodded. Oscar climbed out of the pit and disappeared into the fog.

Frank turned his attention back to Clay. He examined the wound in his chest closely. Torn flaps of skin fluttered around the opening as Clay tried to breathe. The light was nearly gone and Frank knew he had to work quickly. He searched the pocket of Clay's shirt until he found his pack of cigarettes. He removed the transparent plastic wrapping and cut it open into a sheet.

Probing the wound gently with his fingers, he worked the wrapping down through the opening until he could feel the laceration where the bullet had torn through Clay's lung. As carefully as possible,

397

working by feel, he manipulated the wrapping, spreading it out over the hole in the lung until it was held in place by the pressure of the lung against the internal chest cavity.

He opened a battle dressing and cut off two small gauze squares which he worked gently into the opening. He opened another battle dressing and, after sprinkling a mixture of herbs onto the wound, he tied the bandage in place.

He took off his own shirt and laid it on the mud, then rolled Clay over onto it as gently as he could, face down. He lifted the shirt from the exit wound on Clay's back. The bullet had somehow missed Clay's ribs and had not flattened too badly before exit. The damage to his back was not as bad as Frank had feared.

He used the remainder of the first battle dressing to clean the wound. He had to get close to it to see in the growing darkness. He probed the wound again, and then tore off a part of the battle dressing wrapping. He worked it into the wound and over the opening torn in the back of the lung. Clay's breathing began to sound stronger.

Frank's only fear was that the internal bleeding would partially fill the lung and start a coughing fit which would tear his work loose. But there was nothing he could do to prevent it. He sprinkled the exit wound with the herbal mixture, and tied the second dressing in place.

He carefully rolled Clay onto his back and covered him with his own wet, muddy shirt. It was all he had to keep off the chill. He shifted his position until he could lift Clay's head and shoulders into his lap. He put his arms around his friend and rocked him, holding him against the night.

The sounds of battle, which had receded down the hill away from them, intensified again and surged back towards them. Flares lit up the night sky and cast an eerie glow through the fog. From the Stronghold, the drums began to sound and were soon joined by the haunting, pulsing voices of the Tinde, honoring the mountains, honoring the ancestors, asking the power of the spirit world to guide them through another night.

Frank's mind raced, trying to figure out what more he could do for his friend. He wanted to sing his Bear song but he dared not. The battle raged closer, up the ridge on both sides of them, and Frank could hear voices all around. He knew they would be surrounded soon, if they weren't already. He thought about moving to the gun, but didn't. He could make no difference in the battle. He could see nothing. He cared only about keeping Clay alive.

More illumination flares went off overhead. Clay moved slightly, groaned, and opened his eyes. ``Doc?''

``I'm here,'' Frank said, fighting back tears of relief and dread. He had been afraid he would never hear Clay speak again, but he also knew it was not unusual for badly wounded men to come back to consciousness just before they died.

``Maria...'' Clay managed to whisper.

``Sorry,'' Frank said. ``Just me.''

Frank checked Clay's pulse. It was stronger and more even than it had been. ``Just rest easy,'' he said. ``You've lost a lot of blood.''

A long machine-gun burst sounded from somewhere nearby, and was answered with the bark and crack of rifle fire.

``It don't sound good,'' Clay whispered.

``We're just where we always seem to be,'' Frank said. ``Right in the middle of things.''

Clay tried to sit up but Frank held him in place. Clay coughed and pain distorted his features. ``Damnit, Frank, get me up behind that gun. We may not win but we'll let 'em know they've been in a fight.''

``If you don't stop jerking around you're going to have all the fight you can handle right here, with me. You're hurt bad, Clay. You know what a sucking chest wound is. I've only done the crudest of patch jobs on you. We've done everything we can. If we're supposed to make it through the night, we will. If not, we won't.''

``I never put much stock in that fatalistic stuff.''

``There's nothing fatalistic about it. The fog is hiding us right now. You fire one round from that gun and. . .''

The sudden snorting and stomping of a horse behind them cut Frank off. He turned to look and his heart raced. He lifted Clay gently.

``Look,'' he whispered.

A lone Apache, dressed in the old way, sat bareback on a black stallion that glistened in the rain. The man handled his horse excellently, with tiny, almost imperceptible movements of his knees as the horse danced nervously along the edge of the gun pit, shying from the sounds of battle all around them.

Lightning flickered overhead, illuminating the man's straight back and proud, sharply-chiseled features. His salt-and-pepper hair fell to the center of his shoulder blades. A lever-action Henry rifle lay across the horse's back in front of him.

The horseman looked at Frank and something in his eyes filled Frank with a quiet reassurance. The figure shifted his gaze to Clay. Incongruous amid the sounds of battle, a wolf howled somewhere nearby. The rider tossed a folded blanket into the pit next to Clay. Frank spread it over him.

``You have led well, Clay Price. You have fought with honor in defense of your land. Now you are wounded and death dances around you. Power teaches us that there are times to fight, and times to pray. Your time for prayer has come.''

Frank felt a trembling start in Clay's body, but it was not fear.

``Cochise,'' Clay whispered.

``The Gahan have spoken of the circle of the Tinde being completed. That time will come with the dawn. Until then, you will be protected.''

The horseman raised the rifle into the air. The wolf howled again. The man lowered the rifle and let it hang easily at arm's length on his right side as he reined his horse away from the pit and rode quietly down the ridge.

Frank's heart pounded as the trees behind them came alive. Hundreds of Apaches walked and rode past the gun pit, armed with a myriad of weapons: Sharps, Spencers, Winchester '66s and '73's, Remington rolling blocks, Springfield muskets, M-16s, bows and arrows, lances, '03 Springfields, and M-1 Garands and Carbines.

There were men in ragged uniforms of World War I, wearing

wide-brimmed helmets and tattered, blood-stained leggings. Others wore the uniforms of World War II, still others the camouflage jungle fatigues of Vietnam. Most were dressed in the old way, and many carried only bows and lances.

Frank, too, was trembling now, and he and Clay sat reverently and in silence until the last man disappeared into the mist.

An illumination flare burst overhead, casting an eerie glow through the fog. The sounds of battle down the slope in front of them intensified. The fog swirled momentarily, and both Frank and Clay caught a final glimpse of the horseman, rifle at his shoulder, before the fog hid him once more.

Again, the wolf howled, east of them this time, down the slope. It was joined by another behind them, and then others to either side until the night rang with the hunting cries of the pack.

``Frank, that. . .'' Clay coughed once and grunted in pain. ``That was Cochise.'' He coughed again, and this time couldn't stop the coughs that followed. He spat blood out into the mud, and wheezed with short, burbly breaths. Frank laid him out on the ground and tucked the blanket around him.

Clay closed his eyes. ``I never hurt so much, Doc,'' he whispered. ``Am I gonna. . .'' His voice faded away.

Frank grabbed Clay's wrist and held his breath until he found a pulse. I was extremely weak, and uneven. He let his breath out slowly. He grasped the shrapnel at his chest with his left hand, and began his Bear song, the cadences blending with the chants of the old ones echoing out into the night from the Stronghold.

The Bear spoke to him from somewhere out of sight in the fog. ``Bury him, Walks-With-Bear. Dig a den in the back wall of the gun pit and return him to the body of his mother.''

``But he's not dead, grandfather. There's a pulse.''

``He will be soon, if you do not do what I say. Dig the den and return him to the body of his mother. He fought honorably for her. If he is to be healed, she alone can do it. Hurry. Death is all around him.''

Frank scrambled around the mud on his hands and knees,

searching by feel until he found an entrenching tool. He dug frantically at the base of the back wall, dragging the dirt out and away. The rain started again, muffling the sounds of the battle as it seemed to peel off the ridge east of them and fall back on both sides down towards the road below.

The rain ran in his face but he continued to dig until he had managed to scoop out a crude den. He checked Clay's pulse again. It was more erratic, and his breath came in short, uneven gasps. Frank moved him as gently as possible, maneuvering Clay into the den on his side, facing out. He grabbed the small shovel and began covering Clay's feet and legs with the wet soil he had scooped from the den. He continued until only Clay's face was exposed.

He sat in front of the den, panting from the effort. Fear coursed through him. ``Hang on, brother," Frank whispered. ``Please hang on."

The rhythms of the chants from the Stronghold changed. They were clearer now that the battle had moved back down the draw. He realized they had switched to the Gahan chant. He joined in quietly, tears mixing with the rain on his face.

``We are blessed in the Mountain Way,
The Gahan sing songs in our hearts.
We are strong in the Mountain Way,
The Gahan sing songs in our hearts."

Frank felt the familiar energies flowing up through him from the earth, easing his fear, rounding the edges of his pain. He continued to chant softly, watching Clay's face. His features seemed to glow, weakly at first, then with more light. Gradually, the lines of pain around Clay's eyes softened and faded. The taut set of his mouth relaxed. His breathing slowed but became stronger and more even.

Frank continued to chant softly as the night wore on. For a time, the battle intensified down the hill and moved back up towards them, then fell away once more. Frank's eyes grew heavy, and his head nodded.

The Bear appeared to him in the timeless space of his half-dream. ``It is time, Walks-With-Bear."

Frank's eyes jerked open. Clay was not yet conscious, but he struggled against the earth packed around him. Frank clawed at it with his hands, forgetting the shovel, pulling the dirt away until he could maneuver Clay out of the hole. He stretched Clay out and rearranged the blanket around him, using a wet corner of it to wipe the mud from his friend's face.

He checked Clay's pulse. It was strong and even now. He leaned down and put his ear near Clay's mouth. His breathing was slower and deeper, with none of the burbling that indicated internal bleeding in the lung. Clay cried out, and was silent again.

Frank moved until he was cradling Clay's head in his lap once more. ``Rest easy, brother,'' he whispered. A relief, bordering on joy and mixed with love, filled him. *It might not make any difference in the long run*, Frank thought, as images of the battle which loomed ahead at dawn flashed through his mind. *But he will be alive to be part of it. And for that I am thankful.*

Pre-Dawn, August 2 --- *The fifty caliber machine-gun pit*

The first faint signs of light in the eastern sky broadened towards dawn as Frank watched. The fog had dissipated. The sounds of battle which had moved down the ravine towards the road during the night, slackened, flared again briefly, and then stopped. An eerie silence took possession of the early morning.

Clay stirred and Frank looked down at him. Clay's eyes opened. ``What the hell is going on? Why is it so quiet.''

``All the firing stopped about two minutes ago. How are you feeling?''

Clay dragged himself into a sitting position, his back against the sandbag parapet of the gunpit.

``Weak as hell. But I'm still alive. That's an improvement over the last thing I remember. I dreamed I had died and you had buried me.''

Frank laughed. ``I did.'' He gestured to the crude den dug into the back wall of the gun pit. ``But I remembered I still owed you a month of dinners, so I dug you back up."

Clay looked at him questioningly. Frank just grinned. Clay tried to pull himself up far enough to see down the slope in front of their position. The effort triggered a fit of coughing. When it subsided, Frank lowered him back against the sandbags again.

``There's no blood, which is a good sign, but that doesn't mean you're ready for the Olympics. Stay put and let me check you out."

He opened the front of Clay's shirt and removed the battle dressings he had applied front and back. The wounds were closed, scabs already forming around the ragged edges of the holes. Frank left the dressings off.

``Looks pretty good. First sucking chest wound I ever treated with a mudpack. We'll have to open you back up to get the temporary internal patch out, but that can be done in an operating room. It'll be a piece of cake."

``That's easy for you to say..." Clay stopped, his head cocked, listening. ``Why is it so goddamn quiet, Doc? Help me up so I can see what's goin' on."

Frank helped Clay across the pit so he could sit supported by the front parapet as he looked down the ravine.

Bodies of Federal Troops lay scattered up and down the slopes of the draw. Medics and recovery details were at work, carrying their grisly burdens back down to the road at the mouth of the ravine where lines of trucks and field ambulances waited.

Clay saw two arrows in the chest of one man as his body was carried away. He saw no sign of dead Apache.

``Did you give me some morphine, Doc?"

"No, We ran out early yesterday. Why?"

Clay shook his head. ``It just seems like I had a lifetime of weird dreams, all in one night."

Frank grinned. ``Sleep in a bear's den, and that'll happen. Henry says Bear knows all the secrets of sleep and dreams."

``What happened last night? I remember waking up and you being there. But everything after that gets a little fuzzy."

``The fighting continued all night, until just before you came to," Frank said. ``Since then, not a shot. Maybe it's a good sign."

``It's always a good sign when nobody's shootin' at me, but take a look down there." Clay pointed at the massed units of Federal troops, stretched out on the dirt road and dug into the hills below their position.

``That's damn near a full division, and who knows how many we can't see. I count sixteen tanks, just on that little stretch of visible road. Looks like the calm before the storm to me, brother."

Clay made a sudden move towards the machine-gun as the faint *thop-thop* of helicopters became audible to the east. The effort started him coughing again. Frank lowered him onto the ground next to the gun.

``Get me up behind that gun, Doc. They're serious this time. They're bringing the choppers in."

``You're in no shape to fire this thing. You feed, I'll fire."

``You got it. Drag the ammo box over here. We've only got three belts left, and I don't know what good it'll do, but it just don't feel right to die with unused ammo."

Frank moved the ammo box next to Clay then moved behind the gun. The sounds of the choppers grew louder as they got closer. More of them appeared over the eastern ridge. Adrenaline pounded in Frank's ears. He looked through the sights and swung the barrel of the gun in line with the general direction of the choppers' approach.

``I've never fired one of these things. How far do I have to lead them?" The tension was evident in Frank's voice.

Clay sat up slowly and gingerly, looking towards the choppers. ``Depends on the range. Look's like about a mile and a half. Aim for. . . wait a minute! Those are med-evac choppers. Look at the red crosses on the sides."

Frank pulled away from the gun sights and stared. ``What the hell. . ."

A momentary ear-shattering shriek of amplified electronic feedback ripped through the still air and reverberated off the mountains around them. The two men looked at each other as an amplified man's voice boomed at them from several locations in the trees below their position.

``This is Marine Brigadier General William Purvis speaking. The President of the United States has ordered me here to speak to you this morning on behalf of the U.S. Government."

Frank looked at Clay questioningly.

``It sure sounds like him."

``The president has asked me to inform you that as of sunrise this morning, he has ordered all United States armed forces to break off hostilities and withdraw from Chiricahua land in a rapid and orderly fashion. The helicopters you hear and see approaching are solely for the purpose of evacuating casualties. They are unarmed."

Frank turned around and looked back towards the Stronghold. He could hear the first hesitant cheers echoing in the canyons. Lines of armed men stood in silhouette against the sky on the rocky ridges on both sides of the Stronghold entrance, their rifles raised in the air.

``Goddamnit, where's my radio?" Clay snapped. ``It isn't over yet. Those guys make great targets up there."

Frank grinned at Clay. ``Don't be too hard on them. Hell, they're veterans, and they never even went through boot camp."

The sounds of the helicopters changed quality. Clay and Frank turned back to the east as the choppers settled towards the road.

Purvis' voice continued. ``The President has also asked me to convey to you that he has officially recognized your claim to independence, and has ordered the State Department to establish the necessary channels to open full-scale public hearings on the matter."

Frank felt a flood of tears rising in him and made no attempt to stop them. He looked at Clay, who also cried unashamedly.

``I am currently positioned just outside the Chiricahua border, east of Portal. A representative from the State Department is with me. He has in his possession a document, signed by the President, stipulating these points and guaranteeing the U.S. will use no further force against the Chiricahua nation. When the U.S. withdrawal is complete, the leaders of the Chiricahua people are invited to set the terms and conditions of a meeting in which this document can be delivered, and formal channels of communication between the U. S. State Department and Chiricahua can be established. Utility and phone service are being restored immediately on a temporary basis, until more formalized arrangements can be worked out."

The sounds of many engines coughing to life filled the silence as Purvis stopped speaking. Clay and Frank watched as tanks and armored personnel carriers jockeyed to turn around on the narrow road, and began grinding their way back down the canyon towards the Research Station and Portal. The Federal troops dug in on the slopes below them cheered and began moving down towards the road.

``One last thing." Purvis' voice echoed against the backdrop of the noise of the Federal withdrawal. ``If you are out there, Clay Price, you are one hell of a Marine, my friend."

Frank started laughing through his tears. Clay joined in until the laughter started the coughing again. Frank sat next to Clay and held him until the coughing fit had passed.

``It's over, brother," he whispered. ``It's over."

Clay looked up at him. ``I know," he said softly. He coughed once.

``Come on," Frank said, getting to his feet. ``Let's get you back where you can rest." He helped Clay to his feet. ``Can you walk?"

``The way I feel right now, I can fly. Let's get movin'. There's somebody up there I wanna see real bad."

They started up the ridgeline towards the Stronghold entrance. People streamed out of the Stronghold and down the ridge towards them. Clay stumbled, and Frank caught him.

``Sorry, Doc. I guess I'm still a little weak."

Frank lowered Clay to the ground and sat beside him. Tears still ran, tears of mourning for those lost in the struggle, tears of relief that the fighting was over, tears of joy for the future.

Clay reached up and touched the tears on Frank's face.

``Apache tears, Doc."

Frank shook his head. ``Not any more, brother. Apache is the

Apache Tears
Spanish word for enemy. These are Tinde tears."

The End

About the Authors

Gordon Mustain a Marine Corps Vietnam veteran, writer, philosopher, and jewelry craftsman, who has been writing professionally for more than thirty-six years. **APACHE TEARS** is his first published novel. ("I expect to become an overnight success any moment now," he quips.) "I have been fascinated by the Chiricahua Apache ever since I saw the film BROKEN ARROW when I was about ten years old. The more I have studied and learned about them over the years, the more convinced I have become that their 400-year long bloody struggle to preserve their homeland is truly one of the most heroic and noble in history."

Stoney Livingston, a Marine Corps Vietnam veteran, is a retired private investigator in Tucson, and a fugitive recovery agent. He is also an independent long-distance truck driver. **APACHE TEARS** is his first published novel."My dream," he says, "is a mountain cabin just at the beginnings of the pines, situated so that it looks out over the desert in the distance; a place where I can sit and write full time."

NOTE: Gordon Mustain passed away on April 13th, 2011. His death was directly attributed to a cancer caused by exposure to Agent Orange. The Viet Nam war belatedly claimed one of my dearest friends.

Rest in peace, Brother.

Stoney

www.ingramcontent.com/pod-product-compliance
Lightning Source LLC
Chambersburg PA
CBHW021642260626
47154CB00016BA/58

* 9 7 8 0 6 9 2 4 4 8 1 2 0 *